戀愛滋味

Flavours

Susan Mehra

~

© Penrose Publishing Ltd

First Published 2013 by Penrose Publishing Ltd, York House, York Road, Felixstowe
IP11 7QG

www.penrose-publishing.co.uk

ISBN-國際標準書號

978-1-909879-00-3 Chinese/English 平裝版

978-1-909879-01-0 Chinese 電子書 Kindle

978-1-909879-02-7 Chinese 電子書 Kobo

978-1-909879-03-4 Chinese 電子書 PDF

978-0-9576201-6-2 English 平裝版

978-0-9576201-7-9 English 電子書 Kindle

978-0-9576201-8-6 English 電子書 Kobo

978-0-9576201-9-3 English 電子書 PDF

~

Chapter One

"You've done what?" Kevin stopped walking and stared at her.

"Joined a dating agency. That new online one that's been advertising a lot lately." She pulled up the neck of her plum-coloured coat, shivering.

"Haven't noticed."

"Their office is just round the corner from work." She was skimming down the messages on her phone. She'd been so busy this morning that this was the first chance she'd had. She looked up, aware that Kevin had gone silent.

"Come on, Kev, it's no biggie. Lots of people do it these days." She pocketed her phone, grabbed his arm and tucked it in her own, dragging him onwards.

"Yes, but not you. Why do you need to join one? You're intelligent, caring..." he cocked his head on one side. "And I suppose you're quite good-looking. If you like that kind of thing."

She elbowed him in the ribs. "Oh, thanks. What's up, used your monthly compliment allowance?" She pushed at the door of the coffee shop with her spare hand, releasing him with a shove once they were inside. "You go find table, hunter man, me go get sustenance. Cappuccino?"

Rebecca fished for her purse as she walked towards the counter. Please don't let it be the oily little bloke serving, she prayed. Tony had employed a couple of temporary staff before Christmas, and one of them gave her the creeps. She kept on hoping his time was up, but he'd still been here yesterday.

Phew, it was the other new guy, the brown-haired one. He had his back to her but that was absolutely fine; Rebecca was happy to admire the view. This one could stay as long as he liked.

"You're still here then," she said as he turned.

第一章

「你說什麼？」凱文停下了腳步，並凝視著她。

「參加了約會機構啊，是網上最新的那種，最近也有很多廣告吧。」她顫抖著把她那紫紅色大衣的衣領拉起來。

「沒聽說過。」

「在辦公室那邊再拐個彎就是他們的公司了。」她在看手機上的短訊，她整個上午都一直在忙，現在才有機會匆匆翻看一下。她抬頭看了一下，發現凱文默不作聲。

「好了，凱文，又不是什麼大事件。這個年頭很多人都會做這種事吧。」她把手機放好，挽起他的手臂，拉他繼續向前行走。

「是沒錯，但你用不著這樣做。為什麼妳需要這樣做呢？妳聰明，又善良...」他側了一下頭說「而且你還蠻漂亮，要是你喜歡的話。」

她用肘撞了他的一下。「噢，真是謝謝啊。發生了什麼事？把今個月的補貼都花光了嗎？」她用另一隻手把咖啡店的門推開，踏進去的時候把他推開。「男人，去找座位吧！我去點餐，卡布奇諾嗎？」

麗貝卡拿出錢包走去櫃檯。她祈求著服務她的不是那個滿臉油光的小伙子。東尼在聖誕節之前聘用了兩個臨時工，其中一個令她毛骨悚然。她繼續祈望他已經離開了，但其實他昨天還在這裡。

喔！是另外的一位有著咖啡色頭髮的新店員。雖然他背對著她但感覺也非常非常好，麗貝卡很開心可以看到此情景，這一位想在這裡待多久也可以。

「你還在這裡啊。」當他轉身時她說道。

「是啊，第三個星期了。」他笑道。

「哇噢，都快是個老手了，很專業的樣子呢。」

他臉上的笑容消失了。「我不是，我要求其實比較高一點，這樣

"Yep. Week 3." He smiled.

"Wow. Almost a veteran. That smacks of vocation, round here."

His smile faded. "Not for me, I'd like to aim a bit higher. It's convenient for now, and Tony's asked me to stay on." His tone was cool. "What can I get you?"

"Sorry," said Rebecca awkwardly. Her and her dumb remarks. "I didn't mean I thought this was the height of your abilities or anything. I've done my share of waiting tables and serving behind counters. It's just that Tony's Christmas people don't normally stay long."

"Sorry, it's okay. I'm only grumpy because you're about the fiftieth person today who's said something along the lines of 'oh, you're still here then'. His mouth quirked.

"Oh." She grinned. "I can see how that would get annoying. Sorry. I'll have one vanilla latte and one hazelnut, please."

He got busy with the coffee machine and lifted the syrup bottles up high to deliver the shots, doing both cups at once.

Rebecca was impressed. "Wow. You look like Tom Cruise."

He smiled at her over his shoulder. "I don't get told that very often, what with having light brown hair and being 6 foot 1, but thanks."

Rebecca laughed. "No, I meant when you do that thing with the bottles. It's like a scene from Cocktail."

"Ah, right." He turned and put the coffees on her tray. "I did work in a cocktail bar for a while. Another one of my dead end jobs," he said, arching an eyebrow, eyes twinkling.

She held up her hands. "Stop! I feel bad enough already."

"Okay. Truce."

Rebecca paid and he put the change on the tray for her. "Thank you... oh, you've got a badge now!" She leaned forward and looked at it. "Stephen Reynolds."

He shook his head and tapped the badge. She squinted at the smaller writing underneath.

"Oh sorry – 'Call me Steve.' Why don't they just put Steve on

只是迎合現在的狀況。東尼也有叫我留下來。」他冷淡地說：「你要點些什麼嗎？」

「對不起。」她對自己的愚蠢言論感到尷尬。「我的意思不是認為你的能力就只有這樣。我已經做了我的那份，就是等待座位和在櫃檯後面服務。只不過是東尼聘請的聖誕節臨時工一般都不會待很久。」

「不好意思，沒問題的。我是有點脾氣，因為你已經是今天第十五位說：『噢，你還在這裡啊！』的人了。」他撇一撇嘴。

「噢。」她笑著說。「我可以明白這樣有多煩擾，真的對不起。我要一杯香草拿鐵和一杯榛子拿鐵，麻煩你。」

他忙著操作咖啡機，舉起糖漿瓶倒進濃縮咖啡中，同一時間在沖製兩杯咖啡。

麗貝卡深深被吸引，「哇噢，你看來很像湯姆·克魯斯！」

他回頭對她笑道，「我沒有聽說過他有咖啡色頭髮和六尺一寸的身高，但還是謝謝你。」

麗貝卡笑了，「不是，我是說你沖泡咖啡的樣子，就像在調配雞尾酒一樣。」

「嗯，對啊。」他轉身把咖啡放在她的托盤上。「我曾經有一陣子在酒吧工作過，是另一份在窮途末路時的工作。」他揚了下眉毛，眨了下眼睛說道。

她舉起雙手，「停！我已經覺得夠差了。」

「好，休戰吧！」

麗貝卡付了錢，他把零錢放在她的托盤上。「謝謝...噢，你現在已經有名牌了。」她俯身向前望了一下，「史堤芬·雷諾茲。」

他搖了搖頭，指了一下名牌。她斜眼看著在下面較小的字。

「哦，對不起 - 『請叫我史堤夫。』那為什麼他們不乾脆把寫史堤夫上去呢？」

「東尼因為特許經營協議，所以這些都是免費的。這個是他們公司的政策，名牌要寫上全名，即使你不曾會用，中間隔著暱稱。神經病。」

她點了下頭。東尼曾告訴她這件事，當時她被嚇壞了。東尼的個性是他最有魅力的地方。「真蠢！要感謝上帝東尼從來不會妥協，正是這樣我才喜歡這裡。」她拿起托盤微微彎身行了個禮。

your badge, then?"

"Tony got these free when he was considering that franchise deal. It was their company policy. Full name on your badge, even if you never use it, and nicknames across the middle. Mad."

She nodded. Tony had told her about it and she'd been horrified. The individuality of Tony's was part of its charm. "Crazy. Thank God Tony never agreed to it, I love this place exactly as it is." She picked up the tray and did a small curtsey. "Thank you, Call Me Steve. And may your days here be happy ones. And short, if you so desire!"

"Thank you... "

"Rebecca."

"Enjoy your coffee, Rebecca."

"Thanks." She walked carefully to the corner where Kevin sat staring out the window. "Penny for them," she said, plonking the tray down and dropping into the seat opposite.

"Oh you know. Just wondering if this dating agency thing means you've taken leave of your senses and I should call a doctor." He prodded her with a wooden stirrer.

"Oh ha ha."

Kevin sniffed his latte appreciatively and took a long drink. "Seriously, though. You don't need a dating agency."

She smacked her forehead. "Of course! You're right. I've had so many dates lately, I can barely fit in time to go food shopping!"

"The only reason you haven't found The One yet is you work too hard." He wiped foam from his mouth with the back of his hand.

"Yeah. And the reason you haven't found The One yet is that you have the manners of a pig."

"All part of my charm." He smiled winningly.

"Is that what it is? Well save it for someone who cares, pig boy." She made a face. "Now I meant to ask, do you want cake? And if I buy you one, can I trust you to keep your mouth shut while you're eating?"

"Yes I do, and yes you could, but no we can't." Kevin tapped his

www.penrose-publishing.co.uk

「謝謝你，『請叫我史堤夫。』，希望你在這裡會開心，總之，如你所願地！」

「謝謝...」

「麗貝卡。」

「請慢慢享用吧，麗貝卡。」

「謝謝。」她慢慢地走到店舖的角落，凱文正坐在那裡盯著窗外。「在想什麼呢？」她說，她放下托盤並坐在對面的座位上。

「哦，你知道的。只是在想約會機構那件事，我覺得你已經瘋了，我應該要叫醫生來。」他拿起攪拌用的木棒戳了她一下。

「噢，哈哈。」

凱文欣賞地聞了聞他的拿鐵咖啡，喝了一大口。「認真的，話雖這樣說。你根本不需要什麼約會機構。」

她拍拍自己的額頭。「對啊！你說得對。我最近有這麼多約會，我幾乎沒有時間去吃飯逛街呢！」

「你有沒有想過，你還沒找到真命天子的原因是你工作太忙了。」他用手背擦去他嘴角的泡沫。

「是啊。那你有沒有想過，你還沒找到真命天子的的原因是你有著豬一樣的態度。」

「這是我魅力的一部分。」他勝利地笑著。

「就是這樣了？那就留給在乎的人吧，豬男孩。」她做了個鬼臉。「現在我想問，你想要蛋糕嗎？如果我給你買一個，我可以相信在你吃的時候會閉上你的嘴嗎？」

「是的，我可以，你也可以，但是我們不行。」凱文指了下手錶。「你不是想去買手袋嗎？就是昨天你說的...咳咳...『緊急員工便箋』。」

「不，我不能再浪費時間了。事實上我們已經遲了離開，但我敢肯定的是，弗蘭的婚禮不會因為我的手提包跟鞋子不配而變成一場災難。」

「很好，正合我心意，我已經極之疲倦了。」他坐了回去，伸出雙腳並嘆了口氣，接著是一陣子的沉默，因為他們都喝著咖啡。

「那麼，那家約會機構叫什麼？」凱文突然問道。

「什麼？哦...」麗貝卡望進她自己的杯子裡頭。「井然配對」她

watch. "Not if you want to go handbag shopping, as discussed in your, ahem, 'urgent staff memo' of yesterday."

"No, I can't be bothered any more. We left late as it was, and I'm sure Fran's wedding won't be a disaster just because my handbag doesn't match my shoes."

"Fair enough. Suits me, I'm shattered." He sat back and stretched his legs out with a sigh, and a companionable silence fell as they both sipped their coffee.

"So what's this dating agency called then?" Kevin asked suddenly.

"What? Oh..." Rebecca looked down into the depths of her cup. "Methodical Matches," she mumbled.

"What?"

"You heard!"

"Methodical Matches? What kind of a name is that?" he exploded.

"Shut up, will you!" she hissed, glancing around. "I know it's not exactly snappy, but I picked them because they work up a really thorough profile on everyone. It's all very scientific. A computer sifts all the variables."

"Ah." Kevin batted his eyelashes. "So you're looking for a man with huge variables, then."

Rebecca whacked him with her purse.

"Ow!"

"I don't know why I tell you anything."

"Come on, I'm only teasing. How does it work then?"

"Well... you know... "

"No, I don't. I've never been on one of those sites myself, and don't know anyone else who has—or admitted to it, anyway."

Rebecca stirred her coffee, avoiding Kevin's eyes. "You answer lots of questions about what you like, what your interests are, your beliefs, what you're hoping for from a relationship. That's your profile. Then the computer compares your profile to everyone else's and generates your ideal matches."

喃喃自語。

「什麼？」

「你聽到的！」

「『井然配對』？這是什麼名字？」他激動起來。

「閉嘴，可以嗎！」她噓了一聲，環視四周。「我知道名字真的不怎麼好，但我選了他們是因為他們為每一位都製作了一個很詳盡的個人檔案，全都很科學化的，可以用電腦篩選了所有可能性。」

「哦...」凱文眨一眨眼，「所以，你要的是一個很有可能性的男人。」

麗貝卡拿起她的錢包擲向他。

「嗷！」

「我不知道為什麼要把什麼都告訴你。」

「好啦，我只是開玩笑。是怎樣運作的呢？」

「嗯...你知道的...」

「不，我不知道。我從來沒有去過這樣的地方，總之就是不知道誰去過，或者有誰想去。」

麗貝卡攪拌著咖啡，避開了凱文的視線。「你會回答很多的問題，你喜歡什麼，你的興趣是什麼，你有什麼信仰，你希望一段什麼關係。這就是你的個人檔案。然後電腦對照其他人的檔案，找出最合適的配對。」

「那你是不是可以去看其他人的檔案？我想你是可以來查看其他人的詳細資料吧！」

「我在想，你不是說你不知道它是如何運作的嗎？」她揚起一邊眼眉。

他扭了一下身體，「你也有聽過有關的東西吧，不是嗎？」

「嗯，但無論如何，我認為你是對的，這就是他們正常的工作模式 - 他們會建議配對，但你也可以自己瀏覽其他人的個人資料，進行篩選等等。但是，這家公司聲稱，他們已經幫你製作了很詳盡的個人資料，非常有系統地做配對，所以根本不需要那樣做。而當你找到了跟自己匹配的人時，就可以互傳短信或見面，他們說這樣很好，因為這樣就可以有話題，而不是早已經知道了對方的一切。這對我來說真的很有意義。」

"Don't you get to look at other profiles? I thought you could to look at other people's details, check them out."

"And I thought you said you didn't know how it works." She raised an eyebrow.

He squirmed a little. "You hear stuff about it, don't you?"

"Hmm. Anyway, I think you're right, that's the way they normally work—they suggest matches but you can browse people's profiles yourself and filter them and everything. But this company claim they profile you so thoroughly, and match you so scientifically, that you don't need that stage. You find out about your matches when you message each other or meet—and they say that's good, because it gives you something to talk about rather than knowing everything already. That really made sense to me."

Kevin looked doubtful. "Not sure what a computer knows about compatibility and love, but it's your life I suppose. But why sign up in the first place? And why now?"

She shrugged, sipping her coffee. "I thought it would help me meet people."

He looked at her keenly. "You meet people all the time, Becs."

"Not the right people."

"Oh, the right people." He rolled his eyes.

"Shush, you. This way, at least the people I meet will be—well, pre-filtered. We'll already have a lot in common."

"Yes, if they can find anyone else like you, that is."

Rebecca looked away, feeling pathetic and a bit panicky. Perhaps he had a point.

Kevin put his hand on her arm. "Sorry, only joking. I'm a bit surprised, that's all."

"I just feel I want to be with someone. I don't know why I suddenly feel like that, but I do." Her voice was a bit quavery. What was wrong with her?

"Ah. The old biological clock ticking?"

"I don't think so. That's not how it feels, anyway. I haven't got cravings for the smell of baby powder or anything." She smiled

凱文充滿了疑問。「我很懷疑那電腦是否真的知道什麼是合適和愛情，但我想，這是你的人生。不過，為什麼你要在第一時間報名？為什麼是現在？」

她聳聳肩，喝著她的咖啡。「我認為這將幫助我結識其他人。」

他用銳利的目光掃了她一下。「你無時無刻都有結識到其他人啊，貝卡。」

「但不是合適的人。」

「哦，合適的人。」他轉了轉眼睛。

「噓，你！應該這樣說，至少我遇到的人會是經過預先篩選，而我們將會有很多共通之處。」

「是的，如果他們能找到其他人像你一樣就是。」

麗貝卡看著遠處，感到有點悲哀和惶恐。也許他是有他的道理。

凱文把他的手放在她的肩膊。「對不起，開玩笑的。我只是有點驚訝罷了。」

「我只是覺得，我想跟別人約會一下。我不知道為什麼突然會有這種想法，但我就想這樣。」她的聲音有些顫聲。她究竟有什麼不妥？

「哎，那個老舊的生理時鐘開始運行了？」

「我不這麼認為。反正就不是那種感覺。我還沒到渴望嬰兒爽身粉氣味的時候。」她無力地笑了笑。「我只是想要一段真正的關係。」

「你已經擁有一段真正的關係。」

「呵呵。主要是跟來自『有感情傷害的男朋友俱樂部』的一些男人。我是希望能遇到一個可以共存的好人。」

「拉爾夫是個好人啊。」

「是的，是很好。但他的問題是跟他母親有關，再加上他會為野餐墊子而興奮。這對野餐墊子來說是種侮辱。」她很高興談話內容已經轉移到更安全地帶。無論如何，比之前安全。

「西蒙。」

「他很可愛的。除了他的前妻每隔幾個月要威脅傷害自己時，而他一定要回到她身邊。在我開始去做同樣的事前，一定要抽身。」

weakly. "I just crave a real relationship."

"You've had real relationships."

"Huh. Mainly with men from Emotionally Damaged Boyfriends R Us. I want to meet someone compatible. Someone nice."

"Ralph was nice."

"Yeah. Nice. But he had issues with his mother, plus he was about as exciting as a picnic rug. And that's an insult to picnic rugs." She was glad the conversation had moved to safer territory. Comparatively, anyway.

"Simon."

"Lovely. Except for going back to his ex-wife every couple of months when she threatened to hurt herself. Had to get out of that one before I started to go the same way."

"Hal. He was okay." He smirked. "More than at some things, I believe."

"But deep, meaningful conversation wasn't one of them, if you remember."

"No. His interests were pretty limited. But if it's scintillating conversation you're after, darling, then I'm your man," he grinned.

"Right. Of course! Silly me."

"Seriously, you know what the real problem is," he sighed, looking sad.

"Come on then, Yoda." She did the voice. "Give me the benefit of your wisdom, you must." She tipped her coffee mug to get the last of the coffee and froth.

"None of them can ever compare to me," he said, leering comically, and slid a hand up her thigh. Rebecca squawked, spluttering froth and latte liberally across the table. By the time she'd cleared up the mess, which took ages because Kevin was being even sillier than usual, they had to settle for a takeaway sandwich. But Rebecca was glad Kevin had made her laugh, and banished that stupid emotional moment she'd been having. It wasn't like her at all.

His teasing hadn't changed her mind though, she thought, as they walked back to work. She was going through with it. Nothing

「哈爾。他不錯。」他冷笑道。「我相信一定比其他的好。」

「如果你還記得的話，跟他不會有深層和有意義的對話。」

「不是，他的興趣是非常有限。但是，如果你想要是我充滿才趣的對話，親愛的，我就是你的男人，」他咧嘴而笑。

「對啊。當然！我真傻。」

「認真的，你知道真正的問題是什麼。」他嘆了口氣，看似很傷心。

「來吧，大師。」她沒氣的說。「你一定要給我拿出你的智慧來。」她把最後一口的咖啡和泡沫都喝完。

「從來沒有人能夠跟我相比。」他說，然後不懷好意地笑，並把手滑到她的大腿上。麗貝卡呱呱大叫，把咖啡和泡沫都噴濺到桌子的對面很遠。她花了很長時間去清理殘局，因為凱文比平時表現得更笨，而他們亦解決了一份外賣三明治。但麗貝卡很高興凱文令她笑了，令她消除了之前那個無聊的情緒。這一點都不像是她。

當他們回去工作時，她在想，他的逗弄並沒有改變她的主意。她下定了決心。正如她爸爸所說：不入虎穴，焉得虎子。也許她真的會找到一位真命天子。

或者至少有一個像樣的約會。

史堤夫再次看了門口一眼。麗貝卡今天還會再來嗎？她不是每一天都會來，但大多數日子裡，她會突然出現買一杯咖啡和糕點，或者，更多的時候是吃午飯。他知道她最喜歡的糕點是杏味丹麥酥，最喜歡的肉卷是香辣雞肉卷。他也知道她最喜歡什麼類型的男人，但很可惜，因為那個高大金髮的家伙幾乎總是跟她在一起。

自從星期一跟她談過之後，他一直看著他們，當然，他假裝他不是。他有的優勢就是可以躲在看似很忙碌的櫃檯後面。他們看起來很要好。她是一個尤物，一頭栗色的頭髮，有時披在她的肩上，又光澤又順滑，而有時用髮夾盤在腦後，留一撮卷鬢出來，如果硬要說有什麼分別，就是更美麗了。羅拉有一次也這樣盤起了頭髮，他想起時心裡一陣劇痛。現在不能為她費心，無論是她的頭髮或其他任何東西。

麗貝卡總是生氣勃勃而且很幽默，但他對這方面一向沒門。很少會見她和那個金髮的家伙分開來，他想他們應該是一起工作的。如果是這樣的話，經常黏在一起似乎並沒有什麼不好。他們在一起時總是很自在，明顯他們之間有良好的化學作用。史堤夫有注意到他把手放在麗貝卡的大腿上令麗貝卡咯咯大笑，並把咖啡噴濺到周圍都是。他意識到自己盯得太顯眼，感到有點心虛，他把

ventured, nothing gained, as her Dad used to say. Maybe she really would find The One.

Or a half-decent date, at least.

Steve glanced at the door again. Would Rebecca be back today? She didn't come in every day, but most days she either popped in for a quick coffee and a pastry, or, more often for lunch. He knew her favourite pastry was Apricot Danish and her favourite wrap was Cajun Chicken. He knew her favourite type of man too, unfortunately, because that tall blonde guy was nearly always with her.

He'd watched them after he spoke to her on Monday, although of course he pretended he wasn't. You got good at that, hiding away behind the counter looking busy. They looked good together. She was a stunner; all that chestnut hair, sometimes lying over her shoulders, shiny and smooth, and sometimes caught up in a barrette at the back of her head, the tendrils that escaped making her look, if anything, more beautiful. Laura had worn her hair that way once, he thought with a pang. Now she couldn't be bothered. With her hair, or anything else.

Rebecca was bright and funny, too, but he was on a road to nowhere there. It was very rare for her and the blonde guy to come in separately; he wondered if they worked together. If they did, seeing so much of each other didn't seem to do them any harm. They seemed very comfortable together but there was obviously good chemistry between them too. Steve had noticed him put his hand on her thigh making Rebecca giggle and splutter her coffee everywhere. He realised he was staring far too blatantly. Feeling guilty, he'd pulled himself together and set about cleaning and tidying everything in sight, this had impressed Tony no end.

So knowing she was off limits, why did he find himself hoping she would come in today? Glancing at the door every other minute? And even worse, asking Neil, the Australian guy working here in his gap year, to swap duties so he could be here now, serving behind the counter? You're a hopeless case Steve, he told himself, just setting yourself up for disappointment.

The door opened and he glanced up. Through the throng of people just leaving, he caught a glimpse of a plum-coloured coat. She was right on time for lunch and there was no sign of her boyfriend. His heart thudded a little faster and he took a deep breath, summoning up his professional here-to-brighten-up-your-day smile as she came towards him.

"Back again?"

視線拉回來，並著手眼前的清潔和整理工作，這樣才可以令東尼不會解僱他。

他所知道她的事情有限，為什麼他會發現自己希望她今天還會再來呢？而且每隔一分鐘就掃視門口一次？更糟的是，他問那位年齡跟他差幾年的澳洲傢伙尼爾去交換職務，令他可以在櫃檯工作呢？他告訴自己：你沒有希望的了，史堤夫。希望可以令自己打消念頭。

門開了，他抬起頭。隨著一大群人剛剛離開，他瞥見了一個穿紫紅色外套的人。這正是她吃午飯的時間，而沒有任何跡象她的男朋友有一起來。他的心呼呼地跳得比平時快了一點，他深深吸了一口氣，來喚醒自己的專業精神，當她走近時，他亮出了親切的笑容。

「又來了？」

「是啊，我又來了。」

「香草拿鐵？」

「是的，麻煩你。」她深深地嘆了口氣。「一個香辣雞肉卷和雙重碎巧克力鬆餅。要大的」。

「就這樣嗎？」他按了一下咖啡機上的按鈕。

「對。我剛才幾乎去酒吧了。」

「唷！有那麼糟嗎？那是什麼改變了你的想法？」

「我今天下午要跟一些非常重要的人開一個會議，所以喝得爛醉就不是那麼好。」

「我明白了。」他輕輕的把拿鐵放到她前面，並把一塊餅乾放在碟子上。

她看著它，揚起了眉毛。　「另外，這裡的員工也比較好。」她淡淡地說。

史堤夫盡力令自己的臉頰不要紅漲起來。　「你不用這樣說，因為我已經給你一塊免費的餅乾了。」

「不，我就是這個意思，不是為了餅乾。」

「呃…謝謝。」他禮貌地笑了笑，把她的雞卷和鬆餅放在托盤上，但他的內心其實激動了一下。她是不是在跟他調情呢？還是她是那種男朋友不在身邊，就會跟她眼前的所有人調情的那種女人呢？他不知道為什麼，這個奇怪念頭令他覺得很失望。而當她只是報以一個微笑就走開了，他不知道為什麼他有鬆了一口氣或

"Yep. A regular bad penny, me."

"Vanilla latte?"

"Yes please." She sighed deeply. "And a Cajun Chicken Wrap and a double choc chip muffin. Large."

"Like that, is it?" He hit the button on the coffee machine.

"Definitely. I nearly went to the wine bar instead."

"Phew, that bad? What changed your mind?"

"I've got a meeting this afternoon with some Very Important People, so getting sloshed wouldn't be good."

"I see." He slid her latte across to her and put a biscuit on the saucer.

She looked at it, raising her eyebrows. "Plus the staff here are nicer," she said lightly.

Steve willed his cheeks not to go pink. "You're only saying that because I've given you a free biscuit."

"No, I mean it. Biscuit aside."

"Er... thanks." He smiled politely, putting the wrap and muffin on her tray, but inside his heart had done a little flip. Was she flirting with him? Perhaps she was one of those women who flirted with everyone in sight once their boyfriend wasn't around? He found that idea strangely disappointing, but wasn't sure why. When she just smiled in reply and walked away, he didn't know if he felt relieved or demoralised.

He watched her sit down and start on her lunch, then frowned. Her boyfriend had just come in and gone straight to her table. He didn't come to the counter. Probably a good thing, Steve thought, because he could feel himself glowering.

The kitchen door squeaked behind him. "Earth to Steve, come in Steve."

"What?"

"I said, is this the first tray of croissants we've got through today, or the second?" said Neil patiently. Steve liked Neil. He was good fun to work with, but he wouldn't be here for much longer. He'd planned 6 months earning and 6 months trekking, and he'd been

是有點洩氣的感覺。

他看著她坐下，並開始吃起她的午餐，然後皺起了眉頭。這時候她的男朋友進來，徑直地走向她，而沒有到櫃檯來。史堤夫心想這可能是一件好事，因為他能感覺到自己正怒視著他。

他身後的廚房門發出吱吱聲。「史堤夫過來一下。」

「什麼？」

「我說，這盤是不是今天第一盤的牛角麵包，或是第二盤了？」尼爾耐心地說。史堤夫喜歡尼爾，跟他一起工作很有趣，但他不會在這裡待很久。他計劃好了賺六個月工資之後就會去六個月的旅行，而他比史堤夫早來這裡工作兩個月。

「對不起。是第一盤。」

尼爾端著托盤到櫃檯。「那我只填滿這盤，然後把剩下拿回去。抱歉打斷你偷瞄美女了。」

「什麼？我沒有啊。」

「找過其他人吧，兄弟，我看到你在偷瞄麗貝卡。你覺得她很好嗎？」他咧嘴而笑。

「什麼…你不覺得嗎？」史堤夫防範地說。

他聳聳肩，看似有點尷尬。

「反正就沒有太大分別。是很好，但可惜名花有主。」史堤夫說著，他的頭向麗貝卡的方向戳了一下。

「她是嗎？」尼爾抬起頭，皺一皺眉頭。「你覺得他們是在一起的嗎？」

「他們總是一起在這裡，似乎非常親密。昨天，他還把他的手放在她的腿上，很高的位置。」

尼爾搖了搖頭。「他們可能只是鬧著玩，他們一起在博物館工作。我覺得你是誤會了，兄弟。」

「為什麼？」

他無法理解是什麼原因，尼爾臉紅了。「因為…呃…我見過凱文，在城外。」

「然後呢？」

尼爾轉身走開，去整理牛角麵包，雖然史堤夫覺得它們仍然很

here two months before Steve arrived.

"Sorry. First."

Neil carried the tray over to the counter. "I'll just fill up the tray then, and take the rest back. Sorry to interrupt when you're staring at pretty girls."

"What? I wasn't—"

"Pull the other one, dude, I saw you looking at Rebecca. You think she's well fit." He grinned.

"What, and you don't?" said Steve defensively.

He shrugged, looking a little awkward.

"Doesn't make much difference, anyway. Well fit but well attached, unfortunately," said Steve, jerking his head in Rebecca's direction.

"She is?" Neil glanced up, frowning. "You think those two are together?"

"They're always in here together, and they seem very close. He put his hand on her leg yesterday. High up."

Neil shook his head. "They were probably just mucking about. They work together at the museum. I think you're barking up the wrong tree there, mate."

"Why?"

For some reason he couldn't fathom, Neil went a little pink. "Cos I've, er, seen Kevin about. Out on the town."

"And?"

Neil turned away, rearranging the croissants, although they looked fine to Steve. "He wasn't acting like he was attached, that's all. A single bloke out on the pull, I reckon."

Steve looked back to Rebecca, laughing at something the blonde guy had just said, and shook his head. "I don't know. Perhaps they've got a very open relationship, but I'd bet you that whole tray of croissants they're together. Not that I'm in a position to care one way or the other."

"Why? Because of Laura?"

好。「他看來不像是名草有主，就這樣。只是一個單身漢罷了，我估計是。」

史堤夫回頭看了看麗貝卡，她正為那個金髮碧眼的傢伙剛剛的說話什麼在笑，他搖了搖頭。「我不知道。也許他們有一段非常開放的關係，但我敢跟你打賭，整盤的牛角麵包是在一起的，而我對這事或其他都不關心。」

「為什麼？是因為羅拉？」

史堤夫聳聳肩。

「兄弟，我認為是時間做個了斷了。」他用肘推一推他，向麗貝卡和凱文方向點了下頭。「如果他們之間的關係是如此開放，你可能就有機會。」

「了斷，哈？你說得蠻容易。」史堤夫輕輕拍了拍肩膀，在櫃檯上噴了下清潔劑。「而且這不像我，謝謝了，我不同意。」

「你真的是太古板了吧？」尼爾向他眨眨眼睛。「我不理你了，爺爺。」

「回廚房去吧，奴隸！」

尼爾一邊大笑一邊回到廚房去。

史堤夫轉過身來，開始清潔糕點櫃，他在櫃子上方偷看他的目標。尼爾一定是錯了，這兩個人總是黏在一起。他永遠不會得到跟她約會的機會。如果他想在生活中多一個全新的女人，那他需要的是停止注視她並把眼光放遠一點。但，他可以嗎？

他若有所思的地看著櫃檯，上面已經不是第一次堆滿了傳單，他拿起其中一張。

【井然配對：「我們懂得用科學去配對。」】

糟透的名字，俗氣的標題。但是內容又好像很有道理，他把傳單折起，放進了口袋。

Steve shrugged.

"Mate, I think it's time to cut the strings there." He elbowed him, nodding at Rebecca and Kevin. "And if their relationship's so open, you might be in with a chance."

"Cut the strings, huh? Easy for you to say." Steve flipped a cloth over his shoulder and sprayed cleaner on the counter. "And not for me, thanks. I don't share."

"Old-fashioned, aren't ya?" Neil winked at him. "I'll leave you to it then, Granddad."

"Back to the kitchen, galley slave."

Laughing, Neil disappeared back to the kitchen

Steve turned and made a start on cleaning the pastry cabinet, watching his targets surreptitiously over the top. Neil must be wrong; those two were joined at the hip. He was never going to get a date with her. He needed to stop mooning over her and look elsewhere, if he wanted a new woman in his life. But did he?

He looked thoughtfully, not for the first time, at the pile of leaflets on the counter. He picked one up.

'Methodical Matches: "We see Suitability as a Science."'

Dreadful name. Tacky tagline. But everything it said inside seemed to make sense. He folded it up and put it in his pocket.

不需要此页

Chapter Two

No time to go to Tony's today, thought Rebecca, sinking into her chair and wrapping her hands gratefully around her coffee mug. Still, at least she could afford a few minutes sitting at her desk, although it was more tempting to hide under it today.

It wasn't that she didn't love her work. Her parents had both been archaeologists; there was nothing else she'd ever wanted to be, and she couldn't be happier with her current role as Project Leader for GLAMAR – the Greater London Anthropology Museum's Archaeological Research team. But today work had been manic.

Every so often the Museum ran family fun days, either for the general public or for corporations. She enjoyed getting the children involved and knew it was important – if she could get them interested, these kids might be the archaeologists of the future—but it meant her days were hectic as she tried to organise activities for the visitors and keep an eye on the everyday work that went on.

She'd left her group in Kevin and Emma's capable hands for a bit, and as this might be the only break she'd get this morning, she'd better hurry up and reply to the supposedly urgent message that had been on her answer phone when she got home last night. She tapped in the number.

"Good morning! Methodical Matches, Nicola speaking, how can I help you?"

"Hello, you left a message on my answer machine yesterday. It's Rebecca Maynard."

"Oh, Rebecca! Hi! Thanks for getting back to me!"

Rebecca pulled the phone away from her ear a little. Nicola was obviously one of those people who only spoke in exclamations. "You said it was urgent?"

第二章

麗貝卡在想，今天沒有時間去東尼的店了，她坐在椅子上滿足地用雙手拿著咖啡杯。儘管如此，至少她有幾分鐘的時間可以坐在她的辦公桌前，雖然今天還有很多事情要做。

並不是她不喜歡自己的工作。她的父母都是考古學家，她沒有想過要做別的工作，她最開心就是可以擔任了「GLAMAR1」的項目負責人，即是「倫敦人類學博物館的考古研究團隊」。但是今天的工作真的夠瘋狂。

幾乎每隔一段時間，博物館就會為公眾或機構舉辦家庭同樂日。她很喜歡讓孩子一起參與，而且她知道這是很重要的，如果她能令他們感興趣，這些孩子可能就是未來的考古學家。但是這也意味著她將會非常忙碌，因為她除了每天的工作之外，還要為參觀者舉辦活動。

她暫時將小組交給了凱文和愛瑪這兩位得力助手，因為這可能是她早上唯一可以休息一下的機會，她最好快點回覆那個所謂的緊急留言，她昨晚回到家時在電話錄音聽到的，她按下了號碼。

「早上好！井然配對，我是妮科拉，有什麼可以幫到你嗎？」

「你好，我是回覆你昨天留言的。我是麗貝卡．梅納德。」

「噢，麗貝卡！你好！謝謝你回覆我！」

麗貝卡把電話拉離開耳邊一點點，妮科拉顯然是那些只會說感嘆詞的人，「你說有急事嗎？」

「是的，我打電話給你是因為我留意到你的個人資料還沒有完成！如果你沒完成它，我們就不能開立檔案，為你找一些絕佳的井然配對了！」

1 　　「Greater London Anthropology Museum's Archaeological Research」的縮寫。

"Yes, I phoned because I noticed your profile is still showing as incomplete! Until you finish it, we can't get on the case and find you some great Methodical Matches!"

Wow. Hardly the end of the world, thought Rebecca. "Oh, right. It's just that—"

Her office door crashed open and Kevin slithered to a halt in front of her. "There's a problem in the Kid's Corner, Becs!" He spotted the phone in her hand and put his hands over his mouth, muttering a muffled "sorry!"

"Excuse me for a moment." She put her hand over the mouthpiece and gave Kevin a cool look. "Where's the fire?"

"One of the kids just peed in a Dig It Sandbox."

She rolled her eyes. "Nicola, something's just cropped up. I could pop in at lunchtime, unless you close then? I'm just round the corner."

"Great! Look forward to seeing you then!" Nicola trilled.

Rebecca slapped the phone down and stood up. "How did a kid pee in the sandbox?"

He spread his hands. "Er, the usual way? He kind of stood up and—"

"They're not meant to get in the box, Kev, they're meant to lean over it! You know that."

"I know, I know. Sorry. I only turned my back for a second."

"Which one was it?"

"Rory – you know, the little one with those dark corkscrew curls and scarily pale blue eyes? Devil child, Emma's been calling him. Not in his parents' hearing, of course."

She stared. "Not which kid. Which sandbox, dumbass."

"Oh... sorry." He looked sheepish. "Roman. He'd got down to the First Invasion era."

She strode past him. "I suppose we need new sand then."

"And a new brooch," he called, hurrying to catch up with her. "That's what you get for using fake artefacts in there, it's gone a

哇，幾乎世界末日了，麗貝卡心想，「噢，對啊。這只是因為…」

她辦公室的門應聲而開，凱文滑行在她面前停了下來。「貝卡！兒童天地出事了！」他發現了她手拿著電話，他隨即摀住了嘴巴，低沉地嘀咕了一聲「對不起！」

「請等一下。」她用手摀著話筒用一副很酷的樣子看著凱文。「哪裡出事了？」

「孩子剛在掏沙池撒尿了。」

她翻了翻眼睛，「妮科拉，剛發生了些事情。我公司就在拐角處，吃午飯的時候我可以過去，除非你午飯時候會關門。」

「太好了！期待見到你！」妮科拉語帶顫音地說。

麗貝卡摔下了電話站了起來，「孩子怎麼在沙池中撒尿？」

他攤開雙手，「呃，一般的方法吧？他站起來，然後…」

「他們照道理是不會入去沙池中，凱文，他們應該只是俯身去看一下！你知道的。」

「我知道，我知道。抱歉。我只是轉了身一秒鐘。」

「是哪一個？」

「羅里－你知道嗎，是個有黑色螺旋捲髮和可怕淺藍色眼睛的小傢伙啊？艾瑪一直叫他小魔頭，當然是在他父母聽不到的時候。」

她瞪大了眼睛，「我不是問哪個孩子，是哪一個沙箱，蠢蛋。」

「噢…對不起。」他羞怯地說。「在羅馬那邊。是第一次入侵的時代那邊。」

她向他大步走了過去，「我想，我們要新的沙子了。」

「還要一個新的別針，」他叫住她，匆匆趕上去。「這就是為什麼你要放些假的文物在那邊，現在它的顏色被弄得非常可笑…」

六小時後，麗貝卡快步沿著街道走，她非常後悔她打電話給那家約會機構。今天簡直像在煉獄一樣，羅裡最終成為了一個連環撒尿鬼，而且午餐時間也沒法停下來。她一直咬緊牙關把工作做完，好不容易可以準時在下班時間離開。她做到了，大致上。現在她只想倒在沙發上喝杯酒，外賣可以很快就送到。但現在，她不得不再等一下。

really funny colour..."

Six hours later, Rebecca was walking quickly along the street, bitterly regretting her promise to call in at the dating agency. She'd had a hell of a day – Rory had turned out to be a serial pee-er—and hadn't managed to stop for lunch at all. It had been easier to grit her teeth and work through it in the hope of leaving on time. She'd managed that, just about, and now all she wanted was to collapse on her sofa with a large glass of wine, happy in the knowledge that takeaway would turn up shortly. But she would have to wait.

She pushed open the door of Methodical Matches and jumped as it made a loud, discordant two-tone beep.

"Oh, sorry about that. We keep saying we'll get a new one!"

Nicola—Rebecca knew it was her before she spotted the name plate—smiled at her from behind a white desk with arty curved shelves on burnished steel supports, devoid of any paperwork or stationery. She wondered if the sole purpose of the desk was to support Nicola's Tango-coloured arms and scarily long mint-green fingernails, which were resting on it in a glowing triangle formation that resembled a fluorescent road sign.

"Hi, I'm Rebecca Maynard. You phoned about my profile?"

"Yes! We're very keen to get started, and wondered if there was a problem. We can't do anything until the profile's completed! We need the whole picture!" Teeth that could have doubled as a Dulux brilliant white sample flashed in Nicola's face.

"I'm nearly finished, it's just that, er..." Rebecca floundered.

"You're having problems with the website?" Nicola supplied. She tilted her head, a tiny, patronising smile on her lips. "It's not always easy for people who didn't grow up in the internet generation, is it?"

Rebecca had never been completely sure what the phrase 'she bridled' meant when she'd read it in books, but she was pretty sure she was doing it now. Yes. Definite bridling going on.

"I'm perfectly fine with the technical aspects, thank you," she replied, in a tone that could freeze polar bears. "But I only registered last week and haven't had time to complete it yet. It's quite long and the website times out after twenty minutes and loses my information. That's happened twice already."

她推開井然配對的大門，被響亮的聲音嚇了一跳，是很不和諧的二重蜂鳴聲。

「哦，對不起。我們一直在說，得要換一道新的門了！」

妮科拉，麗貝卡在看到名牌前已經知道是她了，她對她笑了笑，她正坐在白色辦公桌後，那桌子用庸風磨光的弧形鋼架支撐，桌上沒有任何文件或文具。她在懷疑，那辦公桌的唯一目的其實只是支撐著妮科拉那探戈橘色的雙臂和長得可怕的薄荷綠色指甲，它們上面還有一個發光的三角形，就像熒光路標一樣。

「你好，我叫麗貝卡·梅納德。是你打過電話來，跟我說有關個人檔案的事嗎？」

「是的！我們很想快點可以開始，但發現有一個問題。如果檔案不完整，我們什麼都不能做的！我們需要的是完整的資料！」兩排像多樂士亮白色的牙齒在妮科拉臉上閃爍著。

「我幾乎就完成了，只是…呃…」麗貝卡有點不知失措。

「你對網站有不明白的地方嗎？」妮科拉問。她偏了一下頭，唇上帶著一個微小而傲慢的笑容。「對於不是在互聯網世代長大的人來說，真的有點難度，是嗎？」

麗貝卡曾經在書上看過，但沒有完全明白那句「暗諷」的意思，但她很確定，妮科拉現在所做的就是「暗諷」。

「在技術上我完全沒有問題，謝謝你。」她回答的語氣像北極熊一樣冰冷。「我上週已經登記好了，只是還沒有時間去完成它。因為要花很長時間，而且每隔二十分鐘，網站就會因為超時而令我輸入的資料都沒有了，已經發生過了兩次了。」

在妮科拉那彈性光滑被曬成棕褐色的額頭上出現一道小皺紋。「超時？我們從來沒這個問題。」

「我已經把那些問題打印出來了，簡單地寫在紙上，只需輸入我的答案就行。」麗貝卡說，「但我到下週都沒時間。」

「下週？」妮科拉重複。她俯身向前，她把聲音降低到好像在說什麼機密似的，「你知道，我們是非常謹慎的。」她嘘了一聲，那刺耳的音調應該連在街上戴著的耳機聽著音樂的人也聽得到。「如果是讀寫的問題，進入辦公室來，有人可以提供幫助…」

她反駁說：「我讀寫能力也很好，謝謝你！」。哪門的神經病！「但食物日記要涵蓋一個星期的，而我只填寫了首四天。」

妮科拉茫然地看著她，「食物日記？」

麗貝卡覺得自己好像在跟一隻鸚鵡談話，真對不起世上所有的鸚

A tiny furrow appeared in Nicola's otherwise stretchy-smooth tanned forehead. "Timing out? We've not had a problem with that before."

"I've printed out the questions now, so I can rough it out on paper, then just type in my answers," said Rebecca. "But I can't finish it until next week. "

"Next week?" echoed Nicola. She leaned forward and lowered her voice to a supposedly confidential whisper. "We're very discreet you know," she hissed, in a penetrating tone that could probably be heard by iPod-wearing passers-by on the street. "If there's a literacy issue, come into the office and someone can help…"

"My literacy skills are fine, thank you!" she retorted. What a nerve! "But the food diary covers a week and I've only filled out the first four days."

Nicola looked at her blankly. "Food diary?"

It's like talking to a parrot, thought Rebecca. Sorry, parrots of the world. "Yes, in the eating habits section. Under lifestyle."

Nicola looked none the wiser.

"I suppose it's so that lovers of daily fry-ups don't get matched up with people whose idea of a big breakfast is a larger slice of watermelon than usual." Why was she explaining the rationale of the profile to someone from the company that had designed it?

"I wasn't aware of a food diary section." Nicola frowned, distracted. "It wasn't there before."

"Perhaps it's new," said Rebecca after a long pause when the only sound was Nicola's nails tapping on the desk. And possibly cogs whirring, if she'd listened closely. "It's very time-consuming. I'm sure some general questions about what people like to eat would be just as useful. Maybe you should suggest it to whoever designs the questionnaire."

Nicola gave a short, sharp laugh, suddenly all attention again. "Oh, that's a great idea." Her tone of voice suggested she thought otherwise. "If I see him, I'll suggest it."

"Er… right. Thanks—"

"Anything else?" Her glare dared Rebecca to say yes.

鵡。「是的，在飲食習慣部分。在生活方式欄下。」

妮科拉看來還沒有明白過來。

「我想它的意思是，每日早餐都要吃煎培根雞蛋的人跟一個認為吃一大片西瓜已經很豐富的人是不匹配的。」她為什麼要向一個設計這東西的公司裡的職員解釋這些？

「我沒有留意食物日記部分。」妮科拉皺起了眉頭，困惑地說。「以前沒有這部分的。」

「也許是新的，」經過一段時間的停頓後麗貝卡說，唯一的聲音是來自妮科拉用指甲敲打著桌面，如果仔細聽的話，又可能是齒輪的颼颼聲。「這是非常費時的，我敢肯定，一般有關飲食喜好的問題已經足夠了。也許你應該給設計調查問卷的人一些建議。」

妮科拉尖銳的笑了一下，突然又再全神貫注。「哦，那是一個很好的主意。」她的語氣明顯表明了她想的跟說的不一樣。「如果我見到他，會告訴他。」

「嗯...那就好。謝謝。」

「還有什麼嗎？」她怒視著麗貝卡像是看她是否還敢說什麼。

「沒有，已經很好...」

「希望很快能看到你的更新。」

「是的，呃...」麗貝卡慌慌張張地走到門口。「盡快吧。」

當她走到安全地帶，她即時鬆了一口氣。哇！好一個反擊。

她剛剛說的會不會令傑基爾小姐變成邪惡女巫海德2？

為何她覺得這樣還是比努力社交簡單多了，而且，為什麼還是會希望最後能遇到一個好男人？

週日晚上，麗貝卡把筆記本電腦放在沙發上，並打開了她的檔案副本。食物日記終於寫完了，但她的個人資料仍然有空白部分。這件事繼續下去，他們可能要挖出她的大腦出來看看，那它應該會轉得快一點，而且不用再這麼痛苦。

哦，不！她忘了這部分。「按字母順序列出你擁有所有專輯的歌手姓氏或樂隊名稱。」究竟跟「你喜歡音樂的類型」有什麼分別？真的有人會說真話嗎？不管怎樣，有人會把在收藏品中最為珍貴的沃澤爾（Wurzel）專輯的整個曲目慎重地放到「W」

2　　　「傑基爾與海德」意為有兩種不同面目（或善惡雙重人格）的人，出處：《Jekyll and Hyde》Robert Louis Stevenson。

"No, that's fi—"

"Hope to see your profile soon then."

"Yes, er..." Rebecca was walking to the door, flustered. "As soon as possible."

Once she was safely outside, her breath whooshed out in a huge sigh of relief. Wow. What a turnaround. What had she said to turn Little Miss Jekyll in there into the Evil Hag Hyde?

And why had she thought this would be simpler than making more effort to socialise and hoping that somehow, eventually, she'd meet a nice guy?

Sunday night. Rebecca stretched out on the settee with her laptop, and opened up the copy of the dating profile. The food diary was finally finished, but there were still blank sections in her profile. This thing went on forever. They might just have well have scooped out her brain and had a good look; it would have been quicker. And probably less painful.

Oh, no! She'd forgotten this part. 'List all albums you possess alphabetically by artist's surname or band name.' What was wrong with 'what genres of music you enjoy?' And did people tell the truth, anyway, or did they get to W and discreetly forget their entire back catalogue of Wurzel albums that had pride of place on the shelf? Luckily—or perhaps scarily, she admitted— she arranged her CDs alphabetically anyway, but she had about 75. Should she confess to Abba?

Twenty minutes later, she'd jotted down a judiciously edited list. Abba had gone the way of Michael Ball, Tangerine Dream and a few others, partly because she persuaded herself they weren't typical of her taste, which was a joke, given how eclectic it was, but mainly because she was worried she'd be matched with someone who owned those albums too. She didn't want to think too hard about what that said about her.

Luckily the reading section was far less detailed, or she'd have been up all night listing books. She owned hundreds; they took up more room than anything else in her small flat, stored on a selection of tall, generally wonky mismatched bookcases. She loved biographies and old dictionaries with archaic words, and had a huge number of books on history, archaeology, anthropology and palaeontology.

But when she was snuggled up in her big armchair relaxing, or chilling out in the bath, she normally chose historical fiction or

入面？幸運地，或者是駭人地，她承認，她的專輯都是按字母順序排列，但她只有大約七十五張。她應該坦白說有阿巴樂隊（ABBA）的嗎？

二十分鐘後，她明智地記下了一個編輯列表。阿巴樂隊已經變成了邁克保爾（Michael Ball）、橘夢樂團（Tangerine Dream）和其他的人了，一方面是因為她說服自己，那其實並不是她喜歡的類型，這只是鬧著玩，讓它看來五花八門。但主要是因為她擔心，跟她配對的人也擁有這些專輯。她不想太確實說有關自己的事情。

幸運的是，閱讀部分是不用那麼詳盡，或者其實是因為她已經用了一整個晚上列出了書單。她擁有數百本書，在她的小平房裡，它們佔用的空間比任何東西還要多，都擺放在以高為主搖搖晃晃不太合襯的書櫃上。她喜歡用古體詞寫的傳記和老字典，還有一大堆歷史學、考古學、人類學、古生物學的書籍。

　但是，當她依偎在那張大扶手椅休息，或在泡浴放輕鬆時，她通常選擇歷史小說或她最喜歡的朱迪·福斯特探險小說。它們通常是要那類解開某種千古懸案，而連接到一個現代化陰謀的劇情，這可以滿足她潛在的強烈「印第安那·瓊斯3」慾望。在填寫「我有史以來排名前十位」和「我讀的最後十本書」的時候，她笑了，想起她與凱文談起她的前男友，原來哈爾從沒有在這些類別，有任何一個在前十位之內。無論如何，也不是那麼難理解的。

下一部分令她感到很不安，他們真的需要知道以前每一段關係的細節嗎？她盡可能簡短把它完成。以十分為滿分來給前男友的特質評分。有些題目是相當私人的，這實在令人生厭。感謝上帝下一部分是最後的了，她迅速完成了她的「道德和信仰」。

當她完成所有答案並複製到線上表格上時，已經是半夜了。她打了個哈欠，點擊「發送」。很想知道那些男人會是怎麼樣的，科學化來配對特質和態度真的可行嗎？還是只會剝奪了約會和約會的浪漫性？當她要以一個預先計劃好的方式來跟一個男人約會時，還會不會感覺坐立不安，還會為一見鍾情而興奮呢？

她合上了她的電腦。但願她很快就能找到。

「那麼，今天要是什麼？哦，拿鐵女皇？你要跟平時一樣，還要想要點不一樣的嗎？」史堤夫不懷好意地俯身向前。「不要跟別人說，」他噓了一聲，「但我們有一款新的糖漿，還沒有開始售賣呢。」

「噢，」麗貝卡吸了一大口氣，睜大了眼睛。「快點告訴我！」

「這是奶油糖果。」史堤夫怪裡怪氣地低聲說道。他做了一個東

3　　　印第安那·瓊斯（Dr. Henry "Indiana" Jones, Jr.）是一個虛構的人物，為冒險電影《奪寶奇兵》（英語：Raiders of the Lost Ark）系列的主角，典型形象特徵為牛仔帽裝扮以及長鞭。

her favourite—a Jodie Forrest thriller. They normally had some kind of ancient mystery to be solved that connected to a modern conspiracy plot, and helped to satisfy her latent Indiana Jones urges. She filled in 'my all time top 10' and 'the last 10 books I read' and grinned, thinking about her conversation with Kevin about her exes. Hal would never have got to 10 in either of those categories—not without some serious head-scratching, anyway.

The next section made her squirm. Did they really need to know the details of every past relationship? She was as brief as possible. Scoring her exes out of 10 on their attributes – some of which were rather personal – was cringe worthy. Thank God the next section was the last. She whizzed through her 'ethics and beliefs'.

It was midnight when she finished copying her answers into the online submission form. She yawned as she clicked 'send', wondering what these men would be like. Did matching attributes and attitudes scientifically really work, or did it just strip dating or all its romance? Would she still get that fluttering in her stomach, that thrill of instant attraction, when she was meeting men in such a pre-planned way?

She closed her laptop. Hopefully, she'd soon find out.

"So what will it be today, oh queen of the latte? Your usual, or something a little more exotic?" Steve leaned forward conspiratorially. "Don't tell everyone," he hissed, "But we've got a new syrup in. It's just not on the board yet."

"Ooh," Rebecca breathed, making her eyes go wide. "Go on. Tell!"

"It's butterscotch," Steve said, in a comical strangled whisper. He made a show of glancing round, then bent down under the counter and let the bottle quickly peep over the top.

"Yum. I love butterscotch. Where did you get that from?"

He shook his head. "If I told you, I'd have to kill you," he rasped. "That would be an awful shame. Bright girl like you."

"Well if I promise not to ask any more questions, can I have some in my coffee?" she whispered back.

"Yes. But remember—tell no one." He glared at her. "Or else..." he mimed cutting his throat.

"Understood."

張西望的動作，然後彎下腰到櫃檯下，並迅速將瓶子放在櫃檯上面。

「美味。我愛奶油糖果。哪裡弄來的？」

他搖搖頭，「如果我告訴你，那我就不得不殺了你。」他粗聲粗氣地說：「這將是非常令人惋惜的事，像你這樣漂亮的女孩。」

「好吧，如果我保證不問任何問題，就可以加在我的咖啡上嗎？」她低聲說。

「可以，但要記住不要告訴任何人。」他盯著她。「否則...」他做了個割喉的動作。

「完全明白。」

「很好。凱文要些什麼嗎？」

「不用了，會冷掉的。」

「他不會過來嗎？」

「我想今天應該都不會來了，他在很遠的地方工作。」

「哦，你自己一個喝咖啡不會覺得寂寞嗎？」

「如果你現在可以小休就沒問題了。然後，我可以給你一分鐘時間聽聽我對奶油糖果的經驗。」她給了他一個俏皮的微笑，史堤夫的胃有翻滾的感覺。

「凱文不會介意嗎？」他脫口而出。

「什麼？不，我不這麼認為。他可以找另一天再跟你一起喝咖啡。」她淡淡地說。史堤夫目瞪口呆看著她拿起托盤，弄清楚她是不是故意誤解了他的問題。

也許他們的關係真的很開放，或許只是很適當地調整到男女之間的友誼，他想。他曾經也有女性朋友，但他已經忘記了怎樣做到。自從他離開大學後，就一直跟羅拉一起。第一時間就去跟其他人保持距離，但是最近，有些困難。

麗貝卡的聲音劃破了他的思緒。「至於奶油糖果，他是不會知道他錯過了什麼的。」她笑了。「因為我不容許任何人告訴他啊！」她走向她慣用的那張桌子，剩下史堤夫困惑地盯著她。

片刻後，他去到小窗口，「東尼！」

「什麼事？」

"Good. What can I get for Kevin?"

"Nothing. It'll get cold."

"Is he not coming in until later, then?"

"Not coming in here at all today, I shouldn't think. He's working miles away."

"Right. Won't you be lonely having coffee on your own?"

"Not if you have your coffee break now too. Then I could give you a minute by minute account of my butterscotch experience." She gave him a teasing smile and Steve's stomach did back flips.

"Won't Kevin mind?" he blurted.

"What? No, I shouldn't think so. He can have coffee with you another day," she said lightly. Steve gaped as she picked up her tray, trying to figure out if she was deliberately misunderstanding the question.

Perhaps their relationship really was open. Or perhaps other people were just better adjusted to the whole man/woman friendship thing, he thought; he used to have women as friends, but maybe he'd forgotten how to. Since he'd left uni, there had always been Laura. Keeping everyone else at arm's length was desirable at first, then recently, a necessity.

Rebecca's voice cut through his thoughts. "As for the butterscotch, he won't know what he's missing, will he," she grinned. "Because I'm not allowed to tell him!" She walked off to her usual table, leaving Steve staring after her and feeling bemused.

After a moment, he went to the hatch. "Tony!"

"What?"

"Can I take my break now?"

"Now? Is bit early, no?" Tony appeared, a stained bright red, green and white striped apron stretched over his bulging middle. He was nothing if not patriotic, thought Steve.

"What is the matter? Is it so busy out there you are worn out?" He stuck his head through, scanning the shop. "No! Is quiet." Then he straightened with a grin. "Ah."

"What?"

「我現在可以小休嗎？」

「現在嗎？還早呢！」東尼走了出來，身穿彩色鮮豔的紅色、綠色和白色條紋圍裙，掛在他鼓脹的腹部上。史堤夫心想，他肯定是愛國主義者。

「發生什麼事？因為太忙而累了嗎？」他探頭去望了一下店。「不是啊！多安靜。」然後他挺起身子笑了，「啊…」

「什麼？」

「我知道你為什麼要小休了。關鍵不是在什麼時候，而是什麼人，是嗎？」他眼睛看似在做什麼壞事。

「什麼？不是啦，我…是的，只是因為那女孩差不多每天都來…」

「可愛的麗貝卡」，他說「可愛」時總會帶上捲舌音，是真正的意大利風格。

「呃…是的，她是。」

「去去去！」當史堤夫在掙扎時，東尼已經解開了圍裙，他把它扔了進小窗口，引起里納爾多在廚房大聲抗議，他跟著從櫃檯下拿出一件乾淨的。「朋友，如果你喜歡，可以休息久一點，也可以用作為午餐時間。」

「謝謝你，東尼。」

「沒問題。東尼也曾年輕過。」

當他走開時，聽到東尼通過小窗口跟里納爾多說了一些話，引起了一陣哄笑，他感覺到自己臉紅耳熱了。剛從櫃檯走了出去，他就停下來。白痴，他還沒拿咖啡呢。他無奈地轉身，東尼假正經地鞠躬。

「先生想要些什麼呢？」

「麻煩你我要一杯奶油糖果拿鐵。」

「對不起，我想先生是搞錯了。如果看下板子，就發覺我沒有什麼奶油…」

「東尼！」

「好啦，」他咧嘴笑了。「我知道先生趕時間。」史堤夫的咖啡迅速地就已經沖好。「就這些嗎，先生？」

「是的，謝謝。」

"I see why you want the early break. Is not the when, it is the who, yes?" His eyes were mischievous.

"What? No, I—yes, it's just that the girl who comes in most days—"

"The lovely Rebecca." In true Italian style he managed to pronounce an r in 'lovely' that wasn't even there.

"Er... yes, she—"

"Go, go!" Tony had undone his apron whilst Steve was floundering. He threw it through the hatch, eliciting a squawk of protest from Rinaldo in the kitchen, and pulled a fresh white one from under the counter. "Take long break if you like, and have the shorter lunchtime, my friend."

"Thanks, Tony."

"No problem. Tony was young once too."

As he walked away, he could hear Tony say something to Rinaldo through the hatch that provoked a burst of laughter, and felt himself flush. He stopped himself just as he walked around the counter. Idiot. He hadn't got a coffee. He turned back reluctantly and Tony gave a mocking bow.

"And what is sir's pleasure?"

"I'll have a butterscotch latte please."

"Sorry, sir is mistaken. If he look at board, he will see we do not have the bu—"

"Tony!"

"Alright," he grinned. "I see sir is in a rush." Steve's coffee swiftly appeared. "Is that everything for sir?"

"Yes, thanks."

"Enjoy."

"Thanks."

Steve did enjoy it. Not just the coffee, but Rebecca's company. It was hard to hold her at arm's length, he thought guiltily. She was warm and witty and broke through any reserve he tried to cling to.

「好好享受吧。」

「謝謝。」

史堤夫一定會好好享受它。不只是咖啡，還有麗貝卡的陪伴。要和她保持一定距離真的很難，他羞愧地想。她又熱情又風趣，令她衝破了他試圖保衛的那道隔閡。

他不太懂得考古學，但當麗貝卡談到她的工作時，她會設法把陌生的名詞用一種方式解釋，令他不覺得她是刻意把詞語笨了下來遷就他。她散發著對工作的熱情。

當在她談到輝煌的日子、失落的日子，以及小男孩在她精心準備的考古活動中撒尿的日子，她的眼睛都閃閃發光。而她就在這時候提到凱文。尼爾是說得對，他們是一起工作的，而且還一起上大學。

他嘗試盡量有禮貌，不要因為純粹聽到那個男人的名字就咬牙切齒。

「當他跑進我的辦公室時，我就知道有事情發生了。」她笑了。「當我給他額外的工作，他一般都不會冒險衝進來，所以我就猜到，這是一場跟撒尿有關的災難。」

他咧嘴笑了，「那麼你們平時會怎樣做？在自己的辦公室打電話給對方？你們只會休息時間碰面嗎？」

「凱文沒有自己的辦公室。」

「我明白了。那是什麼讓你那麼幸運？」

「我是他的老闆，算是吧。」她笑了。「不要跟他這樣說。我是比他高級，這樣說才對。」

「那麼，你是從上級那裡得到自己的辦公室。」

「是的，而他沒有。」

「這是怎麼回事？」

「你的意思是，怎麼一個女人可以贏了一個男人而得到提拔嗎？」她眨了眨眼睛。

「不是！你覺得我是這麼守舊的嗎？我只是在想，你們是一起讀大學的…」

「嗯，但我是唸碩士學位，而凱文還沒有，他那時才剛剛開始唸學士學位。他比我年輕幾年。」

He didn't know much about archaeology but when Rebecca talked about her work, she managed to explain unfamiliar terms in a way that didn't make him feel she was dumbing things down for him. The enthusiasm for her work shone out of her.

Her eyes sparkled when she talked about the brilliant days, the disappointing days, and the days when small boys peed in her lovingly prepared archaeological activities. That was when she mentioned Kevin. Neil was right; they worked together, and they'd been at uni together too.

He tried to be polite and not to grind his teeth together at the mere mention of the man's name.

"I knew something was wrong when he ran into my office," she laughed. "He doesn't normally venture in, in case I give him extra work to do, so I should have guessed it was a pee-related disaster."

He grinned. "So what do you normally do, call each other in your separate offices? Do you only talk face to face at break times?"

"Kevin doesn't have an office."

"I see. What makes you the lucky one then?"

"I'm his boss. Kind of." She grinned. "Though don't repeat that to him. I'm more senior, let's put it that way."

"So you get an office to boss people about from."

"Yep, and he doesn't."

"How did that happen?"

"You mean, how did a woman get promoted over a man?" Her eyes twinkled.

"No! What kind of dinosaur do you think I am? I just thought, if you two were at Uni at the same time..."

"Ah, but I was doing my master's—something Kevin hasn't got—when he was just starting his degree. He's a few years younger."

"Right. A masters, eh? Impressive."

"Thanks. Kevin got a good degree, don't get me wrong, but he's not interested in going for his Masters—not yet anyway—and he's happy to jog along where he is. I went to workshops, conferences,

「沒錯。碩士學位，啊？令人欽佩啊。」

「謝謝你。凱文也有一個很好的學歷，不要誤會我的意思，但他沒有興趣去唸碩士學位，反正還沒有，他總喜歡在原地慢跑。我參加很多研討會、會議、專業培訓，你可以這樣稱呼。我對於可以去加強自己的知識很熱衷，加上...」她做了一個警告的手勢，「不許你在這裡亂說話啊，『請叫我史堤夫』。我很愛說話，總是突然就提出意見，無論沒有人要問我。」

「一個字都不會說。」史堤夫說，呆呆地盯著她。

「很好。其實凱文的才華在於他做什麼。他能只看一眼溝渠的泥土，在你說『讓我們拿去實驗室檢驗』之前，他就明確地告訴你它的成分。他是這領域真正的專家。」突然，她咯咯地笑，差點把咖啡噴出來。

「有什麼好笑的？」史堤夫把餐巾紙遞給她。

「這不是好笑，是可怕。泥土？在這領域的專家...」

史堤夫咧嘴笑了。「是很有趣。」

「哦，不用這麼客氣，真的是可怕啊。我很容易被逗樂，僅此而已。」

「太好了，我有一本書關於聖誕節的小笑話。我一直在等待有人可以試驗一下。」

「應該不會有人在家閱讀吧？」她問，並非常謹慎看著他。

「我所認識的人中沒有對笑話有興趣的，」他淡淡地說，迴避了問題。「除了尼爾，是他給我這本書。但尼爾已經讀過了，所以沒有樂趣。」

「那麼在這種情況下，我看來要注定當你的聽眾。」

「嗯，我想你會成為一個俘虜。我可能會鎖上門一整天，不讓你出去，直到我給你讀完整本書。當然，你不得不笑，而且每個都要笑一遍。」

「你開始討價還價了。」

「這就是我。」他站起身來。「我得回去了，我已經盡量拖長我的小休時間。」東尼看到他來，就跟他使了個眼色並消失在門後。史堤夫認為他太多眉毛在動了，不禁笑了。

她拿著托盤跟著他走到櫃檯。「我想下次會是一個很有趣的禁閉期，是麼？」

specialised training, you name it. I was very keen to deepen my knowledge. Plus—" she raised a warning finger, "and you're not allowed to say anything here, Call Me Steve—I've always been mouthy, always springing up with suggestions whether they're asked for on not."

"Not saying a word," said Steve, staring at her woodenly.

"Good. Kevin's brilliant at what he does, though. He can look at soil in a trench and practically tell you its composition before you can say 'let's get this to the lab'. He's a real expert in that field." Suddenly she giggled, nearly spilling her coffee.

"What's so funny?" Steve passed her a serviette.

"It isn't funny, it's awful. Soil? An expert in that field..."

Steve grinned. "Very funny."

"Ooh, don't be so polite, it was terrible. I'm easily amused, that's all."

"Great, I got a book of one-liners for Christmas. I've been waiting for someone to try them out on."

"Nobody at home to read them too, then?" She seemed to be watching him very carefully as she asked.

"Nobody I know is into one-liners," he said lightly, side-stepping the question, "except Neil, and he gave me the book. But being Neil he read it first, so no joy there."

"Well in that case, it looks like I'm doomed to be your audience."

"Hmm. I think you'd have to be a captive one, literally. I might lock the door one day and not let you out until I've read the entire book to you. Of course you'd have to laugh at them all, as well."

"You strike a hard bargain."

"That's me." He got to his feet. "I'd better get back. Think I've stretched my break as far as I can." Tony saw him coming and disappeared through the door with a meaningful wiggle of his eyebrows. And he's got a lot of eyebrow to wiggle, thought Steve, smiling to himself.

She followed him to the counter with the tray. "I suppose next time it's the comedy lockdown, then, is it?

史堤夫繞到櫃檯後面，並穿上他的圍裙。「或者，我會把你剁碎。」他在製作奶油糖果糖漿，在她手不可及的地方擺動著瓶子。「沒有史堤夫或的奶油糖果拿鐵了。」

「哦，你是真是個殘酷的人啊，我必須確保我下次不會單獨來。如果我要遭受這種命運，凱文也應該要。」

史堤夫的心情像一個碰到玫瑰的氣球一樣洩了氣。「是的，我敢肯定，他會保護你。」他不確定地說。他轉過身來，假裝是很忙碌地補充巧克力碎，讓她看不到他的臉。他相信他現在把所有情緒都寫在他的額頭上。來吧，史堤夫，成熟點。你是不能恨他的，因在你認識這位女孩之前，他已經認識她了。友善點吧。「那凱文的專長就是泥土，是嗎？」他問，試圖令聲音輕一點。

「不是真的，不，那是…」

「不，不，不，」他嚴肅地說。「你必須說是，他的專長是泥土。」

「但不是啦，因為…」

他嘆了口氣。「請說是吧。」

「好吧。是的，史堤夫。凱文的專長是泥土。」

「那麼難怪他是一個考古學家，」他說，揚起了眉毛，「他一定很認真去發掘它了。」他鞠了一個躬。

麗貝卡一臉茫然。

「噢，來吧。」他兩手扠腰。「這是搞笑的點子啦。」

「什麼？」她一臉困惑。

「泥土？發掘它？…」他停下來，皺著眉頭，因為麗貝卡已經在咔的一聲笑了出來，「哈哈。」

「對不起。非常不錯，尤其是演示部分。呃，其實主要是演示部分。」

「謝謝你。我對我的笑話很自豪的…」他皺起了眉頭，盯著糖漿瓶。「對了，是時機問題。」他咧嘴笑了。「要再來一杯奶油糖果拿鐵嗎？給你這位觀眾的。」

「不了，謝謝，我要走了。我有會議在三點，我現在要先去場地會合凱文。」

「對啊，」他說。「你的騎士與閃亮的鐵鍬。你還沒有告訴我，他真正的專長到底是什麼。太可惜了。」儘管他盡了最大的努

Steve walked round the counter and put his apron on. "Either that, or I'm cutting you off." He produced the butterscotch syrup and waggled it just out of her reach. "No more Butterscotch Latte á la Steve."

"Ooh, you're a cruel man. I'll have to make sure I don't come in alone then. If I have to suffer this fate, then Kevin should too."

Steve's spirits deflated like a balloon in close proximity to a rose bush. "Yes, I'm sure he'll protect you," he said lamely. He turned so that she couldn't see his face, pretending to be very busy refilling the chocolate sprinkles. He was sure his feelings were written in inch high letters across his forehead. Come on, Steve, grow up. You can't hate him because he got the girl before you even knew her. Be nice. "So Kevin's speciality is soil, is it?" he asked, trying to keep his voice light.

"Not really, no, it's—"

"No, no, no," he said severely. "You have to say yes, his speciality is soil."

"But it's not, because—"

He sighed. "Please. Just say it."

"Okay. Yes, Steve. Kevin's speciality is soil."

"Well no wonder he's an archaeologist," he said, raising his eyebrows, "he must really Dig It." He took a bow.

Rebecca looked blank.

"Oh come on." He put his hands on his hips. "That was comedy gold."

"What was?" Her face was all innocent confusion.

"Soil? Dig it?—" He stopped, frowning, because Rebecca had let a snigger escape. "Huh."

"Sorry. Very good, especially the presentation. Er, mostly the presentation, actually."

"Thank you. I pride myself on my comic..." he frowned, and stared at the syrup bottles. "Ah yes. Timing." He grinned. "Another butterscotch latte? Since you're such an appreciative audience?"

"No thanks, I should go. My meeting's at three, and I'm got to

力，但聽起來還是有點諷刺的味道。

麗貝卡奇怪地看著他。「沒關係，也許下次吧。」她冷冷地說。

「對。」他感到很尷尬。「那再見吧。」

「再見。」

當他看著她離開時，他心想，做得好史堤夫！真的很好。

meet Kevin at the site first."

"Right," he said. "Your knight with a shining spade. You never did tell me what his speciality actually is. What a pity." Despite his best efforts, he sounded sarcastic.

Rebecca gave him an odd look. "Never mind. Perhaps next time," she said, a little coolly.

"Yes." He felt awkward now. "See you then."

"See you."

Way to go Steve, he thought, as he watched her leave. Nice one.

不需要此页

Chapter Three

He knew she was in the minute he opened the door. It was the smell. He pushed the door shut behind him, taking a minute to lean back and take a deep, steadying breath. Right. He could handle this. He slung his rucksack over the hook in the hallway and stopped at the door of the lounge, listening.

Nothing. Maybe she was asleep. He put his hand on the door handle and pushed it down slowly.

"For chrissake, Steve, stop poncing about out there." Laura's voice lashed out into the silence, making him jump.

As he walked in, all he could see of Laura was a hand laying on the back of the couch. Two steps more and he could see the whole sorry sight. She was sprawled along the sofa, feet bare, legs encased in skin-tight jeans that had started life black but were now covered in stains. Her hair was a mess, the blonde waves flattened and dulled by grease and... Well, he didn't want to think what else. She was wearing one of his best t-shirts. Great.

He didn't say anything, just let his eyes wander over the coffee table and the floor. Over the empty glasses, cans and wine bottles.

She followed his gaze. "Yeah. Sorry 'bout that. I'll wash up later, I had a fwew, few drinks."

And that wasn't all she'd had, he thought grimly, judging by all the empty crisp packets that littered the floor. If she'd had an attack of the munchies, you could bet it was more than just alcohol that had got her in this state.

"You had to use all those different glasses, did you?" he asked coldly.

She blinked at him. "Course," she said. "I had wine in that one—" she lurched sideways and jerked a finger down into the nearest, "and those two—" she waved at hand at two on the edge of the coffee table and they crashed to the floor. "Whoops s'okay it they

第三章

他打開門，他知道她在。有一陣氣味，他推開在他身後剛關上了的門，用了一分鐘時間往後靠，並深呼吸了一下，穩住呼吸。對，他可以應付的。他把背包掛在走廊的掛鉤上，並在客廳的門前停了下來，聽著。

沒有聲音，也許她睡著了。他把手放在門把上，並慢慢拉下。

「天哪，史堤夫，別再在外面閒逛了。」羅拉的聲音劃破了寂靜，嚇了他一跳。

當他走進去，他能看到羅拉一隻手在沙發背面。再走兩步，他就看到整個不堪入目畫面。她趴在沙發邊沿，裸著腳，穿著緊身牛仔褲，褲子已經開始發黑，而且佈滿著污漬。她的頭髮一塌糊塗，金色的曲髮已經變直了，而且滿佈油脂...嗯，他不想再多想了。她還穿著其中一件他最喜歡的汗衫。實在太好了。

他沒有說什麼，只是把目光游移在茶几和地板上，看著空酒杯、酒罐和酒瓶。

她順著他的視線，「是啊。對不起，我會洗乾淨的，我只是喝...喝了幾杯。」

由所有散落在地上空清了的脆片包裝來判斷，她不只是喝了酒，他默默地想。如果她出現極度的饑餓感，可以肯定不僅僅是酒精就能令她在陷於這種狀態下。

「你是否一定要把所有不同的杯子都用一遍嗎？」他冷冷地問。

她眨了眨眼看著他。「當然啦，」她說。「有這杯酒...」她歪向一邊猛然指住旁邊，「和這兩杯...」她伸手揮向茶几邊緣的兩杯酒，它們砸到在地上破了。「哎呀，沒關係，都是空的...我還有伏特加在那邊和那杯蘋果酒，還有啤酒。」她拿起一個罐子，對它皺了皺眉頭。「很好喝，在你的冰箱內找到的，它叫......」她用手指空寫著，將它拿到自己的臉前。「福斯特！」她得意地喊道，並向著空中猛烈揮拳。「是藍色的。是雞尾酒，不是啤酒。」她搖擺著罐子，金色的液體從罐子裡濺出來，濺到她穿著的

wereempty... I had vodka in those and cider in that one. Had beer too." She picked up a can and frowned at it. "Nice, it was in your fridge, wasssit called..." she ran her finger down the writing, bringing it ridiculously close to her face. "Fosters!" she shouted triumphantly, punching an arm in the air." It's blue. Blue can, not beer." She waggled the can and a spurt of golden liquid leapt out of the can onto the t-shirt she was wearing. His t-shirt. "Oh," she looked like she would cry for a second. "Sorry, this is your shirt... where's mine?" She frowned, turning her head unsteadily. "Tha'sright, spilt wine on mine so I borrowed yours!" She looked up at him suddenly with a dazzling smile, which slid from her face just as quickly. "Eww, shouldn't twist my head round," she said, her eyes suddenly losing focus, "think I'm a bit poorly..."

But Steve was already in the kitchen grabbing a bucket. He got back just in time to thrust it into her lap, then walked out, slamming the lounge door behind him. He ran upstairs, desperate to get rid of that foul smell from his nostrils, and headed for his tiny ensuite shower room. But the smell seemed stronger than ever. He frowned, noticing Laura's t-shirt in a heap on the floor. He moved it cautiously with his foot and was glad he'd been careful. Laura hadn't just spilt her drink over it. And she hadn't just spilt drink down the toilet, either.

Steve felt his stomach heave and turned on his heel, shutting the door and fighting back tears of frustration. He couldn't deal with this now. In fact, why the hell should he deal with it at all? Sod her. She could clear up after herself later. He grabbed fresh clothes and a Jodie Forrest novel, and headed for the bathroom.

An hour later, the warm bath and a little pure escapism had worked their magic and he felt he could handle Laura and the mess now, though he was still reluctant to get back to the real world. On balance he'd rather be accompanying the novel's hero on his trek through the jungle to find a buried Mayan temple, because it sounded less stressful. But he had to face Laura sometime.

Not without a cup of tea first, though. Sometimes after smelling coffee all day tea was all he fancied. In the kitchen he filled a large mug with strong, sweet tea, and then opened the lounge door. Quietly.

Laura was asleep on the sofa. There was a trail of vomit on the armrest where her head lay and some in a pool on the floor. Thank God for laminate floors, he thought dispassionately, drinking his tea as he took in the scene. Back in the kitchen, he finished his tea in one gulp and armed himself with disinfectant, a cloth, a dustpan and a mop. He pinged on plastic gloves. He had no illusions about her Laura's lifestyle. Best not to take any chances.

汗衫上。是他的汗衫。「噢，」她看起來像要快哭出來。「對不起，這是你的汗衫……我自己的呢？」她皺起了眉頭，把她的頭搖了幾下。「對了，酒濺到我的汗衫了，所以我才借你的來穿！」她突然抬起頭來看著他，給他一個燦爛的笑容，然後很快又從她的臉上消失了。「噁，我不應該擺動我的頭，」她說，她的眼睛突然失去焦點，「我覺得有點不妥…」

然而，史堤夫已經在廚房裡揪出一個桶，及時回來並擠在她的膝上，然後走開去，砰的一聲把他身後的客廳門關上。他跑到樓上，拼命將那臭味從他的鼻孔趕走，並走進他那個小小的獨立淋浴間。但味道似乎比之前還要厲害。他皺起了眉頭，注意到羅拉的汗衫堆在地板上。他小心翼翼用腳把它移到一旁，還好他一直都很小心。羅拉似乎不只是吐在汗衫上，而且也不只是吐到馬桶內。

史堤夫有反胃的感覺，他急向後轉並關上了門，強忍住失意的淚水。他現在處理不了。事實上，到底為什麼他要處理呢？討厭的傢伙，應該讓她自己去清理。他抓住了乾淨的衣服和朱迪·福斯特的小說，走向浴室。

一個小時後，暖水浴讓他逃避了現實片刻，這發揮了魔力，他覺得自己現在可以處理羅拉和她的爛攤子了，但他仍然不願回到現實世界中。

相比之下，他寧願伴隨著小說的主角長途跋涉地穿過叢林，尋找被埋的瑪雅神廟，因為聽起壓力比較少，但這時他不得不去面對羅拉。

並不是連喝杯茶的時間都沒有。有時侯，當聞著咖啡味道一整天後，他會特別想喝茶。在廚房裡，他倒滿了一大杯濃茶，然後打開客廳的門。靜靜地。

羅拉睡在沙發上。在她躺在的扶手上有嘔吐物的痕跡，有的是一灘一灘的在地板上。要感謝上帝那只是複合木地板，他冷靜地想著。他一邊環視現場，一邊喝他的茶。他回到廚房裡，將茶一飲而盡。他拿起了消毒液、抹布、簸箕和拖把，穿上塑膠手套，他對羅拉的生活方式已經沒有任何幻想，最好不要有。

他從客廳的地板開始，盡量避免不要呼吸到那強烈的酸臭味。然後，他把抹布浸泡在消毒液中，開始清潔扶手。至少在她移動時不會弄髒頭髮。

她彷彿聽到他的思想，羅拉呻吟了一聲並微微動了一下。史堤夫坐在自己的後腳跟上，維持著平淡的表情。幾分鐘後，她的眼皮徐徐張開。她矓朧地盯著他，努力找回焦點。嘴角有點不平衡地

He made a start on the lounge floor, trying not to breathe in the rank acid smell. Then he soaked the cloth in disinfectant and started to clean the armrest. At least she wouldn't get any more in her hair when she moved.

As though she'd heard his thought, Laura groaned and stirred. Steve sat back on his heels, keeping his expression neutral. After a few moments her eyelids slowly opened. She stared at him blearily, struggling to focus. A lopsided grin appeared.

"Hi Steve."

He didn't answer her; not because he was giving her the cold shoulder, but because he felt empty, as though he had run out of words to say to her.

"Are you cross with me?"

He sprayed the laminate with disinfectant. Got to his feet and started mopping.

"I know I'm a mess, Steve."

His jaw tightened. Here comes the whiney voice. It was like nails down a blackboard. Just mop and walk away, Steve, because you haven't got this under control at all.

"I've been trying, honestly. I've been really good. I just screwed up last night, that's all."

Steve mopped, willing himself not to respond, but he couldn't help himself. "What went wrong last night then?"

"Mike made me cross. You know, Mike from work."

"You don't go to work, Laura. Not anymore."

"You know what I mean Steve," she smiled, raising her hand to slap him playfully, but missing.

Steve wondered how many versions of him she was seeing right now. He felt like there were at least two inside his head, and neither of them knew how to handle her.

"My old work. You remember Mike."

He remembered Mike, alright. Some friend he had been. Mike was a borderline alcoholic himself, albeit a 'social alcoholic'. But he knew Mike wasn't good to be around when he'd been without

笑了笑。

「嗨，史堤夫。」

他沒有回答她，並不是因為他要冷淡地對待她，而是因為他真的很空洞，吐不出一個字來回應她。

「你很生我的氣嗎？」

他在地板上噴上消毒劑，站起身來開始抹地。

「我知道我糟透了，史堤夫。」

他收緊下頜，地上開始發出了嘎嘎聲，就像用釘子刮在黑板上。抹地然後就走開，史堤夫，你還不可能控制這個情況。

「我一直很努力，真的。我一直都做得很好。我把事情搞砸了，在昨晚，僅此而已。」

史堤夫繼續抹地，但願自己不要去回應，但他實在無法控制自己。「那究竟昨晚發生了什麼事呢？」

「是邁克令我這樣。你認識的，那個同事邁克。」

「你沒有工作，羅拉。再也沒有。」

「你知道我是什麼意思，史堤夫。」她笑了笑，舉起手調皮地拍拍他，但落空了。

史堤夫不知道她現在看到多少個版本的他，他覺得至少有兩個自己在腦袋裡面，但沒有一個知道要如何應付她。

「是以前的工作，你記得邁克的。」

他記得邁克，當然。曾經算是朋友。邁克是一個在酗酒邊緣的人，儘管是個「交際酒鬼」。但他知道邁克不好的是他不可以連續兩天不喝酒。他也知道，邁克慫恿羅拉在午餐時間喝得醉醺醺，以及下班後去喝酒。可能還有其他下班後的嗜好。

a drink for a couple of days. And he also knew that Mike had encouraged Laura in the boozy lunches and after work drinks. And probably other after work indulgences too.

"I remember Mike. I don't think he's good for you."

"Good for me? You make it sound like I'm playing with a naughty child."

"So why did Mike annoy you?"

"Asked him for a favour but he said no." Her eyes slid away.

"Did you ask him for money?" his voice was harsh.

"No."

"Because you should be coming to me for money, Laura. We're meant to sort these things together."

"I told you, I didn't ask him for money! And you don't let me have money, except my JSA. I haven't got a bank card for the main account, have I?"

"No, and you know why."

"Oh yeah. I can only have money if you approve of how I spend it. A really equal relationship."

Steve's grip on the mop handle tightened. "I'm the one who earns it, so I should have some say on how it's spent, particularly when I find myself scraping thirty quid's worth of it off my floor!"

"Don't take it out on me because I lost my job!"

"And whose fault is that?"

"They had no right to fire me!" she stormed, tears gathering in her eyes. "I worked really hard for that company."

""Yes, until your wages started going up your nose," he ground out.

"They didn't! I always did my job properly!" she screeched. "But they threw me out! Hated me, all of them! Bitches. Bastards!"

"Yes, after informal warnings, formal warnings, written warnings, and even offering you counselling on their bloody time and money!" Steve roared. "And you didn't go to half the sessions

「我記得邁克。我不認為他對你有好處。」

「沒有好處？聽起來好像我在跟一個頑皮的孩子玩。」

「那麼，為什麼邁克惹惱了你？」

「請他幫一個忙，但他說不行。」她的視線溜走了。

「你問他要錢嗎？」他的語氣很苛刻。

「不是。」

「因為你要錢應該來問我，羅拉。我們應該要一起解決這問題。」

「我告訴你，我沒有問他要錢！而且你也不會給我錢，除了我的求職津貼。我甚至沒有賬戶的銀行卡，是嗎？」

「沒有，你知道是為什麼的。」

「哦，是的。我用錢要先得到你批准。這段關係真是平等啊。」

史堤夫握緊手中的拖把柄。「錢是我賺的，所以我應該可以決定如何花費，尤其是當我發現自己把價值三十鎊的地板刮花了！」

「不要因為我失業而拿我來出氣！」

「那是誰的錯？」

「他們沒有權利開除我！」凝聚在她的眼睛裡的淚水湧出來。「我在那家公司工作真的很努力了。」

「是的，直到你對你的工資不屑一顧。」他沙啞地說。

「沒有！我由始至終都有做好我的工作！」她尖叫著。「但他們

because you were out your head!"

She started sobbing. "That's not fair! I was ill."

Steve shook his head in disgust, feeling his heart pound against his ribs. He'd told himself he wouldn't get mad at her. It was pointless. They'd been down this road a hundred times before, and it always ended up with her drowning in a welter of self-pity.

How had things gone so wrong so quickly? He'd tried to guide her, not condemn her, when he'd seen her going off the rails. She was a lot younger than him and he didn't want to become some kind of domineering father figure; he wanted to help her, and to do that he needed to keep her trust. But any trust between them had completely degenerated, on both sides, and the love and respect were going the same way.

"I'm going out," he said abruptly.

She rubbed at her eyes. "We haven't had any dinner."

"I'm eating out."

"But what am I going to eat?" she said pathetically, staring at him, all big eyes.

"It's your house too, Laura. You know where the food is. There's pizza in the fridge—if you're really still hungry." He looked pointedly at the floor.

"But I'm not well—"

"But finish disinfecting the floor first, and wash out your clothes before your vomit gets spread everywhere." He didn't look at her, busying himself with putting his jacket on, and gathering his phone, keys and wallet. On an afterthought, he picked up his laptop too, slipping it into its bag.

She started to sob again. "But Ste—"

He slammed the front door. He wasn't usually a door slammer, but today it felt good. Therapeutic. He'd go back to Tony's and spend the evening there. It would be familiar and comfortable, and smell a lot better than home.

He was right. It smelled a hell of a lot better than home. The deep aromas of coffee and warm pastry and the light, fresh smells of the cucumber and salad made him feel better – and hungry!—the moment he walked in. Sipping a cappuccino and tucking into one

把我扔出去！討厭我！所有人都一樣！母狗！混蛋！」

「是的，是在給你非正式的警告、正式警告、書面警告，甚至用他們珍貴的時間和金錢去為你提供輔導之後！」史堤夫大吼。「有一半的會議你沒有去，因為你的腦袋掉了！」

她開始抽泣。「這不公平！我當時生病了。」

史堤夫厭惡地搖了搖頭，他感覺到他的心臟猛烈地撞擊著肋骨。他告訴自己，不要為她憤怒，因為這是毫無意義的。他們之前已經試過這情況一百次了，到最後總是在她一大堆自怨自憐中結束。

為什麼事情會這麼快就變得如此惡劣？他曾經嘗試在她做錯事的時候引導她、不罵她。她比他年輕很多，他不想像個專橫的父親一樣。他只想幫助她，為此他需要保持對她的信任。但他們之間的信任已經完全變質了，雙方也是，而他們之間的愛和尊重亦然。

「我要出去一下。」他突然說。

她揉揉眼睛。「我們還沒有吃晚餐。」

「我吃了。」

「但是，那我該吃什麼？」她可憐巴巴地說，睜大眼睛盯著他。

「羅拉，這也是你的家。你知道哪裡有食物，冰箱裡有比薩餅，如果你真的還覺得餓的話。」他刻意地望著地板。

「但我不舒服...」

「但請你在嘔吐物被弄得周圍都是之前，先把地板清潔消毒好，把你的衣服洗乾淨。」他沒有看她，忙著穿上他的外套，並拿起他的手機，鑰匙和錢包。之後，他拿起他的筆記本電腦，放入袋中。

她再次抽泣起來。「但是，史堤...」

他砰的一聲關上門，他平時不會用力關門，但今天感覺很好。很有治療性。他會回去東尼的店待一個晚上。那裡感覺熟悉和舒服，而且聞起來也比家裡好多了。

of Tony's handmade sausage rolls, he felt the stress flow out of him. The café was quiet this evening and Steve set himself up in a corner, facing out, near a radiator. He finished his sausage roll and wiped his hands on a serviette. Time to get busy on the laptop.

If today had shown him one thing, it was that he couldn't keep on living his life for Laura. He felt drained. He had given her all the help he could, but she didn't want to help herself. He'd lived like a monk, devoting himself only to her for too long.

He'd saved the dating site to his favourites the other night after wimping out at the last moment. There were lots of internet dating sites to pick from, but he'd gone with Methodical Matches in the end. Their claim that they matched people accurately and scientifically was appealing, particularly as there had been a rumour at university that some dating sites employed students, who spent their evenings matching clients on a drunken whim and posting the worst of the profile photos on the internet for everyone to see.

The downside was, the Methodical Matches profile form was so long that his session timed out way before he had time to complete it. That interruption that had stopped him in his tracks, giving him time to reconsider. He'd wimped out in the end; convinced himself that he was being irresponsible and uncaring. Laura would come out of this; she was young, it was a phase. She needed him to be around for her, not off with someone else. Hadn't he promised to support her, whatever happened? Signed his name to say he would?

But she needed to be responsible for herself now. If he asked her to move out and she refused, what would he do He had no idea. But he knew he needed to find himself a new life.

He copied the profile form into a new document on his laptop. Now he could take his time, thinking about each question carefully. He drained the dregs of his cappuccino and made a start.

His relationships? Well that was easy. He'd only managed a three month romance in sixth form—with a girl he didn't really fancy, but she was quite good-looking and very keen, so it seemed the thing to do—and spent a passionate if turbulent nine months with a French girl in his first and only year of Uni, before she returned to Paris and he got saddled with Laura. Voluntarily, he reminded himself. Yeah. What a mistake that had been.

He scrolled through the rest of the form. It went on forever, but it didn't matter, he was in no rush to get home. He found the next

他是正確的，這裡的氣味的確比家裡好很多。深層的咖啡香味和溫暖的糕點，還有清淡又新鮮的黃瓜和沙拉讓他感覺好多了，當他一踏入門口，餓了！喝著卡布奇諾咖啡和吃著東尼的手作香腸卷，他覺得壓力都從他身上流走了。這個晚上咖啡店很安靜，史堤夫坐到一個角落裡，面朝外，靠近暖氣機。他吃完了香腸卷，用餐巾紙擦了擦手，就在筆記本電腦上忙碌起來。

今天的事讓他明白到，他根本無法再繼續跟羅拉一起生活。他已經心力交瘁了。他可以幫助的，已經盡力幫助她了，但她根本不想幫助自己。他活得像一個僧人，為她奉獻出自己太長時間了。

在另一個逃出來的晚上，他保存了一個約會網站到我的最愛列中，從很多的網絡約會網站挑出來的，他最後還是選了「井然配對」。他們聲稱，他們可以準確和科學化地進行配對，這樣很有吸引力。尤其在大學時曾有過一個傳聞，說一些交友網站僱用學生，他們會用晚上的時間跟配對的客戶喝得爛醉，然後將最糟糕的個人資料照片張貼在互聯網上給大家看。

但井然配對的缺點是，那份個人資料的表格真的太長了，在他把它完成之前就已經超時了。這間斷讓他停了下來，給他時間再考慮。他終究還是逃出來了，他對於自己這樣不負責和不關心有點悔悟。羅拉還年輕，她一定可以走出來的，這只是一個階段。她需要的是他的陪伴，而不是其他人。他從來沒有答應不管發生什麼事也要支持她吧？難道有簽過什麼契約說他要這樣做嗎？

由現在開始，她需要對自己負責。如果他叫她搬出去，她拒絕了，他會怎麼做呢，他不知道。但他知道的是，他需要去尋找自己的新生活。

他把那個個人資料檔案複製到他電腦上的一個新文件檔中。現在他可以用時間仔細思考每條問題。他把他的卡布奇諾喝得點滴不剩，並開始作答。

他的戀愛關係？嗯，這個很簡單。在六年級的時候，他用了三個月時間跟一個他沒有真正看中的女孩談戀愛，但她挺好看的，而且非常熱情，所以他跟她一起似乎是應該的。之後在他大學的第一年，也是唯一的一年，他付出了既熱情又動盪的九個月時間跟一個法國女孩在一起，是在她要回到巴黎之前。再之後，他就一直背負著羅拉這個沉重的包袱。你是自願的，他提醒自己。嗯，是一個錯誤，一直都是。

他翻閱剩下的表格部分，它看似沒完沒了，但不要緊，他並不急著回家。他發現有一個空白欄位，要填寫每一張他擁有的專輯嗎？他不知道他坐在這裡能不能記得所有的。在家中，它們都是按字母順序排列的，然而，所以他可以嘗試順著架子去想一下。嗯…他真的要承認自己有阿巴樂隊（ABBA）的專輯嗎？

blank section. Every album he owned? He wasn't sure he could remember them all, sitting here. They were in alphabetical order at home, though, so he could try and think his way along the shelf. Hmm. Should he really admit to Abba?

不需要此页

Chapter Four

She should go home and cook, but she had been on her feet all day and they didn't feel like they belonged to her any more. She already knew there was nothing in the freezer that she could pop in the microwave and leave for ten minutes, collapsing on the settee until she heard the magical 'bing'. Anyway, she had a strong craving for one of Tony's hot Southern Fried Chicken Wraps, full of delicious crunchy bacon bits, and just the thought of it was making her mouth water as she pushed open the café shop door.

Inside there were only a few occupied tables but that wasn't unusual in the evenings, not at this time of the year anyway. A group of girls chatted quietly at a table near the window, there were a handful of couples scattered about and a few people sitting by themselves-

She stopped. What was Steve doing here, in civvies, all by himself? He was the last person she would have expected to see here in the evening, this side of the counter, anyway. He was at the small table with just two seats, usually favoured by couples because it was tucked away between the big supporting column in the wall and the alcove with the tall curved bench seat, giving it a sense of seclusion and privacy.

Obviously Steve wanted the privacy rather than the intimate company, she thought, amused. He was sitting with his back to the wall, and she was guessing it was him who'd pushed the other matching chair just far enough away from his table so that it looked like it didn't belonged there. She should probably leave him alone then, especially since he had a laptop in front of him. He must be busy.

She started towards the counter, one eye still on Steve. He looked good out of uniform. Whoops, lucky she hadn't said that one out loud! Good in his own clothes, she'd meant. That denim blue shirt suited him, the sleeves tighter than his white work shirts, showing that his arms were more muscular than she'd thought. Not that she'd been thinking about it. Particularly.

第四章

她應該要回家做飯，但她今天一整天都在走路，她已經感覺不到雙腳是否屬於她自己了。她知道冰櫃裡沒有能用微波爐十分鐘就煮好的食物，好讓她可以倒在長椅上，直到她聽到那奇妙的「叮」一聲。不管怎樣，她突然很渴望能吃到東尼熱騰騰的南方炸雞卷，充滿美味鬆脆的培根碎，只想想就令她在吞口水了，她推開咖啡店的門。

店內只有少數位子有人坐著，但這情況在晚上不算稀奇，反正每年的這個時候都一樣。一群女孩靠窗的桌子靜靜地聊天，有極少數夫婦分佈店內，也幾個人獨自坐在…

她停了下來。史堤夫在這裡做什麼？穿便服？一個人？不管怎樣，她本來預計在晚上會在這裡遇到的就是他，但應該是在櫃檯的另一邊。他坐著那小桌子只有兩個座位，通常夫妻比較喜歡，因為它夾在牆壁的柱子之間，壁凹放著高的弧形長條座椅，給人一種與世隔絕和很隱私的感覺。

很明顯，史堤夫想要的是隱私，而不是陪伴，她在想，而且覺得好笑。他背對牆壁坐著，她猜測把另一張椅子推開到另一邊的就是他，所以它看起來像不屬於那裡。她應該讓他獨個兒坐，尤其是他面前有一台筆記本電腦，他一定在忙著。

她一邊開始往櫃檯走過去，但一邊仍然看著史堤夫。他不穿制服很好看。哎呀，還好她並沒有說出聲來！她的意思是，他穿自己的衣服很好看。牛仔藍襯衫適合他，袖子比他白色的工作服襯衫緊一點，突顯了他手臂上的肌肉，比她想像更強壯。並不是說她一直特別地想著它。

她冒險也要直接看一下他。他凝視著遠方，就像這個晚上都一直凝視著桌子的另一側，無所事事地把空的鬆餅盒折疊成很小的三角形。他看起來並不是忙著，他看起來是非常苦惱。

她驚訝地發現自己正向他的方向走過去，衝動似乎已經完全避開了她的大腦，直接控制著她雙腿。

She risked a direct glance. He was staring into space, which seemed to live on the floor to one side of his table this evening, and idly folding an empty muffin case into smaller and smaller triangles. No, he didn't look busy; he looked thoroughly miserable.

She was surprised to find herself making her way between the tables towards him. The impulse seemed to have gone straight to her legs, completely circumventing her brain.

"Hi."

He jumped. "Oh—Rebecca. Hi."

He closed his laptop quickly, looking flustered, and she wondered what he had to hide. Perhaps he'd been looking at porn, she thought, having a mental giggle. But somehow she doubted it. He didn't seem the type to browse x-rated websites in the café where he worked, even if it was outside his working hours.

"Don't tell me, by day you serve in here, latte-maker-extreme, but by night you work for the Food Hygiene Board or whatever it's called and you're here to investigate."

He smiled, relaxing a little. "You got me."

"Now that must be a conflict of interest. You think they'd send someone else." She smiled back. "Are you okay?"

"Fine, thanks."

"Good. Sorry, by the way, I didn't mean to make you jump. You looked a bit fed up, that's all"—gross understatement – "so I thought I'd come over and say hi."

"That's alright. I don't know why I did it, you're not that shocking." He grinned. "And you know how it is. Working here all day, then spending all evening investigating for the—"

"—Food Hygiene Board."

"Exactly. Tires a man out, after a while." He paused and then blurted, "Can I get you a coffee? Or do you have to get home?"

"No, no! I can see you're busy, I was just saying hi."

"Busy? Oh... that." Steve's eyes flicked down to his laptop and Rebecca thought she detected a little pinkness creeping into his cheeks. "That's nothing important."

「嗨。」

他跳了起來，「噢...麗貝卡。嗨。」

他迅速把筆記本電腦關上，看來很慌張，她不知道他要把什麼藏起來。也許他在看色情的東西，她在想，白痴般傻笑著。但不知為何她又懷疑，他似乎不會在他工作的咖啡店裡瀏覽限制級網站，即使是他工作以外的時間。

「不要告訴我，白天你在這裡工作，而到了晚上，你就在食品衛生局或什麼的部門工作，在這裡進行巡查。」

他笑了，放鬆了一點。「被你逮到了。」

「那就有利益衝突了。你是否認為他們應該派其他人來？」她回了他一個微笑。「你沒事吧？」

「很好，謝謝。」

「那就好。順便說一下對不起，我不是有心讓你嚇一跳。只是你看上去有點情緒低落，就這樣而已。」她輕描淡寫地。「所以我想過來打個招呼。」

「沒關係。我也不知道我為什麼會這樣，你不用驚訝。」他咧嘴而笑。「你知道是怎麼回事，在這裡工作了一整天，然後又要花一個晚上來巡查，替...」

「...食品衛生局」

「沒錯。一會兒就覺得很累人了。」他停頓了一下，然後脫口而出，「我可以請你喝杯咖啡嗎？還是你要回家了？」

「不用，不用！我看到你在忙，我只是過來打個招呼。」

「忙嗎？哦...這個。」史堤夫的眼睛瞟一下他的筆記本電腦，而麗貝卡發覺到他的臉頰悄然泛紅了。「那不是什麼重要的東西。」

「好吧這樣，我不喜歡令你對你的摺紙分了心。」

「我的什麼？」

她向折疊的鬆餅盒點點頭，它正在桌子上慢慢展開，試圖彈回成原形。」

"Well even so, I'd hate to distract you from your origami."

"My what?"

She nodded at the folded cake case, which was sitting on the table slowly unfolding, trying to spring back into shape."

"Good point. It might never be a swan, now."

"There you go then," she smiled. "I'd better leave you to it." She turned towards the counter, glad she'd at least been able to put a smile on his face, but he called her back.

"Seriously, would you like a coffee? I could do with the company." He looked suddenly awkward, as though he'd revealed a bit too much. He smiled feebly. "It's a lonely life, being a Food Hygiene Inspector on the evening shift."

"Alright. I was going to grab something to take away and then slob out in front of the TV in my PJs all evening, but you've twisted my arm."

"So you're by yourself this evening then?"

"I'm by myself most evenings," said Rebecca with a theatrical sigh. She saw a small frown cross Steve's face and wondered what she'd said. "I'm going to get a coffee and a wrap, otherwise known as dinner. Do you want anything?"

"No. But take a seat, I'll get it." His eyes twinkled as he got to his feet. "I know the manager, you know."

"Ooh, does that mean I get extra chocolate sprinkles?"

"Maybe si, maybe non."

"Anyway, let me give you some money—"

"I'll pay—"

"No, it's not fair you should pay for my dinner."

"Hey, I'm the one forcing you to sit with me."

"You're not forcing me. You've saved me from an evening of laziness, loneliness and bad TV. All that, and I would still have had to pay for my dinner," she said firmly.

"Fair enough. Coffee's on me though. What do you want?"

「好了。它現在永遠都不能成為一隻天鵝了。」

「那你繼續，」她笑了。「我還是離開好了。」她轉身走向櫃檯，她很高興至少能夠讓他笑了，但他把她叫回來。

「說真的，你想喝杯咖啡嗎？我可以去做一杯。」他突然看似有點尷尬，他好像透露了太多，有氣無力地笑了笑。「當食品衛生局的晚班，是很寂寞的。」

「好吧。我本來打算買點東西就走，然後就整晚穿著睡衣在電視前面當個大懶蟲，但你令我猶豫了。」

「所以這晚只有你自己一個人嗎？」

「我大多數晚上都自己一個人，」麗貝卡說，誇張地嘆了口氣。她看到史堤夫皺了皺眉頭，好像在懷疑她說的話。「我想要一杯咖啡和一個肉卷，作為另類的晚餐。你想要什麼？」

「不。你坐下來休息，我去。」他眨眨眼睛，站起身來。「你知道，我認識這兒的經理。」

「哦，那我是不是就可以得到額外的巧克力碎灑？」

「或許吧，或許沒有。」

「無論如何，讓我先給你錢…」

「我會付…」

「不，這是不公平，要你替我付晚飯錢。」

「嘿，是我逼你陪我坐的。」

「你沒有逼我。你從懶惰、孤獨和糟透的電視節目的一個晚上救了我出來。這樣一來，我不得不自己付晚飯錢。」她堅定地說。

「那很公平。咖啡就由我付吧。你想吃什麼？」

「南方炸雞沙拉卷，和藍莓鬆餅，麻煩你。」

「不錯的選擇。奶油糖果拿鐵？」

「嗯，是的。你真夠了解我。」

他臉上又有一點泛紅了，他拿起她的錢走向櫃檯。

"Southern Fried Chicken Salad Wrap, please, and a blueberry muffin."

"Good choice. Butterscotch latte?"

"Mmm, Yes please. You know me so well."

He went a little pink again as he pocketed her money and made for the counter.

Rebecca was soon sinking her teeth into the hot, fragrant, spicy wrap. "Mmm-mmm." She closed her eyes for a second. "Tony's wraps are just the best."

"They're unholy magic," Steve agreed. "He won't let anyone else make them. I'm starting to wonder if they're drugged." Suddenly his face darkened, but Rebecca was mid-bite and before she could ask what was wrong, creamy salad dressing burst from her wrap, some dribbling inelegantly down her chin and the rest landing on her jeans.

"Oh great! Now that's too much sauce, that is. I can't believe I'm saying that because it's gorgeous, but you can have too much of a good thing."

Steve grinned and passed her a serviette. "I'll pass that on to the chef. Less sauce."

There was silence for a while as Rebecca did serious damage to the wrap, but happily, no more to her clothes. "What does he make it out of, or does he buy it in?" she asked, after she'd taken the edge off her hunger.

"He makes it himself. Out of exactly what, I don't know. And even if I did, I couldn't tell you."

"Why?"

"Because I'd have to kill you," said Steve sadly. "That's the way Tony rolls."

"Only if you knock him over," giggled Rebecca.

"Ouch! Meow!"

"Sorry. Bless him, he wouldn't look half so cuddly if he was skinny. It's a shame about the sauce, I'd love to have some at home. A girl needs some incentive to eat salad."

麗貝卡的牙齒很快就沉沒在溫熱之中，又香又辣的肉卷。「嗯，嗯。」她閉上了眼睛一秒鐘。「東尼的肉卷是最好的。」

「是邪惡的魔法，」史堤夫同意。「他從來不會讓別人來做。我開始懷疑他下了藥。」突然他的臉色陰沉下來，但麗貝卡還沒來得及問什麼問題之前，已經咬下去了，奶油沙拉醬從她的肉卷漏出來，有點不優美地順著她的下巴滴下，落在她的牛仔褲上。

「哦，太棒了！就是太多沙拉醬了，真的是。我簡直不敢相信我正在說著呢，因為太引人入勝了，但你真的吃到好東西了。」

史堤夫笑了笑，遞給她餐巾紙。「我會告知廚師，減醬。」

沉默了半晌，麗貝卡令肉卷嚴重破壞了，但令人高興的是她的衣服沒有被沾污到。「他是怎麼做出來的，還是他買回來的？」當在飢餓邊緣回來之後，她問。

「他是自己親手做的。實際從哪裡來，我不知道。但即使我知道了，也不能告訴你。」

「為什麼？」

「因為我就不得不殺了你。」史堤夫黯然地說。「就是因為這個，東尼卷。」

「那你只會嚇壞他了。」麗貝卡咯咯地笑了。

「哎喲！喵！」

「對不起。祝福他，如果他是骨瘦如柴的，就不會有現在一半的可愛。這是令人難為情的沙拉醬，我很想家裡可以有一些。女孩子吃沙拉總需要一些激勵。」

「所以你不是一個生蔬菜支持者？」

「不能沒有沙拉醬，不可以。」

「我跟你一樣。更柔軟滑膩，效果更好。」

「嗯，我的味蕾很同意你，但我的腰圍沒有。當我把沙拉醬加上沙拉上，我總是感到內疚。因為在內心深處，我知道我可能令吃沙拉這事變得毫無意義。我一定把熱量數量提升了約百分之五百了。」

"Not a fan of rabbit food then?"

"Not without some kind of sauce on it, no."

"I'm with you on that one. The creamier, the better."

"Hmm, my taste buds agree with you but my waistline doesn't. I always feel guilty when I put creamy dressings on my salad, because deep inside I know I'm probably making the salad-eating pointless in the first place. I must put the calorie count up by about five hundred percent."

"But you're still getting your fibre," said Steve, nodding wisely. "Very important, fibre."

"True, I hadn't thought of that," she said solemnly. "Thanks, Doctor Steve."

"Any time, any time." He leaned back and gestured around him. "My surgery is always open."

"Yep," said Rebecca, nodding as she swallowed her last mouthful. "You're not kidding." She licked her fingers. That sauce really did get everywhere. "What are you doing here? Don't you have evenings off?"

His eyes darkened and Rebecca cringed inwardly.

"Sorry, none of my business."

"No, it's okay, I just..." He shrugged. "I don't come here every night, believe me. I'm not that sad, but I wasn't having a very happy evening at home and didn't want to stay in. I didn't want to go anywhere full of noise and strangers, so I came here." He looked at her and gave a small smile. "My second home."

"Ah, so it's stuff at home that making you look gloomy." Stop prying right now, Bec, she scolded herself.

"I didn't know I looked so gloomy, sorry. But yes." He picked up his coffee, probably hoping she'd leave the subject there.

She didn't. Rebecca firmly believed that bottling up problems only made things worse. Time to change tack. "Gloomy? You looked like your kitten had died!" She started to laugh, but his face didn't change.

"Oh God, I've put my foot in it, haven't I? Please don't tell me your kitten actually has died? Or your puppy, or—"

「但是，你仍然得到纖維，」史堤夫說，若有所悟地點著頭。「纖維是很重要的。」

「真的，我沒有想到啊。」她一本正經地說。「謝謝，史堤夫醫生。」

「任何時候，任何時間。」他靠在椅背上，向周圍示意著。「我的診症時間是常開的。」

「沒錯，」麗貝卡說，她點頭，她把最後一口吞下。「你不是在開玩笑吧。」她舔她的手指。沙拉醬真的沾到四處都是。「你在這裡做什麼？難道你晚上不下班嗎？」

他的眼神變得憂鬱，麗貝卡內心畏縮了一下。

「對不起，不關我的事。」

「不是，沒關係，我只是...」他聳聳肩。「我晚上一般都不會來這裡，相信我。我不是那麼傷心，但我今天晚上在家裡發生了非常不愉快的事，而令我不想留下來。我又不想去又吵又人多的地方，所以我就來了這裡。」他看著她，給了一個小小的微笑。「我的第二個家。」

「啊，所以是家裡的事，讓你看起來如此沮喪。」不要再打聽別人的事了，貝卡，她在罵自己。

「我不知道，我看起來有那麼沮喪。對不起。但是，你對了。」他拿起他的咖啡，可能是希望她不要再繼續這個話題。

她沒有停下來。麗貝卡堅信逃避問題只會令事情變得更糟。是時侯會改變策略了。「沮喪？你看起來就像你家的小貓死了！」她開始大笑，但他的臉上並沒有任何改變。

「哦，上帝，我是不是說錯話了？請不要告訴我你的小貓真的去世了？或許是你的小狗，或...」

「沒事！」史堤夫笑著。「沒關係，什麼都沒有死。甚至沒有一條金魚。我沒有飼養任何寵物，死的還是活的都沒有。」

「唷！」她慢慢地倒在椅子上。「感謝上帝。」

一個短暫的沉默之後，伴隨是他們的笑聲。但史堤夫始終沒有主動說出影響他心情的真正原因。她決定，只好直接問了。

"It's okay!" Steve grinned. "It's fine, nothing died. Not even a goldfish. I don't have any pets, dead or alive."

"Phew!" She slumped back in her chair. "Thank God for that."

Their laughter left a small silence behind, but Steve didn't volunteer the real reason for his mood. She decided there was only the direct approach left.

"Do you want to tell me what made you gloomy then, if it's not your mythical kitten? It might help."

"Not really, thanks." He fiddled with his coffee cup. "Sorry."

"That's okay. I just thought, you know, a problem shared..."

"I'm afraid it's one those insoluble, grin-and-bear-it-and-hope-it-improves problems," he said quietly, "So I don't think sharing it would halve it. But thanks for the offer."

"No problem." She felt strangely disappointed that Steve didn't want to confide in her, but she wasn't going to push it. Instead, she looked at the blueberry muffin and sighed. "That seemed like such a good idea. Before I ate the wrap."

"Don't tell me you're full up."

"Not quite. But I don't think the space I have left is blueberry muffin sized. Want to share?" she looked at him hopefully.

"I've already had a muffin."

"Only a small one." She nodded at his 'swan' cake case. "You could only make a cygnet out of that, not a full-grown swan."

He smiled. "True."

"And you bought me the giant size. Wicked man, not thinking about my waistline."

"Alright, anything to help a damsel in distress. Although there's nothing wrong with your waistline," he said with a smile.

"Thanks." Her stomach gave a tiny flutter. Was he flirting with her? Concentrate Rebecca, he's still talking.

"I'll go and get a knife; otherwise it's going to get messy. Actually..." he leaned over. "Talking of messy," he hissed, "Would you like some cream on top? Being as I know the manager, 'n all."

「如果不是因為你虛構的小貓，那麼你想告訴我是什麼令你如此沮喪嗎？會對你有所幫助的。」

「不必了，謝謝。」他擺弄著他的咖啡杯。「對不起。」

「這沒關係。我只是想，你知道的，把問題說出來...」

「恐怕是不能解決的了，只能逆來順受，並希望這樣可以令事情好轉。」他平靜地說。「所以，我不認為說出來就可以令問題減半。但是，還是要謝謝你的好意。」

「沒關係。」她感到出乎意料的失望，史堤夫沒有信任她，但她不打算強迫他了。相反，她看著藍莓鬆餅，嘆了口氣。「在我吃肉卷之前，這個似乎還是很好吃的。」

「不要告訴我，你已經吃飽了。」

「也不是。但我不認為我還有這般大的空間可以吃得下這個藍莓鬆餅了。想要一半嗎？」她抱有希望地看著他。

「我已經吃過鬆餅了。」

「只是一個小的。」她向他的『天鵝』鬆餅盒點點頭。「你只能做一隻幼天鵝的，而不是一隻成熟的天鵝。」

他笑了。「真的。」

「而你還給我買巨型的。邪惡的男人，完成不顧及我的腰圍。」

「好吧，讓我來幫助這個在危難中的年輕女士。雖然你的腰圍沒有什麼問題。」他笑著說。

「謝謝。」她心有點撲通撲通地跳。他在跟她調情嗎？集中一點麗貝卡，他還在說話。

「我去拿刀子，不然它會變成一團糟的。其實...」他俯身。「說到一團糟，」他發出噓聲，「你想在上面加點奶油嗎？我認識這個經理，和其他人。」

她環顧四周。「好啊。」她發出噓聲。

「好吧。那我要拿一些勺子和盤子。」

一個非常混亂而愉快的二十分鐘過去，麗貝卡看了看手錶。「哎呀，現在是什麼時間了？我得要回家了。在我睡我的美容覺之

She looked round. "Yes please," she hissed back.

"Okay. I'll get some spoons and plates too."

A very messy but pleasant twenty minutes later, Rebecca looked at her watch. "Oops, is that the time? I should head for home. I've got lots to do before I get my beauty sleep."

"Yes, I'd better be off too." Steve slipped his laptop back inside his case. "Tony will be closing up in a minute, and if I'm still around he might rope me in to help."

"Heaven forbid!" laughed Rebecca. "You'd have to call in the union." She pulled on her coat. "Thanks for the coffee, Steve. And the cream!"

"My pleasure. Thanks for the company."

She looked up at him. Normally there was a certain reserve in his eyes when he spoke to her, but it wasn't there now. In fact, there was a very different look in his eyes that surprised her. "And thank you for your company, too. It was far better than spending the evening by myself." Another impulse circumvented her brain, and she found herself stretching up to give him a fleeting peck on the cheek. For a split second she wanted to stay there rather than rock back on her heels where she could see the look on his face. Why had she done that?

When she did move back, she was relieved to see that he looked startled but not horrified. She didn't want to give him time to say anything, though, or think too much. "I'll see you soon," she said quickly, grabbing her coat and bag as though they were lifebelts and she was drowning in the deep end. Hmm. Maybe you are, she thought.

"Soon? So not tomorrow, then?"

Was she imagining the disappointment in his voice? "Probably not. I need to be on site this week."

"I see. See you when I see you, then."

"Thanks. Night, then."

"Night."

You're a bit of an enigma, Call Me Steve, she thought as she walked towards the door. But definitely one worth getting to the bottom of. She couldn't remember the last time she'd enjoyed

前，還有很多事情要做。」

「是的，我也最好要離開了。」史堤夫把他的筆記本電腦放回入袋中。「東尼將會在一分鐘內就關店了，如果我還在，他可能會逼迫我去幫忙。」

「但願不會如此！」麗貝卡笑了。「那你就要打電話給工會了。」她拉一拉上衣。「謝謝你的咖啡，史堤夫。還有奶油！」

「這是我的榮幸。非常感謝你作伴。」

她抬頭看著他，通常他對她說話的時候，他的眼裡總會有點保留，但現在沒有了。事實上她很驚訝，他的眼神變得有點非常不一樣。「我也非常感謝你的陪伴。這比起整個晚上都自己一個人好多了。」另一個衝動繞過她的大腦，她發現自己伸長脖子並很快的在他臉頰上親了一下。就那麼一瞬間，她呆在那裡像有塊石頭綁住她的腳跟一樣，她能清楚看到他臉上的表情。她為什麼要這樣做呢？

當她稍稍後移動，她很欣慰地看到他臉上只有震驚，而不是驚嚇。她不想給他時間多說什麼或想什麼。她說：「我們很快就會再見。」她很快速地說，抓起大衣和手袋，彷彿她快淹死時抓住救生圈一樣。嗯，也許你就是，她想。

「很快？所以不是明天嗎？」

他的聲音好像很失望，是她錯覺嗎？「大概不會了。這個星期我都要去別的場地工作。」

「我明白了。那再看到你的時候，就再見吧。」

「謝謝你。晚安了。」

「晚安。」

你真是個不可思議的人啊，『請叫我史堤夫』，她邊想邊朝著門外走去。但他絕對是值得深交。她已經記不起，最後一次跟別人結伴而這麼開心是什麼時候了。

在她身後，她聽到廚房的門打開了，還有東尼轟隆隆的呼喚聲，「史堤夫？你要走了嗎？」

「是的。」

being in the company of just one other person so much.

Behind her she heard the kitchen door open and Tony's rumbling voice call out, "Steve? You are going?"

"Yes."

"Here I have two syrup muffins left, you would like to take them home to Laura, si?"

There was a pause. Rebecca paused too, one hand on the door, and her heart seemed to join in. Open the door and stop eavesdropping. It's none of your business.

"No thanks Tony."

"No? Well, you please yourself! They go in bin, then, is terrible waste!" she heard Tony grumble, as the door closed behind her.

It was bitter outside and she turned her collar up, setting off briskly along the road and nearly bumping into someone looking in a show window further along, huddled down under an umbrella. But she paid little attention. She was going over what she'd heard.

There was a Laura? At home? Oh, God. She'd completely misread the signals there then, hadn't she. She couldn't believe she'd kissed him. Okay, only in a friendly way, on the cheek, but still...

And if this Laura lived with Steve, was she the cause of his bad evening at home? It seemed likely. Perhaps they were heading for a break-up. Rebecca realised that a tiny part of her – a selfish, undoubtedly foolish part, that she wasn't particularly proud of— was hoping that was true.

「我還有兩個糖漿鬆餅剩下來，你想帶回家給羅拉嗎？」

一陣子的停頓。麗貝卡也停頓了一陣子，一隻手在門上，她的心似乎想繼續聽下。把門打開，不要再偷聽了，這不關你的事。

「不用了，謝謝東尼。」

「不用麼？那你自己拿吧！丟掉真的太浪費了！」在她把身後的大門關上時，她聽到東尼抱怨著。

外面很寒冷，她把衣領拉起來，迅速地沿路起步走，差點撞到在櫥窗前和擠在太陽傘下的人。但她只是有點在意剛才聽到的對話。

羅拉？在家嗎？噢，上帝。那麼是她完全會錯意了。她簡直不敢相信她吻了他。好了，那是友好的方式，在臉頰上，但是...

如果這個羅拉是跟史堤夫同住，那她就是令他在家裡不愉快的原因嗎？似乎是的。也許他們快要分手了。麗貝卡意識到有一小部分的她，希望這是真的。那是自私及絕對愚蠢的那部分，雖然她沒有對這部分特別感到自豪。

Chapter Five

Rebecca fired up her email and waited for her messages to download, greedily scooping sweet and sour noodles out of a bowl. Her eyes flicked down the screen as the messages popped up, her finger hovering over the delete button to weed out the ones about Viagra, foreign brides, online casinos and PPI. She almost deleted the email from the dating agency; she was so used to deleting the spam invitations from dating agencies that habit nearly took over.

"Great news from Methodical Matches! You have a message from THRILLER-MAN, 32, from FARRINGDON. Click here to read the message from your Hot Match. We already know you two are a great match, so don't hang around!"

"Thriller-man? What kind of a username is that?" she muttered. Did it indicate he was a Michael Jackson fan or that he liked watching Prime Suspect? Although she had to admit, choosing a username that gave the right impression was tricky. She'd spent ages thinking up something suitable and ended up with Digger Girl. It was only later that it occurred to her people might think it indicated she was a gold-digger, only after someone rich.

She logged into her mailbox on the website. There was the message, flashing to show it was unread. Rebecca clicked on the thumbnail of his profile photo, wanting to look at that first. Hmm. Dark blonde hair, glasses, not bad looking.

The message didn't tell her much. "Hello. My name's John and I'm 35. I live in Farringdon. I'm a business analyst in the City. Your profile is showing as a hot match so hopefully we will have much in common. Perhaps we could meet for lunch?"

She gritted her teeth. She knew it was unreasonable, but she hated it when people spelt city with a capital C, it seemed so pretentious. It wasn't a good reason to dismiss John from Farringdon out of hand. If he was her perfect man in every other way, having to put up with his capital Cs would be a small price to pay, she thought, sucking up her last noodle. Who knows, maybe

第五章

麗貝卡一邊處理她的電子郵件，一邊等待著電郵下載，她貪心地舀了一大碗酸甜麵條。她的眼睛掃視著屏幕彈出的電郵，手指懸停在『刪除』按鈕上，準備清除那些關於偉哥、外籍新娘、線上賭場和生產者價格指數的電郵。她差點把約會機構的電子郵件都刪除了，她習慣刪除由約會機構發出的垃圾邀請電郵，已經是習以為常的事。

「井然配對寄來的好消息！你有一個消息從『戰慄者』寄出，三十二歲，來自法靈頓。點擊這裡閱讀你的熱門配對者發出的信息。我們已經知道你們兩個是絕佳配對，所以請不要呆著了！」

「戰慄者嗎？是個什麼用戶名？」她喃喃自語。那是不是表明了他是個邁克爾·傑克遜迷，還是他喜歡看頭號嫌疑犯？雖然她不得不承認，選擇一個用戶名而要給人良好印象是很棘手的事。她也花了好幾年時間才想出合適的，就是『掘土女孩』。只是後來在她身上發生了一些事，就是有人可能會認為這是指她是一個淘金者，只是一些一身銅臭味的人。

她登錄到電子郵箱的網站上。有電郵閃爍著為未讀。麗貝卡點擊他的個人資料照片縮圖，想先看看他的樣子。嗯，暗金色的頭髮，戴眼鏡，並不難看。

該電郵沒有告訴她很多東西。「你好。我的名字是約翰，三十五歲，住在法靈頓。我是一個住在城市的業務分析員。你的個人資料顯示為熱門配對，所以希望我們會有很多共同點。也許我們可以碰面吃個午飯？」

她咬緊牙關，她知道這是不合理的，但她真的很討厭有人拼寫「城市」時用大寫「C」看來就像太自負了。但如果立即回絕法靈頓的約翰，這又不是一個很好的理由。她想，如果他在其他每一方面都是完美的，那麼他的大寫「C」就作為小小的代價，她吃掉最後的一條麵條。誰會知道，也許我可以把他訓練得好好吧。

I can train him out of it.

Where should they meet? She wasn't sure she should do lunch on the first meeting. Okay, he looked pleasant enough: tidy (if boring) hair, cheerful expression, plain shirt. But say he had terrible breath or a weird voice that reduced her to fits of giggles? And his email sounded really stilted, although some people did sound very formal when they wrote anything.

She took a deep breath, fingers on the keyboard. Stop being an idiot Rebecca and type the message. "What about starting with a coffee first? Are you free on Saturday morning?"

There, that hadn't been so hard. She only had a few other emails to read, so she flicked through them quickly and was about to shut her computer down, when a reply pinged back.

"What were you doing, sitting on the keyboard?" she muttered crossly, feeling unaccountably like her space had been invaded.

"That's fine. What time? And where?"

Hmm. Too late and it would be difficult to get out of progressing naturally on to lunch. Too early, and it might be awkward to suggest extending it until lunch if she did want to. And she might, she thought, forcing herself to think optimistically. They must have a lot in common and if sparks flew when they got together, then who knew what could happen. Where? Not Tony's, definitely. Too many people there she knew; she'd be self conscious.

"10.30? At Café d'Italia?"

"Certainly. Although can I ask that if we decide to have lunch afterwards, we go elsewhere? I'm not fond of Italian food."

Oh great. She loved Italian. She typed 'yes, that's fine', and then stopped. How should she sign off? Best wishes? Naff. Kind regards? Hmm. All the best? No, that's what salt-of-the-earth-type older men said when they shook the hand of someone whom they hadn't seen for ten years (and probably wouldn't see for another ten years). Damn it! She wouldn't put anything. She typed her name underneath and hit send.

She found herself rushing to the kitchen to boil the kettle, wondering what 'John' would say in reply. Just as the kettle clicked off, she heard the sound that told her a message had been received. She bounded back into the lounge.

"I look forward to meeting you on Saturday. John."

應該在哪裡見面好呢？她不知道第一次見面是否應該在午餐時間。好吧，他看起來也挺討人歡喜，有整齊的頭髮（雖然單調）、開朗的表情、素色的襯衫。但如果他有可怕的口氣或奇怪的聲線，會不會令她咯咯地笑個不停？他的電子郵件看起來真的有點做作，雖然有些人在寫東西的時候，的確會用很正規的語言。

她深吸了一口氣，手指放在鍵盤上。不要再白痴了麗貝卡，並鍵入信息，「不如先去喝杯咖啡吧？週六早晨你有空嗎？」

已經沒這麼難熬了，她只有剩下幾個電郵要閱讀，所以她迅速地翻閱完，準備把電腦關上的時間，一個回覆電郵的聲音響起。

「你在做什麼的呢？坐在鍵盤上等著嗎？」她生氣地嘀咕著，她感到好像私人空間莫名其妙被入侵。

「這很好。什麼時候？在哪裡？」

唔…太晚了，又很難避免到繼續進展到吃午飯時間。太早了，又可能很難建議延長直到吃午飯，如果她想的話。她想，她應該要強迫自己向樂觀方向想。他們一定有很多共同之處，當他們聚在一起一定會有火花，那麼誰知道會發生什麼事。在哪裡？東尼那裡肯定不行，太多認識的人在那裡，她知道，她意識到。

「十時三十分？意大利咖啡廳？」

「當然可以。雖然我想問，如果我們之後決定吃午飯，我們可以去別的地方嗎？我不喜歡意大利菜。」

噢，太棒了。她愛意大利菜。她輸入「是的，那很好。」然後停下。她應該如何擱筆？謹致問候？糟透了。親切問候？嗯…一切順利呢？不，那是像個社會中堅分子的老年男子說的話，他們沒見十年有多（也可能之後十年也不會見到），然後會握一下手。該死的！最後她沒有鍵入任何字，只輸入了她名字，點擊發送。

她太趕緊到廚房燒水，好奇不知道約翰會回覆什麼。正當她按下水壺開關時，她聽到的聲音，通知她收到電郵。她立即彈回客廳去。

「我期待著在週六跟你見面。約翰。」

嗯，這是一個令人掃興的結尾，貝卡。白痴。你期待什麼呢？回覆你一首愛情詩嗎？她自己傻笑起來。真可悲。當她在沖咖啡時，她試圖在腦中作一首有關約翰的詩來逗樂自己，但她很快用

Well that was an anti-climax, Becs. Idiot. What were you expecting? A love poem in return? She giggled to herself. Pathetic. She amused herself by trying to compose a poem about John in her head as she made herself coffee, but she soon ran out of things that rhymed with John and gave up. Now what should she wear to a weekend, mid-morning,first, blind, date? She had no idea.

The rest of the week flew by. Work was manic and by the time her head hit the pillow on Friday night, a mixture of nerves and exhaustion meant that all she longed for was a long lie-in the next morning, followed by a wander through the market and a leisurely late lunch. She resented the thought of having to get up and go for coffee with someone she didn't know. Still, she couldn't back out now.

By 8:30 the next morning she'd had breakfast and was out of the shower, towel-drying her hair with one hand while flicking though her clothes with the other. What impression did she want to give? Fun? Sophisticated? Both? She didn't want to look OTT, but not like she hadn't made any effort at all, either.

She sighed. This had seemed like a good idea, but if she was so desperate for someone to share her life with, why did it feel like a chore now? She faced herself in the full length mirror. "You have to do this," she told herself sternly. "Otherwise you'll end up an old batty woman muttering to yourself as you polish the skeleton you've stolen from the Museum for company.

In the end she chose smart indigo blue jeans, slim-fitting but not skin tight, and a blue, white and lilac check shirt over a white vest top with a funky neckline. She could wear her fitted lilac denim jacket over the top. Not too formal or too trendy; it was only a Saturday morning coffee, after all, although the lilac-tinted fake pearls that dangled by intricately twisted dark silver strands from her ears were more dressy than anything she usually wore for daytime. She hoped it said 'fun and stylish—pleased to meet you but not desperate'.

She used more products on her hair—i.e., some—than she normally would before venturing out on a Saturday morning, applied barely-there make-up and sprayed on a light, fresh fragrance. She hesitated by her jewellery box a few times as she scuttled back and forth gathering her phone, purse and keys, eventually muttering, "no, it's only coffee!" to herself. But when she locked the door behind her, the silver and amethyst bracelet that Hal had brought her was on her wrist. It was fairly flashy, she admitted, but it went well with her outfit and added a little more glamour, something she feared she was sadly lacking.

完跟約翰押韻的字，放棄了。現在應該想一下，週末她應該穿什麼，上午，第一次，沒見過，約會？她不知道。

本週剩餘時間飛快地過了。工作一直很忙亂，直到週五晚上她的頭終於可以擱在枕頭上的時候，神經和疲憊交織在一起，令她很渴望可以一直躺臥到第二天早上，之後可以閒逛市場和吃個悠閒的午餐。她抱怨著她得要起床去跟一個不認識的人喝咖啡。儘管如此，她已經無法打退堂鼓了。

到第二天早上八時三十分，她吃過早餐，走出淋浴間，一隻手用毛巾把頭髮擦乾，另一隻手在翻她的衣服。她要留下一個什麼印象給他呢？有趣？成熟？兩者兼而？她不想看起來太誇張，但也不喜歡不作出任何努力。

她嘆了口氣。之前認為這是一個好主意，但如果她如此渴望有人與她分享自己的生活，為什麼現在感覺就像苦差事？她對著全身鏡中的自己。「你必須要做到，」她嚴肅地告訴自己。「否則，你就會跟一個又老又古怪又咕嚕的女人一起終老，就像你每天擦拭那個從博物館偷來的骨骼一樣。」

最終，她選擇了時髦的靛藍牛仔褲，貼身剪裁但不會太緊繃，在一件有時髦領口的白色背心外套上了藍色、白色和淡紫色的運動衣。她可以穿淡紫色牛仔外套在上面，不太正式也不太新潮，到底只是星期六的早晨咖啡。雖然精細地掛在扭紋暗銀色鏈子的淡紫色假珍珠耳環看起來比她平時白天穿的更時尚。但她只想表現得「有趣而時尚，很高興見到你，但不是極之渴望。」

她用了點造型產品在頭髮上，也是比她平常會在星期六早上上街前做的多一點點，化了幾乎看不見的淡妝和噴了微微清香的香水。她猶豫了好幾次，但都沒有打開她的首飾盒，她拿起手機、錢包和鑰匙，最後喃喃地對自己說，「不，這只是一杯咖啡！」。但是，當她把門鎖上時，她的手腕上戴著一條哈爾送她的紫水晶手鍊。她承認是很華而不實，但跟她的衣服很配合，而且能夠加添幾分魅力，她不想看起來什麼都沒有很可悲的樣子。

站在大門外，她幾乎喪失了勇氣，她是不是要先告訴別人她要去哪裡？別傻了，這是一個星期六的早晨，你要去一家繁忙的咖啡店。你不是單獨與他見面，即使他突然變成了一個精神病患者。儘管她堅定地告訴自己，她雙腳仍有點兒發顫，已經有很多年沒有試過這樣了。從來沒有在約會之前，她會把勇氣都留在考試和駕駛考試。但她從來沒有試過跟一個她知道得這麼少的人約會。她知道他長什麼樣，理應是的。他可能是跟照片完全不同的人，

Outside her front door her nerve nearly deserted her. Should she have told someone where she was going? Don't be daft, it's a Saturday morning and you're going to a busy coffee shop. You won't be alone with him, even if he does turn out to be a psychopath. Despite the stern talking to, her legs felt wobbly in a way they hadn't done for years, and never before a date; she had saved her nerves for exams and her driving test. But then she'd never faced a date with a man she knew so little about. She knew what he looked like – supposedly; it could be a picture of someone completely different, or a 10 year old picture. But if he'd used a false picture, how would she recognise him?

Oh God, perhaps that was the whole point! Luring women to different places and ogling them whilst remaining incognito, getting some weird stalkerish thrill out of it. What was she doing?

The blare of a car horn brought her to her senses. She'd been so busy fretting that she hadn't looked properly as she crossed the road. Come on woman, get a grip. This is worst case scenario stuff. He's probably perfectly normal.

As the coffee shop came into view her mouth went completely dry and she tried to control her quivering legs, determined to walk in looking like a confident, professional woman.

A head swivelled to look at her as she came in. Thank goodness! It belonged to a man sitting two tables back, and he looked as similar to his summer holiday photograph as anyone else would to theirs. She smiled tentatively in his direction and he half rose.

"Rebecca, I presume?"

She nodded, suddenly tongue tied.

"Do join me."

Hugely self-conscious, she attempted an elegant walk, which was difficult for someone who spent most of her life in wellies or walking boots.

He held out a hand which was strangely light and dry when she took it, holding hers for longer than she was comfortable with. "You look even lovelier in real life." His voice was thin, the voice of a far older man, but strangely silky too.

"Thank you." She did her best to smile graciously as she sat at his table, but she already felt repulsed, and the feeling didn't go away when she realised he wasn't taking his eyes off her for a second as he sat down, moving his coffee and reaching for the

或者那是十年前的照片。但是，如果他使用假照片，她又怎能認出他呢？

哦，上帝，就是這樣了！引誘女士們到不同的地方，並擠眉弄眼而隱姓埋名，令你沈醉於不尋常被人暗戀的快感。這就是她在做的事嗎？

刺耳的汽車喇叭聲把給她拉回現實。她一直心不在焉，沒有看清楚就過馬路了。來吧女人，控制住自己的情緒。這只是最壞的情況，他可能是完全正常的。

隨著咖啡店進入視線，她的嘴唇已經完全乾透，她試圖控制住正在顫抖的雙腿，決定要走得像一個自信而專業的女人。

當她走進去，有一個人轉過來看著她。謝天謝地！那個人坐在兩張桌子後面的位置，他看起來就跟他那夏季假期的照片一樣，其他人應該都會這樣認為。她向他的方向勉強地笑了笑，他準備起身。

「我猜是麗貝卡嗎？」

她點點頭，舌頭突然打結了。

「一起坐吧。」

非常不自然地，她試圖用優雅的步伐走過去，但對於一個在一生中最常穿是長靴或登山靴的人來說，這是很困難的。

他伸出一隻手，當她搭上去，感覺異常地單薄和乾爽，拖著再久一點也會覺得舒服。「你在現實生活中看起來更可愛。」他的聲音很薄弱，就一個年長的男人的聲音，但出奇地細膩。

「謝謝你。」當她坐在到他的桌子時，她使出渾身解數擠出親切的笑容，但她已經感到反感了，而且揮之不去，就是她意識到他的視線一秒鐘都沒有離開過她，縱使他拿起咖啡或伸手去拿蛋糕菜單，他的眼睛也在緊盯著她的臉。

「我已經在這裡一段時間了，所以我冒昧地點了自己的咖啡。我希望你不會介意。」

「不會，一點都沒有。」

「我的擔心不是遲到，我是怕我或者會太早。但這裡的咖啡和蛋糕菜單相當豐富，令人眼花繚亂，所以足夠的閱讀材料，讓我有

cake menu with his eyes glued to her face.

"I have been here a while, so I took the liberty of ordering myself a coffee. I hope you don't mind."

"No, not at all."

"In my concern not to be late, I am afraid I was rather too early. But the coffee and cake menu is quite extensive, if bewildering, so I had plenty to reading material to keep me occupied."

She wasn't sure how to respond to that. Say something, Rebecca, for goodness sake. "What did you choose?"

"An espresso. I'm afraid I'm not keen on all these unnaturally flavoured, sweetened, frothy or all-milk coffees." He gave a delicate shudder. "It seems sacrilege to me. The ruination of a perfectly good beverage. I found it hard to believe they had nothing on the menu that was simply labelled 'coffee'."

Oh. My. God. Great start.

He smiled, blinking in a way that was disturbingly reptilian. "What will you have?" He offered her the menu, but Rebecca shook her head. "I'll just have the same as you for now, thanks."

He smiled a smile that met his eyes, yet seemed to be a very different type of smile when it got there. He slid up rather than stood up; there was something snake-like about him that definitely hadn't come across in his photograph. She gave a little shiver.

"Are you too cold, my dear? We will move to a table further away from the door before I order for you."

She raised a hand in protest but he completely misread the cue and took her hand, pulling to her feet. "Let's remove ourselves to the corner over there. It looks far more snug and secluded."

Protesting feebly, Rebecca trailed after him, her hand still firmly in his grasp. Snug and secluded with him was the last place she wanted to be.

He left her briefly to order her espresso and she sat there eyeing the distance to the door. Could she make it without him seeing her? Doing a runner before things could get any worse was very appealing.

Too late. He was back.

事可做。」

她不知道如何回應。說些什麼吧，麗貝卡，出於友善地。「那你選了什麼？」

「義大利濃縮咖啡。我不太喜歡不自然的口味，含糖、泡沫或全奶的咖啡。」他微妙地顫了一下。「就好像冒犯了我，令一個非常好的飲料滅絕了。我很難相信，他們的菜單上居然沒有『咖啡』這樣簡單的東西。」

噢，我的天。真是個好開始。

他笑了，眨眼的時候看起來幾乎像隻令人不安的爬行動物。「那麼你要點些什麼？他給她菜單，但麗貝卡搖搖頭。「我要跟你一樣的，謝謝。」

他笑了一笑，跟他碰上了視線，但似乎是一個非常不同類型的微笑。他滑起來而不是站起來了，就像蛇一樣，這肯定不是他的照片給人的印象。她不禁顫抖。

「你冷了嗎，親愛的？在我幫你點餐前，我們可以先換個位子，移離門口一點點。」

她舉起一隻手以示拒絕，但他完全誤解了。他拉起她的手，拖著她的腳。「讓我們移到那邊的角落，看起來更舒適和更隱蔽的。」

她已經無力拒絕，麗貝卡跟在他後面，她的手仍牢牢握在他手裡。舒適和隱蔽的是她想跟他最後會面的地方。

他暫時離開了她，為她點咖啡。她坐在那裡，審視著跟大門之間的距離。她可以在沒讓他看見的時候做到嗎？在事情可能變得更糟之前先逃之夭夭，似乎是個十分吸引人的想法。

但太遲了，他又回來了。

「你想要些蛋糕或糕點嗎？我總是擔心在這些地方的衛生，甚至在每年的這個時候，總有幾隻蒼蠅在周圍亂飛。但至少在這裡他們的糕點是蓋著的。我也看到他們有用鉗來處理蛋糕，所以我認為你會安全的。我從來不認為只用手套就足夠，你呢？除非他們是每一次觸碰另一樣東西或做其他事之後都會換上另一對新的。」

麗貝卡目瞪口呆。「不用了，謝謝，或許遲一步。」她喃喃自

"Would you like a cake or pastry? I'm always rather concerned about the hygiene in these places, even at this time of year when there are few flies around, but at least here their patisserie section is covered. Also I see they have tongs to handle the cakes too, so I think you will be safe. I never think gloves are really adequate, do you? Unless one was to remove them and put on another pair every time one touched something new or turned to a different task."

Rebecca gaped. "No thank you, perhaps later," she mumbled.

He gave her a wide smile in return. Argh. She'd said the wrong thing, unwittingly suggesting she was pleased with what she saw so far and planning to hang around! No, she wasn't.

She picked up her coffee and tried to hide behind it, which would have been a lot easier to do if she'd asked for the large, frothy, sweetened, all-milk caramel latte that she'd really craved. Shallow espresso cups weren't really fit for the purpose.

"So Rebecca. What exactly do you do?"

Oh no. She didn't want to tell him. If he knew where she worked, he might turn up, and GLAM wasn't exactly an inconspicuous place to work.

"Sorry, do you mind if I just take my jacket off..." She got up, surreptitiously sliding a hand into her jacket pocket as she turned away.

"Of course not, of course not, dear lady. I want you to be comfortable."

I couldn't be more uncomfortable, she screamed internally, as she slid her thumb across the screen of her Smartphone. Dear lady? What century was this man from? She pretended to drop a tissue and bend down to retrieve it. That gave her time to activate her 'staff meeting 10:50' alarm on her phone, and pop the phone back in the pocket of her jacket which hung on the back of her chair.

"Can we talk about you first?" she asked, trying to smile. "Only my throat's dry. I've had a bit of a cold. Hopefully the coffee will help."

"Of course, of course." He smiled but looked rather anxious, edging away from her a little as he settled back in his chair. Excellent. She faked a cough and he visibly paled.

語。

他給了她一個大大的笑容。啊，她說錯了話嗎？不自覺地暗示了她很滿意到目前為止在這裡的東西，並打算經常泡在這裡嗎？不，她沒有。

她拿起她的咖啡，並試圖躲在它後面，這本來很容易做到，如果她要的是大杯、有泡沫、加糖的全脂牛奶焦糖拿鐵咖啡，是她真正想要的。淺而短的義大利濃縮咖啡杯子沒有做到真正切合的功能。

「所以麗貝卡，其實你是做什麼的呢？」

噢，不，她不想告訴他。如果他知道她在那裡工作，他可能會在那裡露面，倫敦人類學博物館並不完全是個不顯眼的工作地點。

「對不起，如果你不介意，我只是想把我的外套脫...」她站起身來，在她轉過頭去的時候，她偷偷摸摸地把手滑進口袋裡。

「當然不要，當然不要，親愛的女士，我想你感覺舒服。」

我不能更不舒服了！她心裡尖叫著，她的拇指正在她的智能手機屏幕上滑動。親愛的女士？這個是什麼年代的男人嗎？她假裝掉落了一塊紙巾，彎下腰來撿它。這給了她的時間，把她電話上「十點三十分員工會議」的鬧鈴啟動了，並把手機放回掛在她椅背的那件外套的口袋裡。

「我們能不能先談談你的呢？」她問，試圖微笑。「只有我的喉嚨乾了。我有點感冒，希望咖啡會有所幫助。」

「當然，當然。」他笑了，但看起來相當不安，緩慢地移離她一點點，直到安定在他的椅子上。好極了，她假裝咳嗽，他明顯有點臉色發白。

「你想知道什麼？」

「哦，嗯...你在空餘時間都喜歡做什麼？」

「哦，是的，當然，當然。雖然我一般都很少有空餘時間，我的工作非常忙碌，確實非常忙。」他挺起了胸部並高人一等地笑著。

當然，她想。「那麼你會做...」她引導著。

"What would you like to know?"

"Oh, um... what you like to do in your spare time?"

"Oh yes, of course, of course. Although naturally I get very little spare time, my job keeps me very busy. Very busy indeed." He puffed up his chest and smiled patronisingly.

Naturally, she thought. "But when you do..." she prompted.

"When I do, I like to read. Mostly, the autobiographies of the great movers and shakers of our time. Sugar, Dyson, Brady, Getty, Hiroshi Mikitani, Branson."

"Uh-huh." Fascinating. Yawn...

He looked awkward. "I'm afraid my secret vice is Jodie Forrest novels. I hesitated to admit that on my profile, knowing how it would look. It's far from sophisticated literature, I am afraid, and I don't imagine you're familiar with her work."

"I've read a couple," she mumbled.

"Really?" he looked down his nose at her and she had the distinct impression that far from delighting him, it had made him disappointed in her. Not half as disappointed as I am in you, she thought.

"Her thrillers do have a certain logic to them that I like. The action sequences and drama, however, are completely far-fetched."

Rebecca gulped. They're my favourite parts.

"Sometimes I find myself skipping over the action sequences and dialogue to the sections where the clues are put together and the characters decide their next logical move."

"I see." Ask him something else, Rebecca. Use up the time. "And do you like to, er, eat out with friends or anything?"

"Very rarely. I'm so busy with work that there's little time to socialise."

Argh! I know! You said!

"I do have a small circle of friends but unfortunately, they tend to favour Indian restaurants." He wrinkled his nose.

"You don't like Indian food?" she asked politely.

「當我有時間，我喜歡閱讀。多數是偉大而有權勢的人的自傳，或是在這個時代很有影響力的人，像休格、戴森、布雷迪、格蒂、三木谷浩史、布蘭森。」

「嗯哼。」真令人著迷。無聊透頂了...

他看起來有點尷尬。「我恐怕我有私密惡習就是讀朱迪．福斯特的小說。我猶豫了一下在我的個人資料中寫上去，不知道看起來會怎樣。不像精緻的文學，我很害怕，我也沒有想像你會熟悉她的作品。」

「我讀過兩本了。」她喃喃自語。

「真的嗎？」他低頭看著自己的鼻子，她清楚地感覺到這跟他喜歡的差好遠，令他對她很失望。但也不及她對他的一半失望，她想。

「她的驚悚小說有一定的邏輯，我是喜歡的。然而，動作情節和戲劇部分就完全不切實際。」

麗貝卡吞嚥了一下。這些都是我最喜歡的部分。

「有時我會跳過動作情節和對話的章節，那部分跟線索放在一起，或當主角要決定他們的合邏輯的下一步的時候。」

「我明白了。」問他別的東西，麗貝卡。把時間用完。「你想，呃，與朋友出來會吃些什麼？」

「非常少的。因為我工作這麼忙，很少有時間應酬。」

哎呀！我知道了！你已經說過了！

「我有一個很小的朋友圈，但很不幸，他們比較喜歡印度餐館。」他皺了皺鼻子。

「你不喜歡印度食物嗎？」她禮貌地問。

他打了一個寒顫。「當然不。我的朋友都知道，但仍然選擇那些地方。」

嗯，麗貝卡想。可想而知。

「不僅我對那裡的衛生標準有保留，我也討厭外國的食物。」

她知道她正盯著他，但她真的忍不住。「什麼？所有外國食品？

He shuddered. "Certainly not. My friends know that, yet still choose these places."

Hmm, thought Rebecca. Surprise, surprise.

"Not only do I have reservations about the hygiene standards in these places, I also detest foreign foods."

She knew she was staring, but she couldn't help it. "What, all foreign foods?" she blurted.

"Yes." he wrinkled his nose. "Indian, Mexican, Thai... if only these places would prepare some plainer dishes. Even other restaurants with less spicy dishes—Greek, for instance, or Italian – will insist on adding so many herbs or peppers to their foods that one can barely determine what manner of food forms the basis of the dish! And the French, of course, simply drown everything in garlic."

"Yes, I suppose they do," she croaked.

"I occasionally take Mother to a nearby hotel for a Sunday roast," he added. "But enough about food. It's only purpose is to fuel one through a hectic day, as far as I'm concerned, and of course, you'll be wondering about my work." He put his coffee down and slopped a little on his fingers. He glanced down with a look of distaste, then quickly swept up a serviette and made a meal out of wiping his fingers. "Firstly, I have a job that, in popular conception, is considered boring."

She nodded, still playing the dry throat card.

"I work as a business analyst. I think I may have told you that in my email."

Nod.

"Is business analysis something you know much about?"

Shake.

"It's a fascinating career, I assure you. Only the other day, I was looking at the projections of a third-world company that a client, Messchler and Messchler, is planning to bid for. And what I found was, that despite—"

John seemed was so fond of the sound of his own voice that he needed no interaction from her, and Rebecca's attention started to drift away; very useful, as she gave a genuine start when her

」她脫口而出。

「是。」他皺了皺鼻子。「印度、墨西哥、泰國...但願這些地方會準備一些簡單點的菜式。還有其他餐館比較少辛辣菜餚的，

例如希臘或意大利，他們會堅持在食物中添加很多的香草或辣椒，那完全決定了菜式本身的食品風格！還有法國菜，當然，都只是將所有東西淹沒在大蒜中。」

「是的，我想他們有這樣做。」她嘶啞地說。

他補充說：「我偶爾會帶母親到附近的酒店吃週日烤肉。食物還可以，唯一的目的是在繁忙的日子給自己一點推動力，這對我來說很重要。當然，你可能對我的工作很好奇。」他放下咖啡，並溢出了一點在他的手指上。他低頭並使出了一個厭惡的神色，然後迅速用餐巾紙擦了手指好一會。「首先，我有一個工作，在大眾的概念中，被認為是枯燥的。」

她點點頭，繼續使出喉嚨乾涸這招。

「我的工作是一個業務分析員。我可能已經在電郵中告訴你了。」

點頭。

「業務分析是不是你熟識的東西？」

搖頭。

「我可以向你保證，這是一個讓人著迷的職業。就在前些日子，我正個跟進一個第三世界公司的方案，那個客戶是曼提斯華，而曼提斯華正打算競買。但是我發現，雖然...」

約翰似乎很喜歡自己說話的聲音，他從不需要跟她有任何互動，麗貝卡的注意力開始漸行漸遠。非常好，她的手機響了，她終於可以真正開始。

「對不起，請原諒我...」她拿起電話，看似很艱難才聽到。「信號很弱。」她嘟囔走近窗口，繼續她的「對話」。

「不，我明白的。」她搖搖頭。「沒有。不要擔心，如果你現在需要我，那麼你現在就需要我。好吧，嗯，我十分鐘就可以到你那邊。再見。」她走回到桌邊，小心地安排了在臉上帶著一個歉意的笑容。

phone rang.

"Sorry, do excuse me..." She grabbed the phone and made a show of struggling to hear. "Low signal," she mouthed and walked closer to the window to continue her 'conversation'."

"No, I quite understand." She shook her head. "No. Don't worry, if you need me right now, then you need me right now. Okay. Well I'll see you in ten. Bye for now." She walked back to the table with an apologetic smile carefully arranged on her face.

"I'm so sorry, John, but I'm afraid I have to go. A friend's babysitter has let her down and she's due at an important meeting."

He raised his eyebrows. "What kind of important meeting can a woman who has a baby possibly have? Or is it with Social Services?"

Rebecca gaped for several moments then narrowed her eyes. "It's a business meeting."

"Really? On a Saturday?"

"Well when you run several companies, you know how it is." Her voice was icy and she'd given up all pretence of having a sore throat. She was making up for it in the pretence department with her fictitious, high-flying friend. "In business, as you said yourself, you have very little spare time."

He looked like he'd just been force-fed a Vindaloo. "Won't you at least finish your coffee?" he said curtly. "After all, espressos aren't cheap here. It seems a shame to waste it."

"No, I have to go straight away. But I'd hate for you to be out of pocket," she said smoothly, slapping a £5 note on the table.

"Oh no, my dear I couldn't accept that. The espresso was not quite that expensive."

"Nonsense. My pleasure." She turned on her heel.

"We must do this again. I'll be in touch!" he called after her. She waved a non-committal hand behind her, already at the door. As it closed, she glanced back through the window. He was squirreling the £5 note away in his pocket with alacrity. He was welcome to it. It was a small price to pay for escape.

「我很抱歉，約翰，但我怕我得走了。一位朋友的保姆要把她的孩子留下，但她正在開一個重要的會議。」

他揚一揚了眉毛。「一個有孩子的女人可以有什麼重要會議要開呢？是跟社會服務部門的會議嗎？」

麗貝卡目瞪口呆了幾秒，然後瞇起眼睛。「是一個商務會議。」

「真的嗎？在星期六？」

「當你要運作幾家公司，你就會知道是怎麼回事。」她的聲音很冰冷，她已經放棄假裝喉嚨痛。她正在編造一個虛假的部門，有一個虛構而有成就的朋友。「在企業中，像你說的，有很少會有空餘時間。」

他看起來就像剛剛被迫吃了印度最辣咖喱一樣。「那你會不會先把咖啡喝完呢？」他簡短地說。「畢竟，特濃咖啡是不便宜，浪費它似乎很令人惋惜。」

「不行，我得馬上去。但我討厭讓你白花錢。」她平靜地說，然後把五元擱在桌子上。

「哦，不，親愛的。我不能接受的，這咖啡不用這麼貴。」

「別胡鬧了。不用客氣。」她轉身就走。

「我們一定要再見面，保持聯絡！」他在她身後叫她。她向身後揚一揚手表示不作承諾，她已經走到門口。關門，她通過窗口回頭望了一眼，他爽快地拿起了五元放進口袋裡。明顯他很樂於取回，而她就當作付了一個小數目去讓自己逃出生天。

Chapter Six

Laura was getting worse and Steve had no idea how to help her. She didn't seem to go more than a couple of days now without coming home drunk, high as a kite, or twitchy and aggressive.

He had tried to get her help in the past, but Laura didn't seem to fit into the right categories. Anyway, the message from all the addiction and mental health services he'd contacted had been the same: she had to be willing to seek help herself. Nobody could forcibly step in unless—or until, as Steve thought more likely—she posed a significant danger to herself or others, or committed a criminal act, and then a referral was likely to come from the court. One of the caseworkers at the local addiction centre, a girl who looked about sixteen to Steve, asked what Laura was taking and how often. He admitted he didn't have a clue. He was sure he'd seen a flash of contempt on her face, but perhaps it was his own guilty paranoia.

"If you're telling me she can go a week without a drink, or any withdrawal symptoms then it's alcohol abuse, not dependence, so drying out won't help," advised the tall, burly man from the Alcohol Dependency Drop-in Centre. "It's what's going on inside her head that needs sorting. She's choosing to binge drink, not drinking because she can't do without it." He gave Steve some leaflets on binge drinking. Laura didn't so much look at them as sneer.

The GP had reiterated what everyone else said, although he did call Laura in on the pretext of a 'Young Person's Health Check.' To Steve's amazement Laura had gone along to the surgery without argument, not only on time but comparatively neat and clean; where, when asked, she'd said without batting an eyelid, that she only drank occasionally—"the odd birthday or leaving party, that kind of thing, and I only have a couple" – and that she'd never touched drugs.

"I'm afraid there's nothing more I can do," said Doctor Anderson regretfully.

"What about a blood test?"

第六章

羅拉愈演愈烈，史堤夫不知道該如何去幫助她。她不出兩天就沒有回家跑去喝酒，而且回來時都是極度興奮、或焦躁、或咄咄逼人的狀態。

他曾試圖幫助她，但羅拉似乎並不能夠重回正軌。總管如此，他接觸的所有成癮及精神健康服務機構回覆他的信息都一樣：要讓她自願尋求幫助。這個階段沒有人能強迫她，除非直到，史堤夫認為更有可能凡是她做了嚴重危害到自己或他人的事，或犯罪行為，然後由法院直接轉介。曾經有個當地的戒毒中心的社工，史堤夫覺得她看來好像只有十六歲，她問到羅拉是何時開始吸毒，以及持續多久了，他完全沒有頭緒。他確信他有看到在她的臉上閃過了一個蔑視的表情，但也許這只是他自己因為內疚而妄想出來的。

「如果你告訴我，她可以一個星期不喝酒，又沒有任何戒斷症狀，那麼她是酗酒，並不是依賴酒精。所以戒酒對她不會有幫助的。」降低酒精依賴服務中心那位高大魁梧的男子建議。「這是她的腦袋裡面需要先整頓一下。她選擇酗酒，而不喝酒，因為她不能沒有它。」他給了史堤夫一些有關酗酒的單張。但羅拉只冷笑而沒有多看一眼。

全科醫生也只是重覆其他人所說的話，雖然他藉以「年輕人士健康檢查」致電羅拉。但史堤夫很驚訝羅拉對這次會診毫無異議，不僅準時到達，而且比平日相對整齊乾淨。在那裡，當她被問及時，她面不改色地說，她只會偶爾喝點，「古怪的生日或告別派對，那種情況下我才會喝兩杯。」她還說她從來沒有碰過毒品。

「我恐怕我沒有什麼可以做了。」安德森醫生遺憾地說。

「血液測試可以？」

「我們已經做了標準的糖尿病、甲狀腺和膽固醇測試。其他的如果沒有預先通知她，我是無法做測試，因為這是完全不道德，我也無法想像如果要求她做藥物測試會怎樣。」

"We did the standard one for diabetes, thyroid and cholesterol. I couldn't test for anything else without informing her, that would be completely unethical; and I can't imagine asking her to submit to drugs testing would go down well."

"No, I think you're right there," Steve said heavily. "Thanks for all you've done."

"No problem, only sorry I couldn't do more. You know where I am if you need me."

"Thanks."

Steve had asked Laura to take a drugs test last week. Yelled it at her, in fact. He wasn't proud of it but she'd got under his skin, despite every effort to keep his cool. On Saturday, she'd come home talking gibberish, eyes unfocussed, pupils dilated and her mouth on overdrive. Not alcohol this time, Steve thought. Her behaviour was different and he couldn't smell booze. His best guess, referring to the leaflet Dr Anderson had given him, was cocaine, but it could be something else. Or a mixture.

She was in no state to have a rational conversation, and Steve knew that when she returned to planet earth, she wouldn't want to talk about it. So he tried to stay calm and ride it out. He switched on the TV watched it with her, keeping as much of an eye on her as he did the programme. It had seemed like a good idea, but Laura had embarked on a jarringly loud non-stop commentary.

Steve got her a glass of water. He knew most of the things she might have taken caused dehydration and a dry mouth. She downed the water and kept on talking. Then he brought her sandwiches, but she flipped the top of the sandwich to see what was inside then brought her hand up sharply underneath the plate Steve still held, crashing it upwards into his nose before it fell to the floor, scattering cheese, coleslaw and salad all over the floor.

"I can't eat that shit. Take it away."

Steve's chest felt tight and his nose was agony. "That hurt."

"What did?" She glared.

"You knocked the plate into my nose." He felt his nose and his hand came away bloody.

She stared at his face. "Doesn't look broken, so what are you whining about?"

「對，我覺得你說得沒錯，」史堤夫沉重地說。「感謝你所做的一切。」

「沒問題，抱歉我不能為你做更多。如果你需要我幫忙，你知道我在哪裡。」

「謝謝。」

史堤夫上週曾經問過羅拉有關藥物測試的事。事實上，她大叫了。他不為這事感到驕傲，但她已經令他惱火了，儘管他已經竭盡全力保持冷靜。上週六，她回到家裡胡言亂語、目光呆滯、瞳孔放大，她的嘴在超高速開動。這次不是酒精，史堤夫認為。她的行為跟平時不一樣，他聞不出酒味。根據安德森醫生給他的小冊子，他猜測應該是可卡因，但也可能是別的東西，或者是其混合物。

她不適宜跟他理性對話，史堤夫知道當她回到地球時，她也不會想談論它。於是，他試圖保持冷靜挺過去。他打開電視機，跟她一起收看，他一面選看節目，一面留意著她。那個節目似乎很不錯，但羅拉已經開始在不停發出高聲刺耳的評論。

史堤夫給了她一杯水，他知道她可能會脫水和口乾。她一口氣喝下水，然後繼續說話。然後他給她三明治，她翻開最頂一層，看下裡面是什麼，然後她在碟子下面的手大幅地伸起，而史堤夫當時依然拿著碟子，在他的鼻子崩潰之前，碟子已經摔在地上，奶酪、涼拌捲心菜和沙拉散落到周圍都是。

「我不吃狗屎，把它拿走。」

史堤夫感到胸部非常繃緊，鼻子極度痛苦。「我受傷了。」

「什麼？」她怒視。

「你把碟子撞向我的鼻子了。」他覺得他的鼻子和手正在流血。

她盯著他的臉。「看來沒有破掉，那你還抱怨什麼？」

「痛死了，你甚至沒有說聲對不起。給你三明治也沒有一個簡單的感謝。」

「這不是三明治，是狗屎。」她把焦點放回在電視機上。

史堤夫盡了最大的努力轉身並走回廚房，否則他可能會握住她的脖子或給她一巴掌。他希望他能出去走走，離開她，但不知怎麼

"It hurts like hell, and you haven't even said sorry. A simple no thanks to the sandwich would have done."

"It wasn't a sandwich, it was shit." She was focussed back on the TV.

With a supreme effort, Steve turned on his heel and walked back to the kitchen because otherwise he thought he might shake her or slap her. He wished he could go out and leave her to it, but how would he feel if she had a bad reaction to whatever she'd taken? He did need to stay away from her though.

He could vacuum upstairs, but there was a watery sun peeping out from behind the clouds and for this early in the year, it was a mild day. Maybe he'd put another layer on and sit in the garden with a book. Just imagining it made him relax a little. But Laura came to find him and wouldn't leave him alone.

He abandoned his book and went to the laptop, expecting her to stay in the garden because she'd finally stretched herself out on their small patch of lawn, and her mouth had slowed down. She looked exhausted. It seemed like a good time to get on with his Methodical Matches profile.

Five minutes later she was at his elbow. "What are you doing?"

"Nothing important." Instantly he minimised the window. "Can you take your boots off, Lor, you're trailing mud everywhere."

"Methodical Matches? Isn't that the dating place that's moved into Cooper's?" Damn it, he must have been too slow.

"I think so." He tried to sound offhand. "I was just seeing what it was all about, because they left leaflets at work."

"So how many dates do you get?"

"No idea."

"Where do the people come from? I mean, do they only pick people from r—"

"I don't know, Laura."

"It's not a hoax, is it? Because Lauren Miller said most of them are hoaxes, the people don't even exist." She was bouncing her legs, letting her ankle bang out a rapid rhythm on the chair leg.

"How would I know? I shouldn't think so, if they've got an office."

他又覺得，她可能會做出什麼激烈的行為，雖然他確實需要遠離她。

他可以到樓上去吸塵，但看到淡淡的太陽從雲層後面鑽了出來，是這年初的第一次，好一個暖溫和的日子。也許他可以穿上外套坐在花園看書。想像一下就已經使他放鬆一點。但羅拉跑了出來找他，不讓他獨自一人。

他放棄看書，打開筆記本電腦，他預計她會一直留在花園裡，因為她在小草坪上躺了下來，她的嘴已經有所放緩。她看上去疲憊不堪。這似乎是一個很好的時間，讓他繼續填完井然配對的個人檔案。

五分鐘後，她走到他身旁。「你在做什麼？」

「不重要的。」他立即把視窗最小化了。「你能不能脫下你的靴子，羅拉，你把泥巴印到周圍都是了。」

「井然配對？他們是不是會把約會的地方安排在庫珀車上？」該死的，他動作一定是太慢了。

「我想是吧。」他試圖裝作若無其事。「我只是在看下它究竟是什麼的，因為他們在我工作的地方留下了傳單。」

「所以你會去多少個約會？」

「不知道。」

「那些人是從哪裡來的？我的意思是，他們是不是只挑選那些人隨…」

「羅拉，我不知道。」

「這不是一個騙局吧？因為勞倫.米勒說，大多數都是騙局，那些人甚至是不存在的。」她晃動著她的腳，腳踝在椅腳上敲出了很快的節拍。

「我怎麼會知道？但我不這麼認為，因為他們有辦公室。」

「那會發生什麼事情？如果…」

「我不知道！我甚至沒有機會看，因為你不閉上你的嘴！」他站起身來，蓋上筆記本電腦。

"What would happen if-?"

"I don't know! I didn't even get the chance to look, because you won't shut up!" He got to his feet, closing down the laptop.

She stared at him, eyes wide, legs temporarily still. "Ooh, someone got out the wrong side of bed. If you're finished, can I play on the laptop?"

"Fill your boots. Since you can't be bothered to take them off." He turned his back on her. Maybe the vacuuming had been the best idea, after all

He wouldn't normally have considered vacuuming as peaceful, but that's how it had felt. For ten minutes, anyway. Until he heard a rhythmic banging on the doorframe.

He looked up. Laura was leaning on the doorframe, banging her still-booted foot against it, hard.

He turned the vacuum cleaner off. "Finished on the laptop?"

"No, but it's crashed, says I've downloaded a virus or something. Piece of shit, you should get a better one. Just wondering when the hell lunch is, it's already half past one. You do a crap job of looking after me, don't you, Stevie Boy."

That was the point when the last thread of Steve's patience had unravelled with an almost audible twang. He yelled first, but who wouldn't. He wasn't a saint.

He accused her of being high. She swore she'd taken nothing. Then swore some more.

"You know what your problem is, don't you, Steve? You just want me to behave like an obedient little girl all the time, because it suits you. Out of sight, out of mind, not seen and not heard!"

"Of course I don't!"

"You do, because the minute I have different opinions to you and I open my mouth about them, you can't handle it! You can't handle it because I don't live my life like photocopy of yours!"

"You're joking! You haven't got a clue what my life's like, and you sure as hell couldn't live it! You're far too selfish and self-centred to ever put your life on hold for someone else!"

"Oh here we go! Ram it down my throat, what you've given up

她盯著他，眼睛睜得大大的，腳仍在晃動。「哦，原來有人從早晨醒來心情就不好。如果你用完電腦了，我可以用嗎？」

「那麼你就穿著你的靴子吧，既然你不想把它們脫下來。」他轉身背對著她。現在最好的主意還是去吸塵。

他沒有想過吸塵可以如此寧靜的，就像現在一樣。但只有十幾分鐘時間。直到他聽到有節奏地敲在門框的聲音。

他抬起頭來。羅拉倚在門框上，她仍然用穿著靴子的腳用力地叩著門框上。

他把吸塵器關上。「筆記本電腦上用完了嗎？」

「沒有，但它癱瘓了，說我下載了病毒或什麼的。真是一塊狗屎，你應該換個好一點的。其實我只是想問一下該死的午餐何時可以吃，已經一點半了。你的垃圾工作就是照顧我，不是嗎？史堤夫男孩。」

就在這一刻，當史堤夫的耐性中最後一道防線被衝破時，就像聽得到了嘣的一聲。他吼叫了，誰不會呢，而且他不是聖人。

他指責她還在興奮狀態，而她就發誓她沒有吸毒，然後再發誓更多。

「你知道你的問題是什麼嗎，史堤夫？你只是想我像一個聽話的小女孩，永遠都是，因為這樣才適合你。眼不見，心不煩，沒有看到，沒有聽到！」

「我當然不是！」

「你是，如果有一刻，我跟你有不同的意見，我一開口說出來，你就不能接受！你不能接受是因為我沒有活得像你一樣！」

「你是在開玩笑吧！你對我的生活根本一無所知，而你肯定會覺得像在地獄一樣受不了！你太自私和自我中心了，只會將你自己的生活套到別人身上！」

「哦，現在就開始吧！向我不斷強調你已經放棄我了！你知道的，雖然我沒有問，我也希望你沒有。那麼你就不會因為我搞砸你的生活而太恨我！」

「我不恨你，羅拉，不要那麼傻！」

for me! You know what, I didn't ask you to, and I wish you hadn't. Then you wouldn't hate me so much for screwing up your life!"

"I don't hate you Laura, don't be so stupid!"

"I am stupid, remember? I must be, because I didn't go to uni, did I? After all that effort he put in I let Stevie down by finally not jumping through one of his hoops!"

He shook his head. "I'm not doing this. You don't know what you're saying, it's the drugs talking." He went to leave the room, but she blocked the doorway.

"That's what you'd like to believe, isn't it! The perfect excuse! God forbid little Laura might actually think these things for real!" She was right in his face now. "I don't TAKE drugs!"

"Bloody well prove it then!" he yelled back, face inches from hers. "Let's book you a blood test, shall we? Right now! I bet Dr Anderson could fit us in!"

"I don't have to prove anything to you, you wanker!" she screeched, and fled.

Steve had stood there for a while, breathing heavily, trying to calm himself down. He could hear her banging about and swearing. Then he heard the front door slam. After a while, he went to check what she'd taken. Not much. Some of her clothes, and her day-to-day toiletries. He wandered to the kitchen in a daze and fixed himself lunch. With no small sense of irony, after a minute's hesitation he'd pulled a can of lager out the fridge too. Then he'd grabbed his book and headed to the garden.

Laura had turned up two days later, looking fine and acting as if nothing had happened. Steve felt wrong-footed. He had no idea how to react. She hadn't answered any of his calls to her mobile, ignoring his voicemails.

He'd been worried sick and on the verge of calling the police and reporting her missing. She'd seemed on an even keel since then. Not that she'd done much to clear up after herself or keep the house clean, and there was no sign she was looking for work. But for now, things were calm, so Steve was letting things ride. He knew he was just sticking his head in the sand though, and he felt a constant tension, as though a thunderstorm was brewing.

He tried to be glad she was back. That she seemed okay. Tried to convince himself it had just been a phase, and now it was out of her system. She would find work soon, get back on her feet,

「我是很傻，你記得嗎？我一定是，因為我沒有上大學，是嗎？付出所有的努力之後，到最後我太令史堤夫失望了，而且根本沒有盡過力！」

他搖搖頭。「我沒有這樣。你不知道你在說什麼，你吸毒了才會說出這樣的話。」他想離開房間，但她堵住了門口。

「這就是你相信的，是不是！完美的藉口！上帝一定要阻止小羅拉相信這些東西是真的！」她把臉湊到他的臉前面。「我沒有吸毒！」

「血液可以證明！」他喊回去，把臉移開了幾英寸。「讓我為你預約做血液測試，好嗎？現在！我敢打賭，安德森醫生可以給我們安排！」

「我不必向你證明什麼，你這個混蛋！」她尖叫著，逃走了。

史堤夫站在那裡了一會兒，喘著粗氣，試圖讓自己冷靜下來。他能聽到她在到處亂敲還大聲咒罵。然後，他聽到前門砰的一聲。過了一會兒，他去檢查了一下她拿了什麼東西。並不是很多，只是一些衣服，和每天用的洗滌用品。他呆呆地走到廚房，並準備了自己的午餐。隨著一點的諷刺感和一分鐘的猶豫後，他從冰箱拿出一罐啤酒。然後他拿住他的書，走出花園。

羅拉在兩天後出現，看起來很不錯而且彷彿什麼都沒有發生過。史堤夫感到措手不及，他不知道應該如何反應。他打電話給她，她都沒有接，而且沒有理會他的語音留言。

他一直擔心得想吐，差點就致電警方報案她失踪了。她似乎從那時起一直都很穩定。不，她還做了很多事，整頓好自己和保持家裡清潔，但仍沒有找工作的跡象。但現在事情安定下來了，所以史堤夫就讓事情這樣了。他知道他只是在逃避現實，像採取鴕鳥政策，但他仍感到一股持續的緊張氣氛，彷彿正在醞釀一場暴風雨。

他嘗試為她回來而高興，而且她看起來似乎很好。他說服自己這只是一個階段，現在她是有點偏離了軌道。她很快就會找到工作，再腳踏實地，並獲得一些尊嚴，她會嗎？這事剛好趕上了史堤夫準備今年去申請上大學，畢竟，他不會再延遲一年，而他會申請本地的大學。如果成功，也許他們就不用搬遷，雖然在倫敦居住不是最便宜的選擇。

他究竟想騙誰，她根本就是一個定時炸彈。

and gain some self-esteem, wouldn't she. Perhaps it might all happen in time for Steve to feel confident applying for uni this year; after all, he wouldn't go for another year, and if he applied to a local one, maybe they wouldn't have to move, although London wasn't the cheapest place to live.

Who was he trying to kid. She was a ticking time bomb.

"How's it going?" Rebecca asked.

Kevin started, the tweezers in his hand jerking and releasing a piece of pottery. "I wish you wouldn't creep up on me like that!"

"I wasn't trying to."

"Can't you wear high heels or something?"

"Yes, because that would be so practical."

"Walk louder, then."

"Walk louder?"

Kevin waved his tweezers at her threateningly. "Back off, lady. I was concentrating. My boss is a real slave driver, you know. Always wandering in here at random to check up on me. Very quietly."

"That must be a burden."

He rolled his eyes comically. "Oh it is, believe me. Anyway, what can I do for you, She Who Must Be Obeyed?"

"I wondered if we'd had results back on those soil samples from last week."

"No, but they should be ready this afternoon, apparently."

"Great. In that case, how about an early lunch?"

"It's barely twelve Bec! I've only just started on this pot."

She stretched over, looking past him. "Huh. Looks like you haven't started at all to me, so you might as well take a break. Besides, I'm starving."

"Do I get a say? Especially as I had a snack half an hour ago and

「怎麼回事？」麗貝卡問。

凱文突然跳起了，拿著鉗子的手猝然一動，掉下了一塊黏土。「我希望你不要這樣突擊我！」

「我沒有想過要這樣做。」

「你不能穿高跟鞋或其他的嗎？」

「是的，因為這樣穿比較踏實。」

「那你走得大聲點。」

「走得大聲點？」

凱文向她揮揮小鉗子威脅她。「退後一點，女士。我在集中精神。我的老闆是一個真正的奴隸主人，你知道嗎？經常徘徊在這裡，然後靜悄悄地突擊檢查我。」

「那一定是一種負擔。」

他滑稽地轉了轉眼睛。「哦，是的，相信我。不管怎樣，我可以為你做什麼呢？她是我必須服從的人。」

「我只是有點疑惑，我們上週就應該要有那些土壤結果了。」

「沒有，但顯然應該是今天下午就準備好。」

「太好了。那麼，不如早點吃個午餐？」

「現在只剛好十二點，貝卡！我才剛剛開始工作。」

她把頭伸過來，看看他。「呵呵。看起來你好像根本還沒有開始，所以你不如先稍稍休息。而且，我餓了。」

「我可以說什麼呢？尤其是因為我有半小時前才吃了一點小食，而我根本並不餓呢？」

「不。」她說，把手穿進他的手臂並把他轉過來對著門口。

他嘆了口氣。「那先讓我洗洗手，然後拿回我的外套。就當是你迫我的，所以午餐是你的。」

她咧嘴一笑，讓他走開了。「很公平。」她停在門口。「很有趣，」她輕描淡寫地說，「我想你會渴望聽到我去了第一個網絡

I'm not hungry at all?"

"Nope," she said, slotting her arm through his and spinning him round to face the door.

He sighed. "Let me wash my hands and get my jacket then. As you're forcing me into this, lunch is on you."

She grinned and let him go. "Fair enough." She stopped at the door. "Funny," she said casually, "I thought you'd be dying to hear how my first internet date went."

"You had a date? When?" he squawked. She could hear him scrabbling about trying to shut his computer down. "Bec, wait—"

"Saturday." She kept on walking. "See you out front."

"So what was he like? Come on!" Kevin put his knife and fork down, clasped his hands and leaned forward, with a daft grin on his face.

Rebecca chased a piece of chicken round her plate. "He was a business analyst."

"Oh dear. Name?"

"John."

"Nothing wrong with that." Kevin went back to his salad.

"No. That was about the only thing that was right with him. He doesn't like any coffee other than espresso; any other variety is a mortal sin—"

"Oh my Lord!" His fork stopped halfway to his mouth.

"He had this really weird handshake; like he didn't really want his hand to be in mine—his hand was all rigid—"

"Oo-er!"

"— but then he wouldn't let it go. And he's a hygiene obsessive." Unlike me," she laughed, scooping up a piece of lettuce that had escaped on to the table. "And he kept calling me 'my dear' like I was his niece or something, although he was looking at me in a decidedly un-uncle-ish way."

約會。」

「你去約會了？什麼時候？」他呱呱大叫。她能聽到他亂抓試圖關閉他的電腦。「貝卡，等等…」

「星期六，」她繼續往前走。「在外面等你。」

「所以他是怎樣的？來吧！」凱文把他的刀和叉放下，緊緊地握住了雙手，俯身向前，一個愚蠢的笑容在他的臉上。

麗貝卡追捕著碟子上一塊圓形的雞肉。「他是一個業務分析員」

「哦，親愛的。他叫什麼名字？」

「約翰。」

「沒有什麼不妥。」凱文又繼續吃他的沙拉。

「沒有。這是他唯一一樣正常的東西。他不喜歡任何特濃咖啡以外的咖啡，好像其他任何款式是不可饒恕的大罪。」

「噢，我的天啊！」他的叉子在送到嘴裡的中途停下了。

「他還有這古怪的握手方式，就像他其實不是真的想要跟你握手一樣，他的手是完全僵硬的。」

「哦…咿！」

「…但他不會放開手。而且他是有潔癖的，不像我。」她笑了，撿起了一塊掉到桌上的生菜。「他不停地叫我『親愛的』，好像我是他的外甥女或什麼的，雖然他一直用一個非叔叔的眼神看著我。」

「好噁心。」

「沒錯。」

「你忍受了多久？」凱文拿起咖啡，眼睛在閃動著。

她覺得他真的有點高興過頭了。「時間不長。我設法去彎腰並設定我手機上的鬧鈴，感謝上帝，因為那時他已經開始叫我『親愛的女士』。」

他鼻子哼了一聲之後就大笑起來，麗貝卡嚴厲地看著他。「這並不好笑。而且他也太吝嗇了。當我說我要走，他說他希望我先把

"Yuck."

"Exactly."

"How long did you put up with it for?" Kevin's eyes were dancing as he picked up his coffee.

He was enjoying this far too much, she thought. "Not long. I managed to bend down and set the alarm on my phone, thank God, because then he started calling me 'dear lady'."

He snorted with laughter and Rebecca looked at him severely. "It's not funny. He was tight, too. When I said I had to go, he wanted me to finish my coffee because he'd paid so much for it!"

Kevin's coffee stopped halfway to his mouth. "No!"

"Yes! And when I offered to pay for it, it was very much a token refusal, let me tell you. He pocketed the fiver quickly enough as I left."

"You sure know how to pick 'em." He shook his head.

"But I didn't pick him, did I! That the whole point."

"You did in a way. Scientifically he's an ideal match, remember. Perhaps it's something you said. Or rather, wrote." His eyes were full of mirth.

She glared at him. "Yes, and perhaps the dumb computer's dyslexic." She stabbed her last piece of chicken with unnecessary force.

He wiped at his eyes and tried, unsuccessfully in Rebecca's opinion, to look serious. "Poor you. Perhaps the next one will be better."

"Next one?" her eyes widened. "Don't even joke about it! You don't honestly think I'm going through that again?"

"To which I say, you're not honestly going to give up after one date? After you've paid good money for all this scientific matching stuff, too?"

"Huh! A fat lot of good that is, if it matches me up with a creep like that." She wiped her fingers on a serviette, folding it with her fingers.

"Come on, Bec, you have to give it another go."

咖啡喝完，因為是他付錢的！」

凱文的咖啡送到嘴裡前停了下來。「不會吧！」

「就是！而當我說我會把錢還他，他象徵式的回絕了，但我告訴你啊，我一離開了，他就很快把錢袋下來了。」

「你肯定懂得如何挑選他們。」他搖了搖頭。

「但我沒有選他，我沒有！這是重點。」

「這是你想要的方式。科學上，他是一個理想的配對，你要切記。也許這就是根據你說的東西，或者更確切地，應該是寫的東西。」他的眼睛充滿了快意。

她瞪了他一眼。「是的，也許啞的電腦有閱讀障礙。」她用不必要的武力在刺最後一塊雞肉。

他擦了擦眼睛並試圖用嚴肅神情看麗貝卡，但並不成功。「真可憐，也許下一個會更好。」

「下一個？」她瞪大了眼睛。「不要開玩笑了！你不是真心地想我去再經歷一遍吧？」

「要我說的話，你不想真心地再去多一次嗎？你已經花了很多錢，在這個科學化配對上，不是嗎？」

「咦！毫無用處，如果它只會配對這種小人給我。」她用餐巾紙擦了擦手指，然後用手指把它折疊起來。

「來吧，貝卡，你必須再去一次。」

「呃，不。我不會。」

「下一個可能就是你理想中的男人。如果現在就放棄，你永遠不會知道。」

她拿起另一張餐巾紙，無視他。凱文當然不覺得有什麼問題，他沒有跟約翰這個蛇人相處過。他真的給她不寒而慄的感覺，她總覺得不應該白費她的週末。生命太短暫了，而你不應該用空餘時間去做你一些不喜歡的事。正如當凱文試圖嘮叨她跟他去看恐怖電影的時候，她總是這樣跟他解釋。

另一方面，好吧，恐怖片總是嚇人的，但男人並不是每個都會像

"Er, no. I don't."

"The next one might be your ideal man. Give up now and you'll never know."

She put another fold in her serviette, ignoring him. It was alright for Kevin, he hadn't been stuck with John the snake man. He had genuinely given her the creeps, and being creeped out wasn't the way she fancied spending her weekends. Life was too short to spend your free time doing things you didn't enjoy, as she always tried to explain to Kevin when he tried to nag her into watching horror films with him.

On the other hand— well, horror films were always scary, but men weren't always snake like. Kevin wasn't, and Steve wasn't, either. She glanced towards the counter but couldn't see him. Perhaps he wasn't in today.

"I suppose you're right," she said, aware she sounded like a sulky child. "I can't presume they'll all be losers, can I. I'll give it another go."

"Hooray! Common sense prevails." Kevin grinned.

"Not with him, though. That was absolutely our first and last date."

"Absolutely. Let him go and try his 'dear lady' on some other sucker."

"I'm not sure I'd wish that on my worst enemy!"

"Not even a certain archaeologist currently digging up random bits of Italy?"

She put her head on one side. "Okay, you've got me there. If anyone deserves John the snake man, it's Marcie."

Kevin chuckled. "That's what we're calling him now, is it?"

She lifted her nose in the air. "I'd prefer that you didn't refer to him at all, thank you. Far too traumatic."

"Your wish is my command. Do you want another coffee?"

"Yes please. Mocha this time."

"Certainly dear lady."

蛇一樣。凱文不是，史堤夫也不是，兩個都不是。她朝櫃檯瞟了一眼，卻不見他。也許他今天不在。

「我想你是對的，」她說，她意識到她剛才就像一個生氣的小孩子。「我不能假定他們全部都會是失敗者，可以的話，我會再試一次。」

「萬歲！常理獲勝了。」凱文笑了。

「但不是他，無論如何。那個絕對是我們第一個和最後一個的約會。」

「當然。他去讓其他傻逼試當他的『親愛的女士』。」

「我不肯定，我希望這已經是最壞的一個！」

「連一個考古學家也不肯去發掘意大利嗎？」

她側了一下頭。「好吧，你令我想起了。如果任何人都應該得到約翰這個蛇人，那個一定是是瑪西。」

凱文笑了。「那我們現在就這樣叫他了，是嗎？」

她抬一抬起了鼻子。「我寧願你沒提到他，謝謝。那實在是一件很痛苦的事。」

「你的願望就等於是給我的命令。你要再來一杯咖啡嗎？」

「好啊。這次要摩卡咖啡。」

「當然，親愛的女士。」

她把餐巾紙飛機扔在他的頭上。

She threw a serviette aeroplane at his head.

不需要此页

Chapter Seven

It was still cold but the sun was dazzling in a clear sky. I should have worn my sunglasses, thought Steve, squinting as he walked along the road to work. He wasn't complaining, though. The sunshine lifted his spirits and when the breeze dropped, he could even feel a little warmth on his face.

But when he pushed open the door of Tony's his spirits sank. Not only because Rebecca wasn't alone, but because Kevin was loading their empty salad bowls and cups on to a tray, meaning they must be about to leave. They looked round and he forced a casual, friendly smile.

"Was it something I said?"

Kevin grinned. "Not unless you're a ventriloquist." God damn him, did he have to be so friendly? And funny? Not to mention good-looking. It was unfair competition. He was allowed to have two attributes out of the three; having all of them was, as Steve's Dad would have said, just not cricket.

"Good one. You two are early."

"Yep. We were hungry."

"Excuse me! I wasn't, but she forced me to come with her, so she could warn me of the perils of internet dating." Kevin rolled his eyes and walked off towards the counter with their tray.

"Perils? Like meeting weirdoes who take you home and show you their collection of false eyes?" asked Steve, smiling.

"No, as in being matched with people you wouldn't even talk to if they were the last person on earth, let alone date," said Rebecca.

"Yes, I suppose that's a risk," said Steve cautiously, wondering why they'd been talking about internet dating. "I suppose it depends how good the agency is and how many people are on their books. If it's only ten, the chances of them finding you your ideal partner are slim, aren't they. They probably just offer the three that aren't completely incompatible."

第七章

天氣仍然冷，但陽光在清澈明朗的天空中顯得很耀眼。我應該戴上太陽鏡，史堤夫在想，他瞇著眼沿著路走去上班。然而他沒有抱怨。陽光提起了他的精神，而當有微風吹過時，他甚至可以感覺到一點點的溫暖在他的臉上。

但是，當他推開東尼的咖啡店的大門時，他的精神完全沉沒了。不僅是因為麗貝卡並不是一個人來，而是因為凱文正把空的沙拉碗和杯放到托盤上，這意味著他們很快就要離開。他們看過來，他擠出一個漫不經心而友好的微笑。

「我說了些什麼嗎？」

凱文笑了。「沒有，除非你會說腹語。」該死的他，他有必要那麼友好嗎？很有趣嗎？更不用說他有好看的外表。這是不公平的競爭，他有三個之中兩種的特質。史堤夫的爸爸會說，如果有齊所有這些特質，剩下的就只有不公平。

「很好。你們兩個來得好早。」

「沒錯。我們都餓了。」

「對不起！我並沒有，但她強迫我跟她一起來，讓她可以警告我網絡約會的危險。」凱文翻了翻眼睛，拿著他們的托盤朝櫃檯走去。

「危險？就像遇到那些很古怪的人，會帶你回家，然後展示自己收集的假眼球一樣嗎？」史堤夫臉帶微笑地問。

麗貝卡說：「不，只是一個跟你配對的人，他可能是地球上最後一個，你也不會想跟他說話，更不用說約會。」

「是的，我想那一定會有風險的。」史堤夫謹慎地說，不知道為什麼他們會一直在談論網絡約會。「我想這是取決於該機構是不是夠好，是不是很多人在他們的名冊內。如果那裡只有十個人，要找到你理想的伴侶的機會就很渺茫，不是嗎？他們可能只會提供三個不是完全不匹配的選擇。」

"I hadn't thought of it like that before."

"Me neither, until now," said Steve with a half-hearted laugh. This was too much like thinking aloud. How many people did Methodical Matches have on its virtual 'books'? He hadn't given it that much thought. "But I don't know anyone who's tried it. Who's fallen foul of internet dating then?"

"Oh, just a friend," said Rebecca casually, blushing. "But it was only her first date. Perhaps she'll have better luck next time."

"Let's hope so." Steve looked at her curiously. "Right, I'd best get to the kitchen and get my gear on, my shift starts in a couple of minutes."

"See you tomorrow," she said, as Kevin reappeared at her elbow.

He smiled. "That depends if you're going to make a habit of these ultra-early lunches! Bye."

He put his jacket and apron on, thinking about what Rebecca had said. Should he check how many people were signed up to the dating agency? Perhaps he should have chosen a better-known, more established one. Say he got a succession of dates with women whom he wouldn't normally give the time of day? Or who were fine in public, but turned out to have freaky habits and hobbies when you went back to their place?

The door swung open and Tony stuck his head into the kitchen. "Steve, some on," he said, his chiding tone belied by a smile. "Let's get moving! Is filling up out here and talking of filling, the coffee machine is needing refill. Bring out pouch of beans with you, please."

"Yes, boss! Sorry." Steve knotted his apron and went to the store, but he was still on autopilot as he dragged out the big silver pouch of Colombian beans. What about bringing girlfriends home? How could he ever do that whilst he lived with Laura? He never knew when she would be at home—or what state she would be in if she was there. The more he thought about it, the more impossible it seemed.

He backed through the kitchen door and into the café, hefting the coffee beans. "That's the end of that batch," he told Tony as he refilled the coffee machine. And the end of my daft idea, he thought. Even if met the girl of his dreams through the agency, there was no way he could start a relationship with her at the moment. He must have been nuts to fill out that profile in the first place. Thank God he hadn't pasted his answers into the website

「我之前從來沒有想過這些。」

「我也沒有，直到現在。」史堤夫說，心不在焉地笑。這太像在自言自語了，井然配對究竟有多少人在他們虛擬的『名冊』內？他沒有太多的想法。「但我不認識有人試過，那麼是誰被網絡約會惹惱了呢？」

「哦，只是朋友，」麗貝卡隨口說，臉漲紅了。「但這是她第一次約會，也許她下一次運氣會好一點。」

「但願如此。」史堤夫好奇地看著她。「好吧，我還是最好先去廚房準備一下，我的當值時間在一兩分鐘後就要開始。」

「明天見。」她說，凱文再次出現在她身旁。

他笑了。「那就要看，你是否打算養成這麼早吃午餐的習慣了！再見。」

他穿上外套和圍裙，想著麗貝卡說了什麼。他應該要檢查一下有多少人參加了那家約會機構嗎？或許他應該選擇一家更有知名度、地位更鞏固的。若然他有一系列的約會，是與一些女人他平常根本就不注意到的呢？或在公共場所時看似很好，但回到她們的地方就發現她們有古怪的習慣或愛好呢？

門開了，東尼頭探進了廚房來。「來吧，史堤夫。」他說，他的笑容掩飾了責罵的語氣。「動起來！到這兒補一下位，說起了補，咖啡機需要補充一下。請拿一袋咖啡出來。」

「是的，老闆！對不起。」史堤夫綁好他的圍裙，走到倉庫，但當他拖出銀色袋的哥倫比亞咖啡豆時，他的自動駕駛模式仍在運行。把女朋友帶回家會怎樣呢？他跟羅拉住在一起，他怎麼可能做到？他從來都不知道她是否在家…或者如果她在家的時候，她處於什麼狀態。當他想得更多，就似乎更不可能。

他走過廚房的門，抬著咖啡豆走進咖啡廳。「這是這批的最後了。」他告訴東尼，他斟滿咖啡機。我愚蠢的想法也是最後了，他在想。即使透過該公司，遇到了他夢想的女孩，在此刻他還是沒有辦法開始去建立跟她的關係。他早就在外面填好那些個人資料。感謝上帝，他還沒有把他的答案貼到網站上和發出去，他們仍然在電腦中的一個文件夾上。下一次，他打開電腦時就把它刪掉。

and sent them off; they were still in a document on the computer. Next time he went on the PC he'd delete it.

Ron stuck his head round the door. "Rebecca, can I have a word?"

She smiled, "Sure. Don't tell me, you're about to haul me over the coals for not having the osteology report on 78C ready."

"No," he replied with a small smile, "I'd forgotten I said today for that. But now you mention it..."

She groaned. "Me and my big mouth."

"It's about the Crossrail project, so not totally unrelated. Could you come by my office in the next half hour? I've got some documents to show you."

"Let me grab a drink and I'll be there."

"Great. Mine's a black coffee. Thanks!" He walked away with a smile. Rebecca grinned. She would get him his coffee, because he was a great boss and was just as likely to get a coffee for her if she asked.

A few minutes later she was sitting opposite him, waiting for him to cut the small talk and get to the point. When he hesitated, she leaped in.

"So what do we need to talk about, Ron?"

"Ah. Yes. I was getting to that." He hesitated. "You know the plan is for you to go back on to the Crossrail project."

"Yes. I've been looking forward to it." Rebecca had been leading the team working with Crossrail's archaeologists for a while. The excavations for new tunnels, ticket halls and elevator shafts at various sites across London were giving them a fantastic opportunity to survey and dig areas and levels they'd never have had access to otherwise. She grinned. "You know I don't fare well stuck indoors for too long. I like to be out there."

"Yes." He picked up a pen and started to tap it on his desk. "But I think you might want to sit this one out."

Rebecca leaned forward. "What? Why? They've just started to uncover skeletons on the Farringdon site—why would I want out

羅恩從門外探出頭來。「麗貝卡，可以借一步說話嗎？」

她笑了，「當然可以。但不要告訴我，你要責備我還沒有把78C的骨科報告準備好。」

「不，」他微笑著回答說，「我都忘了今天我說過。但現在你提起…」

她呻吟著，「我和我的大嘴巴。」

「這是關於東西橫貫鐵路的項目，所以是完全無關的。你半小時後可以來我的辦公室一下好嗎？我有一些文件要給你看。」

「讓我先去買喝的，然後就過去。」

「太好了，那我要一杯黑咖啡。謝謝！」他笑著走開了。麗貝卡咧嘴笑了。她會給他買咖啡的，因為他是一個很好的老闆，他只會要求她買杯咖啡，而且是她問到的時候。

幾分鐘後，她坐在他對面，等著他閑聊完再開始真正的話題。當他停頓了一下，她立刻坐直了身子。

「那麼我們需要談些什麼，羅恩？」

「嗯，是的。我得到聊一下這點。」他猶豫了一下。「你知道，計劃是讓你去負責那個東西橫貫鐵路的項目。」

「是的。我一直期待著它。」麗貝卡已經帶領團隊與東西橫貫鐵路的考古學家工作了一段時間。在可以貫穿倫敦各地的場地，發掘新隧道、售票廳和升降機井，令他們有絕佳的機會調查和發掘這種他們從來沒有獲得過的領域和層次。她咧嘴一笑。「你知道我的狀況不太合適停留在室內太久，我比較喜歡到那裡去。」

「是。」他拿起了筆，開始輕敲他的辦公桌。「但我認為你可能不會想參與了。」

麗貝卡俯身向前。「什麼？為什麼呢？他們剛剛在法靈頓的場地發現骸髏，為什麼我會想退出呢？」

「正如你所知，格林威治至斯特拉特福那一段由其他小隊發掘。」

「是在我們和東西橫貫鐵路的監督下。」

of that??"

"As you know, the Greenwich to Stratford section is being excavated by other teams."

"Under our oversight and Crossrail's."

"Yes... and you know that Swindon Archaeology's are our main partners." Ron was starting to look a bit pale.

"And Royal Surrey, yes..." She frowned. "Ron, what's going on? We've worked with all of them before—I worked with Swindon on my first dig in my teens, on the Jubilee Line Extension project. What's the big deal?"

"Stan Laurence is leaving," Ron broke in flatly.

"I know."

"They've just announced who's taking over."

"Who?"

The words were being wrung out of him. "Marcie King."

She felt her stomach plummet. "But she can't—I thought – isn't Marcie still in Italy on secondment?"

"No. She's back, the Italian team decided to end the exchange early."

"Why?"

"I'm not sure, but Stefano's gone back. Marcie takes over next week."

Her fingers gripped the arms of the chair and left sweaty indentations as she pushed them back and forth along the leather. "Shit."

"Shit indeed."

Silence fell. Then Ron muttered, "I can ask Kevin to oversee her team—"

"She'd eat Kevin for lunch and you know it."

He spread his hands. "Just making the offer. What do you suggest? Business as usual?"

「是的...你也知道史雲頓考古團隊是我們的主要合作夥伴。」羅恩的臉看起來開始有點發白。

「還有皇家素裡,是的...」她皺起了眉頭。「羅恩,究竟是什麼回事呢?我們之前也有與他們合作過,在我十幾歲第一次做發掘的時候,就已經是跟史雲頓合作,是銀禧支線項目。有什麼大不了的?」

「史丹·勞倫斯離開了。」羅恩平淡地說道。

「我知道。」

「他們剛剛宣布了誰來接管。」

「誰?」

他將那名字慢慢地吐出來,「瑪西.京」。

她感到肚子驟然墜落。「但她不能...我想...瑪西不是依然被調派到意大利嗎?」

「沒有。她回來了,意大利團隊決定提前結束交流。」

「為什麼?」

「我不知道,但斯蒂法諾已回去了。瑪西下週會回來接管。」

她抓住椅子扶手的手指留下了汗痕,不停在皮革上來回推著。「可惡。」

「真是可惡。」

沉默片刻,羅恩嘀咕著,「我可以安排凱文去監督她的團隊...」

「她會把凱文當作午餐吃掉,你知道的。」

他攤開雙手。「我只想提出一個方案,那你有什麼建議嗎?要跟平常一樣嗎?」

「我不知道,但這是行不通的,羅恩。你知道這一點。」

「但工作一定要做的,否則我將不得不把你拉出來。讓你在實驗室裡寫完所有的報告,或轉去做另一個項目。」

「除非我死了。」

"I don't know, but this isn't going to work, Ron. You know that."

"It has to work, otherwise I'll have to pull you out. Keep you here in the lab, doing all the write ups. Or move you to another project."

"Over my dead body."

"Or hers?" He gave her a grim smile. "I'm not sure which I'm most concerned about." He looked at her intently and she met the look for a while before launching herself back in the chair and throwing her hands up in resignation.

"Okay. I'll work with the woman. I don't have much choice, do I? But I want minimal contact with her."

"I'll do my best, you know that. But you'll have to meet face to face sometimes."

"And when we do, I'll make sure I meet with Mike from the Surrey team too, and I'll probably take Kevin."

Ron shook his head. "Rebecca—"

"I'm serious, Ron. I won't be in a room by myself with her. She's poison."

"Fair enough." He sighed. "That's all I had to say, really."

She got to her feet abruptly, striding to the door without a word.

"I am sorry, Rebecca. If it was up to me..."

She gave the briefest of nods in acknowledgement, shutting the door behind her. She needed to find Kevin.

He was bent over a long document spewing out of the fax machine, but looked up as she opened the door. "Great timing Becs, we've got the dendro results back from the timbers in 425, and they're really interesting because—"

He stopped because she'd leaned over, identified the end of the document and ripped across the perforations in one aggressive sweeping motion. "Leave it," she said, slapping the paper down on the bench. "I'll look later."

"Why, what are we doing?"

"Early lunch." She swept out the door towards her office.

「還是她？」他給了她一個猙獰的笑容。「我不太肯定，我最關心的是什麼。」他目不轉睛地看著她，當她坐回自己在椅子上，她跟他對上視線一陣子，並舉起雙手投降了。

「好吧。我會跟那個女人一起工作。我沒有太多的選擇，是吧？不過，我想跟她少點接觸。」

「我會盡我所能，你知道的，但你們有時候是必須碰面。」

「當有需要時，我確保我會跟素裡隊的麥克一起會面，而且可能也會帶上凱文。」

羅恩搖了搖頭。「麗貝卡…」

「我是認真的，羅恩。我不能跟她獨自留在一個房間裡，她是毒藥。」

「很公平。」他嘆了口氣。「實際上，以上就是我要說的話了。」

突然，她站起身來，一言不發，大步走到門口。

「我很抱歉，麗貝卡。如果可以由我決定…」

她簡短地點點頭以示了解，就關上了身後的門。她需要去找凱文。

他俯身拿起從傳真機湧出來的一串文件，他正看著文件時她就打開了門。「來得真合時啊，貝卡，我們已經得拿到了425木材的聚類分析結果了，它們真的很有趣，因為…」

他停了下來，因為她俯身確認報告的結尾位置，然後俐落地沿著紙孔撕了下來。「先放一邊，」她說，啪地一聲把報告丟在板凳上。「我待會就看。」

「為什麼？那我們要做什麼？」

「早點去吃午餐。」她掃視了一下她辦公室的門口。

「又來？又有災難性的約會要仔細地分析嗎？我才剛小休完…」

她已經踏出了走廊上，他趕上了她，把外套搭在肩膀上，「…但我想我也可以喝杯榛子拿鐵咖啡。」

「我們不會去東尼那邊。」她嚴厲地說。

"Again? Not another disastrous date dissection? I've only just had my coffee break..."

She was already marching away down the corridor but he caught up with her, jacket over his shoulder, "... but I suppose I could manage a hazelnut latte."

"We're not going to Tony's," she said tightly.

"Oh? Where we off to, then?"

"The pub." She stopped to grab her own jacket from the back of her office door and slammed the door behind her.

Kevin winced. "Had a bad morning?"

"No, just a bad ten minutes."

"Can I ask why?"

He opened the foyer door for her and out on the pavement she stopped a moment, taking a lungful of air and forcing her shoulders to relax.

"Don't worry. I'm going to tell you all about who's heading up the Greenwich to Stratford dig. And then you'll want to go to the pub too."

She'd delivered the news over the big, saturated fat laden burgers that they allowed themselves occasionally, and now Kevin was staring morosely into his lager. "Jeez. That will be a barrel of laughs."

"Yep. I can't wait," she said curtly. "But there's not much I can do about it. Except to avoid her as much as possible."

"I take it she—"

"Still hates me? I can't see that changing, can you? It was bliss while she was away, not worrying about when I'd bump into her next. I was hoping she'd love Italy and never come back." She swirled the Merlot in her glass and took a long drink.

"No such luck. I guess it lost its appeal."

"She's back early but Ron doesn't know why." She sighed heavily. "I feel like the woman's an albatross around my neck. If

「哦？那麼我們去哪呢？」

「酒吧。」她停下來，在她辦公室的門後面抓起了外套，在身後關上了門。

凱文畏縮了一下。「這個早上有這麼糟糕嗎？」

「沒有，只是非常糟糕的十分鐘。」

「我可以問為什麼嗎？」

他為她打開了前廳的門，在人行道上她停了片刻，深呼吸了一下，迫使自己的肩膀放鬆下來。

「別擔心，我會告訴你所有關格林威治至斯特拉特福發掘項目的所有事，然後你也會想去酒吧了。」

她一面說一面吃了一個巨大、充滿飽和脂肪的漢堡，他們偶爾會允許自己吃一次，凱文正愁眉苦臉地盯著他的啤酒。「哎呀。這真的是非常有趣。」

「沒錯。我已經急不及待了。」她簡短地說。「但我沒有太多可以做的事，只能盡可能避開她。」

「我想她是…」

「還恨我嗎？我不覺得會有改變，是嗎？很幸運她走了，不用擔心有一次我要遇到她。我希望她會喜歡意大利，永不回來。」她旋動著杯子裡的墨爾樂紅酒，喝了一大口。

「沒那麼走運。我猜那裡失去吸引力了。」

「她提早回來了，但羅恩不知道為什麼。」她重重地嘆了口氣。「我覺得那個女人的大包袱就在我的脖子上。如果她真的回來了，也許我需要到別的地方找過一份工作。」

他坐直了身子。「告訴我，你是在開玩笑。」

「相信我，我現在沒有開玩笑的心情。」

「來吧，貝卡，你想得太遠了。如果她在GLAM找到了一份工作，我可以理解，但…」

「如果她在GLAM找到了一份工作，凱文，你將會一個老闆都沒有。」她又喝了一大口紅酒，看到凱文畏縮了一下。「應該是沒

she's back for good, maybe I need to find a job somewhere else."

He sat up straight. "Tell me you're joking."

"Believe me, I'm not in a joking mood."

"Come on, Becs, that's going a bit far. If she got a job at GLAM I could understand it, but—"

"If she got a job at GLAM, Kev, you'd be without a boss." She took another big gulp of red wine and saw Kevin wince. "Probably without two bosses. I'd either kill her, or kill Ron if I saw him first, for taking her on. Whichever, I'd go to prison."

"I'm sure with our forensic experience we could commit the perfect crime." He smiled tentatively. "They'd never catch you."

Rebecca didn't smile. "Kevin, be practical," she said quietly. "More and more of these projects are being shared between different teams now. Eventually we'll finish the Crossrail project, but what then? A few months down the line there will be another project where we're asked to collaborate with another team—and you know how often that's Swindon. "Oh God," she smacked a hand down on the table, "even worse, what if there's a project in future where they oversight?"

"In fairness, I doubt if she's thrilled at the prospect of you bossing her about either."

She glared at him. "Yes, but I haven't got some misbegotten, mentally messed-up grudge against her, have I?"

"You don't like her much."

"No, I don't," Rebecca ground out, "but with good reason. It's hard to form a good working relationship with someone who's accused your father of being responsible for her father's death."

He nodded. "I know how difficult it is."

"Sorry but you don't. Kev, Marcie and I used to play together all the time. My parents weren't only David King's colleagues; they were his best friends, and his wife's. I saw Marcie's Mum all the time too, because she was always there, doing all the secretarial stuff, getting the day-to-day things sorted. We were like one big, happy family. Mum, Dad and David were like the Three Musketeers. They did everything together, and it was their joint projects that made their names internationally known."

有兩個老闆。我要麼就殺了她，如果我先看到他，我就先殺了羅恩，再跟她較量。無論如何，我都會坐牢去。」

「我敢肯定，以我們的法醫經驗，我們可以來個完美犯罪。」他很勉強地笑了笑。「他們不會捉到你的。」

麗貝卡沒有笑。「凱文，實際一點，」平靜地說。「越來越多這種項要跟不同的團隊合作。我們最終會完成東西橫貫鐵路項目，然後呢？幾個月下來就會有另一個項目，我們會要求與另一支團隊合作，你知道很多時候都是史雲頓。噢，我的天呀！」她使勁地拍了一下桌子，「更糟糕的是，如果將來有一個項目是由他們來監督呢？」

「平心而論，我懷疑她是否恐懼，一想到你會對她呼來喝去。」

她瞪了他一眼。「是的，但我沒有這麼可鄙、精神失常地對她懷恨在心，我會嗎？」

「但你不喜歡她了。」

「不，我沒有，」麗貝卡苦心地說，「但有一個很好的理由。這樣很難可以有一個良好的工作關係，跟一個指責你父親要為她父親的死負責的人。」

他點點頭。「我知道有多困難。」

「很抱歉，但你不知道。凱文，瑪西和我一直都是一起玩的。我父母不僅是大衛．京的同事，他們也是他最好的朋友，還有他的妻子。瑪西的媽媽，我也是常常見到，因為她總是在那裡做秘書的事務，每天在整理東西。我們就像一個又大又幸福的家庭。爸、媽、大衛就像三劍客。他們做所有事都一起行動，他們合作的項目令他們的名字變得國際知名。」

「我知道。我有一個考古學學位，貝卡，記得嗎？我說，那時候在教科書中讀有關你父母的事是多麼奇怪。我也知道對你來說是很困難。」

「那天你見到我的時候，我再一次克制住自己。我是花了那麼久，凱文，是六年。那一天我失去了一切，不僅是我的父母，還有我最好的朋友和我第二個媽媽。」

「我很遺憾。」

她聳了聳肩，她的眼睛閃著淚光。「這應該是無法改變的事了，

"I know. I did do an archaeology degree, Bec, remember? I said at the time how strange it was to read about your parents in a textbook. And I know that makes it hard for you too."

"By the time you met me, I'd got a grip on myself again. But it took me that long, Kevin. Six years. I lost everything that day. Not just my parents, but my best friend too. And my second mum."

"I'm sorry."

She shrugged, her eyes glistening. "It should be water under the bridge now, but Marcie won't let it lie. That's why it might be easier to go somewhere else. Start again up north somewhere, perhaps. Or right down in the South West. Anywhere too far for the Swindon team to be involved."

"I'd miss you."

With difficulty, she found a small smile. "I'd miss you too. But you could visit. Or come with me! Leave all this behind." She waved her hand around rather unsteadily. "Make a new life in the country, with me."

"Ooh, would we make our own cheese and keep chickens?" he mocked gently.

"Definitely. Fancy it?"

He shook his head with a quickness and finality that shook her. "Not me, I'm afraid. I'm an urbanite through and through."

It was stupid but that hurt. "I see," she said, trying to keep her tone light, "you care more about the bright lights than your friend, huh?"

Kevin looked at her, his face serious. "No, I care about you far more. But you don't need me, Rebecca. You're a very independent woman, and would make new friends wherever you go, because that's what you do."

"Not close ones like you, though." She tried to laugh but it stuck in her throat and threatened to become a sob. "You're my best bud," she said huskily.

He took her hand. "Like you say, I could visit. And so could you, whenever you got fed up with your chickens and yearned for civilisation. Providing you're not moving to the Outer Hebrides or anything."

但瑪西不肯讓它過去。這就是為什麼我去別的地方可能會更簡單。也許啟程去北部某處，或下去到西南部，總之是任何遠離史雲頓有份參與的地方。」

「我會想念你的。」

雖然有點困難，但她還是擠出了個小笑容。「我也會想你。但你可以去探望我，或者跟我一起去！離開這裡。」她搖搖晃晃地揮動著手，「去一個新的國家建立新生活，跟我一起去吧。」

「哦，那我們會做自己的奶酪和養雞嗎？」他溫和地嘲弄道。

「當然。想嗎？」

他快速而斷然地搖頭嚇到了她。「我不行，我很害怕。我是一個徹徹底底的都市人。」

這是很傻，但很傷人。「我明白了，」她試圖放輕語調地說，「比你的朋友，你更關心明亮的燈光，嘿？」

凱文一臉嚴肅地看著她，「不，我關心你多得多了。但你並不需要我，麗貝卡。你是一個很獨立的女人，無論你走到哪裡，都可以交到新朋友，因為那就是你。」

「不過不可能像你一樣親密。」她想笑，但卡在她的喉嚨，更可能會變成了嗚咽。「你是我最好的老友。」她沙啞地說。

他握住她的手。「像你所說，我可以去探望你。所以你能不能，如果你有一點厭倦你的雞或開始想念文明，就不要去到外赫布里底群島或其他地方了。」

「那裡比我腦子裡想的有更多農村。」

「很好。」他把他一隻手搭在在她的手上。「對不起，但我喜歡城市生活，貝卡。我喜歡倫敦，其他城市也很適合去渡過一個美好的週末，但我所有的朋友都在這裡，不像你，我不能那麼容易可以認識新朋友。我很喜歡我的工作，也沒有要提升職級的野心，雖然我不排除有一天會做到你現在的位置，我認為更可能的是我會一直在GLAM，直到我可以爬出這個沒有自動樓梯的溝渠。」他咧嘴笑了。「即使如此，我可能會不斷地嘮叨負責人，好讓我調派到平面設計部門，那我就可以整天都坐著了。」

「但你的技能會過時的，」她笑了。「每個人都會像湯姆．克魯斯在未來報告裡，用魔術手套在大屏幕上移動上面的所有信息。

"That's a bit more rural than what I had in mind."

"Good." He put his other hand over hers. "Sorry but I love the city life, Bec. I love London. Other cities are great for a weekend, but all my friends are here, and unlike you I don't make them that easily. I'm happy in my job, have got no ambitions to rise up the ranks—although I'm not ruling out being where you are now, one day—and I think it's more than likely I'll be at GLAM until I can't climb out of a trench without a stair lift." He grinned. "And even then I might nag whoever's in charge to let me move to the graphic design department, so I can sit down all day."

"Your skills will be out of date by then," she smiled. "Everyone will be like Tom Cruise in Minority Report, moving all the info around on a big screen with a magic glove."

"Oh I'm not daft. I keep in with all those bright young things down there, just so I can stay on top of it all."

There was a pause.

"So that's your master plan, is it? I didn't know you had one."

"And I didn't know Marcie bothered you so much that you'd rather move miles away than risk working with her sometimes."

They sat where they were for a while, Kevin still holding her hand.

"Well that's that then."

"Yes," said Kevin quietly. "All done with your lunch?" He released her hand.

"Yes thanks." She was fighting to keep her tears at bay as they left, and she was winning the battle until Kevin slipped his arm through hers as they walked back to work. "Wherever you go, whatever you decide to do, I'll always be here if you need me, Becs. You know that, right?"

Her throat was too tight to answer. She nodded and laid her head on his shoulder a moment, a single tear escaping down her cheek. That was the trouble, she thought, as she wiped her cheek. She wasn't sure there was enough to hold her here anymore. Kevin would always be here. But she didn't think she would.

」

「哦，我不愚蠢的。我一直有跟進那些明亮而年輕的東西，好讓我可以與時並進。」

沈默了片刻。

「所以這就是你的博士學位計劃，是嗎？我都不知道你有這樣的計劃。」

「而我也不知道瑪西對你來說有這麼困擾，令你寧願走到英里遠而避開跟她合作的風險。」

他們在那裡坐了一會兒，凱文仍然握著她的手。

「嗯，就這樣了。」

「是的，」凱文悄悄地說。「吃完你的午餐了嗎？」他放開了她的手。

「是的，謝謝。」當他們離開時，她盡力把她的眼淚留在眼眶內，直到他們走回去工作時，凱文的手臂溜進了她的臂內。「無論你走到哪裡，無論你決定做什麼，我會一直在這裡，只要你需要我的時候，貝卡。你知道的，對吧？」

她的喉嚨緊得答不出來，她點點頭，把頭靠在他的肩膀了一陣子，一滴眼淚在她的臉頰流下。真是麻煩，她想。她擦了擦臉頰，她不肯定這裡還有沒有她的位置。凱文將一直在這裡，但她沒有想過她會。

Chapter Eight

She'd not been able to shake the cold sensation, floating somewhere between her stomach and her chest, all day. She'd thought that pouring her worries out to Kevin and burying herself in a mountain of work would dispel it, but no such luck. She was dreading working with Marcie; more than dreading it. It filled her with a bizarre sense of foreboding that was very un-Rebecca-ish.

She wasn't convinced coffee and a cake would help, either, but it was worth a try—and the phrase 'comfort food' had originated for a reason. Rebecca hadn't fancied sitting in Kevin's flat as he either minutely dissected the situation or tried to jolly her out of her dark mood, and she knew he would have done either or both if she'd accepted his offer of Chinese at his place. So she'd said no and walked wearily to Tony's instead.

She laid her head back against the wall behind her chair and stretched out her legs under the table. In a minute she'd go and get a coffee and pick something fattening, but right now it was good to just sit. It was weird, this sense of impending doom. If she was in a fantasy film right now, some old crone—or a bloke in a cloak and a funny hat—would be waggling their finger at her and cackling (or pompously declaring, in cloak bloke's case,) 'no good will come of this, mark my words! I have Seen the Signs!' before retreating into their cave or disappearing in a swirl of magical mist. Her instincts were telling her to run in the opposite direction, but she couldn't run from this any more than she could run from the unpleasant memories that another confrontation with Marcie would stir up. She closed her eyes for a moment. Deep breaths, Rebecca.

When she opened them, Steve was standing by her table.

"What the—! Oh, hi."

"Sorry, only me. Didn't mean to make you jump, it wasn't revenge or anything. I was already on my way over to you when you closed your eyes. Felt like a bit of a berk then. I wasn't sure whether to cough loudly, or what." He grinned.

She noticed his coat and rucksack. "Going home?"

第八章

她無法擺脫冰冷的感覺，整天在她的肚子和胸部流動著。她以為把她的憂慮告訴凱文和把自己埋在堆積如山的工作中就可以消除，但她始終沒有這麼好運氣。她很害怕跟瑪西一起工作，是超越了害怕。她有一種不祥的預感，這樣非常不像麗貝卡。

她不是很相信咖啡和蛋糕會對她有幫助，無論如何，還是值得一試。名詞「溫馨食品」的起源真的是有原因的。麗貝卡沒有想過要去凱文的家裡，或者他會仔細地分析情況，或試圖令她趕走壞心情，而她知道如果她接受了他的提議吃中餐的話，他會在家裡任意做一款，或者兩樣都做。所以，她拒絕了，並疲憊地走到東尼的咖啡店。

她把頭倚在她的椅子後面的牆上，在桌底下伸出她的腿。在一分鐘內，她會去叫杯咖啡和一些油膩的東西，但現在最還是先坐著。這瀕死的感覺有點不可思議。如果她現在是在一齣奇幻電影中，就會有一些老太婆或一個穿著斗篷和奇怪帽子的傢伙，擺動著他們的手指，指著她咯咯大笑（穿斗篷的傢伙或會傲慢地大聲說話明，）「不會有什麼好東西了，記住我的話！我見到了徵兆！」之後他們就會撤退回洞穴，或消失在奇幻的霧漩渦之中。她本能告訴她，要向相反方向逃走，但比起那裡，她更想逃出跟瑪西對峙這個不愉快的回憶。她閉上了眼睛一會兒，深呼吸，麗貝卡。

當她打開眼睛，史堤夫就站在她的桌子旁邊。

「什麼…！噢，嗨。」

「對不起，是我。我不是故意嚇到你，亦不是報復或其他的。當我正在走過來了的時候，你閉上了眼睛。然後感覺有點像個傻瓜，我不知道是否應該要大聲咳嗽或者是什麼。」他咧嘴而笑了。

她留意到他的外套和背包。「要回家了嗎？」

「是的，然後我發現你在這裡，如果你不介意我這樣說，看來就

"I was. Then I spotted you over here looking, if you don't mind me saying, like the world had fallen on your head."

"Or like my kitten had died?"

"Can't use that one, that's your metaphor." He grinned. "So I thought I'd come over and check if you were okay."

"Well this all seems strangely familiar."

"Yeah, just in reverse." He smiled. "So are you?"

"Am I what?"

"Okay?"

"Oh. Yes, thanks. Well, not really, no."

He put his head on one side. "And what I'm meant to deduce form that is...?"

She sighed. "I'm not okay."

"I see. Suspected as much. You looked gloomy, and we know that's a dead giveaway," said Steve lightly. "Do you want some company for a bit? I need to be home by seven, but—"

"No, you go home. Your company will be good, but I guarantee mine will be bloody awful."

"I'll be the judge of that." He dumped his rucksack on the floor and pulled up a chair. "So what's it going to be? Do you want to 1, tell me what's wrong—in as little or as much detail as you want, 2, listen to a succession of hilarious one liners, or 3, just sit in companionable silence? With perhaps a blueberry muffin for company?" He put on the kind of overly-bright voice heard in adverts. "The blueberry muffin is available with all options!"

The icy feeling was still there, but she grinned. "Well as tempting as option 2 sounds..."

"Knew it would, knew it would. Everyone's favourite."

"Perhaps we could start with the blueberry muffin and work our way backwards."

"Okay." Steve leapt to his feet. "Large or small? With cream or without? Sharing it or pigging it all yourself?"

像整個世界掉在你的頭上。」

「或者像我的小貓死了嗎？」

「不能使用那一個，那是你用的比喻。」他咧嘴笑著。「所以我想我要過來檢查一下，你是否還好。」

「嗯，這一切似乎都似曾相識。」

「是啊，只是相反了。」他笑了。「那麼，你如何？」

「我什麼？」

「還好嗎？」

「哦。還好，謝謝。嗯，不是真的，不。」

他側一側頭。「那麼我應該推斷你的意思是…？」

她嘆了口氣。「我不好吧。」

「我明白了，跟我猜想的一樣。你看上去很憂愁，而且我們都知道這已經洩漏了馬腳，」史堤夫輕輕地說：「你想我陪伴你一會嗎？我需要七點回家，但…」

「不行，你回家吧。如果有你陪伴會很好，但我保證我的事是非常血腥恐怖。」

「我會判斷的。」他把背包甩在地板上，拉一把椅子過來，「那麼你想做什麼？一、告訴我是什麼問題，只說你想說的細節，無論多或少。二、聽一系列極有趣的笑話。三、只是靜靜的坐著？或者還可以要個藍莓鬆餅作伴？」他用那種在廣告中才會聽到的那種非常明亮的聲音說道，「藍莓鬆餅是最好的選擇！」

冰冷的感覺依舊存在，但她咧嘴笑了。「選項二聽起來很吸引…」

「它是的，它是的。大家的最愛。」

「也許我們可以先由藍莓鬆餅開始，然後再繼續。」

「好吧。」史堤夫的腳迅捷地動起來。「大還是小？要不要加奶油？一起吃一個或是你自己吃一個？」

「大的，自己吃。但如果你打算坐在那裡又不吃東西，我會被內

"Large, with, and pigging it all myself, please. Although if you're going to sit there and not eat, I'll be racked with guilt. Then I'll feel worse than I do now, and it'll be your fault."

"Suppose I'd better get myself one too then."

Ten minutes later, Rebecca sat back with a satisfied sigh, wiping her fingers and mouth on a serviette. "Well I have to confess, it's hard to keep the gloomy expression going when your stomach's full of delicious, moist blueberry muffin and cream."

"And butterscotch latte," Steve reminded her, raising his coffee cup.

"And butterscotch latte," she agreed, leaning forward to chink her cup against his.

"So," he said, settling back in his chair, "now we've got rid of the glooms, do you want to tell me what caused them in the first place?"

She hesitated. "It's about work. Well, kind of."

"Right. I don't know much about archaeology, but I could try and make some suggestions." He raised an eyebrow comically. "How about 'use a bigger spade?'"

She smiled. "Thanks, I'll bear that in mind. Actually, it is about work, and it isn't."

"Glad we've got that clear."

She looked at him sternly. "Shh! Do you want me to tell you, or not?"

"Sorry."

"And it will sound minor at first, but you'll see it's quite major, really."

"Understood. Often the way with stuff that makes us miserable, I find." He smiled. "Go on."

"To summarise the boring stuff: the team I lead will be working again with the Swindon team on another site for the Crossrail project."

"I read about that in the paper. What's the problem? Have they all got terrible B.O? Not good."

疾折磨的。然後，會感覺比現在更糟糕，而且會是你的錯。」

「那我自己也要一個比較好。」

十分鐘後，麗貝卡坐著並滿意地鬆了口氣，用餐巾紙擦拭她的手指和嘴巴。「好吧，我不得不承認，這個時候很難繼續維持陰鬱的表情，當你的肚子充滿了美味、濕潤的藍莓鬆餅和奶油。」

「奶油糖果拿鐵。」史堤夫提醒她，舉起咖啡杯。

「奶油糖果拿鐵。」她同意說，身體傾前去跟他碰了一下杯子。

「那麼，」他說，並坐穩在他的椅子上，「現在我們已經擺脫了鬱悶，你要告訴我當初是什麼原因令你那樣嗎？」

她猶豫了一下。「這是有關工作。好吧，差不多是那一類。」

「對。我不是認識很多關於考古，但我可以嘗試並提出一些建議。」他滑稽地揚起一邊眉毛。「關於『如何使用一個更大的鐵鍬』？」

她笑了。「謝謝，我會記住這一點。實際上，它是關於工作，但又並非如此。」

「很高興我們已經很清楚。」

她嚴肅地看著他。「噓！你想讓我告訴你，還是不？」

「對不起。」

「一開始聽起來會是一些小事，但之後你會看到這是相當嚴重，真的。」

「明白。通常情況下，這種東西才讓我們苦不堪言，我認為。」他笑了。「繼續吧。」

「先概括了無關痛癢的事情：我帶領的團隊將再次跟史雲頓團隊合作在東西橫貫鐵路項目的另一個場地工作。」

「我讀了有關的文件。有什麼問題嗎？他們都有可怕的體臭嗎？那就不好了。」

「不是，雖然你是正確的，但這只是小事。他們的團隊現在正在由一個叫瑪西．京的人帶領。」

"No, although you're right, that would be gross. Their team's now being led by a Marcie King."

"And she's the problem?"

"Yes. She hates me."

"Professional jealousy?"

"Hardly, she's done at least as well as me. I suspect more people have heard of her, anyway."

"Why does she hate you, then? What's her beef?"

"Her beef, as you put it, although I never had you down for a cockney, Call Me Steve"—she grinned and he rolled his eyes— "Is that she thinks my father killed her father."

Steve stopped mid-gulp and put his cup down, giving a low whistle. "Okay, of all the things I expected you to say, that's not one of them. A more major beef than I was expecting."

"Sorry. I did warn you."

He nodded slowly. "I take it we're not talking about a cold-blooded, pre-meditated act of murder here?"

"No. Causing death by negligence, I suppose you'd call it." She sighed. "Although I suppose to her, the outcome's the same. Her father was in a car with my parents. They worked together, they were all archaeologists. Quite well-known ones. They were working on a site in Thailand with another archaeologist, Francois Villeneuve. He was a very close friend of my parents, he's kind of an honorary uncle to me, or a big brother, though I don't see him often. He lives in Paris."

"Anyway, they'd had a hugely successful day, digging up some really significant finds. Francois went straight back to the hotel where they were staying, but my parents and Marcie's father drove to a bar first to celebrate. On the way back to the hotel, there was a terrible rainstorm. The mountain road they were on was partially washed away. Their car came off the road and rolled down the mountainside. The roads were horrendous out there then—well, a lot of them still are—in the rural areas, many of them are more or less mud tracks to start with."

"I see. Were they all killed in the crash?" he asked gently.

She nodded. "If the roads were as bad as you say, how can

「她有問題嗎？」

「是的。她恨我。」

「專業上的嫉妒？」

「很難啊，她做得至少跟我一樣好。無論如何，我猜想會有越來越多的人都認識她。」

「那為什麼她討厭你呢？她怨恨的是什麼？」

「她怨恨的，正如你所說的那樣，雖然我從沒有把你看成一個倫敦佬，『請叫我史堤夫』，」她咧嘴笑了，他翻了個白眼，「是的，她認為我父親殺害了她父親。」

史堤夫正在喝咖啡的手停了下來，並把杯子放下，吹了一聲口哨。「好了，我希望你能說出的所有事情，但這不是其中之一。比我所期待的更加怨恨。」

「對不起。我已經提醒過你。」

他慢慢地點了點頭。「我在想我們是不是正談論一個冷血、有預謀的謀殺案呢？」

「不是，是疏忽而導致死亡，我希望你會這樣說，」她嘆了口氣。「雖然我也希望她是這樣想，但結果還是相同。她父親與我父母在車上。他們一起工作，他們全部都是考古學家，也頗為知名的。他們跟另一位考古學家弗朗索瓦．維倫紐夫在泰國的場地工作。他是我父母一個非常親密的朋友，他就像是我的名義上的叔叔，或者是一個大哥哥，雖然我不是經常見到他。他住在巴黎。」

「不管怎麼說，那一天他們得到了巨大的成功，發掘到一些真正重大的發現。弗朗索瓦直徑回到酒店，就是他們住的地方，但我父母和瑪西的父親開車到了酒吧慶祝。回酒店的路上，發生了一場可怕的暴雨。他們在山區道路被沖走了，他們的車被沖離了公路，滾下山腰。那裡的道路是很可怕的，那裡很多仍然是農村地區，有許多都是泥濘道路。」

「我明白了。他們都在事故中喪生了？」他輕輕地問。

她點點頭。

「如果如你所說是因為道路損毀，瑪西怎麼能怪你父親呢？」

Marcie blame your father?"

"Because she claims he was drunk."

"And what do you think?" asked Steve gently. "Could he have been?"

She shook her head. "Never. He abhorred drunk drivers; in fact he wouldn't drive if he'd had any drink at all. He always said that other people's lives deserved his maximum concentration and his sharpest reflexes. He didn't care about what the legal limit was in whatever country he was in, because he said even a small quantity of alcohol impairs your reactions. He had a real thing about it. Dad said people shouldn't be given advice on safe limits to drink and drive; the message should be 'drink or drive—not both."

"Does Marcie know all this?"

"She must do. We basically grew up together. We spent hours around each other's houses in England, and if our parents were abroad and we were with them, normally we'd all share the same house or stay at the same hotel. We were very close."

"So why is she so convinced he was drunk?"

"Because her mother claims that my Dad phoned to tell her they were starting back to the hotel, and he sounded drunk, apparently."

"I see. And your Dad was found in the driving seat?"

"No. It was a huge drop they went over." Her voice quivered and she swallowed hard before carrying on. "They were thrown out of the car at various points, except my mother. She was partly pinned under the car at the bottom."

"So how does anyone know who was driving?"

Rebecca stared at him. "Dad nearly always drove," she said, her voice barely more than a whisper. "He could handle the roads best."

"Did the police report say who was driving?"

"I don't think there was much of an investigation, not back then. They put it down to an accident caused by the state of the roads. They were just some foreigners caught out when the road washed away, and everyone had died; it didn't matter who was driving, I

「因為她聲稱，是因為他喝醉了。」

「那你有什麼想法？」史堤夫輕輕問。「他會嗎？」

她搖搖頭。「從來不會。他憎恨酒後駕車，事實上，只要他有喝過一點點，他就不會開車。他總是說，其他人的生命應該得到他最高度的關注和最敏銳的反應。無論在任何國家，他都不理會那裡的法律限制，因為他說，即使少量的酒精也會損害你的反應。他有真正關注這事件。爸爸說，根本不應該給予人們酒後駕駛的安全限制，正確的應該是：喝酒或駕駛，兩者不能並存。」

「瑪西知道這一切嗎？」

「她一定知道。我們基本上是一起長大的。在英格蘭的時候，我們有很多時候都在對方的房子附近玩耍。如果我們的父母要去外地，而我們跟他們一起去，我們通常會住在同一間房子，或者同一家酒店。我們是非常親近的。」

「那麼，為什麼她如此深信是他喝醉了呢？」

「因為她的母親聲稱，他們準備回去酒店的時候，我爸爸有打電話去告訴她，那時候他聽起來明顯是喝醉了。」

「我明白了。那你爸爸被發現在駕駛座位上嗎？」

「沒有。他們在那裡掉了下去。」她的聲音顫抖著，繼續說下去之前艱難地吞一下口水。「他們被拋出車外，並在不同的地點，除了我的母親，她有部分卡住在汽車的底部。」

「那麼，根本沒有人知道是由誰來駕駛嗎？」

麗貝卡盯著他。「爸爸幾乎總是開著車，」她說，她的聲音幾乎比之前更小。「他比較懂得處理的道路狀況。」

「警方的報告說誰在駕駛呢？」

「我不認為有很多的調查，至少沒有收到過。他們只當作是道路狀況造成的意外事故。他們只知道有一些外國人在道路上被沖走了，而所有人已經死了，所以不會關心要誰在駕駛，我想。」

「所以有可能是，你爸爸已經喝了幾杯酒，所以由其他人來駕車回去？」

「我也這樣認為，是的。」她搖搖頭，一臉茫然。「我只是一直

suppose.

"So it's possible that your Dad could have had a few drinks, but someone else could have driven the car back?"

"I suppose so, yes." She shook her head, dazed. "I just always presumed that Marcie's mother was mistaken, or that my Dad hadn't sounded drunk at all, but that her grief made her desperate for someone to blame."

"Sorry. I didn't mean to confuse things."

"No, it's okay. You've given me something to think about. I've been making assumptions all these years that might be wrong."

"Why blame you, though? Even if your father was to blame, there's nothing you can do; it's not your fault."

"She just does."

"And it's how long ago?"

"Twelve years."

"So it should be water under the bridge. Yes, it's awful and sad, but hating you isn't going to bring her Dad back."

"She always talks about it as though it happened last week. I don't know why she's transferred the blame to me, but she's gone out of her way to make my life a misery. Yet I lost more than she did," said Rebecca bitterly. "She still had her mother."

"How old were you?"

"Sixteen."

"Poor Rebecca." His eyes were full of sympathy, "That must have been tough."

"It was. At least I had my Gran then, though. I lived with her whilst I was in sixth form, but she died before I went to Uni. I sometimes think that's where I made my mistake, because I'd never have gone into archaeology if I'd known it would bring me into contact with Marcie."

"You didn't know she'd followed in her father's footsteps, then?"

"She didn't, at first. Didn't want anything to do with archaeology. She was three years older than me, so she was already at uni when

在推測是瑪西的媽媽錯了，或許我爸爸聽起來沒有醉，只是她的悲痛使她絕望地怪罪別人。」

「對不起。我不是故意把事情搞得複雜。」

「不是，沒關係。你給了我一些東西思考。這些年來我一直在假設的可能全部是錯的。」

「但為什麼要怪罪你？就算真的是你父親咎由自取，你也沒有什麼可以做，這不是你的錯。」

「她就是這樣。」

「這是多久以前？」

「十二年。」

「所以，這都是過去的事了。是的，是很可怕和很可悲，但恨你並不會把她的爸爸帶回來。」

「她總是談論著它，就好像在上週發生的事。我不知道她為什麼要把所有罪名都推給我，她自己走出來了，而讓我活在悲痛之中。但其實我失去的比她更多，」麗貝卡苦澀地說。「她還有她母親。」

「那時你多大？」

「十六歲。」

「可憐的麗貝卡。」他眼神充滿著同情，「那一定是很艱難。」

「是的。但無論如何，至少我還有我的祖母。當我是在六年級的時候，我就跟她住了。但我在上大學之前，她就已經去世了。我有時會想，我做得最錯的是考進了考古學，如果我知道這會令我要跟瑪西接觸，我永遠也不會讀考古學。」

「那你不知道她會承繼父親的事業？」

「她一開始沒有，沒有想過要讀考古學。她比我大三歲，所以我們的父母去世的時候，她已經在上大學，是讀物理的。我失去了她的消息好幾年，只從其他人那裡聽到她的事，因為之後無論是她還是她的母親也不會跟我或我的祖母說話。接下來我知道的事情，就是她在一個團隊中負責發掘一個在布里斯托爾附近的場地。原來她去了蘇格蘭讀考古學，所以我一直在這裡都沒有遇到

our parents died, doing physics. I lost track of her for a few years – I only heard about her through other people, because neither she nor her mother would talk to me or my Gran afterwards—and next thing I knew, she was on a team digging a site near Bristol. She'd gone to Uni in Scotland to do archaeology so I hadn't come across her on digs down here. She took the job at Swindon three years ago. I barely saw her then though and about eighteen months ago Swindon agreed to exchange her with a member of a Florence team. She went out there and Swindon got Stefano."

"Will you see a lot of her when you work on this project?"

She shrugged. "I'm not sure yet. She's in charge of their team, but I don't know how much time she'll spend at the site, or how hands-on she'll be."

"You can't ask to be assigned to something else?"

She squirmed. "I could, but..." She could feel her cheeks flush.

"It's your baby," he said wryly.

She nodded. "Pathetic, isn't it."

"No, not if it really matters to you. I can understand wanting to see something through."

"Good, because I'm not sure I completely understand it myself. I'm dreading it."

"So what are you going to do? Grit your teeth and see how it goes?"

"I think I have to. My boss, Ron, is going to do what he can to reduce the contact between us, but we're going to have to work together sometimes, and make some decisions together. It's not feasible, otherwise."

"He sounds like a good guy to have as a boss."

"He is. He's the best." She grinned. "A bit like Tony."

"You may laugh, but you have no idea. Tony really is the best," said Steve with feeling.

She searched his face for clues as to what lay behind that comment, but found none. "Well that's good," she said lightly. "Some of my friends work for monsters. It's nice to know you don't."

她。直到三年前，她接受了在史雲頓的工作。但我也幾乎沒有遇到她，因為約十八個月前，史雲頓跟佛羅倫薩團隊同意進行一個交流計劃，她換過去了，而斯蒂法諾就來了史雲頓。」

「當你在進行這個項目時，你會經常見到她嗎？」

她聳聳肩。「我還不能確定。她掌管他們的團隊，但我不知道她會花多少時間在現場，或者她會親自動手。」

「你不能要求負責別的項目嗎？」

她扭動著。「我可以，但是…」她感覺到她的雙頰開始漲紅。

「這是你的孩子。」他開玩笑地說道。

她點點頭。「很可悲，是不。」

「不是，如果它真的對你很重要。我能理解你無論如何也想看著。」

「好的，因為我不敢肯定我完全瞭解狀況，我非常害怕。」

「那你打算怎麼辦？咬緊牙關，看看會發生什麼事嗎？」

「我覺得我一定要。我的老闆，羅恩，打算做些什麼可以減少我們之間的接觸，但我們有時一定要一起工作，做一些決定。無論如何都是無可避免的。」

「他聽起來是一個好人，身為一個老闆。」

「他是，他是最好的。」她咧嘴笑著。「有點像東尼。」

「你可能會笑，但你不了解。東尼真的是最好的。」史堤夫很有感情地說。

她在他的臉上搜索著，想找出這說話的背後隱藏著什麼，但沒有發現。「嗯，很好，」她輕輕地說。「我的一些朋友跟怪物一起工作。很高興知道你不是。」

他笑了。「這聽起來似乎你已經將我跟你的朋友混為一談了。」

「當然。這是奶油糖果拿鐵而且是你做的。」

「我還以為是因為我這雙有同情心的耳朵。你想再要嗎？」

He smiled. "That almost sounds like you're lumping me in there as a friend."

"Definitely. It was the butterscotch latte that did it."

"And there was me thinking it was my sympathetic listening ear. Would you like another one?"

"What, another ear? Crikey, how many have you got?"

"Ha ha. You've missed your vocation there, the comedy world has no idea what it's missing," he said, rolling his eyes. "Another latte, Miss Facetious?"

She glanced at her watch. "No thanks, Steve, but I'd best be going. Thanks for listening. Sorry to waste your evening." She stood up, and Steve did too. They'd both launched themselves in the same direction and suddenly they were very close, Steve looking down at her very intently.

"That's okay, any time," he said gruffly, holding her arm for a moment. "Happy to step in if you can't talk to Kevin."

For a split second – a glorious split second, she admitted to herself – she'd thought he was going to kiss her.

"Oh, I've already bent his ear on this one today," she said ruefully, and saw Steve's eyes narrow. What had she said wrong?

"He thinks I'm just being stupid though. Thinks I should just ignore her. I don't think he realises just how dangerous Marcie can be, particularly when she's in a position to meddle with my work. Or how hurtful it can be, dredging up all those memories."

"Sometimes when you're close to things, it can be hard to see them clearly."

She wasn't sure quite what he meant by that, but a wave of tiredness was crashing over her and suddenly all she wanted to do was go home. "I'm dead on my feet, so I'm going. Thanks again for listening."

"No problem." He smiled in response but didn't meet her eyes, sweeping up their things and heading off with the tray. "See you," he said casually over his shoulder.

She stared after him. "Yes... right. Bye."

He reached the counter, put the tray down and without so much

「什麼，再要多雙耳朵？唉呀，你究竟有多少耳朵？」

「哈哈。你錯過了你的天賦，在喜劇世界裡永遠不知道會錯過了什麼，」他說，翻了翻白眼。「再要杯拿鐵嗎？詼諧小姐。」

她看了一眼手錶。「不了，謝謝，史堤夫，我最好還是回去了。感謝你的聆聽。很抱歉浪費了你一個晚上。」她站起身，史堤夫也站了起來。他們都向同一個方向邁步，突然間令他們非常接近，史堤夫很專注地低著頭看她。

「這沒關係的，任何時候都可以，」他生硬地說，抱著她的胳膊好一會。「很開心可以參與，如果你有不能跟凱文談的話。」

一秒鐘的靜止，在美好的一瞬間。她確定她以為他將會吻她。

「哦，我今天已經令他的耳朵變形了，」她沮喪地說，看到了史堤夫眼睛瞇了起來。她說錯了什麼嗎？

「他認為我很蠢，認為我應該做的只是不理會她。我不認為他意識到瑪西可以有多危險，尤其是當她的位置是可以插手我的工作。以及重拾那些所有的回憶對我有多大的傷害。」

「有時候，當你很接近一樣東西，你就很難看清楚它們。」

她不太肯定他的意思是什麼，但一陣疲倦的浪潮湧至，令她突然崩潰了，她最想做的是回家休息。「我已累得不得了，所以我要回去了。再次感謝你的聆聽。」

「沒問題。」他笑著回應，但沒有望到她，眼睛掃視著他們的東西，並拿起托盤。「再見。」他回過頭簡單地說。

她盯著他。「是的…對，再見。」

他走到了櫃檯，把托盤放下來，甚至沒有回過頭看她一眼，就開始跟尼爾談話，那個在清洗架子的人。

麗貝卡站在那裡一會兒，感覺像個傻瓜。他明顯不會再轉過身來，她拿起她的外套離開了。

as a glance over his shoulder, got into conversation with Neil, who was cleaning the shelves.

Rebecca stood there for a moment, feeling like an idiot. When it was obvious he wasn't going to turn round, she picked up her coat and left.

www.penrose-publishing.co.uk

不需要此页

Chapter Nine

The door of Tony's banged shut so hard that their table shook. Kevin frowned but stayed glued to the article he was reading in the paper. Rebecca looked up from her salad. A girl was leaning back against the door, pouting. That was the only word for it. Not sexy pouting, thought Rebecca, but proper, cross pouting. She would have been pretty, with that mass of wavy blonde hair, if it weren't for the thick, smudged black eyeliner and general grubbiness. From here the girl whiffed a bit, too. She hadn't moved, but was just turning her head, sullenly surveying everything. Rebecca nudged Kevin.

"Mmf?" he grunted around his sandwich.

"That one looks like trouble," she said quietly.

Kevin swallowed and wrinkled his nose. "Smells like it too."

"Hmm, obviously doesn't follow the 'not before lunch' rule."

"Either that or she's had a really early lunch," he muttered.

The girl pushed herself off the door and started to walk to the counter, an easy enough task as Tony arranged his tables so that there was a clear route straight to the counter, always maintaining that it was more convenient for people in a rush and takeaway customers. But the girl seemed to be finding it difficult to walk in a straight line, and lurched into their table as she passed. "Oops, sorry," she said, trying to focus on them but not quite managing it before she carried on.

"And our next model is wearing Eau de Brewery," said Kevin, raising an eyebrow as he watched her progress. "Eww."

Steve appeared from the kitchen with a fresh batch of pastries. Rebecca was close enough to see his face darken as he caught sight of the girl, and her interest was piqued. She picked up her magazine and tried to watch the action unobtrusively from behind it.

"There you are, Steve!" The ringing but slurred tones backed up

第九章

東尼咖啡店的大門重重地被關上，他們的桌子震動了一下。凱文皺起了眉頭，但仍然繼續閱讀報紙上的文章。麗貝卡的視線從她的沙拉離開了並看過去。一個女孩靠在門口，撅著嘴。唯一可以說得上的是，不是性感的撅嘴，麗貝卡認為，更適當的應該是壞脾氣的撅嘴。她說得上漂亮，有質量的波浪金髮，如果沒那麼厚就更好。暈開了的黑色眼線，一般看上去都是髒髒的。有一陣從她身上吹送過來的氣味。她沒有動，但只是轉著頭，沉著臉觀測周圍。麗貝卡碰一碰凱文。

「唔？」他吃著三明治咕噥道。

「這位小朋友看來是來找麻煩的。」她平靜地說。

凱文咽下了三明治，皺一皺鼻子。「聞起來也是。」

「嗯，顯然她做了『不能在午餐前做的事』。」

「如果不是這樣，那可能她吃了一個非常早的午餐。」他喃喃地說。

女孩推了自己一把移離了大門，開始步向櫃檯，這是一件很容易的事，因為東尼把座位安排好，由大門到達櫃檯的路線非常清晰，而且一直保持如此以便匆忙和買外賣的顧客。但那個女孩似乎很難走出一條直線，她走過時撞上了他們的桌子。「哎呀，對不起。」她說，並試圖注視著他們，但焦點還沒對好之前，她又繼續開始走。

凱文說：「我們下一個的模特兒是穿著『淡香水釀酒廠』品牌的。」當看著她繼續前行，他揚起了眉毛。「呃...」

史堤夫拿著一批新的糕點從廚房出來。麗貝卡坐得夠近，足以看到他看見那個女孩的時候，他的臉色驟然變暗了，這引起了她的興趣。她拿起雜誌，並試圖悄悄地從後面看著他們。

「你在這裡，史堤夫！」響亮但口齒不清的音調，加上那些氣味和雜亂無章的步伐，足以証明這個女孩喝了很多酒。

「我是在這裡。」史堤夫的表達方式就像教科書中的例子一樣，麗貝卡認為，或是有些人說的木無表情。

the evidence provided by the smell and the haphazard walking. This girl was tanked.

"Here I am." Steve's expression was a textbook example, thought Rebecca, or what people mean when they call the look on someone's face 'stony'.

"Uh-oh. Looks like Steve's got girl trouble," murmured Kevin.

She peered over her magazine to see Kevin twisting round, staring towards the counter with undisguised interest. "Nosey!" she shot at him.

He raised his eyebrows. "Look who's talking!" he mouthed. But a minute later, every head was turned towards the counter.

"I wunnered where you were, Steve!" The girl's voice was loud and harsh. She took the final step towards the counter, leaning heavily against it then lurched forward to try and kiss Steve on the cheek.

He didn't move his feet, just quickly leant back out of the way, his eyes not leaving her face. Like Neo from the Matrix, thought Rebecca. Neat move.

"I'm at work, Laura," he said, curt but quiet. Rebecca was straining to hear him.

"I know that now, silly," Laura laughed, wobbling on the spot. She lifted a hand as though to rest it on Steve's shoulder but missed.

This time he was too slow to move and her nail raked down his cheek. He wiped his cheek with his hand, smearing the bright red beads of blood that had appeared. He was way beyond stony now, thought Rebecca. His face was like thunder; she wouldn't want to be the woman who made him look like that.

"Oh, Steve, I'm sorry, sorry..." Laura looked wildly around her and spotted serviettes further along the counter. She grabbed a huge handful, trying to reach up and wipe his cheek.

He batted her away. "That's enough. Go home."

"But, but..." Her voice got even louder and she sounded tearful. "I was only trying to help. It's your faul, your fault, Steve, I woke up and you wern there. You left without saying g'bye!" She threw her hands up in protest and wiped out two plates of takeaway flapjacks displayed on the counter cabinet. The plates hit the floor, one rolling to a halt against the counter and the other

「嗯，哦。看來史堤夫惹上了這個女孩。」凱文喃喃地說。

她凝視著她的雜誌，看到凱文扭轉身子，毫不掩飾地朝櫃檯盯著。「多管閒事！」她炮轟他。

他揚起了眉，嘟囔著：「你看是誰在說話！」但一分鐘後，所有頭都轉向了櫃檯。

「我在想你在哪裡呢，史堤夫！」女孩的聲音響亮而苛刻。她向櫃檯踏出最後一步，但身體又嚴重地向反方向傾斜，然後蹣跚地向前，嘗試上前去吻史堤夫的臉頰。

他沒有移動他的腳，只是迅速傾斜了身子，他的眼睛也沒有離開她的臉。麗貝卡覺得他就像《駭客任務》中的尼歐一樣，乾淨俐落地閃身。

「我在上班，羅拉。」他生硬但安靜地說。麗貝卡使勁地才聽到他說話。

「我當然知道，傻瓜。」羅拉笑了，然後在原地搖擺著。她舉起一隻手，好像想搭在史堤夫的肩膀上，但落空了。

這時他正緩慢地移動著，而她的指甲正好擦過了他的臉頰。他用手摸一下臉頰，一抹鮮紅色的血珠出現了。

麗貝卡覺得現在的他遠遠超出木無表情，他的臉色如雷，她不會想成為一個令他看起來這樣的女人。

「哦，史堤夫，對不起，對不起...」羅拉瘋狂地看著周圍，發現沿著櫃檯放了餐巾紙。她抓起了為數不少的一疊，試圖去擦拭他的臉頰。

他推開了她的手。「夠了，回家吧！」

「但是，但是...」她的聲音變得更響亮，而聽起來帶著哭腔。「我只是想幫忙。這是你的錯，是你的錯，史堤夫，我醒來的時候，你就在那裡，你連再見沒跟我說一聲！」她甩她的手以示抗議，並掃落了在櫃檯陳列櫃上展示用的兩盤外賣煎餅。盤子砸在地板上，一個滾到櫃檯旁就停了下來，另一個就打碎了，瓷器的碎片跟煎餅混在一塊。她低頭盯著這片殘局，然而她好像還是想不出為何會弄成這樣。「哎呀。」過了片刻之後她說。

「羅拉，馬上回家，」史堤夫咆哮著。「你知道我在工作，我就告訴過你不要來這裡打擾我。」他開始繞過櫃檯走向她。

她向後退去一點點，「但你星期三是不用工作的，史堤夫，」她說，用不穩定的手指指向他。「我知道你不用。」

「今天是星期四。」

shattering, shards of china scattered amongst the flapjacks. She stared down at the mess as though she couldn't work out how it had got there. "Whoops," she said, after a moment.

"Laura, go home right now," Steve growled." "You knew I was at work, and I've told you not to bother me here." He started to walk round the counter towards her.

She backed away a little, "But you don't work on Wednesdays, Steve, "she said, pointing an unsteady finger at him. "I know you don't."

"It's Thursday."

Her forehead creased. "Thursday?"

"Yes, so I'm where I should be. Where you should be is at home in bed, sleeping it off."

"Sleepinitoff? I'm n'drunk, if thas what you're tryin t'say." She planted her hands on her hips.

The kitchen door swung open. Tony came to stand beside Steve and put his hands on the end of the counter, shoulders squared. "What is it we can for you, Laura? You have not bought anything, I think, and Steve needs to get on his work. Si?"

Rebecca stared. Oh my God. She'd never heard Tony take that tone with anyone.

Laura stared at him, and instantly became a little girl. "I haven't brought any money, Tony," she said pathetically.

"Why are you in my café, then?"

"I came to see Steve." She was half-sobbing. "He didn't say goodbye to me!"

"You have seen him. My café is for people to sit, eat my food or drink my coffee. If you are not here to do these, leave, please."

Laura went completely still for a minute, tears stopped. Rebecca found she was holding her breath. Would she just turn and walk out?

With a screech, Laura's arm lashed out, trying to claw at Tony's face. With a dexterity Rebecca would never have suspected of him, Tony grabbed both her wrists. "If you do not stop right now, I call the police." He still hadn't raised his voice. The kitchen door

她的額頭起了皺紋。「星期四？」

「是的，所以我應該要在這裡。而你就應該在家中的床上睡覺。」

「睡覺消酒氣嗎？我喝醉了，這是你想說的話。」她雙手扠腰。

廚房門開了。東尼走出來站在史堤夫旁邊，雙手放於櫃檯上，擺正肩膀。「我們有什麼可以幫你，羅拉？我想你並沒有買東西，而史堤夫需要繼續他的工作。嗯？」

麗貝卡瞪大了眼睛。噢，我的天。她從來沒有聽說過東尼用這種語氣跟任何人說話。

羅拉盯著他，瞬間變了一個小女孩。「我沒有帶錢過來，東尼。」她可憐巴巴地說。

「那你為什麼會在我的咖啡店呢？」

「我是來看看史堤夫。」她在半抽泣。「他沒有跟我說再見！」

「你已經看見他了。我的咖啡店是供人坐下來吃我的食物或喝我的咖啡。如果你不在這裡做這些，那就請你離開。」

羅拉有一分鐘完全靜止了，眼淚也停止了。麗貝卡發現她屏住了呼吸。她會轉身離開嗎？

隨著尖叫，羅拉的手臂猛烈揮動，試圖去抓東尼的臉。麗貝卡沒有懷疑過他的靈巧，東尼抓住了她的手腕。「如果你還不馬上停下來，我就打電話報警了。」他依然沒有提高嗓門。廚房的門再次打開，尼爾出現了，詫異地看著東尼。東尼向他輕輕的搖了搖頭，尼爾就留在原地。

「小子，東尼真的很酷。」凱文低聲說。

麗貝卡無言地點了點頭。她的眼睛望著史堤夫，心思已經走向他了。他僵在原地看著，咬緊牙關，臉是紅色的，可能是因為憤怒、尷尬或二者的混合，她不知道。

「放開我！」羅拉尖叫著，她另一隻手腕再次揮動。

這一次東尼攔住了她的手，就在他臉前一毫米。他轉頭望向尼爾。「尼爾請你去撥一下電話，我想警察應該要過來一下，是嗎？」

尼爾轉身，但史堤夫突然活了過來。「不要，東尼，求你...」

「我很抱歉，但如果她不肯離開。」

opened again and Neil appeared, looking questioningly at Tony. Tony gave a small shake of the head. Neil stayed where he was.

"Boy, Tony's a cool customer," whispered Kevin.

Rebecca nodded speechlessly. Her eyes had gone to Steve, and her heart went out to him. He looked frozen to the spot, jaw rigid and his face red—whether from anger, embarrassment or a mix of both, she wasn't sure.

"Get off me!" Laura shrieked, freeing one of her wrists and lashing out again.

This time Tony stopped her hand only millimetres from his face. He looked over his shoulder at Neil. "You make the call please Neil; I think police should be here, yes?"

Neil turned, but Steve suddenly came back to life. "Stop, Tony, please—"

"I'm sorry, but if she won't leave—"

"I'll get her to! I'll take her home. I'm sorry."

"Go on then," said Tony through gritted teeth, "is against my better judgement, but as it is you..."

Steve moved behind Laura. "Come on, time to go home." He brought his arms down over hers in the kind of locking manoeuvre Rebecca had seen used on violent teens when she'd done a stint of work experience in a youth custody centre. That experience had helped her opt firmly for an archaeology degree and not the psychology degree she'd been toying with.

"But I want a coffee," said Laura, quieter now, turning round in Steve's hold to face him. "Can't you buy me a coffee?"

"I haven't got any money with me, Lor." He pulled her to the side of him, against his hip, one arm firmly around her shoulders.

Her face dropped and her eyes sparked.

"I'll tell you what," said Steve quickly, "I'll make you a special coffee at home. I bet Tony will let me borrow a bottle of syrup."

"Really?"

"Really. What one would you like?"

「我來帶她走！我會帶她回家，我很抱歉。」

「那就去吧，」東尼咬牙切齒地說，「這是有違我的原則，但這次就只因為你…」

史堤夫走到羅拉的背後。「走吧，是時候回家了。」他把他的手臂放在她的手臂下面，像那種反鎖式的。麗貝卡曾經看過有人使用在暴力少年身上，是她以前在青少年拘押中心的工作經驗，她在那裡工作了一段時間。這經驗令她斷然地選擇考古學學位，而不是心理學學位，她曾經非認真地考慮過這個選擇。

「但我想要一杯咖啡，」羅拉說，她已經安靜下來了，在被史堤夫抓住的狀況下轉身過去面對著他。「難道你就不能給我買杯咖啡嗎？」

「我沒有帶錢，羅拉。」他把她拉到他身邊，跟他的臀部並排，一隻胳膊緊緊摟著她的肩膀。

她的臉下沈了，眼睛閃爍著。

史堤夫很快說道：「我告訴你，回家我會為你做一杯特別的咖啡。我猜東尼會借我一瓶糖漿。」

「真的嗎？」

「真的。你想要那種？」

羅拉雙膝突然發軟，她轉過頭看架上的瓶子。「哦，我頭暈了…」

「好了，不用回頭，我可以告訴你有那些口味。榛子、薄荷還是香草？」

「哇，真的是簡短。」麗貝卡喃喃地說。

「嗯。薄荷。」

東尼從櫃檯下拿了一瓶新鮮的糖漿往史堤夫的手裡塞。

「謝謝。」史堤夫聽起來就像一個被拯救了的人。

「現在，你帶她離開這裡。」東尼的眼睛閃爍著。

「我們現在回家了。」他帶領羅拉走向門口，眼睛盯著前方。可憐的史堤夫，麗貝卡在想。我也不會想看任何人的眼睛。

東尼一直看著史堤夫帶著羅拉出了門口。凱文幫了他一把，他躍起腳把門打開，因為在附近的人都陷入癱瘓了。東尼轉身，向尼爾不耐煩地揮手叫他返回廚房。他砰一聲關上身後的門，幾乎跟

Laura's knees sagged as she turned her head to look at the bottles on the shelf. "Oooh, I feel dizzy..."

"Okay, don't turn round, I can tell you the flavours. Hazelnut, mint or vanilla?"

"Wow, that's the short version," Rebecca murmured.

"Mmm. Mint."

Tony produced a fresh bottle from under the counter and thrust it into Steve's hand.

"Thanks." Steve sounded like a man who'd had his life saved.

"Now, you get her out of here." Tony's eyes glittered.

"Home we go." He steered Laura towards the door, eyes fixed ahead. Poor Steve, thought Rebecca. I wouldn't want to look anyone in the eye, either.

Tony watched them go, and as Steve got Laura out the door—aided by Kevin, who'd leapt to his feet to open it because everyone closer seemed paralysed—he turned on his heel, waving Neil into the kitchen before his with an impatient flick of his hand. The door banging behind him was nearly as loud as Laura's entrance a few minutes earlier.

Kevin turned to Rebecca with eyes like dinner plates. "Oo-er, missus."

"Poor Steve."

"Yeah. Poor Steve," Kevin agreed, picking up his abandoned coffee. "Eww. Cold. Never can understand how people can drink iced coffee."

"Philistine. It's gorgeous."

Neil appeared, and the heads of everyone in the shop whipped round to see what was happening now. He walked to the nearest table and squatted down on his haunches, talking quietly to the customers.

"What's going on?" Kevin hissed.

"Dunno, I can't hear. Are you done?"

"Just want to finish my muffin," said Kevin, watching Neil curiously

羅拉幾分鐘前進來的時候一樣大聲。

凱文轉向麗貝卡，她的眼睛像碟子一樣大。「哦…呃，女士。」

「可憐的史堤夫。」

「是啊。可憐的史堤夫，」凱文同意，他拿起被遺棄了的咖啡。「呃，冷掉了。永遠無法理解人們怎麼可以喝冰咖啡。」

「那非利士人。很享受地。」

尼爾出現，店內的每一個人都猛然轉身看發生什麼事。他走到最近的桌，一屁股坐了下來，靜靜地跟客人說話。

「這是怎麼回事？」凱文小聲地說。

「不知道，我聽不到。你吃完了嗎？」

凱文說：「我只想把鬆餅吃完，」他好奇地看著尼爾，他移到下一張桌子。「至少，冷了味道也不錯。」

「你比較想多管閒事，」麗貝卡反駁說。「快點，我們要回去了。」

「為什麼？沒有什麼要趕。這比肥皂劇更好看。」

她揚起眉毛。「好吧，我知道你很無聊…沒關係，這個下午我可以找到很多工作給你做。我有一堆現場的調查報告，就在我的辦公桌上，全部都需要歸檔。」

「不，不，不無聊，我只想指出…」

「閉嘴，麥肯齊，吃你的鬆餅。」

「是的，老闆。」他滑稽地大大的咬了一口，當尼爾來到他們的桌坐下，他假裝驚訝。

他笑了。「嗨。」

麗貝卡輕笑。看著凱文試圖用有禮貌的方法把整個鬆餅在兩秒內吞掉，使她心情平伏了，她覺得在她的肚子裡的結稍微鬆了一下。看到史堤夫心煩是非常可怕。

凱文向尼爾揮揮手，滿臉歉意地聳聳肩。

「白痴！」她轉過身來望向尼爾。「請原諒我家的猴子，尼爾，我們能為你做什麼？」

尼爾努力地板著臉。「是我們能為你做什麼，首先要為剛才的混

as he moved to the next table. "At least that tastes good cold."

"Just want to be nosey, more like," Rebecca retorted. "Hurry up then, we need to get back."

"Why? There's nothing urgent on. This is better than soap."

She raised her eyebrows. "Well if I'd known you were bored... never mind, I can find plenty for you to do this afternoon. I've got a stack of site surveys on my desk that all need filing."

"No, no, not bored, just pointing out that—"

"Button it, McKenzie, and eat your muffin."

"Yes, boss." He'd just taken a comically huge bite, pretending to panic, when Neil arrived at their table and hunkered down.

He smiled. "Hi."

Rebecca chuckled. Watching as Kevin tried to look polite while swallowing his muffin practically whole in two seconds flat was making her day, and she felt the knot in her stomach relax a little. Seeing Steve so upset had been horrible.

Kevin waved a hand at Neil and shrugged apologetically.

"Idiot!" She turned to Neil. "Excuse the tame monkey, Neil, what can we do for you?"

Neil was trying hard to keep a straight face. "It's more what we can do for you, which is firstly, to apologise for the disruption."

Kevin made a choking noise and Neil thumped him on the back.

"Are you alright, dude?" He looked concerned.

Kevin nodded.

Rebecca grinned. "You look like a giant tomato."

Kevin glared at her and did a giant swallow. He turned to Neil, his face all innocence. "What disruption?"

This time, Neil allowed himself a grin. "The young lady who was – how do you say it politely over here, rather worse for wear...?"

"Oh, the one who was drunk as a skunk," said Kevin. He smiled. "That's alright, not your fault."

亂道歉。」

凱文發出被噎到的聲音，尼爾幫他捶背。

「你還好嗎，伙計？」他關心地看著他。

凱文點了點頭。

麗貝卡咧嘴笑著。「你看起來像一個巨型番茄。」

凱文瞪著她，並做了一個巨大的吞嚥動作。他轉身對著尼爾，一臉無知地說：「什麼混亂？」

這一次，尼爾允許自己笑了，他說，「那位年輕女士，你會怎麼把它說得有禮貌一點，比差勁更加糟糕的…？」

「哦，就是一個醉得像隻臭鼬的人，」凱文說，笑了。「沒問題的，不是你的錯。」

「不是任何人的錯，」麗貝卡堅決地說，她壓低了聲音，「史堤夫還好嗎？」

尼爾向周圍掃了一眼。「我也希望他沒事。這不是第一次了，像這樣的事情已經發生過。」他不好意思地抬起頭。「呃，請忘了我說的話。」

「她必定是很難伺候。」凱文說。

「有一點。」尼爾同意。

「我很驚訝他居然可以忍受得了。」

「你不得不佩服他可以容忍她。」麗貝卡說。她覺得自己的聲音聽起來異常地高。她感覺突然有點想哭，控制你的情緒，女人。

「我同意。他是一個非常忠誠的傢伙，但應該要對自己好一點。無論如何，不應該說別人閒話的，這是史堤夫自己的事。」尼爾站起身來，看似不太舒服。「哦，差點忘了。東尼說，今天的午餐是免費的，他希望很快再見到你們。」

「嗯。威逼和利誘，我媽媽這樣叫它。」凱文笑了起來。

「對啊，跟你們兩個說有點徒勞，你們幾乎每天都在這裡。無論如何，給你們的。」他從圍裙口袋裡拿了兩張優惠券出來給凱文和麗貝卡。

凱文看著。「哦，謝謝！」

「是我們的榮幸。」尼爾說，拿走了他們的托盤。

"Not the fault of any of the staff," said Rebecca firmly. She lowered her voice. "Will Steve be okay?"

Neil glanced round. "I hope so. It's not the first time stuff like this has happened." He looked embarrassed. "Er, forget I said that."

"She certainly looks high maintenance," said Kevin.

"And some," Neil agreed.

"I'm surprised he puts up with it."

"You have to admire him for sticking by her," said Rebecca. Her voice sounded unusually high, she thought. She felt suddenly tearful. Get a grip, woman.

"I suppose. He's a very loyal bloke, but too nice for his own good. Anyway, shouldn't be gossiping, it's Steve's business." Neil got to his feet, looking uncomfortable. "Oh, almost forgot. Secondly, Tony says today's lunch is on the house and he hopes to see you again soon."

"Ah. Flannel and flattery', as my Mum would call it," Kevin laughed.

"Yeah, well with you two it's wasted, you practically live here. There you go, anyway." He produced two vouchers out of his apron pocket, giving one to Kevin and one to Rebecca.

Kevin looked. "Ooh, thanks!"

"Our pleasure," said Neil, carrying away their tray.

Kevin waved his voucher under Rebecca's nose. "Look, Bec, ten percent off our next bill!"

"Whoopee."

"Well don't sound so enthusiastic," said Kevin, affronted. "Ten percent off is ten percent off. Us more lowly workers can't afford to look a gift voucher in the, er..."

"Voucher code?"

"Exactly. We need every penny—Bec?"

She was on her feet, pulling on her coat. "Time we we're going."

He got to his feet. "Right," he said, sounding crushed. "Bec?"

凱文在麗貝卡的鼻子前揮舞著優惠券。「你看，貝卡，下次的帳單有九折！」

「放屁。」

「那好吧，不應該說得那麼熱烈的，」凱文輕蔑地說，「九折就是九折，我們這麼卑微的工人買不起這個，呃…」

「禮券代碼？」

「沒錯。我們需要每一分錢…貝卡？」

她站了起來，拉一拉上衣。「是時候走了。」

他站起身來。「沒錯，」他說，聽起來很消沈。「貝卡？」

「怎樣？」

「什麼事？」

「沒事。」她拿起手袋，沒有望他一眼。

「不要瞞我了。」

「我真不敢相信你所關心的就只有你的折扣代碼，我我我先生。已經夠荒謬了，只要我有這種心思，我會更關心那個人類小悲劇，就是剛在這裡上演的那個。」她嚴厲地說。「

嘿，不要說得我像個壞人似的！」凱文抗議後，跟著她走到門口。「我有關心。史堤夫似乎真的是一個非常不錯的傢伙，但這裡沒有很多我們可以做的事，不是嗎？根本不關我們的事。」

「不，我知道。抱歉。只是…可憐的史堤夫。他一定是真的很關心和支持她。大部分男人一早就已經跑了一英里。她可能會令他失去工作。」他們朝著門外走去，但她猶豫了一下，她的手還在門的把手上。「不知道我是否應該跟東尼說一下？」

「說什麼？」

「當然是史堤夫，如果東尼要解雇他呢？」

「麗貝卡，這是由東尼決定，而且那裡所有的員工都有權去胡言亂語，他不得不先去處理，你知道的。」凱文走過了她去打開門，迫使她走到街上。

「但是，這是史堤夫需要的最後一件事。我敢打賭，她不能保住她的工作，她是，如果她經常處於那個狀態！」

"Yes?"

"What the matter?"

"Nothing." She picked up her bag, not meeting his eyes.

"Could have fooled me."

"I just can't believe all you care about is your discount code, Mr Me Me Me. Strangely enough, as I have a heart, I'm more concerned with the little human tragedy that's just played out here," she said tightly.

"Hey, don't make me out to be the bad guy!" Kevin protested, following her to the door. "I do care. Steve seems like a really nice bloke, but there's not a lot we can do about it, is there? None of our business."

"No, I know. Sorry. It's just... poor Steve. He must be really caring to support her like that. Most men would run a mile. She could lose him his job." They walked towards the door but she hesitated, her hand on the handle. "I wonder if I should talk to Tony?"

"What about?"

"Steve, of course. Say Tony gives him the sack?"

"Rebecca, that's up to Tony, and there's all sorts of employee rights rigmarole he'd have to go through first, you know that." Kevin reached past her and opened the door, forcing her out of it and on to the street.

"But that's the last thing Steve needs. I bet she's not holding down a job, is she, if she regularly gets in that state!"

"I'm sure Tony wouldn't do anything without giving it serious thought, Bec, he's a good guy. And he must know Steve pretty well by now, as you don't really know him from Adam. Now come on, it's nearly—"

"Actually I've had coffee with him. And lunch. And dinner, kind of." She rushed out the door, hoping he wouldn't see the blush she could feel rushing up her face.

Kevin stopped and faced her just outside.

"Really?"

「我敢肯定，東尼沒有認真思過是不會做任何事的，貝卡，他是一個好人。他一定知道史堤夫是相當不錯，而你不知道他是否真的由亞當造的。來吧，差不多…」

「其實我已經跟他喝過咖啡，吃過午餐和晚餐之類的。」她衝了出門口，希望他看不到她的臉，她能感覺到她的臉紅了。

凱文停了下來，在外面面對著她。

「真的嗎？」

「是的。我們是相當不錯的朋友，如果你一定要知道的話。」她並沒有望他的眼睛，她開始走著，並擺弄在她的手袋裡一些不必

要的東西。「我知道東尼是一個好心人，但他也有古老的意大利人想法…」

「和神氣十足的警覺！」凱文把她的手臂塞進他手臂內，就跟他平常做的一樣，雖然她仍在跟他爭論，她還是讓他這樣做。她不想當眾大吵大鬧。

「沒有，但他可能會認為史堤夫只應該趕她出去，或者送她到出國或其他…」

「麗貝卡，你生活在什麼世紀呢？」

「…可憐的史堤夫，他不值得…」

凱文突然停了下來，令麗貝卡被強行拉停了。

「嗷。」她怒視，並把胳膊拉出來。

「對不起。麗貝卡聽著，東尼只是個經營小咖啡店的傢伙，就這樣而已。他不是我們的叔叔，也不是朋友，甚至不是朋友的叔叔，看在上帝的份上。所以你不能干涉。」

「我通常都不會，我只是覺得這次不同。」

「可憐的史堤夫…又，史堤夫只是一個不錯的傢伙，他負責招待我的午餐。而且是你的朋友，很顯然是。但無論這種事在什麼時候發生，都肯定只是偶然。」他用銳利的目光看著她，她別過頭去。

但已經太遲了，這一次。不只是臉紅了，她能感覺到自己的臉頰被火燒一樣。

「貝卡，你不用那麼認真。史堤夫似乎是一個可愛的小伙子，而我真的很替他難過，但如果你認為那個小狀況顯示了什麼事情，這肯定是他，一、自找的，二、跟那個女人的關係亂七八糟，而

"Yes. We're quite good friends, if you must know." She wasn't meeting his eyes, fiddling with something unnecessary in her bag as she started to walk. "And I know Tony's a sweetie and everything, but he's got all these old-fashioned Italian ideas—"

"Patronising alert!" Kevin tucked her arm in his as he often did, and although she was cross with him, she let him. She didn't want to make a scene.

"No, but he might think Steve should just chuck her out, or send her to the country or something—"

"Rebecca, what century are you living in?"

"— and poor Steve, he doesn't deserve—"

Kevin stopped dead, bringing Rebecca to an abrupt halt by default.

"Oww." She glared and pulled her arm out of his.

"Sorry. Listen Rebecca, Tony is the guy who runs out local cafe. That's all. He's not our uncle, or a personal friend, or even a personal friend's uncle, for God's sake. You can't interfere."

"I wouldn't, normally. I just think this is different."

"And all this poor Steve... again, Steve is just a nice guy who serves me lunch. And your friend, apparently, whenever that happened, but surely only a casual one." He looked at her piercingly, and she looked away.

Too late. This time it wasn't just a blush, she felt her cheeks burn.

"Bec, you're not serious. Steve seems a lovely guy and I feel really sorry for him, but if that little scene showed you anything, it's that he's a, taken and b, in a mess with that woman, a mess that you, I, and everyone else is best staying out of. It's their business."

Rebecca's stomach was churning. Have you quite finished lecturing me like I'm a wayward teenager?" Her tone was cutting and she knew she was behaving badly, but for some reason she couldn't stop herself.

Kevin's mouth opened, closed, then opened again. "Look, Bec, I didn't mean it like that, I—"

你、我和大家都一樣最好遠離一點。這是他們自己的事。」

麗貝卡的胃在翻騰，「你對我說完教了嗎？我是一個任性的少年嗎？」她的語氣很刻薄，她知道自己表現得極為無禮，但出於某種原因，她無法阻止她自己。

凱文打開口，閉上，然後再次打開。「你看，貝卡。我也並不是這個意思，我...」

「你最好回去工作，你快遲到了。」她突然轉身跑到馬路邊，在找可以走過去的空隙。

「你要去哪裡？」他的聲音聽起來很憂慮而不高興，她穿過馬路離他而去。麗貝卡．梅納德，你是個婊子，她告訴自己。當她到達另一面，她看著對面的他，給了他一個小小的微笑。

「我要坐公車去埃德巴斯頓的場地，我需要作最後的檢查，明天就要封閉了。」她叫著然後開始走。

「但是，你的東西...」

「我已經拿了我的東西。」這是真話。「我在午飯前早就計劃了要過去，但我忘了說，就因為那齣鬧劇！」這是謊話。

「那好吧。」凱文開始慢慢地沿著他那邊的路走，但她迅速拋離了他，加快了速度是因為她看見公車正在路的盡頭轉彎，正開始向她駛過來。

她揮揮手。「再見！」公車已經停了下來，她現在作最後衝刺。只有兩個人在車站等候，第二個剛剛上了車。她祈禱，司機有看到她。

幾秒鐘後，她跳上了車，付了錢，撲入第一個空座位。作為她的朋友，凱文有時表現得更像她的親生母親，她想。當公車沿著街上蹣跚行駛，她的靜脈裡的腎上腺素仍在快速流動。淚水刺痛了她的眼睛，就在那個諷刺的念頭一下子閃過的一剎。她不希望有人能像她的母親，而是希望她能夠回來。也許她會明白麗貝卡有時候是多麼的孤獨，即使有朋友在身邊。以及當你不能夠得到一個你想要的人的時候是有多麼的難受。

羅拉走了。在跟平常一樣的大吵大鬧之後的下午，他讓她去睡覺，而他就出去買一些食品。當他回來的時候，幾乎她所擁有的物品都消失了，他相信她有留下什麼是她不想要的，其中許多是他送的禮物。他想她應該是坐出租車或有人接送她的，因為她是無法一個人帶所有的東西離開。

史堤夫把頭靠在沙發上。他本來預期自己會感到如釋重負、或煩

"You'd best get back to work, you'll be late." She turned abruptly and went to the kerb, looking for a space in the traffic.

"Where are you going?" He sounded worried and unhappy as she crossed the road away from him. Rebecca Maynard, you are a bitch, she told herself. As she reached the other side, she looked across at him and gave him a small smile.

"I'm getting the bus to the Edgbaston site, I need to check how that last trench is going. They're closing up tomorrow," she called, starting to walk.

"But your stuff—"

"I've got everything with me." Truth. "I had this planned before lunch but I forgot to say, what with all the drama!" Lie.

"Okay then." Kevin started to walk slowly along his side of the road, but she was rapidly leaving him behind, speeding up as she saw the bus turn the corner at the end of the road and start coming towards her.

She waved a hand. "Bye!" The bus had stopped and she was sprinting now. There had only been two people waiting at the stop and the second had just got on. She prayed the driver had seen her.

Seconds later she jumped on the bus, paid the driver and threw herself into the first empty seat. Sometimes Kevin acted more like her bloody mother than her friend, she thought, adrenaline still racing through her veins as the bus lurched off along the street. Tears pricked her eyes as the irony of that thought struck her. She didn't want someone to act like her mother, she wanted her Mum back. Perhaps she would have understood how lonely Rebecca sometimes was, even amongst friends; and how tough it was to want someone you can't have.

Laura was gone. After the usual massive row, he'd left her to sleep it off for the afternoon and gone out to do some food shopping. When he got back, nearly everything she owned had disappeared and he presumed what she'd left behind were things she no longer wanted – many of which seemed to be gifts from him. She either taken a cab or someone had picked her up, he figured, because she couldn't have carried all that stuff away by herself.

Steve rested his head back on the sofa. He would have

惱、或內疚。

奇怪他沒有，他只是覺得麻木。

expected to feel either relieved, worried sick or guilty.

Strange then that instead, he just felt numb.

不需要此页

Chapter Ten

Laura opened the back door cautiously. By rights Steve shouldn't be here, he should be at work. But she needed to be sure. She left her boots outside on the step and padded round the house in her socks.

Ok, she was safe. He was gone and so were his work clothes. She pulled a carrier bag out of her rucksack and filled it with clothes. Then she went to the bathroom. In the cabinet was a bag she could guarantee Steve wouldn't snoop in, because it was full to the brim with tampons. She groped around at the bottom, pulled out a tampon box and removed the roll of £10 notes inside. That would do for today.

Kitchen next. She took all the multipacks from the cupboard—crisps, mini cheddars, cereal bars and a bumper bag of min rolls—and took one or two of everything. Steve rarely ate snacks himself, but she wouldn't take too many, just in case. She stashed the food in her rucksack along with a couple of juice cartons from the fridge, and then placed the bags and boxes back again with military precision. She grinned. She should apply for a job in MI5.

She was about to retrieve her boots and leave when she spotted the laptop on the dining room table. Why not check her email while she was here? It was more private than the library and cheaper than an internet café, too. She sat down and flipped the laptop open.

There weren't many messages on her webmail. She didn't dare use Outlook because then Steve would know she'd been home as soon as he got his own email. He checked it most days. She answered two messages, then looked at the third. Someone had offered her good money for a very specific set of addresses a few weeks ago; she'd put the information into a word document (with an innocuous title to prevent Steve becoming suspicious) but hesitated about sending it. Money was going to be tight now though, so she found the document, attached it to her email and hit send. Then she deleted the document, just to be on the safe side. Was there anything else she should delete?

第十章

羅拉小心翼翼地打開了後門，按理史堤夫不應該會在這裡，他應該去了上班。但她還是需要確定一下。她脫下靴子放在外面的台階上，穿著襪子放輕腳步在房子裡走了一圈。

好吧，安全了，他不在，工作服也不在。她從她的背包中拉出一個手提包，塞滿了衣服。然後她去了洗手間，櫃內是一個袋子，她可以保證，史堤夫不會去看，因為只會看到滿滿都是衛生棉條。她摸索著底部，拿出一個衛生棉條盒子，並在裡面拿出一卷十元的紙幣，是為了今天而準備的。

下一步是廚房，她從櫥櫃拿出所以大包裝的薯片、迷你切德乾酪、穀物棒和一個特大裝的小卷，每款都拿了一或兩小包。史堤夫很少吃零食，但她也不會帶太多，只是拿來以防萬一。她把食物和從冰箱拿的兩包紙盒果汁一起放進背包，然後剩下的就用軍事精確度來放回櫥櫃內。她咧嘴笑了，她應該可以申請到軍情五處工作。

她準備穿回靴子離開的時候，她發現筆記本電腦在餐桌上。為何不在這裡檢查一下電子郵件呢？這裡比圖書館和網吧更私隱，而且便宜得多。她坐了下來，翻開筆記本電腦。

她的網絡郵箱不是有很多的郵件。她不敢使用電郵軟件，因為史堤夫收到自己的電子郵件，就會知道她在家。他大部分的日子都會檢查郵箱。她回覆了兩封郵件，然後看著在第三封。有人在幾個星期前，提出一個很好的價錢來買一些非常具體的地址，她把那些資料轉換成文字檔（改了一個無關痛癢的標題，以防止史堤夫懷疑），但在發送前猶豫了。但現在她的錢將會很緊張，所以她找出那個文件，貼到她的電子郵件上並點擊發送。隨後，她把文件刪除掉，只為了安全起見。還有別的她要刪除嗎？

她皺起了眉頭，史堤夫很少把文件保存在筆記本電腦上，但是這個不是她的。「井然簡介」，她不應該，但是...

她眼睛掃描了一下文件檔，有一整頁的。用戶名、出生日期、年齡範圍廿三至廿五歲、最喜歡的電視節目...「噢，我的天啊。認真的嗎？」她大聲地說。為什麼他完成了最繁複的部分，但又不發送出去呢？

She frowned. Steve didn't often save documents on the laptop, but this wasn't hers. 'MM Profile'. She shouldn't, but...

Her eyes scanned down the document—God, there were pages of it. Username, date of birth, age range 23-35, favourite TV shows... "Oh my God. Seriously?" she said out loud. Why had he gone to all this trouble but not sent it off?

She looked at her watch. Steve wouldn't be back for ages yet, even if he was on a short shift. She brought up the Methodical Matches website and logged in using the username Steve had thoughtfully noted. A-ha: 'profile status: incomplete'. She split the screen so she could see Steve's completed form at the same time, and started copying and pasting. She was tempted to change the odd detail to something outrageous, but decided not to. She wanted it to get some interest.

Perhaps a few dates would keep him off her back for a while.

Derek. She said it a few times, but it didn't get any better. You could quote Shakespeare's line about 'a rose by any other name would smell as sweet' as much as you liked, but there was no denying that your opinion of someone was swayed by their name. It wasn't fair, but it was a fact. Some people out there—people who knew delightful Dereks—probably thought Derek was a wonderful name, perfectly capable of conjuring up a man 'sexy, suave, great with kids and a dab hand at cooking, who independently remembers and marks their mother's birthday but is in no way tied to her apron strings'.

In Rebecca's mind, however, Dereks were the polar opposite of this ideal hero. Dereks were overly-skinny, slightly stooped contestants for 'most neglected hair' awards, sporting glasses seemingly picked for their inability to flatter the human face. In the winter they wore worn out poo-brown cords and hideously baggy, knitted-by-their-mother jumpers that had seen better days twenty years ago, swapping to knee-length beige shorts, mid-shin length socks and brown sandals in the summer. So she was almost too scared to click on the link to Derek's profile photo, because she'd had a bad day and wasn't in a rush to have her worst fears realised. She braced herself with a large glass of wine first.

Wow. Derek was a bit of a hunk. Muscles—large enough to impress but without giving him that deformed, out-of-proportion look she hated—stretched the sleeves of his t-shirt in a pleasing manner, and there was the hint of a six pack, which made perfect sense with those arms. He had sandy, spiky hair, broad shoulders

她看了看手錶，史堤夫應該短時間內不會回來，即使他今天是上短班。她打開了井然配對網站，使用史堤夫的用戶名來登錄，仔細地看了一遍。呀...啊，「個人資料狀態：不完整」。她把視窗縮小並排，這樣她就可以同時看到史堤夫的文件，並開始複製和貼上。她很想將那些奇怪的細節改成駭人的東西，但最後決定了不這麼做，她希望它真的會有用。

也許幾個約會可以讓他遠離她一會兒。

德瑞克。她讀了幾次，但也好像沒有好了點。如果你喜歡，你可以引述莎士比亞的名句「玫瑰不叫玫瑰，依然芳香如故。」，但也無可否認，你會因為他們的名字而動搖。這不公平，但卻是事實。那裡有些人認識很討人喜歡的德瑞克們，大概都認為德瑞克是一個美妙的名字，完全會令人聯想到男人的「性感、風流倜儻，對孩子有愛心和烹飪能手，會自發地記低其母親的生日，但又並不是因為是過於依賴母親。」

但是在麗貝卡的心中，德瑞克是跟這個理想的英雄截然相反。德瑞克是一個過於消瘦，並微微駝背的，是「最不重視頭髮」獎的參賽者，運動眼鏡看起來也遮掩不了平坦的臉。在冬天，他們穿著破舊、像便便的褐色和寬大得嚇人的線衫，是母親織的，那至少已經穿了二十年。在夏季會換上米色及膝短褲，中脛長襪子和棕色的涼鞋。所以她很害怕去打開鏈接去看德瑞克的個人資料照片，因為今天已經夠糟糕了，而且她並不急於去令可怕的事情出現。她準備先去喝一大杯酒。

哇。德瑞克是一位猛男。大塊肌肉足以令她留下深刻的印象，但並沒有令他變形，她討厭看上去不合比例的。他的汗衫那彈性的衣袖令人賞心悅目，還有隱隱約約的六塊肌肉，是非常屬害的武器。他有沙色、高低不平的頭髮，寬闊的肩膀和一個友好的笑容。當然，也許他是很養眼，但然後沒有太出眾的智慧，否則電腦應該不會配對他們，不是嗎？無論她對蛇人有多不安，但肯定他有足夠智慧。

信息是簡短和親切。

嗨，麗貝卡。

今天早上你現出在我的熱門配對列表上，我真的很喜歡你的相片（你的頭髮很美麗！）。想見個面嗎？迪恩僅致（我的朋友都這樣叫我，我討厭德瑞克！）

她一直都知道網絡約會是會有命中和不命中的機會。畢竟，在世界最好的資料配對並不等於人與人之間就可以起化學作用。但直到她的第一次約會，並沒有出現什麼「不正確」而是「完全讓人不寒而慄」。但凱文是正確的，她必須再嘗試一次，而且德瑞克–應該是迪恩，看起來很適合，她點擊回覆。

and a friendly smile. Of course, perhaps eye-candy was all he was, but then he couldn't be too intellectually superior, otherwise the computer wouldn't have matched them. Would it? Whatever her qualms about the Snake Man, he had certainly been intelligent enough for her.

The message was short and sweet.

Hi Rebecca

You came through on my hot matches list this morning and I really like your picture (you have gorgeous hair!). Would you like to meet up? Regards, Dean (that's what my friends call me. I hate Derek!)

She'd always known that there would be hits and misses with internet dating. After all, the best profile matching in the world didn't mean there would be the right chemistry between people. But until her first date, it hadn't occurred to her that 'not right' might be 'downright creepy'. But Kevin was right, she had to give it another try, and Derek—or rather Dean—looked pretty fit. She hit reply.

'Are you free on Saturday? What about lunch at Frisconti's? It's on Parson Street.'

His reply pinged back almost instantly. 'Great. Just looked it up, I love Italian. 1pm?'

'1p.m. is fine, but not sure you'll find a parking space nearby.'

'Thanks for the heads-up. Look forward to seeing you Saturday.'

As she walked towards the restaurant on Saturday, she couldn't help looking at her reflection in shop windows as she passed. She hoped she'd got it right. This was the trouble with internet dating; there was so much pressure when it was a first meeting and a first date all rolled into one. She hadn't realised what how tense she would feel each time, although she'd never been keen on blind dates and never agreed to any suggested by well-meaning friends.

She preferred to meet people in a natural way, even if it was spotting them at the edge of a crowd and deciding that by the end of the evening she'd like to know them better. There was a whole language of eye contact and subtle signals that let you show you were interested, and told you they were too. But then if meeting

「你週六有空嗎？在法斯高蒂餐廳吃個午餐如何？就在帕森街。」

他的回覆幾乎立刻就彈了出來。「太好了，我剛好在看電郵，我喜歡意大利餐。下午一點好嗎？」

「下午一點很好，但不知道你在附近能否找到停車位。」

「感謝你的提醒。期待星期六看到你。」

週六當她在去餐廳的途中，她忍不住看著自己在商店櫥窗反射的倒影。她希望這樣打扮沒有問題。這就是網絡約會麻煩的地方，第一次見面和第一次約會在同一時間發生，真是很大壓力。她不知道每一次她究竟會有多緊張，雖然她從來不贊成相親，亦從沒有答應過朋友熱心的介紹。

她寧願自然而然去地遇上一個人，即使要在擁擠的人群中搜尋，而且可能到了最後才知道結果，但她至少可以了解他。眼睛接觸所發出的訊息和微妙信號，可以表達出你對他有意思，也知道他是否一樣。她只是覺得很遺憾，如果自然而然的方式對她有用的話，她當初就不會轉到互聯網來。

只差幾步就到法斯高蒂餐廳。她深吸了一口氣，打開了大門。不入虎穴，焉得虎子。

談話過程很流暢，酒也喝得很暢快。這是非常好。

迪恩是個很出色的伙伴，甚至比他的照片更好看。他有自信，機智幽默，對任何傳統或是不同口味的咖啡都沒有絲毫不安，更沉迷於有風味、泡沫或全脂牛奶的款式。麗貝卡放心了，知道如果之後再有任何約會的話，她的巧克力碎灑也安全了。迪恩顯然是一個肉桂男子，當麗貝卡說她烤蘋果和肉桂片的時候，他給了她一個迷人而調皮的笑容。

「太好了。我急不及待想要試試。」

她的肚子有點欣喜地跳動著。她可能對做法已經生疏了，但肯定這個是重要的暗示，他想再次見到她嗎？而且這個建議，可能是要到她家裡，似乎很…親密。更重要的是，她意識到，她很開心也很期待可以再次見到他。

他似乎真的對她的工作感到興趣，並對她的成就留下深刻印象。他也熱切地談到自己的工作，而且並不自負，蛇人一定要改善一下。迪恩頭腦很冷靜，而且獨立，履行到自己的生活，很熱衷與別人分享，是特別喜歡，她更正。因為聽起來他好像有很多朋

people in a natural way had been working for her, she thought regretfully, she wouldn't have turned to the internet in the first place.

Frisconti's was just a few steps away. She took a deep breath and opened the door. Nothing ventured, nothing gained.

The conversation flowed. The wine flowed. This was going amazingly well.

Dean was excellent company and even better looking than his photo. He was confident, he was witty, and he had no qualms whatsoever about ruining the pure heritage or taste of coffee by indulging in flavoured, frothy or full milk versions. Rebecca relaxed, safe in the knowledge that if any subsequent dates involved imbibing coffee, her chocolate sprinkles were safe. Dean was a cinnamon man apparently, and when Rebecca mentioned that she baked a mean apple and cinnamon slice, he had given her a charming, cheeky smile.

"Great. I can't wait to come round and try it."

Her stomach had done a delighted little flutter at that. Out of practice she might be, but surely that was a major hint he'd like to see her again? And the suggestion that might be at her house seemed quite... intimate. Even more significantly, she realised that she was happy at the prospect of seeing him again, too.

He seemed genuinely interested in her work and impressed by what she'd achieved, and talked enthusiastically about his own work without being patronising. A definite improvement on snake-man there. Dean was level-headed. Independent. Fulfilled in his own life, but keen to share it with someone else. Well a special someone else, she amended, because it sounded like he had plenty of friends. Hooray! Not a recluse. It sounded like they all spent a lot of time at his stepfather's farm, where Dean kept his two horses.

"So your friends ride too?" she leaned forward, smiling.

"God, yes! Nearly all of them, they're horse mad. Mark's horse—he calls it Ninja, would you believe, it's black—" he rolled his eyes and she chuckled,"— has gone lame. It's going to be out of action for a while, so I've lent him Salt."

"Salt's your grey mare, you said?"

友。萬歲！他不是一個隱士。聽起來他們都花了很多時間在他繼父的農場裡，迪恩在那裡養了兩匹馬。

「所以，你的朋友都會騎馬嗎？」她俯身向前，微笑著。

「天啊，沒錯！幾乎所有人都會，他們都是馬癡。馬克的馬，他叫牠忍者，你相信嗎？是一隻黑色的...」他翻了翻眼睛，她呵呵地笑，「牠是跛腳的。已經有一段時間不便行動，所以我借了鹽巴給他。」

「鹽巴是你灰色的母馬？你剛才說的。」

「這是正確的。」他的嘴暗藏著笑容。「你知道這是意味著她是白色的嗎？」

她咧嘴一笑。「是的，我不是馬的專家，我知道就這麼多。」

「太好了。我想我應該注意一下，不是每個人都能意識到。」

「你覺得我是一個典型的城市人。」她戲弄地說。

他笑了。「我也是，在一周內。」

「我猜辣椒是不是灰色的嗎？」

「不，我的大傢伙是非常深的赤褐色。他看起來幾乎是黑色，直到你看到牠跟忍者對比。」他喝光了他的酒。「你下個週末應該要一起來跟和他們見面。」

「誰？你的朋友或你的馬？」麗貝卡笑了起來。

「都是！」他爽朗地笑著。「人與野獸一樣，他們都會在那裡，在酒吧外見面。」

「你酒吧外見面？所有的馬呢？你在那裡找到了一個很通融的店主！」

「每兩星期，這是一個傳統，我們也是在那裡跟獵犬碰面。店主確實很好，一直都是。」

麗貝卡的腦袋因為他的說話而半凍結了，最後勉強地說道，「獵犬？」她有氣無力地說。

「是的，獵犬。沒有他們，去打獵就會毫無意義！」他笑了。「馬有自己的優良本能，但他們敵不過小個頭的獵犬，尤其是嗅覺方面。」

「所以，你會去打獵？」她的聲音出奇地保持平靜。

"That's right." A smile lurked round his mouth. "You do know that means she's white, don't you?"

She grinned. "Yes, I'm no horse expert but I do know that much."

"Great. I thought I should check, not everyone realises."

"You think I'm a typical townie," she teased.

He laughed. "So am I, during the week."

"And I'm guessing Pepper isn't a grey?"

"No, my big fella is a really dark bay. He almost looks black, until you see him against Ninja." He drained his wine. "You should come along next weekend and meet them."

"Who, your friends or your horses?" Rebecca laughed.

"Both!" He smiled broadly. "Man and beast alike, they'll all be there, meeting outside the pub."

"You meet outside a pub? With all the horses? That's one accommodating landlord you've found there!"

"Every fortnight. It's a tradition, that's where we meet the hounds. The landlord does well enough out of it, both before and after."

Rebecca's brain had frozen halfway through his sentence, barely registering the end of it. "Hounds?" She said faintly.

"Yes, hounds. A bit pointless going hunting without them!" he chuckled. "Horses have got fine instincts of their own, but they're no match for a fine pack of beagles when it comes to a sense of smell."

"So you go hunting?" Her voice was still calm. Miraculously.

He nodded. "The best way to give a horse real exercise, great combination of flat gallop and fences. It doesn't do me any harm either. It's the best thigh workout known to man!" he laughed, refilling both their glasses, and winked. "Or woman!"

She stared at him blankly. "And the hounds, I suppose they're chasing a, a—"

"Fox? God, of course! None of this poncey dummy scent nonsense, if you've got the horses and the hounds out there working, what the devil's the point in not ridding the countryside

他點點頭。「這是讓馬兒真正鍛煉的最好方法，馳騁和障礙賽的完美結合。牠們不會令我受傷。這是對男人來說一個最好的大腿鍛煉！」他笑了，斟滿了他們的水杯，眨了下眼睛。「對女人也是！」

她茫然地盯著他。「獵犬，我以為牠們會追逐...」

「狐狸？上帝，當然了！別胡說牠們是造作的蠢貨，如果你已經有了馬和獵犬，魔鬼的主意就不是想趕走農村的害蟲嗎？那些假狩獵是多麼噁心的浪費資源。還不如把狗拿下，這是一種對牠們的智慧和生育的侮辱。」

她吞嚥了一下，不太相信這些令事情有了個災難性逆轉。「你不覺得會有更好的方法來控制狐狸群嗎？」

「天啊，沒有。這可以讓很多人就業，而且是傳統的就業機會，一方面，就是那些笨蛋誰認為是很殘忍，然後他們就在大口大口地吃鹿肉，或牛肉，他們令我作嘔，他們真的是血淋淋的偽君子！他們根本沒有理解現實情況。」他深深地喝了一口。

「我認為抗議者很理解死亡的殘酷，」麗貝卡冷冷地說。「以及狐狸在牠們的最後一刻感到的恐懼和絕望。總言之這就是我一直在活動中爭取的。」

迪恩臉色發白，他拿著的杯子停止他的嘴前。「活動？你的意思是...」

「我是一個反狩獵抗議者？笨蛋？」她從手袋中拿出她的錢包，沒有看他一眼，掏出二十元的紙幣。「天啊，是的。」她知道她的模仿技巧很刻薄，但她控制不了自己。

「呃，這...這很好。很顯然你不是笨蛋。每個人都應該為他們所相信的東西站出來，不是嗎？每件事情總有不同的觀點與角度。」

「我恐怕我不會同意。對於我來說，在這個問題上的就只有一個角度。看不起手無寸鐵的動物對死亡有不必要的留戀和痛苦。」她站了起來，把大衣放在她的手臂上。「聽起來反正就是你不會真的尊重其他人的看法。」她把二十元放在桌子上。

「等等，麗貝卡，我...我的意思是，我們剛才還好好的...」

「是的，我們是。很奇怪，我真是一個笨蛋。但我不是一個偽君子，我沒有吃鹿肉或牛肉。」她緊緊地微笑著和盡量保持所謂的禮貌。「相信我，我很失望你令到事情進展到這個地步，有誰想到一句說話可以毀了整個晚上呢？」

「但是，這重要嗎？我們可以不談論它。」他的眼睛閃過一絲希望。

of some vermin? Such a disgusting waste of resources, those dummy hunts. Might as well put the dogs down, it's an insult to their intelligence and their breeding."

She swallowed, not quite believing the disastrous turn the conversation had taken. "You don't think there are better ways to control the fox population?"

"God, no. This keeps lots of people in employment, traditional employment, for one thing, and all those lame-brains who go on about it being cruel—and then sink their teeth into a nice piece of venison, or veal, come to that—they sicken me, they really do. Bloody hypocrites! They've no grip on the reality of the situation." He drank deeply.

"I think what the protesters have a grip on is the cruelty of the death," said Rebecca coldly. "The fear and desperation the foxes feel in their last moments. "That's what I've always written about when I've campaigned, anyway."

Dean paled and his glass stopped halfway to his mouth. "Campaigned? You mean—"

"That I'm an anti-hunt protester? A lame-brain?" she took her purse out of her handbag, not looking at him, and pulled out a £20 note. "God, yes." She knew that bit of mimicry was bitchy, but she couldn't help herself.

"Er, that's... that's fine. Obviously you're not a lame-brain. Everyone has to stand up for what they believe in, don't they? There's always room for more than one point of view."

"I have to disagree, I'm afraid. For me, there's only room for one point of view on this issue. The one that despises unnecessarily lingering, painful deaths for defenceless animals." She stood up, her coat over her arm. "And by the sound of it, you don't really have that much respect for anyone else's view anyway." She laid the £20 note on the table.

"Look, Rebecca, I—I mean, we were getting on so well—"

"Yes we were. Surprising, really, lame brain that I am. Not a hypocrite by the way, I don't eat venison or veal." She smiled tightly and-ever-so-politely. "Believe me when I say I'm as disappointed at how things have turned out as you are. Who would have thought that one sentence could ruin a whole evening?"

"But does this have to matter? We can agree not to talk about it." A tiny glimmer of hope sparked in his eyes.

在其他情況下，這種希望會奇妙地安撫了她的自尊心，她認為，但不是現在。「這不會改變的事實，你所做的事完全違背我的原則。我不能忽視它。」她皺起了眉頭。「不像你。你為什麼不在你的個人資料上說你會狩獵？這本來可以省回我們的時間。那裡應該有特別問到有關『道德和觀點』之類的東西。」

「我知道，我有啊！」他看上去真的很困惑。　「這就是為什麼我很驚訝你的反應。」

麗貝卡搖搖頭。「我開始認為那家公司根本是沒用的。」

他遺憾地點點頭。「他們似乎喜歡配對兩個極端的人。我上次約會的那個人討厭意大利和中國食物。而我就很少吃其他別的東西。」

「這聽起來很熟悉。」她嘆了口氣，她推回她的椅子。「很開心可以認識你，迪恩。對不起，我不是你預期的。」

「不，你很好，我的意思是...非常好，」他有點不知所措。「但很明顯我們不是很匹配。我希望你在下一個約會時運氣會更好。」

這是不太可能，她離開時在想。因為不會再有下一個約會。

In other circumstances, that eagerness would have been fantastically flattering for her ego, she thought. Not now. "That wouldn't change the fact that you do something that's completely against my principles. I can't ignore it." She frowned. "Unlike you. Why didn't you say you were into hunting on your profile? It would have saved both of us time. It specifically asked about things like this under 'ethics and viewpoints'."

"I know, and I did!" He looked genuinely perplexed. "That's why I was surprised by your reaction."

Rebecca shook her head. "I'm starting to think that agency couldn't organise a piss-up in a brewery."

He nodded ruefully. "They do seem to like matching polar opposites. My last date hated Italian food, and Chinese. I rarely eat anything else."

"That sounds familiar." She sighed as she pushed her chair in. "It was interesting to meet you, Dean. Sorry I wasn't what you were expecting."

"No, you were fine, I mean I... more than fine," he floundered. "But obviously we're not a good match. I hope you have better luck with your next date."

That wasn't very likely, she thought as she left. Because there wasn't going to be a next date.

不需要此页

Chapter Eleven

"Steve Reynolds?"

Steve, busy cleaning a sticky nozzle on the coffee machine, turned back to the counter with a smile. "Yes?" He took in the uniforms, and behind them, the craning necks and curious faces of all the customers, including Kevin and Rebecca. Not surprising. He didn't think the man and woman in front of him were here for a latte and an Eccles cake, somehow. They didn't usually get police officers in Tony's. "How can I help?"

"I'm Sergeant Duffy," said the male officer, and this is Sergeant Peebles." We've just got a few questions, if that's okay. Is it alright if we talk here? It will only take a minute."

"Of course." This would be about the robbery along the road last week he thought, watching Sergeant Peebles flip open a notebook. The police had phoned him afterwards, but finding out that he'd seen so little, they'd said they probably wouldn't have any more questions, as they had far better witnesses. Obviously they'd changed their minds.

"We're looking for Laura Reynolds. Is she still living with you, at—" he glanced down briefly at Sergeant Peebles' notepad, "—53 Dreadnought Road?"

Steve's stomach hit the floor. "Er... I'm not sure."

The sergeant raised his eyebrows. "You're not sure?"

He flushed. "Sorry, yes, I live at 53 Dreadnought Road but I think she's moved out. She's taken a lot of her belongings." back."

"I take it you parted on unfriendly terms?"

"You could say that, yes."

"And when did you last speak to her?"

第十一章

「史堤夫．雷諾茲？」

史堤夫正忙著打掃咖啡機上粘手的噴嘴，面帶微笑地轉身回到櫃檯前。「你是嗎？」他們穿著制服，而在他們身後，所有的客戶，其中包括凱文和麗貝卡都伸長脖子並展示出好奇的臉孔。這並不出奇因為在他面前的男女，應該不是來買拿鐵咖啡和埃克爾斯蛋糕的，不知什麼緣故，警察通常不會出現在東尼的咖啡店。「我有什麼可以幫忙嗎？」

「我是達菲警長，」男的那位說，「這是皮伯斯警長。我們只是有幾個問題，如果可以的話。我們可以在這裡說幾句嗎？只需要一分鐘時間。」

「當然可以。」看著皮伯斯警長翻開了筆記本，他在想，這應該是為了上週公路沿線的搶劫案。警方之前已經打過電話給他，但查不到什麼，因為他看到的不多。而他們說應該不會再有任何問題，因為他們已找到更好的證人。但很明顯現在改變了主意。

「我們正在尋找羅拉．雷諾茲。她是不是跟你一起生活，在…」他低頭短暫地看了看皮伯斯警長的筆記本，「…無畏艦道五十三號嗎？」

史堤夫的肚子好像突然被重擊了。「呃…我不肯定。」

警長揚起了眼眉。「你不肯定？」

他滿臉通紅。「對不起，是的，我是住在無畏艦道五十三號，但她已搬走了，她把很多東西都拿走了。」

「我想你的意思是指你們並不是很和睦？」

「你可以這樣說，是的。」

「你最後一次跟她說話是什麼時候嗎？」

「上週二。」

"Last Tuesday."

Sergeant Peebles was scribbling away. What was she finding to write about? Steve wondered. He'd barely said anything. He took a deep breath, dropping his eyes. His knuckles were white around the cloth he still held and he made a conscious effort to relax and unclench his hands a little.

"And did you speak to her in person last Tuesday, or was it over the phone?"

"In person."

"Has she called or texted you since?"

"No. She hasn't answered my calls to her mobile either."

"Okay, and can I just verify that since she left your home you haven't seen her at all, or had any indication of her whereabouts, activities or who she has been with—via someone else who knows her, for instance?"

"That's correct. I've called a couple of people she knows, but they claim they've not seen her or heard from her either."

"We'll need the details of the people you contacted. Sergeant Peebles?"

She gave him a sympathetic smile. "Name first, then address, then phone number, if you don't mind."

"Of course." He rattled off the names of the two ex-colleagues of Laura's. "If they're telling the truth, then God knows where she's gone. It's like she's disappeared off the face of the earth."

"We're fairly sure that's not the case, sir. We think she may have been involved in criminal activity."

Steve braced his hands on the counter, hanging his head. "I daren't ask what." His voice was low.

"We can't tell you anyway, sir. Not until we've confirmed a few things," said the officer gently. "I'm sorry, I understand this isn't welcome news."

"No, it isn't."

"Well thank you for your help, sir. We need to follow up some enquiries, but we'll probably have to speak to you again. Will you

皮伯斯警長在抄寫。她發現了什麼需要抄下來嗎？史堤夫很想知道。但他幾乎沒有說什麼，只他深吸了一口氣，垂下了眼睛。他看到自己拿著布的手指關節都發白了，他有意識地努力放鬆自己，鬆開緊握著的手一點點。

「你最後在星期二跟她說話時，是跟她本人還是通過電話？」

「本人。」

「她之後有打電話或發短信給你嗎？」

「沒有。我甚至打她的手機，她都沒有接聽。」

「好吧，我只是確認一下，自從她離開你的家，你再沒有見過她，或有任何跡象顯示她的行踪、活動、或她有跟她認識的人在一起，比如誰？」

「完全正確。我打過電話給她認識的幾個人，但他們都聲稱從來沒見過她或聽過她的消息。」

「我們需要你聯絡過的人的詳細資料。皮伯斯警長？」

她給了他一個同情的微笑。「首先是姓名，然後地址、電話號碼，如果你不介意的話。」

「當然。」他給了兩位羅拉前同事的名字。「如果他們說的是實話，那麼，上帝才知道她去哪兒了。她就像在地球表面消失了。」

「我們相當肯定，並不是這樣，先生。我們認為她可能有份參與犯罪活動。」

史堤夫的手緊靠在櫃檯上來支撐著自己身體，垂下了頭。「我不敢問是什麼。」他的聲音很低。

「無論如何，我們也不能告訴你，先生。直到我們已經確認一些事情，」警長輕輕地說。「對不起，我知道這不是一個好消息。」

「對，不是。」

「嗯，謝謝你的協助，先生。我們需要先追查一些事情，但我們可能會再找你問話。今天晚上你會在家嗎？」

「會的。」

「那我們會再與你聯繫的。」他點點頭，向門口走去了。

be at your home address this evening?"

"Yes."

"We'll contact you there, then." He nodded and made for the door.

Sergeant Peebles lingered a moment, packing her notebook back in her pocket. "Thanks again for your time, Mr. Reynolds. Sorry to disturb you at work."

"No problem." He stared after her as she left. His stomach felt strange.

Tony approached him hesitantly. "Steve, I just—"

His stomach gave an almighty heave. He pushed past Tony and just made it to the staff toilet in time. What would his parents have said if they could see what Laura had become under his guardianship? He retched again until there was nothing left and then sank on to the toilet seat, holding his head in his hands. This was his worst nightmare come true.

Rebecca's hand hit the glass door with some force and she sailed through as it swung back on its hinges. It was the same girl behind reception. Nicola, the patronising one. Oh goody.

Nicola looked up and gave her an agonisingly wide smile, her Minnie-Mouse-pink lip-sticked lips a fluorescent slash in her tanned face.

"Good morning, how can I help?" Her brow wrinkled as she looked up at her. "Ah! Rebecca, isn't it?"

Rebecca hadn't expected that, and it threw her for a moment. "Yes, Rebecca Maynard."

"What can I do for you today, Rebecca?"

Rebecca rested the heels of her hands on the reception desk and Nicola pulled back a little, her smile slightly less certain.

"I went on my second date last night."

Nicola clapped her hands together, obviously deciding she'd read the body language wrong. "That's marvellous! So the relationship's progressing!"

皮伯斯警長徘徊了一會兒，然後把筆記本放進口袋裡。「再次感謝你的時間，雷諾茲先生。很抱歉打擾你的工作。」

「沒關係。」當她離開時，他凝視著她的背面。他的胃有些奇怪的感覺。

東尼走近他欲言又止，「史堤夫，我只是…」

他的胃劇烈地翻騰起來。他推開東尼並衝向職員洗手間。他的父母曾經說過，他們已經能看到在他的監護下羅拉會變成怎樣？他再次嘔吐，直到胃裡什麼都沒剩，然後坐在馬桶上，用手抱著頭。最可怕的噩夢居然成真了。

麗貝卡用手大力地撞向玻璃門，在它再次關上前順利穿進去了。又是同一個女人坐在接待處後面。妮科拉，那個刻薄的人，好極了！

妮科拉抬起頭來，給她一個大大的笑容，她的米妮老鼠唇膏畫了一個閃閃發亮的缺口在她曬得黑黑的臉上。

「早上好，我有什麼可幫你嗎？」她的眉頭緊皺，她抬頭看著她。「啊！麗貝卡，是不是？」

麗貝卡沒有預期她會記得自己，她停頓了一會兒。「是的，麗貝卡．梅納德。」

「我今天能為你做什麼，麗貝卡？」

麗貝卡把手肘放在接待處的桌子上，而妮科拉稍稍退後了一點，笑容也稍微少了一些。

「我去了我的第二次約會，在昨晚。」

妮科拉拍一拍手，顯然她錯誤閱讀了身體語言。「這真的是了不起！關係有進展啊！」

她的反應真的夠驚喜但又實在令人感到不安。究竟實際上井然配對成功配對過多少次？真是遺憾要讓妮科拉的泡沫破滅了。

「不，我的意思不是與同一個人的第二次約會。我已經跟兩個不同的男人去過兩個不同的約會了，而我不期望再有下一個。」

妮科拉臉像升降機一樣直線下滑。「哦，千萬別這樣說！我肯定，你的清單上會有更多熱門的配對呢？」她開始奮力地打字，但麗貝卡伸出一隻手。

There was an element of surprise in her reaction that was unnerving. How much success had Methodical Matches actually achieved? What a shame that she was about to burst Nicola's bubble.

"No, I don't mean a second date with the same person. I've had two single dates with two different men, and I don't expect to be having any more."

Nicola's face dropped like an elevator in freefall. "Oh, don't say that! Surely there are more hot matches on your list?" She began to type furiously, but Rebecca stuck out a hand.

"Stop—please. Yes, there are more hot matches, but I don't think I want to meet any of them."

"Well you can hardly expect to meet Mr Right straight away," said Nicola, half-chastising, half-wheedling. "Just give it a bit lon—"

"I didn't. Expect to meet Mr Right straight away, that is. I'm not stupid. But I also didn't expect to be matched with people who have nothing in common with me."

Nicola looked aghast. "Nothing? At all? Really?"

Rebecca squirmed. "Well okay, not nothing at all. The first man liked my favourite author but it's his guilty secret, because her stuff's so low brow, apparently. He barely has a social life, hates the food I love, calls his Mum Mother, and generally comes across as a male chauvinist Victorian relic. Oh, and he's—" a tight-arse, she was about to say, "— a penny pincher too."

"Oh." Nicola looked downcast. "What about, er, the second match?"

Rebecca counted points off on her fingers. "Good-looking. Intelligent. Good sense of humour. Loves his career. Didn't patronise me because I'm a woman. Loves Italian food, just like me."

Nicola's face brightened. "Great! But you said none of your matches are any good! This one sounds really promising!"

"You'd think so, wouldn't you? Except that he spends his weekends in Surrey with his friends and his stepfather, seeing how many defenceless foxes he can slaughter before it's time to come back to London for work on Monday morning."

"I take it you don't?"

「停止...請。是的，會有更多熱門配對，但我不認為我想跟他們見面了。」

「嗯，你也很難期望馬上可以找到真命天子吧，」妮科拉半怪責半哄騙地說。「只要再給多一點...」

「我沒有想過真命天子馬上就出現在我面前。我並不愚蠢。不過，我也沒有期望過要跟一個與我沒有任何共同之處的人配對。」

妮科拉看上去驚呆了。「沒有？完全沒有？真的嗎？」

麗貝卡扭動著。「好吧好吧，不是完全沒有。第一個男人，他也喜歡我最喜歡的作家，但那好像是一個令他覺得有罪的秘密，顯然是因為她寫的東西是如此低俗。他幾乎沒有社交生活，討厭我喜歡的食物，叫他的媽媽做母親，大致上是於維多利亞時代的一具盲目愛國主義的男性遺跡。噢，他是...」緊屁股，她差點就說了出來，「...吝嗇鬼。」

「哦。」妮科拉有點垂頭喪氣。「那麼，呃，第二個呢？」

麗貝卡算著手指。「好看、有智慧、幽默、熱愛自己職業。沒有自命不凡，可能因為我是一個女人，喜歡意大利食品，就跟我一樣。」

妮科拉的臉上露出了光彩。「太好了！但是你說你的配對沒一個是好東西！這個聽起來真的大有希望啊！」

「你會這麼認為，是嗎？除他會花整個週末在薩里跟他的朋友和他的繼父，去看有多少手無寸鐵的狐狸可以屠殺，就在他在週一上午回到倫敦工作之前。」

「我想你是不會這樣做嗎？」

麗貝卡冷冷地看著她。「沒有。事實上，我也花了好幾個週末，去參加反殘活動。」

「反殘活動？」

「反對殘忍活動聯盟。」

「我明白了。這可能有點兒問題。」

「你覺得呢？」

Rebecca looked at her coldly. "No. In fact I've spent several weekends campaigning with LACS."

"LACS?"

"The League Against Cruel Sports."

"I see. I suppose that could be a problem."

"You think?"

Nicola blushed, shoulders drooping. "I don't understand. The program's meant to be set up to look at the whole person, to take notice of everything. If it doesn't find a good enough match, an alert should come through. I don't know why it keeps on doing this." She suddenly clamped her lips together.

Rebecca swooped. "Keeps on doing this? You mean it's happening to other people?"

There was a pause, and then Nicola sighed and slumped back in her chair. "Not at first. But you're the third complaint I've had today."

"Maybe someone needs to take a look at your program, then."

"Yes. We are trying our best to resolve the technical problems."

"What happens in the meantime?"

"I can refund your registration fee," said Nicola tentatively. "And extend your trial by a month? We could call this a dummy run."

"Very appropriate."

Nicola winced. "Is that what you'd like me to do?"

Rebecca tapped her fingers on the desk. "I'm just wondering if I can actually put myself through that again. I'm not sure I've got the willpower."

"Please carry on!" Nicola was welling up. "It might be third time lucky. Keep the first date brief—"

"Oh believe me, I've been trying to!"

"—And that way, if you don't get on, there's no harm done. Is there?" Nicola summoned up an encouraging smile.

妮科拉臉一紅，垂下肩膀。「我不明白。該程式的設定是看整個人，看所有東西。如果它沒有找到足夠匹配的東西，應該會有警示。我不知道為什麼它不斷這樣做…」她突然緊閉嘴唇。

麗貝卡俯衝而問，「不斷這樣做？你的意思是，也有發生在其他人身上？」

停頓了一會兒，然後妮科拉頹然地嘆了口氣，坐回到她的椅子上。「一開始沒有。但是，你已經是我今天收到的第三個投訴。」

「也許有人需要去檢查你的程式。」

「是的。我們正在盡力解決技術上的問題。」

「在這期間會發生什麼事？」

「我可以退還註冊費給你，」妮科拉試探性地說。「並延長你的試用期一個月？我們可以稱這個為虛擬運行。」

「非常合理。」

妮科拉退縮了一下。「那麼你希望我這樣做嗎？」

麗貝卡用手指敲在桌子上。「我只是在想，我是不是真的想要再經歷一遍。我不肯定我有如此大的毅力。」

「請堅持！」妮科拉湧了上來。「可能第三次會好運的。保持第一次約會的…」

「噢，相信我，我一直都很努力！」

「這樣一來，如果你不肯嘗試，就不會造成傷害。是這樣嗎？」

妮科拉堆出一個激勵的微笑。

她嘆了口氣。「好吧。我就再試一次。但是，如果第三次也只是一場災難，那就是這樣了。」

妮科拉鼓起掌來。「太好了！我很高興你已經決定堅持下去！我會用電子郵件確認你的退款和延長試用期的安排。」

麗貝卡簡單點了點頭以示回應，然後就離開了。我一定是為了自己的未來而瘋了，或者真的是太心軟。

史堤夫在回家之前，先去了超級市場，然後就直接出去跑步。當他洗完澡，換上舒適的汗衫和牛仔褲之後，他已經餓壞了。他翻

She sighed. "Okay. I'll give it another try. But if my third guy is a disaster, that's it."

Nicola clapped her hands. "Wonderful! I'm so glad you've decided to stick with it! I'll confirm your refund and trial extension by email."

Rebecca nodded briefly in response and left. *Either I'm mad, desperate or too soft for my own good.*

Steve had gone to the supermarket before he came home, then straight out for a run. By the time he'd showered and changed into a comfy t-shirt and jeans, he was ravenous. He nuked a curry ready meal, switched on the laptop and opened his email, taking a mouthful of food.

"Ow!" *Was this really meant to be a Rogan Josh? It was more like Madras.* He went to the kitchen for a lager and took a huge, neutralising gulp. By the time he'd settled himself back at the table, there were 15 unread messages sitting in his inbox. He started to work his way down them, deleting all the spam and invitations to place his first bet free on the best online casino ever. It didn't leave him with that many to read.

He stopped. There were three emails form Methodical Matches. *Strange. He guessed that at least one of them would say something along the lines of 'Hi, we notice you haven't completed your profile yet. Click here to complete it NOW, and start meeting your hot Matches!' But what were the other two?* He clicked on the first one. And frowned.

'Congratulations on completing your profile. Now it's time for us to do the hard work! Sit back, relax and wait for your first Hot Matches email. *You should receive your first Hot Matches email within 24 hours. If you have not received it within 48 hours, please contact us.'

What? He hadn't completed his profile, and he sure as hell hadn't submitted it. It must be an error—yeah, that must be what the next email was about, it was probably an apology. The third one was more than likely to confirm he didn't have a live profile and everything was sorted.

He clicked on the second email. 'Congratulations! Your profile is live and can now be viewed by other clients who can see you in their Hot Matches list. Below are your first Hot Matches!' Underneath were two photographs. One was a dark haired woman

熱了咖哩速凍食品，打開筆記本電腦，開啟了他的電子郵件，塞了滿嘴的食物。

「噢！」這真的是羅根喬希羊肉咖哩嗎？它更像是馬德拉斯咖哩。他走到廚房拿了一罐大裝的啤酒，一飲而盡以中和口中的味道。他重新回到桌前，有十五個未讀信息在他的收件箱中。他開始以他的方式解決它們，首先刪除所有的垃圾郵件和那些邀請他去有史以來最好的網上賭場押上第一個賭注的郵件。之後沒有留下許多要他閱讀的。

他停了下來。這裡有三封郵件來自井然配對的。很奇怪。他猜測，那裡至少有一個郵件會說「嗨，我們注意到你還沒有完成你的個人檔案。請點擊這裡去完成，並開始遇上你的熱門配對！」但是，其他兩個是什麼呢？他點擊開啟了第一個。皺起了眉頭。

「恭喜你完成了個人檔案。現在是時候讓我們為你效勞了！請坐下來，放鬆點，等待你第一個熱門配對的電子郵件。　*你應該會在廿四小時內收到第一個熱門配對的電子郵件。如果你在四十八小時內還沒有收到，請跟我們聯繫。」

什麼？他還沒有完成他的個人檔案，他非常地肯定他沒有提交到。這肯定是個錯誤，對了，下一封郵件肯定是關於這事，它可能是一個道歉。第三個可能是再確認他沒有有效的個人資料檔案，以及問題已經解決了。

他點擊開啟了第二封電子郵件。「恭喜你！你的個人資料已經生效，現在其他客戶可以看到你在他們的熱門配對名單上了。下面是你的第一個熱門配對！」下方的兩張照片。一個是黑頭髮的女人，看上去年紀比史堤夫大一點。根據標題說，她的名字是蘇珊，二十五歲，是一個銀行職員。另一個金髮的叫埃莉諾，她看起來比較年輕，但實際上卻是二十九歲。據說是個教學助理。

他想，還是要徹底地搞清楚，他打開第三個電子郵件，搖搖混亂的頭，也許會解釋這到底是怎麼回事。

但事實並非如此。

「嗨，史堤夫，我是蘇珊，我今天上來看到你在我的熱門配對名單上。我真的很感興趣。請你聯繫我。」

史堤夫看一下時間。下午五時廿四分，運氣好的話，可能仍然在辦公室。他拿起電話，他打了個號碼。

「下午好，井然配對，我是妮科拉，有什麼可以幫到你嗎？」一個顫聲。

哎呀。這個女人發生什麼事？「嗨，我希望你可以幫到我。」

who looked a little older than Steve. According to the caption, her name was Susan, she was 25 and she was a bank clerk. The other was a blonde name Eleanor, who looked younger but was actually 29. A teaching assistant, apparently.

Might as well go the whole hog and open the third email, he thought, shaking his head in confusion. Perhaps it would explain what the hell was going on.

It didn't.

'Hi Steve, I'm Susan and I saw your profile come up today on my Hot Matches. I'm really interested in meeting you. Please get in touch.'

Steve checked the time. 5.24p.m. With any luck, there might still be someone at the office. He punched the number into his phone.

"Good afternoon, Methodical Matchezz, Nicola speaking! How may I help you?" a voice trilled.

Jeez. What was the woman on? "Hi, I hope you can help me—"

"I hope so too!"

Steve cringed. "Er, yes... I registered on your website a while ago but haven't submitted my profile yet—"

"Do you need some help with it? We're always happy for clients to come into the office, if you're local. The questionnaire can seem long-winded, so we're recommending that you print—"

"No, that's fine. I pasted it into a blank document and filled it in there, but—"

"The online submission form timed out on you, didn't it?" she burbled. "We are trying to fix that, but if you bring the form and your completed profile up on your screen, you can cop—"

"No, that's not it," said Steve sharply. He must have made his point this time because he heard a quiet "oh."

"The problem is, I changed my mind about submitting my profile. I haven't submitted it."

Silence. Then Nicola cleared her throat. "That is of course completely your choice sir, you're not under any obligation. Do you want me to cancel your registration?"

「我也希望如此！」

史堤夫覺得有點難為情。「呃，是...我前陣子在你們的網站上註冊了，但還沒有提交我的個人資料。」

「你需要這方面的幫助嗎？我們一直很高興客戶來我們的辦公室，如果你是在本地的話。問卷似乎有點長，所以我們建議你先打印...」

「不，這很好。我把它貼上到一個空白文字檔，並在那裡把它填好，但是...」

「是在線上提交表單時遇到超時問題嗎？」她喋喋不休地說。「我們正在努力修復它，但如果你已在你的屏幕上完成了表格，你就可以貼...」

「不，不是這樣的，」史堤夫嚴厲地說。他現在必須說清楚他的論點，因為他聽到一個安靜的「哦。」一聲。

「問題是，我改變了主意並不打算提交我的個人資料，而且我還沒有提交它。」

沉默片刻，然後妮科拉清了清嗓子。「這當然完全是你的選擇，先生。你沒有任何義務要完成它的。你想讓我幫你取消註冊嗎？」

「不，我的意思是，但是...問題是，你們發了電子郵件給我說，你已經收到我完成的檔案，並放上網站了。」

「可是你剛才說你改變了主意。你的意思是提交後，你改變了主意？」

史堤夫翻了個白眼。雖然她看不到，但這讓他感覺好點。「不，我沒有。」

「你肯定你沒有發送出去？會不會是按錯了？」

「絕對肯定。我甚至沒有開始填寫線上的表格，因為第一次填的時候就出現了超時的情況，我就複製到一個文字檔，就像我剛才說的，我正想複製和貼上它。」

「直到你改變主意。」她疑惑地說。

「是。」他竭力抑制聲音並保持平靜。「直到我改變了主意。」

"No, I mean yes, but... look, the problem is, you've emailed me saying you received my completed profile and it's live on the site."

"But you just said you had changed your mind about submitting it. Did you mean you changed your mind after you submitted it?"

Steve raised his eyes heavenward. She couldn't see it, but it made him feel better. "No, I don't."

"And you're sure you haven't sent it? By mistake?"

"Absolutely sure. I hadn't even started filling out the online form—as soon as it timed out first time round, I copied in into a word document, as I said. I was going to copy and paste it in."

"Until you changed your mind," she said doubtfully.

"Yes." He fought to keep the irritation from his voice. "Until I changed my mind."

"You're sure you didn't paste it into the online form and just forget? Or hit send without realising?"

Steve held the handset away from his ear and stared at it. Took a deep breath. Put it back against his ear.

"Nicola—can I call you Nicola?"

"Yes, of course," she answered, in a tone still filled with sunshine and fluffy bunnies.

Time to make rabbit pie, thought Steve. "Have you seen how long the form is?" he asked. Quiet. Calm.

"Yes, of course—"

"And do you think Nicola, that you yourself could forget copying and pasting that many pages of text into an online form?" A little louder.

She sensed the danger now, she was blustering. "No, er, of course not, I only, er, wondered if—"

"And do you think there's a chance that, having somehow mysteriously forgotten you'd spent hours copying and pasting all that text into the form, you might forget, at the same time, that afterwards you'd clicked on the submit button?"

"It doesn't seem likely, but—"

「你肯定你沒有貼到線上的表格嗎？會不會是忘了呢？或者不由自主地點擊了發送呢？」

史堤夫把手機拿遠耳朵，盯著它。深吸了一口氣，再把它放回耳朵上。

「妮科拉，我可以叫你妮科拉嗎？」

「是的，當然。」她回答的語氣中仍然充滿了陽光，像一隻愚蠢的兔子。

是時間做兔肉餡餅了，史堤夫在想。「你見過表格有多長嗎？」他問。安靜地。平靜地。

「是的，當然...」

「妮科拉那你認為你是不是會忘記，如果你要複製並貼上許多頁的文字到一個線上的表格上呢？」比之前大聲了一點。

現在她感覺到危險了，她叫嚷道。「沒有，呃，當然不是，我只是，呃，想知道如果...」

「那你覺得有機會是，因為鬼使神差你忘記了自己花了幾個小時，複製並貼上所有文字到線上的表格，而你在同一時間也可能忘記了，你點擊了『提交』按鈕嗎？」

「這似乎沒有可能，但...」

「不，沒有。我不是老糊塗，妮科拉，我也沒有患上失憶症或任何種類的精神病。在你問到之前，我要告訴你，我的頭部也沒有曾經有過任何嚴重的碰傷。」

「嗯，這是，這是很好的。」他能聽到她吞了一下口水，並深吸了一口氣。然後，就這樣，愚蠢的兔子又回來了。男孩，她是天生做這份工作的。「哦，親愛的。那麼似乎是電子郵件發送錯誤，對嗎？」

「我覺得這應該是最有可能的解釋吧？」史堤夫說，用最僅僅的一點嘲諷。但有一個奇怪的小疑問是在他的腦海裡閃過。「雖然...」

「是？」

「如果是這樣的情況下，如果電子郵件只是發送錯誤，它似乎很奇怪，因為我之後再收到兩封你們發出的電子郵件。」

「哦。是什麼時候？」

「就跟隨第一個之後。一共三封電郵件，一起發過來的。就在今

"No it doesn't. I'm not senile, Nicola, nor do I suffer from amnesia or any kind of mental illness. I also haven't had any nasty bumps on the head, before you ask."

"Well that's, that's good." He could hear her swallow, and take a deep breath. Then, just like that, the fluffy bunnies were back. Boy, she was made for this job. "Oh dear. It seems like the email has been sent in error then, doesn't it?"

"I think that seems the likeliest explanation, don't you?" said Steve, with the merest trace of sarcasm. But an odd little doubt was nagging at his mind. "Although..."

"Yes?"

"If that's the case—the email's just been sent in error—it does seem strange that I've had two more emails from you."

"Oh. When?"

"Straight after the first one. Three emails, all together. They came through this morning, around 9.30."

"Right." He could hear the frown in her voice. "And were they duplicates of the first one?"

"No, the next one said it was my first Hot Matches email, and the third one was from a lady called Susan, presumably the Susan that came up on the email before. She was asking me for a date."

"Oh, lucky you!" She chirruped. "She must be very keen, that's quick off the mark. She would only have got your details a few hours ago."

"But I haven't submitted my profile, have I! There shouldn't be any Hot Matches. I don't want to go on any dates!"

"No, no, I see." She was quiet for a moment. When she spoke again, the fluffy bunnies had seemingly bolted and he could actually envisage her as a human being. "But really, I don't see. Excuse me asking, but if you didn't want to go on dates, why did you register with a dating website?"

"It was, er, just a whim."

"It must have been a long-lasting whim, if you got all the way through the questionnaire."

Suddenly, he was on the back foot here. "Yes. Look, I did want

天上午九點半左右。」

「沒錯。」他能從她的聲音中聽得出她在皺眉。「是跟第一個完全相同的嗎？」

「不是，下一封是說，這是我的第一個熱門配對電郵，第三封是一個叫蘇珊的女士寄來的，很可能蘇珊就是上一封電郵所說的人。她在邀請我去約會。」

「噢，你真幸運！」她尖聲叫道。「她一定是非常熱衷，快得離譜。她應該是在幾個小時前才看到你的資料呢。」

「但我還沒有提交我的個人資料，沒有！不應該有任何熱門配對。我不想去任何約會！」

「不，不，我明白。」她沉默了片刻。當她再開始說話的時候，那隻愚蠢的兔子逃竄了，他實際上可以見到她變回一個人。「不過說真的，我不明白。對不起，我想問如果你不想去約會，你為

什麼去一個約會網站註冊呢？」

「那是，呃，只是一時心血來潮。」

「那一定是一個很長時間的心血來潮，如果你已經把所有問題都答完。」

突然，他處於不利的境地。「是的。你看，其實我也想去，你知道，約會，和某人見面。但只是現在不是一個好時機。」他斷斷續續地。

「很難得的，是嗎？」他能在她的聲音聽得出笑容。「這就像一對夫婦等待多年，然後開始去建立一個家庭。而他們總是說，等待直到他們有間更大的房子，或者一輛更大的汽車，直到他們搬到一個更好社區，或者他們再過得更好，或者直到他們爸媽的病完全好過來…」她嘆了口氣。「然後有一天，他們發現，他們已經沒有時間了。或者，甚至更殘酷的，我的朋友就發生這種情況，他們發現當初他們沒有要到孩子。而他們已經沒有更多寶貴時間去做任何事情了。」

史堤夫吞嚥了一下，很驚訝居然被她的軼事所感動了。「我明白你的意思，但是…」

「這很有趣，不是嗎？但通常人們總是在他們的生活中最不方便的時候遇到他們的伴侶，往往是最意想不到的方式和地方。」

「有時候，是的，我想。」

停頓。他可以想像她是故意留下一分鐘的寂靜。「你為什麼不嘗試一次，那麼？」她哄著他說。「只是一個約會，又不會傷人

to go, you know, on dates, meet someone. But it's just not a good time right now," he said lamely.

"It rarely is, is it?" He could hear the smile in her voice. "It's like these couples who wait for years to start a family. They always say they'll wait until they get a bigger house, or a bigger car, until they move to a better area, or they're better off, or until their Mum or Dad just gets over this illness..." she sighed. "And then one day they find they've run out of time. Or, the even crueller irony—this happened to friends of mine—they find out they couldn't have children in the first place. And they've left themselves precious little time to do anything about it."

Steve gulped, surprisingly moved by her anecdote. "I see what you mean, but—"

"It's funny, isn't it, but people usually seem to meet their partners at the most inconvenient points in their lives, and often in the most unexpected ways and places, too."

"Sometimes, yes, I guess."

Pause. He could tell she was deliberately leaving it to sink in for a minute. "Why don't you give it a try then?" she coaxed. "Just go on one date. It's not going to hurt, is it? You won't be engaged to her or anything! If there's a lot going on in your life, you can take things slowly. Although sometimes I think someone else in your life is exactly what you need when your life is, well, busy."

She was making sense, reluctant though he was to admit it. His mouth certainly thought so. "I suppose I could give it a go." Have you finally lost it?

"That's the spirit!"

Oh Lord, thought Steve, the bloody bunnies are going to trample me now. Look at them, running down the hill towards me.

"So I'll leave your profile status as live, then, shall I?"

"You might as well—hey, hold on. I mean, thanks for the pep talk – I see your point and it was very good, by the way—"

"Thanks!"

"—but we're no nearer to working out how you got hold of my completed profile. If it is mine, because I can't see for the life of me how that's possible."

的，是嗎？你又不會跟她建立什麼密切關係！如果在你的生活中有很多事情在發生，那麼你可以先慢下來。然而有時候我覺得其實你現在正是需要一些人，尤其在你的生活…嗯…忙的時候。」

她說得很有道理，雖然他不願意去承認。但他的嘴肯定是這麼認為。「我想我可以去一下。」終於輸了？

「就是這種精神！」

哦老天，史堤夫想像到，血腥的兔子現在就要來踐踏我了。看看牠們，正朝我的方向跑下山來。

「所以，我會把你的個人資料留下，可以嗎？」

「你可能，哎，等一下。我的意思是，感謝你一番鼓舞士氣的說話…我明白你的意思而且非常好，順便說一下…」

「謝謝你！」

「但我們還沒解決到你們怎麼會拿到我完成的檔案。如果它是我的，因為我看不到我現時的生活有什麼可能做到。」

「那似乎很奇怪。」

「也許，我的個人資料跟別人的混在一起，如果有的話，那麼我的熱門配對可能就不是那麼熱門了，如果你明白我的意思。」

「好的。我最好還是檢查一下。」

「麻煩你。」

「你的用戶名是什麼？」

他清了清嗓子。「呃，藍眼睛史堤維。這只是鬧著玩。」他覺得有點難為情。

「是嗎？」她含糊地說。他能聽到她敲擊著鍵盤。

史堤夫有點挫敗，感覺需要為自己辯護。「是的，你知道的，就是休.格蘭特的電影《藍眼睛米奇》，我媽媽半個西西里島人，而

電影推出的時侯，她覺得極之有趣。所以她開始叫我藍眼睛史堤維，她有用一點口音和其他的。」

「什麼口音？」

他嘆了口氣。「你有沒有看過《藍眼睛米奇》？」

"It does seem odd."

"Perhaps my details have got mixed up with someone else's, and if they have, my Hot Matches might not be all that hot, if you see what I mean."

"Good point. I'd better check."

"Please."

"What's your username?"

He cleared his throat. "Er, Stevie Blue Eyes. It's a joke." Cringe.

"Is it?" she said vaguely. He could hear her tapping the keyboard.

Steve plunged on, feeling the need to justify himself. "Yes, you know, like the Hugh Grant film—'Mickey Blue Eyes'? My mum was half-Sicilian and when that film came out, she thought it was hilarious. She started to call me Stevie Blue Eyes, you know, she did the accent and everything."

"What accent?"

He sighed. "You haven't seen Mickey Blue Eyes?"

"No, I don't think so."

"Never mind."

"Let's see... yes, the profile's under your username. Steve Reynolds, age 29, Capricorn..." She read out the whole thing, on Steve's insistence. Partly because he couldn't believe that what Nicola had in front of her really was his profile—how could it be? And partly because, once he knew that all the basic details were correct, he still needed to know that the rest were—if even a tiny part had been altered, he wanted to know. Otherwise, God knows who he might end up with. It was a hugely embarrassing experience, but by the end of it, one thing was for sure. It was his profile.

"Which still beggars the question—if you'll pardon my French—how the hell did you get my profile?"

"That's still a mystery, I'm afraid. All I can tell you from this end is that it went on the system yesterday afternoon. Perhaps it was a good Samaritan?"

"What?"

「不，我想是沒有。」

「沒關係。」

「讓我們看看…是的，你的用戶名下的個人資料。史堤夫．雷諾茲，二十九歲，摩羯座…」在史堤夫的堅持下，她讀出了全部資料。部分原因是因為他不敢相信，在妮科拉面前的真的是他的個人資料，這怎麼可能呢？另一部分原因是因為，他要知道所有的基本細節是正確的，他還需要知道剩餘部分被修改了，這也是他想知道的。否則，天也知道他一定會叫停。這是一個非常尷尬的經驗，但結束了之後，有一件事是肯定的，就是這真的是他的個人資料。

「仍然難以解釋的問題，請你會原諒我說髒話，去你的究竟是怎麼弄到我的個人資料？」

「這仍然是一個謎，我恐怕是。為此，我可以告訴你的只是，系統是昨天下午收到的。也許這是一個好心的撒瑪利亞人吧？」

「什麼？」

「也許有人幫你發出去的。一個覺得你的生活需要多一些愛的人。」

「有趣的理論，但沒有人可以存取我的…哦，渾蛋。噢，對不起。」

「你想起了誰嗎？」

「是的，我會殺了她。」

「我敢肯定誰也好，她只是為你的最佳利益著想！」

史堤夫在想，上帝一定要保佑她和她的小兔子，要好好住在妮科拉的世界。「嗯…」

「至少解決你的疑惑了。現在，如果就是這樣，那麼，雷諾茲先生，對不起，但辦公室需要關門了。」

他看了看手錶。下午六時五分。「天哪，很抱歉！我沒有要阻你這麼久的意思。」

「沒問題，我在這裡就是為了這樣。祝你的約會順利！」

「謝謝你。再見。」

一定是羅拉，雖然他一直在想她的動機是無私的，正如妮科拉認為。但他仍然開始建立一個單獨的用戶名和密碼去保護他所有在筆記本電腦上的東西。為什麼他之前沒有想過要這麼做呢？

"Maybe someone else sent it in for you. Someone who thought you needed some love in your life."

"Interesting theory, but nobody else has access to my... oh, bugger. Oh, sorry."

"You've thought of someone?"

"Yes, and I'm going to kill her."

"I'm sure whoever it was only had your best interests at heart!"

Bless her and her bunnies, thought Steve. It must be good to live in Nicola world. "Hmm."

"At least that's your mystery solved. Now, if that's all then, Mr. Reynolds, I'm sorry, but I need to lock up the office."

He looked at his watch. 6.05pm. "God, I'm so sorry! I didn't mean to keep you that long."

"No problem, that's what I'm here for. Good luck with your date!"

"Thanks. Bye."

It must have been Laura, although he doubted her motives had been quite as altruistic as Nicola believed. He started setting up a separate user name on the laptop to password protect all his stuff. Why hadn't he done it before?

Of course, if Laura had discovered that document and filled in his profile, that meant that at some time yesterday, she'd been back to the house – and stayed some considerable time. He wondered what else she'd got up to while she was there. What other nasty surprises he might have in store?

當然，如果羅拉已經發現了該文件，並填寫了他的個人資料，這就是意味著，昨天有一段時間，她曾經回到家中，而且停留了一段相當長的時間。他在想她究竟在這裡還幹了什麼壞事。還會有什麼討厭的驚喜嗎？

Chapter Twelve

"Morning, Rebecca Maynard speaking."

"Ms. Maynard, it's Marcie King."

Ooh, subtle. Don't stoop to using my first name. Fine, if that's the way you want to play it Marcie, but I'm not calling you Ms. "Good morning, Miss. King. What can I do for you?"

"Nothing, thank you," said Marcie crisply. "I was asked to phone you in order to arrange a mutually convenient time to meet the head of the surveying team."

"Yes, Simon said he wanted a meeting this week." Rebecca hoped she sounded breezy, because that's what she was going for.

"If that is Mr. Holland, then yes." Marcie's tone would give a penguin the chills, thought Rebecca.

"Oh sorry, do you not know Simon? I thought everybody did. We go back quite a way. Very easy to work with." That was unworthy of you Rebecca.

"Yes, you seem to go back quite a way with everybody. I'm sure that's very useful."

Bitch! Rebecca seethed. "Well I always find it useful, and more pleasant, to build up good working relationships with people when I can. People skills are just as important in archaeology as technical skills, I find."

"Doubtless that's why you've had fewer papers published than many of your peers," said Marcie smoothly. "You've put your energies into other areas."

"Precisely. It's far more important to me to lead good digs and develop the skills and success of my team, rather than garner personal glory." Rebecca treated the phone to a razor-sharp sarcastic smile down the phone, wishing Marcie could see it. Marcie was obsessed with getting her name, preferably on its

第十二章

「早上好，我是麗貝卡．梅納德，請說。」

「梅納德女士，我是瑪西．京。」

噢，妙極了。不服氣地叫我的姓氏。好吧，如果你要玩，瑪西，就這樣，但我不會叫你做女士：「早上好，京小姐。我可以為你做什麼嗎？」

「沒有，謝謝你，」瑪西清脆地說。「是有人叫我打電話給你，來安排一個雙方都方便的時間，跟調查隊的負責人會面。」

「是的，西蒙說他希望在本週舉行會議。」麗貝卡希望她聽起來很明快，因為她打算要這樣。

「如果你是說霍蘭先生，是對的。」麗貝卡認為瑪西的語氣令企鵝也會覺得寒冷。

「哦，對不起，你不認識西蒙嗎？我以為每個人都認識他。我們合作很長時間了，工作起來很方便。」不值得你這樣啊麗貝卡。

「是的，你似乎與大家都合作很長時間。我敢肯定，這是非常有用的。」

婊子！麗貝卡強壓著怒火。「嗯，我一向都覺得很有用，如果可以跟別人建立良好的工作關係，就更開心。我發現人際交往能力是跟考古學的技能同樣重要的。」

「毫無疑問，這就是為什麼你比很多跟你同齡的人發表較少的論文，」瑪西流利地說。「因為你已經把精力投入到其他領域。」

「正是。對我來說更重要的是，指揮我的團隊來進行良好的發掘、發展技能以達到成功，比起獲得個人的榮耀更加重要。」麗貝卡對著電話銳利的嘲笑了，她希望瑪西可以看到。瑪西很迷戀

own, on to as many news items and publications as possible.

There was a silence. "Yes, obviously those things are important. But we seem to have deviated from the purpose of this call. Do you have time for a meeting with Simon in the next two days?" Marcie snapped. "Or are you too busy developing your team?"

Rebecca decided to let that one go. "Let me just check my schedule." She rustled some papers on her desk and hit a few random keys on her laptop, muttering about fictitious tasks under her breath. "I'm afraid I can't do the next two days, not on this short notice."

"Are you sure? I can't do the end of the week. I have to go to Luxembourg for a few days."

"Now that is unfortunate," said Rebecca, exulting inside. "I'll ring Simon, and ask if it's okay with him if he sees us separately. He can tell me what you two discussed when I meet up with him, and then between us we can make the final plans."

"I thought we were all to be involved in the final planning," said Marcie, a note of panic creeping in under the anger. "It's hardly appropriate to have two separate meetings."

"Well as that's impossible, we will just have to work around it," said Rebecca brightly. "I'm sure it won't be a problem. We're all adults."

Silence again.

"Very well. I'll ring Mr. Holland now, and see it that meets with his approval."

"Great. Thanks, Marcie. Give Simon my love, will you?"

There was no proper reply, just a barely growled "goodbye," and the resounding thump of the phone being slapped down.

Rebecca didn't feel great about herself when she put the phone down. Granted, it was unusual for her to start the sly digs first; Marcie normally had her, metaphorically, by the throat in the first minute of any conversation. And granted, Marcie usually said things far worse than anything Rebecca would ever say, many of them not-so-thinly-veiled threats. She made no secret of her hatred for Rebecca, only pretending a borderline civility towards her when absolutely necessary.

But two wrongs didn't make a right, and Rebecca hadn't meant

可以令自己的名字盡可能有更多機會在新聞或報章出現。

一陣沉默。「是的，很明顯那些東西是很重要的。不過，我們似乎已經偏離了這次通話的目的。在接下來的兩三天，你有時間與西蒙會面嗎？」瑪西惡聲惡氣地說。「或是你要忙於發展你的團隊？」

麗貝卡決定讓步。「讓我看一下我的日程表。」她弄一下辦公桌上的文件做出沙沙聲，並按了幾下在她的筆記本電腦的鍵盤，低聲地自言自語，說了幾個虛構的工作。「我恐怕在未來兩天都不可以，太倉卒了。」

「你確定嗎？在週末我要去盧森堡幾天，我沒有時間。」

麗貝卡說：「很遺憾，」她內心欣喜著。「我會打電話給西蒙，並詢問他可不可以分開地跟我們會面。到我跟他見面時，他可以告訴我你們討論了什麼，然後，我們就可以作出最後的計劃。」

一陣恐慌在憤怒之下蔓延，瑪西說：「我想我們都要有份參與最後的計劃。兩個獨立的會面似乎不太恰當。」

「嗯，但就是因為不可能，我們就只好這樣解決，」麗貝卡巧妙地說。「我敢肯定不會有問題的，我們都是成年人。」

又是一陣沉默。

「很好。現在我會打電話給霍蘭先生，看他會否批准這樣做。」

「太好了。謝謝，瑪西。請代我問候西蒙，可以嗎？」

她沒有回覆她，只是勉強地咆哮道：「再見。」響亮地摔下了電話。

當麗貝卡放下電話，她感覺沒有些很好。的確，她首先開始暗中地挖苦她是很不尋常。瑪西通常於任何對話中都要在第一分鐘就完全掌控情況。而且，瑪西通常說的東西都比麗貝卡曾經說過的任何說話更惡劣，麗貝卡說的幾乎都不是什麼威脅性的說話。她會毫不掩飾對麗貝卡的仇恨，在絕對必要時才會假裝有限度的禮貌。

但兩個錯誤加在一起決不會變得正確起來，麗貝卡並不是想令局勢火上澆油。然而當她聽到瑪西的聲音，知道這是她一直害怕的一天要開始了，就很衝動地覺得要在被壓倒性的襲擊之前，先來個猛烈反擊。

to inflame the situation. When she heard Marcie's voice, though, and knew this was the start of what she'd been dreading for days, the compulsion to lash out before she was attacked was overwhelming.

How was she going to work with her? If this was what a brief phone call was like, how the hell would they get on once they were both on the same dig site?

She found out soon enough. Over the next fortnight Marcie took every opportunity to contradict her and twist everything she said, especially when relaying it to someone else. She stirred up trouble wherever she could and Rebecca's stress levels went up on a daily basis.

Kevin thought she should let Marcie have more control and defer more to her opinion.

"Working for you makes her feel belittled and undermined. Don't forget she's used to leading projects herself. It can't be easy for her, having to follow orders from someone she hates."

"Oh, thanks!"

"You know what I mean. Go on, try it. Give her some responsibility. What have you got to lose? Either things will improve, or you'll have given her enough rope to hang herself."

Rebecca took his advice. Later on that week she told Marcie that she wouldn't be around the next day. "Two new trenches need to be placed, marked out and started tomorrow, but I know I can leave that in your capable hands."

"Yes of course."

"I should be around the day after to give some practical help, so you can tell me what you'd like me to do then."

"That's a good idea, since it's a situation we'll have to get used to."

Rebecca frowned. "Pardon?"

"There are some changes afoot at GLAM," said Marcie. "They'll affect the leadership and the middle management. I'm sure you'll hear about them shortly, but it's on a need to know basis. But based on what I know, the boot will be on the other foot very soon. Learning to follow my instructions will come in very useful to you."

她究竟要如何與她合作呢？如果這一個簡短的通話就已經這樣了，他們到底要如何在同一個發掘現場工作？

她很快知道結果了。在接下來的兩週，瑪西抓住每一個機會來反駁她和扭曲她所說的一切，尤其是在傳達說話給別人的時候。她在任何可以的地方興風作浪，麗貝卡的壓力水平每天持續上升。

凱文認為她應該讓瑪西有更多的控制權，並多點順從她的意見。

「為你工作讓她覺得自己被貶低和削弱了。不要忘了她曾經自己帶領一個項目。對她來說，要服從她討厭的人的命令，這絕對是不容易的事。」

「哦，謝謝！」

「你知道我的意思。去試試吧。給她一定的責任，你有什麼損失呢？事情要麼會變得更好，要麼讓她自我暴露弱點、不擊自破。」

麗貝卡聽從了他的建議。後來那個星期，她告訴的瑪西，她之後的一天不會去現場。「有兩個新的坑道需要安置，明天開始就標註

出來，但我知道有你的幫忙，我可以放心。」

「是的，當然。」

「後天我可以過去實際地幫助一下，所以你能告訴我你想我做什麼。」

「這是一個好主意，因為這類情況，我們一定要習慣。」

麗貝卡皺起了眉頭。「什麼？請再說一遍。」

「在GLAM將會有一些變化，」瑪西說。「是會影響領導和中層管理人員。我敢肯定你很快就會聽到消息，但還是需要知道基本的。但是，根據我所知道的，形勢已經完全不同了。學習遵循我的指示對你會非常有用的。」

麗貝卡沒有回答就走開了，並試圖把它那些說話後腦海中殲滅。瑪西肯定是在說謊，這只是另一種技倆去拉她的後腳。如果博物館有領導職位空缺，而瑪西又知道的話，她一定會聽說過的。

難道不是嗎？

Rebecca walked away without answering, and tried to put it out of her head. Marcie must be lying, it was just another ploy to put Rebecca he back foot. If there was some kind of leadership vacancy coming up at GLAM, and Marcie was in line for it, she would have heard.

Wouldn't she?

Steve slowed as he got to the restaurant. He'd never been here before. Was the tie too much? He was early, so he could always take it off if he got inside and everyone else was in jeans and t-shirts.

He scanned the restaurant as he went in and saw a few men without ties, but no jeans in sight. He'd got it right then, which was lucky because a woman with long dark hair was casually raising a hand. Susan was already here. He headed towards her but a waiter intercepted him.

"Have you booked a table?"

"No, I, er..." he felt flustered with Susan's eyes on him. "I'm joining the young lady over there."

"I see. Shall I bring the wine list over?"

"Could you give us a minute?"

The waiter's eyes narrowed. "We are quite busy this evening, sir. Do you mean literally a minute, or did you want me to wait longer? You only have the table until 9.15."

"A few minutes will be fine," said Steve abruptly. The prices here certainly didn't include service with a smile, he thought.

Susan was looking away as he came up to the table. Probably expecting me to get caught up with the waiter, Steve thought. She'd chosen a table in a little alcove with orange leather bench seats.

Steve smiled. "Susan?"

She glanced up, with just the hint of a smile. Maybe she was shy. "Hi."

Steve sat down and slid around the curved seat until he was a little closer, but not too close. The walls of the alcove were high

史堤夫到了餐廳門口放慢了腳步。他從來沒有來過這裡，不知道領帶是不是多餘的呢？他早了，所以如果他發現裡面大家都是穿牛仔褲和汗衫的話，還可以把它除下。

他進去掃視了一下餐廳，有幾個男人沒有打領帶，但在眼前也沒有牛仔褲。那麼他這樣做就是正確的了，很幸運因為有一個黑色長頭髮的女人正對他舉起一隻手。蘇珊已經在這裡，他走向她，但有個服務員把他截住了。

「你有訂到位嗎？」

「不，我，呃...」蘇珊望著他令他到有點慌亂。「跟我一起的年輕女士就在那邊。」
「我明白了。我拿酒單過去好嗎？」

「你能給我們一分鐘時間嗎？」

服務員瞇起了眼睛。「我們晚上是相當繁忙的，先生。你的意思是字面上的一分鐘，還是你要我等更長時間呢？你的座位只到可以用到九點十五分。」

「幾分鐘就可以了。」史堤夫硬生生地說。他在想，這裡的價格肯定不包括有親切的服務態度。

當他走到桌子前面，蘇珊望著遠處。史堤夫認為她大概是以為他被服務員纏住了。她選擇了在一個小涼亭內，有橙色皮革板凳的座位。

史堤夫微笑。「蘇珊？」

她抬頭，只是淡淡的微笑。也許她是害羞。「嗨。」

史堤夫坐下，下滑到弧形座椅中比較緊貼一點點，但又不太緊貼。小涼亭內的牆壁太高，他覺得有點透不過氣來。這不是他選擇的座位，這裡不太看到餐廳內的情況，感覺有點太親密。

「點了喝的沒有？」

「不，我不是來了很久。我想應該要等你的。」她的眼睛盯著他的肩膀。

史堤夫轉過身來，但什麼也看不到。當他回頭一看，她正看著她

and he felt smothered. This wasn't the table he'd have chosen—you couldn't see much of the restaurant and it felt a little too intimate for a blind date.

"Have you ordered a drink?"

"No, not been here long. Thought I'd wait for you." Her eyes were fixed on a point over his shoulder.

Steve turned but could see nothing. When he looked back, she was looking at her mobile.

"Right. Shall I order us a drink from the bar?"

She shrugged, not lifting her eyes. "If you want, but the waiter will bring the wine list."

Steve was wishing he'd let that waiter follow him with the wine list after all. At least they'd have something to talk about. His tongue was paralysed and his brain wasn't far behind. Ask her about herself then, moron. Let her do the talking.

"So which bank do you work for?"

"I don't, now."

"Oh. Should I say 'sorry to hear that', or 'congratulations'?"

She shrugged. "I wasn't fired." She put her phone away in her bag.

"Ah. You decided to leave?"

She nodded.

"Right. I suppose it's congratulations, then." He smiled. "Where's your new job?"

She shrugged again. "Haven't got one."

"Oh, so you're looking for something?"

"Not really."

Steve's nails dug into his palms. This is real blood from a stone stuff, he thought grimly. I'm all for using body language but speaking is good too. Preferably with the odd full sentence thrown in.

的手機。

「沒錯。那我去酒吧去點杯酒？」

她聳了聳肩，但沒有提起她的眼睛。「但如果你想要的話，服務員是可以把酒單拿過來的。」

史堤夫希望那個跟著他的服務員會拿酒單過來。至少他們有些東西可以談。他的舌頭已經癱瘓，而大腦也差不多。白痴，應該問她關於她的問題，讓她負責說。

「所以你在哪家銀行工作？」

「我沒有，現在。」

「哦。那我應該說『抱歉』還是『恭喜』？」

她聳聳肩。「我不是被解僱的。」她把她的手機放回手袋裡。

「嗯。是你自己決定要離開的嗎？」

她點點頭。

「沒錯，那我想應該是恭喜，」他笑了。「那麼你的新工作呢？」

她又聳了聳肩。「還沒有。」

「哦，那麼你正在找嗎？」

「也不是。」

史堤夫的指甲挖進了手心。真是要從石頭裡擠出血來，他冷冷地想。我已經用盡所有的肢體語言，說話也不錯。最好還是隨口說些奇怪的完整句子就算了。

「你打算去旅行嗎？還是為自己工作？」

「不知道。」她聳聳肩，凝視著他背後。

史堤夫抽搐了一下。如果她再聳肩一次，我會用膠帶把她的肩膀粘貼在椅子上。這可能會把她折斷成一半，她的手臂很骨感。但她看來沒有照片上的那麼瘦，全黑的衣服沒有一點幫助。他尋找著一個適當回應。

"Are you planning to travel? Or perhaps work for yourself?"

"Dunno." She shrugged, gazing past him.

Steve twitched. If she shrugs once more I'll stick her shoulders to the chair with duct tape. That would probably snap her in half though, her arms were stick thin. She hadn't looked that skinny in her picture and all the black clothing didn't help. He groped round for an appropriate response.

"Oh. I'm sure you'll find something to keep you busy."

She nodded and blew a huge bubblegum bubble.

Steve stared at her in horror, which wasn't a problem because she was looking anywhere but at him. He wished they had agreed on lunch at a café. It could have been over and done within an hour.

She shifted on her seat. "I'm hungry."

"I'll get a menu," said Steve hurriedly, raising his hand and trying to catch the eye of the waiter who'd just emerged from the kitchen. How quickly would she eat? He wondered if this potentially three course nightmare could modified into just a main meal, preferably from the 'lighter selection', if this restaurant had such a thing. If he said he wasn't hungry and didn't know if he could manage a starter, would she follow suit out of politeness? It had to be worth a shot.

The waiter slid up to the table. Oh great. It was the one who had accosted him. "Is sir ready for the wine list now? Or appetisers? Or both?"

Oh God! There were appetisers! "The wine list, please, I don't think we want app—"

"Both please," said Susan, with alacrity, coming out of her stupor briefly to smile. Even as the waiter turned, she sank back against the seat and got her phone out again.

Steve cleared his throat and tried again.

"So Susan, what kind of books do you like to read?"

"Don't read, usually" Her eyes were fixed on her phone screen. She appeared to be playing a game.

"What, not at all?" He tried to turn the shocked tone into a teasing

「哦。我肯定你會找到讓你忙起來的東西。」

她點點頭，吹了一個巨大的泡泡糖波波。

史堤夫震驚地盯著她，這完全沒有問題，因為她一直在看著什麼東西，但肯定不是他。他希望他們是約在咖啡店吃午飯，那麼就可以在一個小時內完成。

她在座位上挪動了一下，「我餓了。」

史堤夫說：「我先要個菜單。」他急忙舉起手，並試圖引起剛剛從廚房走出來的服務員的注意。她吃的速度有多快？他不知道三道菜的噩夢有沒有可能修改成為一道主餐，最好是「輕便選擇」，如果這家餐廳有的話。如果他說他不是很餓，不知道如果他首先點菜，她會出於禮貌地跟隨嗎？但也值得一試。

服務員走到桌前。哦，太棒了。這是剛才跟他搭話的那位。「先生現在準備要酒單了嗎？或是前菜？或者兩者都要？」

哦，上帝！還有前菜！「酒單，拜託，我不認為我們需要前...」

「都要，請。」蘇珊爽快地說，露出她僵硬而短暫的微笑。直到服務員轉身，她又靠回在座位上，再次拿出她的手機。

史堤夫清了清嗓子，再次嘗試。

「蘇珊，你喜歡看什麼書嗎？」

「通常都不看。」她的眼睛盯著她的手機屏幕，她似乎在玩遊戲。

「什麼，一本都沒有嗎？」他試圖在句中流露震驚的語氣來揶揄她。

「上個月看過朱迪．福斯特的小說，儘是廢話。」她吹起另一個波波。

史堤夫把他的頭放在他的手上。這將是一個漫長的夜晚。

為什麼鬧鈴關上了？他沒有設定到是因為昨晚他需要睡個懶覺。蘇珊是一個噩夢，只有當食物出現，她才會有生命跡象，包括在配菜之後出現的那三道主菜上的伴菜。

她大口地吃著，一直沒有跟史堤夫說話，就算是回答他越來越少

one, mid-sentence.

"Read a Jodie Forrest novel last month. Crap though." She blew another bubble.

Steve put his head in his hands. It was going to be a long night.

Why was the alarm going off? He hadn't set it because after last night, he needed a lie-in. Susan had been a nightmare, only showing signs of life when the food appeared—including all the side dishes she'd ordered with each of the three courses that followed the appetisers.

She'd eaten every mouthful of food and hadn't spoken to Steve other than to answer his increasingly sparse questions with monosyllables, grunts and shrugs. She hadn't offered to go halves on the horrendous bill, and when he'd commented how expensive it was and looked at her meaningfully, she'd revealed she only had enough money for the cab fare home.

He reached out a hand towards his alarm clock, but then his sleep-fogged brain worked out the ringing was from the phone. He struggled upright.

"Hello?"

"Hi, bruv.' Laura's voice sounded high and strained.

"Laura? I've been worried sick, why didn't you call?"

"Sorry. Don't worry, I'm safe."

"Good. Where are you? I've been looking everywhere."

"I know. I heard."

Steve gritted his teeth. So some of her friends he'd contacted had known exactly where she was. Now she was safe, he felt the anger kick in.

"The police have been looking for you too. But not as a missing person," he said coldly.

There was a short silence. "I know. They found me."

"They—Laura, what's happening?"

的提問，也只是會用單音節詞、呼嚕聲或聳聳肩。她沒有提出付一半的賬單，當他想著那是多麼昂貴，意味深長地看了她一眼，她就透露她只有足夠的錢付出租車車費回家。

他伸出手去關上他的鬧鈴，但隨後他缺乏睡眠的頭腦意識到那是來電的振鈴。他奮力坐直身子。

「喂？」

「嗨，兄弟。」羅拉的聲音高而緊繃。

「羅拉？我一直擔心得要命，你為什麼不打電話給我呢？」

「對不起。不用擔心，我很安全。」

「好。你在哪裡？我一直在到處找你。」

「我知道。我聽說了。」

史堤夫咬了咬牙關。所以他聯絡過她的一些朋友中，有人確切地知道她在哪裡。現在她是安全的，他開始感到憤怒了。

「警察一直在找你。但不是作為一個失蹤人口。」他冷冷地說。

一陣短暫的沉默。「我知道。他們已經找到我了。」

「他們…羅拉，究竟發生了什麼？」

「他們已經逮捕了我，史堤夫，」她說，聲音在顫抖。「我不認為只是象徵性的懲戒。」她的聲音變成了嗚咽。

「你做了什麼，他們要逮捕你呢？」

「藏毒。」沉默。「搶劫。」她說完了，聲音小得只勉強讓史堤夫聽得見。

他坐了起來。「搶劫？你搶劫別人？天啊，該死的！羅拉！」

「我知道很愚蠢。」

「愚蠢嗎？就這樣嗎？為什麼，因為你被抓住了？」史堤夫站了起來，在踱步，他緊握著身旁那隻閒置的手。

"They've arrested me, Steve," she said, her voice quivering. "I don't think it will b-be just a s-slap on the wrist." She disintegrated into sobs.

"What have they arrested you for?"

"Possession." Silence. "And mugging," she finished, barely loud enough for Steve to catch.

He sat bolt upright. "Mugging? You MUGGED someone? Bloody hell, Laura!"

"I know it was stupid—"

"STUPID? That's all? Why, because you got caught?" Steve was on his feet, pacing, his unoccupied hand clenched by his side.

"No, I know it was wrong, too. I wasn't thinking straight—"

"Oh and I wonder why THAT was!"

"I was with this guy, but he ran—"

"I'm coming down there." He grabbed his jeans and started to pull them on, hunching his shoulder to hold the phone against his ear.

"No! Steve, please don't—"

"Course I bloody well am, Laura. I'm legally in charge of you—"

"You're not any more. I'm nineteen, remember?" He could tell she was gulping back tears.

"I need to know you're alright."

"I am. Don't come today. Please! B-but can you come tomorrow? I really want you there."

"What's happening tomorrow?"

"I'm in court." he voice was flat now, although she'd run out of tears. "To see if they'll grant me bail."

Steve drew in a slow breath. He hadn't thought that far.

"Bail?" His voice dropped as anger gave way to a grim disbelief. He shook his head as though that would make this nightmare go away. "Jesus Christ, Laura..."

「不，我知道這是很錯。我沒有想到…」

「哦，而我真的不知道是為什麼！」

「我跟了個傢伙，但他逃跑了。」

「我現在過來。」他抓起並開始穿起他的牛仔褲，拱起的肩膀把手機對著他的耳朵。

「不！史堤夫，請不要…」

「因為最好是我，羅拉。我在法律上是要看管你的。」

「你已經不是了，我十九歲了，還記得嗎？」他聽出她把淚水咽了回去。

「我需要知道你沒事。」

「我沒事。今天就不要過來。求你了！但…但明天可以過來嗎？我真的很想你在那裡。」

「明天有什麼事發生嗎？」

「我要上庭。」現在她聲音平靜了，可能是因為眼淚已經耗盡。「要看看他們會否讓我保釋。」

史堤夫緩慢地呼吸了一下。他沒有想到那麼遠。

「保釋？」他的聲音降低了，是因為憤怒已被滿腹的疑惑取代。他搖搖頭，彷彿可以令這個噩夢消失。「耶穌基督，羅拉…」

「等一下。」他能聽到她在跟別人說話，然後她又回來了。「我得走了。警員希望跟你談談明天的安排。」

「好…那我們明天見。多多保重。如果你需要我，你知道我在哪裡。」

「再見。」

即使在他已經知道了事實，但是這一切似乎不是真實的，很模糊，好像是別人的聲音在討論羅拉和她要跟與警方人員上庭似的，平靜而不帶感情。後來他走下樓，還是赤裸上身，給自己倒了一杯威士忌。還好羅拉不在這裡，他帶著一點諷刺地想。作為一個好的示範，我要把鬧鈴設置到早上十點。

"Hold on." He could hear her speak to someone else, then she was back. "I have to go. The officer wants to talk to you about tomorrow."

"Right... I'll see you tomorrow. Take care of yourself. You know where I am if you need me."

"Bye."

Even after he'd been given the facts, but it all seemed unreal, a blur, as though it was someone else discussing Laura and her court appearance with the police officer in that calm, matter-of-fact voice. Afterwards he walked downstairs, still bare-chested, and poured himself a whisky. Good job Laura isn't here, he thought with some irony. A fine example I'm setting at ten in the morning.

Life seemed to be running in slow motion. He drained the glass and took it to the kitchen to rinse out, then remembered there was something more urgent to do. He grabbed the handset mounted by the kitchen door. Punched in a familiar number. Waited, rigid, until a voice answered.

"Tony, it's Steve. Sorry, but I won't be in tomorrow." He knew he sounded curt and unapologetic. But his throat was tight and his mouth felt dry, even after the whisky. It was an effort to form a sentence, use the niceties.

He steeled himself to answer the inevitable questions, walking back into the lounge with his glass. It would have been a waste to rinse it, because it was easier to answer Tony with a little help. He poured his second whisky of the morning.

生命似乎慢速地運行。他喝完了一杯酒，並拿到廚房沖洗杯子，然後想起有什麼急事要辦。他抓起掛在廚房門的聽筒。猛擊了一個熟悉的號碼。等待，僵住，直到聽到回答的聲音。

「東尼，我是史堤夫。對不起，但我明天不可以來上班。」他知道他聽起來生硬，而且毫無歉意。但是，他的喉嚨很緊，他覺得嘴裡很乾，雖然他已經喝了一杯威士忌。這是已經是他盡力用細節組成的句子。

他準備應付回答不可避免的問題，拿著酒杯走回客廳。沖洗它本來就無謂的，因為只有這可以令他容易點回答東尼的問題。他倒了今個早上的第二杯威士忌。

Chapter Thirteen

"Hi Tony."

He nodded. "Rebecca. What would you like?"

"Butterscotch latte, please."

He gave a small smile. "You like the butterscotch, eh? Is very popular. Steve made good decision to buy it." He busied himself at the coffee machine.

Rebecca fidgeted. "Talking of Steve, where is he today then? Don't tell me you've let him have a day off." She hoped she sounded casual.

"Yes. He had day off."

"Oh? Is he going somewhere nice?"

"I couldn't say. What he does when he is not here, it is his business," replied Tony curtly.

Rebecca flushed. "I didn't mean to pry. I thought you two were friends." She slapped some coins down on the counter and grabbed her tray, spilling some of her coffee.

"Rebecca!"

She turned.

"Sorry. I am being rude. It's just, I worry about him." He said quietly.

"Why?" She leaned against the counter again.

"Because he risk everything for that ungrateful bitch!" he snapped suddenly, throwing his hands up in the air.

Rebecca flinched.

第十三章

「嗨，東尼。」

他點點頭。「麗貝卡。要些什麼？」

「麻煩你要奶油糖果拿鐵咖啡。」

他給了一個小小的微笑。「你喜歡奶油糖果，嗯？非常受歡迎的。史堤夫買它是個明智的決定。」他忙著操作咖啡機。

麗貝卡有點坐立不安。「說到史堤夫，今天他在哪裡？不要告訴我，你讓他休息一天。」她希望她聽起來漫不經心的。

「是的。他放假。」

「哦？他有好地方去嗎？」

「當他不在這裡時，我不能說在他做什麼，這是他的事。」東尼簡短地回答說。

麗貝卡滿臉通紅。「我不是故意探聽什麼。我只是以為你倆是朋友。」她摑了一些硬幣在櫃檯上，並拿起她的托盤，溢出一些咖啡。

「麗貝卡！」

她轉過身來。

「對不起。是我無禮。只是，我有點擔心他。」他平靜地說。

「為什麼？」她再次靠著櫃檯。

「因為他不顧一切為了那個忘恩負義的婊子！」他突然失控，在空中扔了一下手。

麗貝卡畏縮了一下。

「對不起。但是，我只看到他在浪費了自己的生命，他讓她走出

"Sorry. But I see him, wasting his life, he's getting her out of trouble again and again. He is always there for her, but who is there for him, eh? Laura, she will not change. He's given her more last chances than she deserve."

"Why doesn't he leave her?"

He shrugged. "Because still, he feels responsible for her. A hard habit to break, I suppose, after all the years."

Rebecca frowned. "All the years? She only looks twenty."

"She is nineteen."

"Well he can't have been with her that long—what were they, childhood sweethearts? How old was she when they married?"

"What?" Tony started at her. "No, I talk about Laura. His sister. Steve is not married! If he is, is big secret he keeps from me."

"His sister," she said faintly. Cogs whirred in her brain. "So how come he's been responsible for her for years? What about his parents?"

"Very sad story." Steve shook his head. "Both are dead. Steve, he is only young when his father die and make them both orphans, and the government want Laura to be—" he frowned "fostered? That is right? But Steve fights and he signs papers, becomes – how you say – legal guardian?" He sighed. "Is big responsibility."

Rebecca was about to ask more, but a family came up beside her to order coffees and milkshakes. She took her coffee over to her usual table and stirred it for a long time, lost in thought.

Rebecca had read real-life internet dating stories and knew, not surprisingly, that most people who had found their perfect partner had lots of dates before they struck lucky. So why was she on the verge of giving up after two? And why was the prospect of a third date, with yet another man, too depressing for words?

She suspected some of her feelings were to do with discovering that Steve was single. Even so, Laura was still a big part of his life; Kevin's warning about getting involved in what was obviously a messy situation was still valid, and she's been adamant that she wasn't getting herself involved with men with complicated lives. She wanted to keep things simple. If only Steve wasn't so darn attractive. Or so funny. Or such a good listener. If only he

困境一遍又一遍。他總是為她著想，但又有誰為他著想呢，嗯？羅拉，她不會改變的了。他給她的最後機會比她應得的多。」

「為什麼他不離開她呢？」

他聳了聳肩。「因為，他仍然覺得要對她負責。一個很難打破的習慣，我想，畢竟這麼多年。」

麗貝卡皺起了眉頭。「這麼多年？她看起來只有二十歲。」

「她十九歲。」

「嗯，他不能一直長時間跟她一起，他們是青梅竹馬嗎？他們結婚時她幾歲？」

「什麼？」東尼看著她。「不，我在說羅拉，他的妹妹。史堤夫沒有結婚！如果他有，他一定瞞著我一個大秘密了。」

「他的妹妹，」她有氣無力地說。她腦袋中的齒輪在響著。「那麼多年來，他一直負責照顧她？他的父母呢？」

「非常悲傷的故事。」東尼搖了搖頭。「兩個都死了。史堤夫，在他年輕的時候他的父親就死了，他們兩個變成了孤兒，而政府希望羅拉被...」他皺起了眉頭。「領養？這是正確的嗎？但是，史堤夫抗爭，他簽署了文件，變成了...你怎麼說...法定監護人？」他嘆了一口氣。「是一個很大的責任。」

麗貝卡正想要問更多的，但一個家庭來到了她的身旁，要買咖啡和奶昔。她把她的咖啡帶到她一貫坐的位子，很長一段時間，在攪拌，並陷入了沉思。

麗貝卡看了一個現實生活中的網絡約會的故事，不出意料地，大多數人誰遇到了他們完美的伴侶，他們在遇到幸運之前都去過很多次的約會。那麼，為什麼她在兩個之後就想要放棄呢？為什麼不憧憬與另一名男子的第三次約會呢？是太令人沮喪了嗎？

她覺得自己發現史堤夫是單身之後，對他有一些感覺。即便如此，羅拉仍然是他生活重要的一部分。凱文警告她不要介入一個明顯是混亂的局面仍是有效，而她一直堅持認為，她並沒有讓自己捲入一個男子的複雜生活。她希望讓事情變得簡單。如果史堤夫是沒有這麼混賬的吸引力，或者沒有這麼有趣，或者不是這樣好的一個聽眾。如果他沒有那個迷人的笑容，令她...那就沒關係了。哎唷！

不管怎樣，她永遠無法肯定他有沒有被她吸引。信號太混亂了。那一刻，很明智地跟他保持距離，明智地利用交友網站。但她前兩次的經歷並沒有令她有多點信心。

儘管如此，一不做二不休，她堅定地告訴自己。好吧，二號不是

didn't have that devastating smile that made her... well never mind. Argh!

Anyway, she could never decide if he was attracted to her or not. The signals were too confusing. At the moment, it would be wise to keep her distance, and wise to make use of the dating website. But her first two experiences hadn't filled her with confidence.

Still, in for a penny, in for a pound, she told herself firmly. Okay, no.2 hadn't been suitable, but at least he hadn't been creepy. Perhaps this time she should look at her hot matches and do the picking herself. Third time lucky.

You have 3 new Hot Matches!' said yesterday's email. Underneath were three sample pictures of suspiciously good-looking people, with a big blue question mark on them; Rebecca doubted any of them had ever been Methodical Matches clients.

She clicked the link and logged in. Stewart, Peter and Malcolm appeared. She didn't like the look of Malcolm; instant reject. Stewart and Peter were both reasonably good-looking and neither looked creepy. So which should she tackle first? She giggled. That sounded like she was bracing herself to climb a mountain, not deciding who to date. Wasn't this meant to be fun?

She clicked on Stewart. He was a 39 year old accountant who ran marathons, apparently. Peter was a fund-raising co-ordinator who belonged to a local history group and he was 34. There was nothing wrong with either of them, but she had to pick one—and Stewart, although undoubtedly fit in both senses of the word, was right at the upper age limit she'd set. If she met someone, liked them, and then found out they were 10 years older, no problem; but a large age gap wouldn't be her first choice. Peter was interested in history, so that would be a good starting point for a conversation; and if he was a fundraising co-ordinator, he must be socially aware and caring. Mustn't he?

"Don't be so naive," she muttered to herself. Still, there was only one way to find out. She clicked on 'Send a message to Peter.' What should she write? What had John and Derek's messages said? After dithering for a bit, she finally wrote: "Hi Peter, I noticed you on my Hot Matches list. Would you like to meet for a coffee?" Short and simple. That would do.

She spent another hour on the computer, surfing archaeology websites and playing a word game, then checked her inbox. Nothing yet, but hey, Peter had a life to live—hopefully. She didn't want to date someone who spent all their life on their computer. After vacuuming the whole flat, she relaxed in a deep bubble bath

很適合，但至少他沒有令人毛骨悚然。也許這個時候，她應該看看她的熱門配對名單，自己來選擇一下。第三次的幸運。

「你有三個新的熱門配對！」昨天的電子郵件寫著。下面三個樣本相片，貌似都很好看，有一個藍色的大問號在上面。麗貝卡質疑他們有沒有一個是井然配對的客戶。

她點擊鏈接並登錄，斯圖爾特、彼得和馬爾科姆出現了。她不喜歡馬爾科姆的外表，即時否決了。斯圖爾特和彼得看去起來都很好，看上去也不會覺得毛骨悚然。所以她應該先選擇那一個呢？她咯咯地笑起來。這聽起來像她在選擇先去爬哪一座山，而不是決定跟誰約會。這不是很有趣嗎？

她點擊斯圖爾特，他是一個三十九歲跑馬拉松的會計師。彼得是一間於當地頗有歷史的組織負責籌款活動的統籌，他三十四歲。兩個都沒有什麼不妥，但她不得不挑一個。斯圖爾特，雖然看來無疑是很適合，但年齡剛好是她設置的上限。如果她遇到了一個人，很喜歡他，然後發現他比她大十歲，那是沒有問題。但一個大的年齡差距不會是她的首選。彼得對歷史感興趣，所以這應該是很好的一個談話起點，如果他是負責籌款活動的統籌，他應該有一定的社會意識和關懷，是嗎？

「不要那麼幼稚。」她喃喃地對自己說道。不過，只有一個辦法可以知道。她點擊「發送一條信息給彼得。」她應該怎麼寫呢？約翰和德瑞克的信息是說什麼的呢？躊躇了一會後，她終於寫了：「嗨，彼得，我看到你在我的熱門配對列表。你想出來喝杯咖啡嗎？」這應該夠簡短直接了。

她花了一個小時在電腦上，瀏覽考古網站和玩文字遊戲，再檢查收件箱。還沒有回覆，但是，嘿，彼得也有自己的生活。她不想跟某人約會而他花光了所有生命在他們的電腦上。她用吸塵器打掃整個單位後，放鬆自己在一個泡泡浴中，然後懶洋洋地穿著睡衣拿著一杯酒在電視前。這不是最迷人的週五晚上，她想，但現在她覺得精神而且輕鬆。但太放鬆而睡著了，在午夜後醒來看到電視在播放一套很老的恐怖片，她昏昏沉沉地拖著自己回到床上。

她沒有收到彼得任何回覆，直到週日清晨。「是的，喝咖啡是一個好提議。你什麼時候有空呢？」

「要到下週末了，」她打字。然後，經過一番思考，她補充說，「我今天有空，如果不太趕的話？」

「對不起，我十點半要回教會。下週六可以麼？」

教會？好吧...這究竟是什麼回事？她有說她沒有宗教信仰，但另一方面，她也不排除約會某人是有宗教信仰的。那裡有個方框，她沒有在那裡打勾。也許電腦有其智慧，覺得宗教差異不是一個問題。這很好，彼得沒有因為她沒有信仰而嘗試改變她。雖然這

and then lounged in front of the TV in her PJs with a glass of wine. Not the most glamorous Friday night, she thought, but now she felt virtuous and relaxed. So relaxed that she fell asleep, waking after midnight in front of what looked like a very old horror film, and dragging herself groggily to bed.

She didn't get an answer from Peter until early Sunday morning. "Yes, meeting for coffee would be good. When are you free?"

"Not until next weekend," she typed. Then, after some thought, she added, "I am free today if it's not too short notice?"

"Sorry, I have church at 10.30. What about next Saturday?"

Church? Okay... how had that happened? She had said she had no religious affiliation, but on the other hand, she hadn't precluded dating someone who had. There was a tick box for that and she'd left it blank. Perhaps the computer, in its wisdom, had decided religious differences weren't an issue. That was fine, providing Peter didn't object to her lack of faith or try to convert her. It made her a little uncomfortable though.

"Next Saturday's fine. 10.30? Where would you like to go?!"

"Do you know Vincenzo's, near the Meredith & Partners on Parson Street? They do coffees, soft drinks and smoothies as well. I was going to suggest a wine bar instead, but I don't want you to think I'm a raging alcoholic!"

Wow. Good taste and a sense of humour. Vincenzo's was lovely, if a bit out of her usual area. The atmosphere was sophisticated but friendly. Not so upper crust that you couldn't pop in at the weekend in smart jeans, but not so lowly as to allow grinning idiots in Hawaiian shorts or girls in fluorescent boob tubes, either.

"Yes, I've been there a couple of times before. Look forward to seeing you there."

So that was it. Date no.3. And nearly a whole week to wait and worry about it.

She needn't have worried. They had a great time. As she suspected, Peter did have a good sense of humour. He liked some of the same music, he tried three different coffees without having a panic attack, and he was enthusiastic but not obsessed with studying the origin of place names. He knew a lot about it – far more than she did – and he talked about it in an entertaining

讓她有點不舒服。

「下週六很好。十點半嗎?你想去哪裡?」

「你知道溫琴佐嗎?在帕森街的梅雷迪思企業附近?他們有賣咖啡、汽水和果汁。其實我想建議去酒吧,但我不希望你覺得我是一個瘋狂的酒鬼!」

哇,品味好又有幽默感。溫琴佐是一個可愛的地方,雖然有一點超出她平時會到的區域。氣氛很高雅時髦但友好的。不至於是上流地方,但也不可以穿牛仔褲在週末出現,當然也沒有卑微到允許穿夏威夷短褲笑嘻嘻的白痴或熒光窄腳褲的女孩。

「是的,我有去過幾次。期待跟你見面。」

就是這個第三次約會。幾乎有整整一個星期的等待和擔心。

她根本不用擔心,他們相處得非常之好。她覺得彼得真的有很好的幽默感。他們喜歡的一些相同的音樂,他嘗試了三款不同的咖啡而沒有恐慌症發作,他非常感興趣,但沒有執著研究原產地。他知道了很多關於它的事情,遠遠超過她所知道的,他用有趣和詼諧的方式去告訴她。麗貝卡被迷住了,和他聊了幾個小時。

他們雙方同意,沒有異議地延長他們的約會到午飯時間,他們走到附近的一家印度餐廳,那裡有自助午餐。

他們說再見的時候,麗貝卡邀請了彼得陪伴她去一個在月內舉行的講座,是有關歷史悠久的行業如何影響地方名稱和姓氏,而且溫馨而舒適地肯定了她交了一個好朋友。

而她可以做的都做了,因為彼得,祝福他,他並沒有用很長時間,但輕鬆而直接地告訴她,他覺得她是個很可愛和有趣的人,他很高興認識她這個朋友,但他的信仰是他生活的基本組成部分。他只想跟一個可以跟他分享這些的人約會,這是完全沒問題,麗貝卡也有同樣的想法。驚喜的是他說了他在井然配對的個人檔案上寫了什麼。

至於是全面損失,在回家的路上她在想。唯一的損失是這家約會機構。這只可以是友誼,但已經是超額完成。

麗貝卡怒視著,而妮科拉萎縮在她的不銹鋼和玻璃桌子後。麗貝卡想,她可能希望她在那些銀行風格的接待處後面,接待員只可以通過一個小窄縫望出去。這是一個相當明智的希望,因為麗貝卡在令自己比較平靜和理智,她非常想伸手過去並扭斷那個蠢女人在紫外線床烤完的脖子。

and witty way. Rebecca was fascinated and they talked for hours. They mutually agreed, without a second thought, to extend their date into lunch and walked to a nearby Indian restaurant that did a lunchtime buffet.

When they said goodbye, Rebecca was left with an invitation to accompany Peter in a month's time to a talk on how historic industries influenced place names and surnames, and the warm, cosy certainty that she'd made a good friend.

And that was all she'd made, because Peter, bless him, hadn't taken long to tell her in his light-hearted but direct way that he thought she was a lovely, interesting person, and would be delighted to be her friend, but his faith was a fundamental part of his life. He only wanted to date people whom he could share that with, which was completely fine with Rebecca and was also, surprise surprise, what he had stated on his Methodical Matches profile.

At least it wasn't a total loss, she thought, as she made her way home. The only thing that was a total loss here was the dating agency. That was one friendship that was definitely over.

Rebecca glared and Nicola shrivelled behind her stainless steel and glass desk. She was probably wishing she was behind one of those bank style reception desks, thought Rebecca, the tall ones where the receptionist was only visible through a small gap. And that was quite a wise thing to wish, because Rebecca, who liked to think of herself as relatively calm and reasonable, was sorely tempted to reach over and wring the bimbo's toasted-on-a-tanning-bed neck.

"It would have been better," she continued, "if I'd wandered out into the street blindfolded, spun around a few times, then grabbed the next three people I laid my hands on. They would have probably have been a better matches. Even if one of them was a dog!" She threw up her hands dramatically. Even if one of them was a dog? You're overdoing it, girl that just sounded daft.

"How you can have the nerve to call your company—and let's be honest, it is your company, isn't it, Nicola? There are no other staff, you're the be all and end all—Methodical Matches, is beyond me. It's about as methodical as a lobotomised hamster on acid."

To Nicola's credit, she attempted to talk to her. "So what I'm hearing is, that you've had three dates but not found Mr. Right?" she said, the quiver in her voice belying the desperate

「本來是可以更好的，」她繼續說，「如果我到街上蒙住眼睛漫步，轉幾圈然後抓住接下來三個人的手。他們將有可能是一個更好的配對。即使其中一隻是狗的手！」她激烈地丟了一下手。即使其中一隻是狗的手？你太誇張了，女孩，聽起來很愚蠢。

「你怎麼能好意思叫你的公司做井然配對...說實話，這是你的公司，是嗎？妮科拉？有沒有其他工作人員？你就是全部和所有人吧？我真的無法理解。這只是跟一隻遲鈍的倉鼠一樣井然有序吧。」

妮科拉值得讚揚的是，她試圖去跟她說話。「所以我聽到的是，你已經有去了三個的約會了，但還沒有找到真命天子？」她說，顫動的聲音掩飾了在她的語氣中極嚴重的樂觀。

「我不會因為我在三個約會內還沒有找到真命天子而抱怨的，這是天真至極的事。但我只是沒想到這三個男人，我都不想花上兩個小時去相處，更別說再見了！」

「所以第三個沒有好點嗎？」

「很好。真是個夠好的人，但他是一個重生得救的基督徒，驚喜吧，他期待跟另一個基督徒共度一生。這似乎是一個足夠合理的要求，尤其是他在他的個人資料已經說得很清楚。」

「我可以鑒別這是我們電腦輔助配套的問題。」

「如果這就是用科學得出的結果，我想我應該要採用相反的做法，就是從電話簿中隨便挑一個。」

「我們正努力解決技術上的問題。」

「這就是你說的最後一次。同時，請不要再說『我們』和『我們的』，你在騙誰啊。」

妮科拉曬得棕褐色的臉顯得很蒼白，但她的表情沒有任何變化。麗貝卡覺得她可能真的是一個芭比娃娃。

「我們希望我們的客戶對我們的服務感到滿意，所以我可以為你提供額外三個月的免費會藉。」

「到底為什麼我會想延長我的會藉？」

妮科拉說：「當然，這是你的決定，如果你想停用你的個人資料。 但是如果你改變了主意，你的會藉將會直至新的到期日之前仍然有效。正如我所說，我們正在努力作出改善。」

「很高興聽到這個消息。但是，是的，我想停用我的個人資料，

cheerfulness of its tone.

"I'm not complaining because I haven't found Mr. Right within three dates. That would be naive in the extreme. But what I didn't expect was three men that I didn't want to spend two hours with, let alone want to see again!

"So number three wasn't any better?"

"No. Nice enough man, but he's a born again Christian who, surprise, surprise, is looking for another Christian to spend his life with. It seems a reasonable enough request, particularly as he made it very clear in his profile."

"I appreciate there have been problems with our computer-aided matching—"

"If this is a result of using science, I think I'll take the opposite approach and just pick someone from the phonebook."

"We are trying our best to resolve the technical problems."

"That's what you said last time. And please don't keep saying 'we' and 'our'. You're not fooling anybody.

Nicola had gone very pale under the tan, but her expression didn't change. She really could be a Barbie doll, thought Rebecca.

"We want our customers to be satisfied with our service, so I can offer you another three months membership free of charge."

"Why on earth would I want to prolong my membership?"

"Naturally, it's up to you if you wish to deactivate your profile," said Nicola. "But your membership will still be valid until the new expiry date, if you change your mind. As I say, we are working hard to make improvements."

"Glad to hear it. But yes, I'd like to deactivate my profile, please."

Nicola tapped away on her laptop for a minute or so.

"There. That's all done for you."

"Thank you." Rebecca marched out. What did computers know about her perfect partner? If she ended up being a batty old spinster, so be it. She was never trying internet dating again.

麻煩你。」

妮科拉在她的筆記本電腦上敲了敲一分鐘左右。

「可以了。一切都為你做好了。」

「謝謝你。」麗貝卡大步走了出去。電腦知道什麼是她的完美伴侶嗎？如果她要成為一個古怪的老處女而終老，就這樣吧。她不會再試什麼網絡約會了。

Chapter Fourteen

"Another busman's holiday?" Steve looked up from his book and instantly wished he'd put a decent shirt on before he came out. Rebecca was smiling down at him and looked, as usual, gorgeous.

"Yeah, I know." He smiled. Great. Now she would think he was really sad. "See? I really can't stay away from the place."

"You must really love it, to choose to spend your Friday night here."

"Says the girl who's at a modest café on Friday night." He wondered where Kevin was but didn't want to ask.

"Fair cop. Although I could be here to meet Tom Cruise, for all you know."

"No. I know you're impressed with his bottle-juggling skills, but he's too short for you."

"True. Cute, though." She fished in her handbag for her purse. "Anyway I'm dying of thirst, and Tom doesn't seem to have made it, so I'm off to drown my sorrows by myself."

"If you fancy some company, I can draw up another chair," he said, hoping he sounded far more suave and sophisticated than he felt. He held his book up. "This is your only competition."

She looked at the cover, then shook her head. "I was going to say pull me up a chair, but I'm not sure I can compete with that."

"Ooh, sarcasm." Good move. Your status as a complete loser, in her eyes, is assured. Young single man alone, reading a book, once again spending his Friday night at the café where he works.

"Nope." She shook her head emphatically. "Not sarcasm. I love Jodie Forrest. Got them all. Grab me a chair. Do you want anything?"

第十四章

「又是另一個照常工作的假期？」史堤夫從他的書中抬起頭，並立即希望他出來之前有穿上一件像樣的襯衫。麗貝卡笑盈盈地看著他，像往常一樣，華麗地。

「是啊，我知道。」他笑著說。太好了。現在她會認為他是真的是很傷心。「看到了嗎？我真的不能遠離這個地方。」

「你一定是真的很喜歡它，而選擇星期五晚上在這裡渡過。」

「比如說有個女孩於上週五晚上在普通的咖啡店裡。」他想問凱文，但又不想問。

「理應如此。因為我可以在這裡遇到湯姆·克魯斯，你知道的。」

「不會。我知道你很欽佩他的耍瓶技能，但他對你來說太矮了。」

「真的。不過可愛，」她在手袋中尋找她的錢包。「反正我渴死了，而湯姆似乎沒有做咖啡給我，所以我只好把自己淹沒在悲傷之中。」

「如果你想找個伴，我可以讓出另一張椅子，」他說，希望他聽起來比他感覺的更風流倜儻和老練。他拿起他的書。「這是你唯一的競爭對手。」

她看著封面，然後搖搖頭。「我正想說我拉一把椅子過來，但我不知道我能不能跟它抗衡。」

「哦，挖苦我啊。」幹得好。在她眼裡你肯定是一個徹底的失敗者的地位。年輕的單身男人獨處、看書、再次在他工作的咖啡店渡過週五晚上。

「不，」她斷然地搖搖頭。「不是挖苦你。我喜歡朱迪．福斯特。我有所有她的書。幫我佔張椅子。你想要什麼？」

Just you, he thought, but unfortunately you're not on the menu. "No thanks, I'm fine."

"Ok."

Rebecca wasn't at the counter long—it was quiet this evening—but it was long enough for him to get nervous. Why had he taken it into his head to ask her to join him? She must know all about Laura by now, which was enough to put any woman off, and nothing changed the fact that she was attached. Normally he would have had the sense –and the decency – to back off long before now.

He looked over at her, in slim fitting black jeans, neat black boots with a small heel and a bright, checked shirt, seeing her smile at Tony and hearing her laugh ring out. He would give a lot to be the person who got to hear that laugh every day. She was nearly finished at the counter so he quickly pretended to be reading his book again, although in reality he was aware of every step she took towards him, watching her from the corner of his eye.

"Mind your book!"

Steve hastily shut it, sliding it into the pocket of his jacket that hung on his chair. Rebecca plonked the tray down without ceremony, and started to transfer everything to the table.

He looked at her latte. "Don't tell me. Butterscotch."

"Oh dear, oh dear. Very poor show. You'll be getting the sack."

He bent forward and sniffed. "Ah. Hazelnut. Didn't know you liked that, I thought that was normally Kevin's—" shut up, Steve! Shut up, shut up, SHUT UP! "...choice," he trailed off.

Rebecca didn't seem to notice, busy unloading the tray. "It is, but I fancied something different. Sometimes butterscotch seems wrong for this time of day, unless I'm really cold – or really fed up! Too sweet, somehow. Don't tell me, I know. I'm weird."

"No, I know what you mean. I never have mocha in the morning. I always wait for lunchtime. Mornings are for cappuccinos."

"Exactly." She took the empty tray and put it on the rack nearby.

Steve looked at the items she'd spread out on the table. "Hungry?" he asked, quirking an eyebrow in amusement.

She pretended to glare and thrust a Southern Fried Chicken

你，他在想，但不幸的是，你不在菜單上。「不，謝謝，我很好。」

「好吧。」

麗貝卡沒有花很長時間在櫃檯，這個晚上很安靜，但還是夠長的時間讓他變得緊張。為什麼他突然想到要叫她跟他一起坐呢？現在，她一定知道所有關於羅拉的事，這足以把任何一個女人嚇走，只要有她跟隨，沒有什麼可以改變的。通常情況下他會意識到，或是更應該做的是，很久以前就打退堂鼓。

他看著她，纖細合身的黑色牛仔褲，俐落有小鞋跟的黑色皮靴和一件明亮的格子襯衫，看到她對著東尼笑，聽到她一串嘹亮的笑聲。他願意付出更多去成為每天都聽到她笑的人。當她準備離開櫃上，他很快就假裝在看書，但實際上，他能在他的眼角意識到她向他走過來的每一步。

「注意你的書！」

史堤夫匆匆把書合上，放回他掛在椅子上的夾克口袋裡。麗貝卡隨意地重重放下了托盤，並開始調動著桌上的東西。

他看著她的拿鐵咖啡。「不要告訴我。是奶油糖果。」

「噢，親愛的！噢，親愛的！非常壞的表現，你會被解僱。」

他彎下身聞了聞。「嗯。是榛子。不知道你喜歡這款，我以為通常都是凱文的…」閉嘴，史堤夫！閉嘴，閉嘴，閉嘴！「…選擇。」他拖長了。

麗貝卡似乎沒有注意到，她忙著處理托盤上的東西。「是的，但我想要點不同的。有時，奶油糖果似乎在這個時間不太適合，除非我真的很冷，或者真的受夠了！是太甜了，不知為什麼。別跟我說，我知道。我很奇怪。」

「不，我明白你的意思。我從來沒有在早上喝摩卡咖啡，我會一直等到午飯時間。早晨應該要喝卡布奇諾咖啡。」

「沒錯。」她拿著空的托盤，並把它放在附近的架子上。

史堤夫看著她攤開在桌子上的東西。「你餓了嗎？」他問，他樂得翹起了眉毛。

她假裝在他面前炫耀和打開一份南方炸雞卷拼沙拉。「這是晚

Wrap with Salad at him. "This is dinner, pal. I'm ravenous." She ripped open the end of the packet.

"I'll let you off then."

"And these—" she waved her hand at two Apricot Danish pastries—are not both for me. One of them's for you."

"Thanks. You shouldn't have, I've already eaten—"

"No problem." She took a big bite of wrap and swallowed it with relish. "It's not kind of me really, it's selfish. I couldn't stuff my face while you just sit here. Think of the guilt! And I know they're your favourite."

"How?"

"A little bird told me."

"Was this little bird about five foot six, measuring nearly the same round the waist, by any chance?"

"Could be. I didn't measure his waist," she said, her eyes twinkling as she picked up the second half of her wrap. "But I think he said his name was Tony."

"There you go then. Proves what I've always said."

"What have you always said?"

"You can't trust birds to keep your secrets."

She giggled. Pushing her plate to one side, she picked up her coffee and took a long drink, sighing in appreciation. "I so need this."

"Dangerous phrase. Saying 'need' smacks of addiction, you know," Steve said solemnly, then cringed. Funny how innocent jokes could be so unfunny in the right circumstances.

But soon he began to relax for the first time in days as Rebecca chatted about her day. She was such good company. So easy to be with. He could happily sit here all weekend with her, given the chance. But he didn't think that was a chance he'd ever get.

"Are you not going to eat your pastry? Please don't tell me you're on a diet," she said, her tone leaving him in no doubt of how she felt about that.

餐，伙計。我非常飢餓。」她撕開包裝的末端。

「那我讓你吃個夠。」

「這些…」她揮舞著她手中的兩個杏味丹麥酥，「…不是全部是我的。其中一個是給你的。」

「謝謝你。但你不用買給我，我已經吃過…」

「沒問題。」她拿著雞卷咬了一大口，津津有味地咽了下去。「實際上並不是因為我客氣，這是自私的。我總不能塞滿我的嘴，而你就只是坐在這裡。想想都覺得內疚！我知道這是你最喜歡的。」

「怎麼知道？」

「一隻小鳥告訴我的。」

「這只小鳥高約五尺六，量一下發現幾乎跟腰圍相同，是嗎？」

「可能是，但我沒有量過他的腰，」她說，眼睛一閃一閃的，她拿起另外半份雞卷。「但我知道，他說他的名字是東尼。」

「那你真的是去了證明我經常說的事。」

「你經常說什麼？」

「你不可以信任的小鳥可以幫你保守秘密。」

她咯咯地笑起來。她的碟子推到一邊，拿起她的咖啡，喝了一大，讚賞地嘆息道：「我需要這個。」

「這是危險的短語。說『需要』亦會成癮的，你知道的。」史堤夫表情凝重地說，然後畏縮了一下。有趣而天真的笑話也可以在恰當的情況下變得如此無趣。

但很快他開始放鬆了，是今天的第一次，就在麗貝卡聊起她的一天時。她就是這麼好的一個夥伴，很容易相處。他能愉快地坐在這裡跟她渡過所有的週末，希望有這個機會。但他不認為他能夠得到這樣的一個機會。

「你不吃你的糕點？請不要告訴我你在節食。」她說，她的語氣令他不知道她真正的感想是什麼。

「沒有，你覺得我需要嗎？」他盯著她，假裝被冒犯似的。

"No, why, do you think I need to be?" he stared at her, mock-affronted.

"Good Lord no. You're not fat! But then you're not too skinny, either. You're just right," she said, laughing. Then she seemed to realise what she'd said and blushed to the roots of her hair.

There was an awkward silence which Steve tried to break quickly, but failed to, his throat suddenly dry. If he didn't know better he would think she was interested in him.

"Good," he managed to croak eventually, "because I was only waiting for you to finish your main course. Just good manners, don't you know."

"Ah, your mother taught you well."

"I'm afraid she can't claim all the credit for that," he said quietly. She died when I was 9."

Rebecca put her coffee down. "Wow. I really am an idiot," she said. "That was a completely insensitive thing to say."

He smiled awkwardly. "What, because I have Laura to advertise my complete ineptitude at being a surrogate parent?"

"Nobody in their right mind would put the blame for that on you," she said, looking stricken. "I can't imagine how tough it must have been, bringing her up alone, especially when you were so young yourself."

"It was. Very tough. Doesn't change the fact that I didn't do a very good job though." He couldn't look at her, and his throat was so tight that for a minute he couldn't say anything.

"Lots of children have two sensible, mature parents who try their best, yet they still go off the rails." Rebecca sat there, looking at a loss for what to say next.

Well done Steve, this is going swimmingly. Now she feels guilty and uncomfortable and you sound bitter and twisted. He blinked hard, cleared his throat and raised a smile. "Sorry. Boy, I bet you're glad you accepted my invitation now, aren't you. I've cheered up your evening no end."

"No, it's fine, it's my fault. It was a thoughtless thing to say."

"It was a perfectly normal, off-the-cuff comment," said Steve. "Now please start on that pastry and then I can start on mine. It's

「上帝啊。你不胖！但你也不是太瘦，剛剛好。」她說，笑了起來。然後，她似乎意識她說了什麼，然後臉紅耳熱起來。

出現了令人尷尬的沉默，史堤夫試圖快速打破它，但失敗了，他的喉嚨突然很乾。如果他不知道，他會認為她對他感興趣。

「好，」他最終設法啞著嗓子地說，「因為我只是在等著你完成你的主菜。這是良好的禮儀，你知不知道。」

「啊，你媽媽教得你很好。」

「我怕她不能邀功了，」他平靜地說。「她去世時，我只有九歲。」

麗貝卡把她的咖啡放下。「哇，我真的是個白痴，」她說。「這是完全不顧別人感受的說話。」

他尷尬地笑了笑。「什麼？是因為羅拉宣傳了我是一個完全不稱職的代理家長？」

「心智正常的人都不會怪罪於你，」她說，看似受了打擊。「我不能想像一定是有多麼的艱難，要獨自把她帶大，尤其是你自己這麼年輕。」

「這是非常艱難的。但我沒有做好我的工作是不能改變的事實。」雖然他沒有看她，但他的喉嚨仍然很緊，不一會兒他就什麼都不能說。

「很多小孩有兩個懂事、成熟的父母盡了最大的能力去教育他們，但他們仍然會走上歪路。」麗貝卡坐在那裡，不知道下一步該說些什麼。

史堤夫幹得好，一切進展多麼的順利。現在，她感到內疚和不舒服，你的聲音聽起來痛苦而扭曲。他努力地眨了眨眼，清了清嗓子，擠出了一個微笑。「對不起。孩子，我敢打賭你現在覺得接受了我的邀請真好，是不是？我就很高興你的晚上沒有結束。」

「不，這很好，是我的錯。我說了有欠考慮的話。」

「這是完全正常的，只是你即席的意見，」史堤夫說。「現在，請開始享用糕點吧，然後我就可以開始吃我的。它在呼喚我了。」

「好吧。對不起。」她拿起丹麥酥順從地咬了一大口。

calling to me."

"Okay. Sorry." She picked up her Danish and dutifully took a big bite.

"I think we need to ban that word," said Steve, picking up his too, "or we're going to spend all our time apologising."

She nodded, mouth full, and they at the rest of their pastries in a companionable silence. Rebecca wiped her hands on a serviette.

"Would it be awful of me to ask what happened to your father?"

"No. But I'd rather not go into details, if that's alright. He died ten years after my mother."

"So you were 19?"

He nodded. "I hadn't been at university very long."

"Which one?"

"Southampton. I took Architectural Technology."

"Ouch. Try saying that when you're drunk."

He smiled. "I did. Several times."

"Did you get your degree?"

He shook his head. "No, otherwise I wouldn't be working here. I'd already been working at MacDonald's quite a while to help me get through uni."

"Oh yeah." Rebecca nodded emphatically. "Been there, done that."

"So has nearly everyone I know!" He fiddled with the pastry crumbs on his plate. "After Dad died and everything was sorted, I begged all the hours I could and dropped out of uni. A few months later they gave me a full time job. I worked my way up and became a manager eventually."

"So that you could support Laura?"

He nodded. "Yes. The mortgage was paid when Dad died, but there wasn't any money for anything else. He only had enough life insurance to pay for funeral expenses, and he had a few debts. He'd been ill for a long time."

史堤夫說：「我認為我們需要禁用這個詞語，」他拿起他的丹麥酥，「不然我們所有的時間都會在道歉。」

她點點頭，嘴裡塞得滿滿的，剩下來吃糕點的時間他們都保持在沉默。麗貝卡用餐巾紙擦了擦手。

「如果我問你的父親發生了什麼事，你會不會覺得不舒服？」

「沒有。但如果可以的話，我寧願不說得太詳細。他在我母親去世後十年後去世的。」

「那麼你當時是十九歲？」

他點點頭。「所以我沒有在大學待了很久。」

「哪一間？」

「南安普敦。我修建築科技。」

「哎喲。請告訴我你喝醉了。」

他笑了。「我做到了。好幾次。」

「那你有拿到學位嗎？」

他搖搖頭。「沒有，否則我就不會在這裡工作。我已經在麥當勞工作了一段相當長的時間，來幫助我讀大學。」

「噢。」麗貝卡斷然地點頭。「我也有做過。」

「幾乎我認識每個人都做過！」他撥弄著他的碟子上的糕點屑。「爸爸去世並安排好一切之後，我要求了所有的工作時間而且輟學了。幾個月後，他們給了我一份全職的工作，我就一直在那裡並最終成為一名經理。」

「你是為了可以照顧到羅拉？」

他點點頭。「是的。當爸爸死的時候按揭已經付完了，但是沒有再剩下錢了。他的人壽保險只足夠用來支付喪葬費，而他還有幾個債務，因為他之前病了一段很長時間。」

「要你放棄你的學位一定是很困難。」

「是的，我真的很享受那些課程。」

"It must have been hard, giving up your degree."

"It was. I was really enjoying the course."

"So how did you end up here?"

"I'd managed to build up some money and I wanted to go back to studying—either distance learning, so I could keep an eye on Laura and work, too, or else doing architecture at UCL. Stay closer to home. I wanted something closer to home, with hours that were a bit more regular, too, because Laura was starting to..." He hesitated.

"Go off the rails?" she said gently.

"Yes."

"And you like it here?"

"Actually I love it. Tony's been so good to me. It's a good place to work, and-," be bold, Steve, "—you get to meet some really nice people."

She met his gaze. "I hope that includes me."

"Definitely." Steve's heart seemed to be thudding very loudly in his chest. He let his eyes linger on hers for a moment. It was no good. He had to broach the subject.

"So where's Kevin tonight?"

She grinned. "D & D, would you believe?"

"D&D?" He frowned. "Am I meant to know what that is?"

"Dungeons and Dragons."

"Ah. Got it. He's into that, then, is he?"

"Madly. He loves his RPG. D&D every Friday. Every Friday."

"I take it you don't share his enthusiasm."

She shuddered. "Wild horses wouldn't drag me there. I can't think of anything worse."

"You don't have shared hobbies, then?"

"Oh we do. We like a lot of the same music, so we nearly always

「所以就這樣結束了？」

「我有儲了一些錢，想回去學習，無論是遠程學習也可以。這樣我就可以同時照顧到羅拉和工作，不然在倫敦大學學院讀也可以。那裡離家更近，我想要離家近一點的，如果可以在一小時內的距離就可以令生活規律一點，因為羅拉開始…」他猶豫了一下。

「走上歪路？」她輕輕地說。

「是的。」

「那麼你喜歡這裡嗎？」

「其實我很喜歡。東尼一直對我這麼好，而且這裡也是一個很好的工作地方，而且…」史堤夫要大膽點，「…可以遇到一些非常不錯的人。」
她對上了他的視線。「我希望有包括我。」

「當然。」史堤夫的心在胸腔裏劇烈地跳動著。他讓自己的眼睛流連在她的眼睛上一會兒。這樣不好，他一定要轉個話題。

「那凱文今晚在哪裡呢？」

她咧嘴一笑。「龍與地，你相信嗎？」

「龍與地，」他皺起了眉頭。「不知道是不是我想的那個？」

「龍與地下城。」

「嗯。猜到了。他很喜歡嗎？」

「瘋狂地，他很熱愛角色扮演遊戲。每個星期五都龍與地，是每個星期五。」

「你看來不太認同他熱衷的事。」

她打了一個寒顫。「八人大轎都請不動我去那裡，我想不出有什麼事情可以更糟。」

「所以你們沒有共同的興趣嗎？」

「哦，我們有的。我們喜歡很多相同的音樂，所以我們幾乎總是一起去看演唱會。雖然他不喜歡羅比．威廉姆斯，所以我不得不叫我的朋友安娜去。」她笑了。「她並不介意的，她有帶花邊內褲到那裡的。」

go to gigs together. He hates Robbie Williams though, so I have to drag my friend Anna out instead," she laughed. "Not that she minds. She takes a supply of lacy knickers with her."

Steve's eyebrows shot up, momentarily distracted from worrying about her relationship with Kevin. "Really?"

"Really. Five pairs, last time, in her jacket pocket."

"How old is she?"

"38."

"Blimey." Steve whistled. "It must be true what they say about women in their late thirties."

"I wouldn't know," she said with a wicked grin. "When I get there, I'll let you know."

I'd rather be around to find out for myself, thought Steve, starting to feel rather hot under the collar. That cheeky smile of hers was killing him. This conversation wasn't helping him keep a friendly distance. He found her presence more disturbing than ever—in the most pleasurable way but dangerous way.

"So have you got any plans for the weekend?" he asked, trying to steer the conversation into safer waters.

"Shopping tomorrow morning—Kev and I have got an engagement party to go to tomorrow evening, so we'll be combing the streets of London for a decent gift."

Gloom settled over Steve. Whatever signals he thought he was getting, they must be wishful thinking. Shopping together sounded a very couple thing to do.

"Who's getting engaged? A friend?" he asked, trying to keep the disappointment out of his voice. Bang went his plan to hint at a possible lunch date, to see how she reacted.

"Anna."

"Anna? Anna throws-lots-of-knockers-at-Robbie Anna?"

"Yep, that's the one."

"Does her boyfriend know? Or doesn't he care?"

"She hasn't got a boyfriend." Rebecca's eyes danced with

史堤夫的眉毛迅速上揚，頃刻之間分散了他對她與凱文關係的擔心。「真的嗎？」

「真的。五件，最後一次是，在她的上衣的口袋裡。」

「她有多大了？」

「三十八。」

「啊呀。」史堤夫吹了一聲口哨。「那一定是真的，他們說的什麼三十有幾的女人。」

「我不知道，」她說，一個邪惡的笑容在臉上。「當我到那個年紀的時候，我再告訴你。」

我寧願留在她身邊到那時候自己去發現，史堤夫開始覺得自己的衣領下相當之熱。她臉上的微笑可以將他殺死。這次談話並沒有幫助他跟她保持友好的距離。他發現她的出現比以往都令人不安，雖然是以最愉快的方式，但卻是危險的方式。

「所以，你週末有什麼計劃嗎？」他問，試圖將話題掌舵到安全的水域。

「明天早上要購物去，凱文和我明天晚上要去一個訂婚派對，所以我們會在倫敦街頭四處搜尋一個像樣的禮物。」

黑暗籠罩了史堤夫。任何信號他接收到的，都一定只是他一廂情願。購物聽起來是一對情侶去做的事情。

「誰訂婚？朋友嗎？」他問，試圖讓他的聲音聽起來不至於那麼失望。看她的反應，原本想暗示有沒有機會跟她來個午餐約會，現在徹底沒戲了。

「安娜。」

「安娜？拋出很多內褲給羅比的那個安娜？」

「沒錯，就是這個。」

「她的男友是否知道？或者他不關心嗎？」

「她沒有男朋友。」麗貝卡的眼惡作劇般跳動著。

mischief.

"What?"

"She's getting engaged to her girlfriend."

"I... see," said Steve slowly. "Actually, no I don't. The knicker-throwing...?"

"To put it in the vernacular," said Rebecca, laughing, "she bats for both sides. But mainly, very mainly, for her own. Robbie's a bit of an exception, really. Him and Daniel Craig, for some reason."

"So she just doesn't date real men?"

"Well she's dated a couple, but—"

Steve put a hand up. "Sorry, I don't know why I asked that. It's really none of my business."

"That's alright. She wouldn't mind! She's always been very open about her sexuality. I find most people are, these days. They make a lovely couple—they're so happy together." She got out her phone, swiped the screen a couple of times with her thumb and then turned it towards him.

Steve looked at the picture. Both women were beautiful; pictured hand in hand on a beach, tanned and relaxed in long, bright summer dresses, wearing big smiles. Rebecca leaned close to him and Steve caught the scent of her perfume. He tried hard to focus as she pointed to the woman on the left, with long, wavy blonde hair.

"That's Anna. The dark-haired one is Jessica."

"They're stunners."

"Aren't they. Sickening." She twisted to put her phone away, and Steve felt emboldened by her turned back.

"You've no need to be envious, have you. You're hardly a wallflower yourself." Oh God. He could feel himself going red.

She turned round quickly. "You're going to make me blush."

Not nearly so much as I am, he thought, trying to look casual as he tidied up his sugar sachets and avoided her eyes.

"Thanks."

「什麼？」

「跟她訂婚的是她的女朋友。」

「我…明白了，」史堤夫緩慢地說。「不，我不明白。拋內褲的…？」

「把它說成白話，」麗貝卡說，笑了，「她兩面都支持的。但主要是，很主要是，憑她自己感覺。羅比是真的有一點例外，還有丹尼爾．克雷格，出於某種原因。」

「即是，她只是不跟真正的男人約會？」

「嗯，她曾經約會過，但…」

史堤夫舉起一隻手。「對不起，我不知道為什麼我要問。其實真的不關我事。」

「這沒問題的，她不會介意！她對於自己的性取向一直是非常開放的，我覺得這個年頭的大多數人都是。她們是一對可愛的情侶…他們真的很快樂。」她拿出她的電話，用拇指在畫面上掃了幾下，然後轉向給他看。

史堤夫看著那幅相片，是兩個美麗的女人的合照，她們手牽手在海灘上，曬得黝黑而輕鬆地，穿著長而明亮的夏季長裙，臉上掛著大大的笑容。麗貝卡湊近他，史堤夫陷入她的香水味之中。他拼命把注意力集中在她指著的那個在左邊有波浪金髮的女人。

「這是安娜。黑髮的是潔西卡。」

「她們都是大美人。」

「她們不是。討厭。」她擰轉手機把它拿開，當她的轉身時史堤夫感到膽子越來越大。

「你沒有必要羨慕，你也是。你要自己當壁花很難啊。」哦，上帝。他能感覺到自己已經臉紅了。

她迅速地轉身。「你要令我臉紅了。」

他認為她的臉根本遠遠不及他的紅，他試圖看起來漫不經心地收拾起小袋糖，避免看到她的眼睛。

「謝謝。」

"My pleasure," he said quietly.

There was a pause. "So what are your plans for tomorrow?"

He sighed. "I'll be visiting Laura."

"She's not back living with you then?"

"Hopefully she will be. She's in a secure drug rehab unit at the moment."

"Oh." Rebecca squirmed. "God, I'm sorry. I didn't know. I seem to be making a great job of putting my foot in it this evening."

"Don't worry, you weren't to know." He smiled at her. This bit's the easy bit in a way. It's what happens next that I'm dreading."

"What's that?"

"When she comes out, her bail conditions mean she has to spend two weeks under the supervision of a named person, whom the court approves, at all times. I can cover most of it if I use my annual leave, but Tony has to go into hospital for some tests. With Neil gone, that leaves me and Rinaldo." He shrugged.

"Can't you ask someone else to supervise her?"

"The police can authorise someone else—it doesn't have to be just me—but who else can I ask? Anyone else has to have a valid CRB check. I haven't exactly got a huge social circle, and everyone I know works. It's a huge ask, even if you're really close to someone. They'd have to come to a meeting before she gets out, have their ID checked..." He shook his head. "And she seems a lot better, but I can't guarantee she won't flip out."

"Poor you." Her eyes were full of sympathy. "That must be really worrying. Have you spoken to Tony about it?"

He shook his head. "Not in any detail, not yet. I was hoping I could figure something out."

"Let's hope something turns up."

"Yes, let's. Anyway," he said, trying to muster a smile and turn the conversation, "I think I can guarantee your Saturday will be fun. Don't do anything too wild."

"Well I hope yours isn't too bad, I really do," she said putting her hand on his for a moment. "I won't be having too wild a time.

「這是我的榮幸。」他平靜地說。

有一陣子停頓。「那麼，你明天有什麼計劃嗎？」

他嘆了口氣。「我會探訪羅拉。」

「她不會回來跟你一起生活嗎？」

「希望她會。她現在在一個安全的戒毒康復單位。」

「哦。」麗貝卡扭動著。「天啊，我很抱歉。我不知道這事。我今晚似乎一直在做偉大的工作就是涉足於這些事。」

「不要擔心，又不是你自己要知道的。」他對她笑著。「這應該已經是一條容易的路了，我在害怕接下來會發生什麼事。」

「會有什麼事？」

「當她走出來，她的保釋條件是她在兩個星期內的任何時候，都要由一名由法院批准的人監督。如果我用我的年假，應該還可以做到，但東尼必須入醫院進行了一些測試，而隨著尼爾走了，留下只有我和里納爾多。」他聳聳肩。

「你不能要求別人來監督她嗎？」

「警察可以授權別人，不一定是我，但還有誰我可以問呢？任何人都必須有先做一個有效的刑事紀錄檢查。而且我完全沒有一個龐大的社交圈子，我認識的人都要工作。還有一個很大的問題，即使我找到一個親朋好友，但在她出來之前，他們都不得來開會，檢查他們的身份…」他搖了搖頭。「雖然她似乎好了很多，但我不能保證她不會失控。」

「真可憐。」她的眼睛充滿了同情。「那一定是非常令人擔憂。你跟東尼談過了嗎？」

他搖搖頭。「沒有談到這麼仔細，還沒有。我希望我能想出辦法。」

「讓我們一起期望吧。」

「是的，一起。無論如何。」他說，試圖擠出一個微笑，換了個話題，「我想我可以保證你的星期六會很好玩，但不要做任何太狂野的事。」

We're going for dinner at Kevin's parents on Sunday, and that makes it my job to keep us both sober. Relatively sober, anyway."

Dinner with Kevin's parents? This was the end of any doubts he had. They were obviously a couple, and she was just one of those open, friendly women to whom a little low-level flirting comes naturally, as part and parcel of their character. Rebecca probably wasn't even aware of the effect she was having. Thank God he hadn't read anything into it.

Yeah right, Steve. You read quite a lot into it. You'd have liked to read the whole damn book, given half a chance.

"Sounds like fun," he said dully.

"Well Kevin's Dad cooks a mean roast and his mum is the queen of puddings. Rumour is she's making a very alcoholic zabaglione, so chances are we might end up more sloshed on Sunday than Saturday!" She grinned. "And talking of Saturday, now that I've refuelled I'd better go, otherwise I'll never face shopping tomorrow. Shopping with Kev is a nightmare. I need to brace myself." She stood up and pulled her jacket on.

"Enjoy your party." Steve tried to summon a bright smile. "And your Sunday dinner."

"I'm sure I will. Saturday should be good, and Kev's parents are lovely." She buttoned her jacket. "They've been like surrogate parents to me, really."

"That's nice." His chest felt tight. What was up with him? He felt jealous of Kevin but envious of Rebecca, too, he realised, with her 'lovely, surrogate parents'. Her weekend sounded idyllic. He wanted Rebecca, and part of him wanted to be Rebecca, and live her life.

"I'm very lucky." She swung her bag on to her shoulder. "I doubt if I'll see you this week. I think we're going to be on site right the way through."

"So you'll be drinking coffee somewhere else, will you? Traitor."

"I'm afraid so." She rested a hand briefly on his shoulder. "I'm sorry about Laura. I really hope she gets better soon. And that your weekend's not too grim."

"Thanks." he didn't know what else to say. "See you."

"Bye."

「好吧，我希望你的也不會太差，我真的希望，」她說，把她的手放在他的手上面好一會。「我這次一定不會很狂野。在週日，還要跟凱文的父母共進晚餐，讓我們都保持清醒變成了我的任務。無論如何要比較清醒。」

跟凱文的父母晚餐嗎？這是他懷疑的最後一步，很明顯他們是一對的，而她只是有些開放，一個友好的女人很自然地用有點低級的手法跟你調情，這是她們性格中不可或缺的一部分。麗貝卡可能甚至不知道她做到了這個效果。感謝上帝，他沒有閱讀太多她的事。

是啊，史堤夫。你已經讀了不少了。你喜歡讀完整本該死的書，給自己一半的機會。

「聽起來很有趣。」他遲鈍地說。

「凱文的爸爸會烤肉，而他的母親是布丁女皇。謠言說她很會做酒精薩白利昂飲料，因此我們的週日有機會最終比週六喝得爛醉！」她笑了。「說起星期六，現在我需要先加油，最好先回去了，否則我永遠不能面對明天的購物。跟凱文購物是一場噩夢，我需要穩住自己。」她站了起來，穿起她的外套。

「享受你的派對。」史堤夫試圖鼓起一個燦爛的笑容。「還有週日的晚餐。」

「我敢肯定我會的。週六應該是很不錯，而凱文的父母亦都很可愛。」她穿好她的外套。「他們已經像我的代理家長了，真的。」

「這一家人真的很不錯。」他感到胸緊張。什麼一回事呢？他很嫉妒凱文，但他意識到他很羨慕麗貝卡有「可愛代理家長」，她的週末聽起來就像田園詩般一樣。他想要麗貝卡，有一部分的他很想成為麗貝卡，住她的生命裡。

「我很幸運。」她把她的手袋擺在肩膀上。「我懷疑我這個星期是否能再見到你。我想我們要直接到在場地去工作。」

「那麼，你會在別的地方喝咖啡了，是嗎？叛徒。」

「我恐怕是。」她把手短暫地放在他的肩膀上。「我很抱歉關於羅拉的事。我真心希望她盡快變得更好，而你的週末不是太嚴峻。」

He sat there for a long time after she left, staring at nothing much at all. After a while he became aware that Tony was standing beside him.

"You want a wrap, Steve?" asked Tony gently. "We've got two left. Or another coffee, if you want? On the house. I'll have to send you home soon though, my friend. Maria's waiting."

Steve looked down at his watch. How had that happened? It was nearly 9. Looking round, he realised the only other customers left, a couple who were sitting near the door, were getting to their feet and putting their coats on. He stood up, shaking his head. "No thanks, Tony. I think I need something stronger."

He went to walk away, but Tony put a hand on his arm.

"Look after yourself, eh? And don't do anything silly. You're a good boy, Steve, but I worry for you. You've got to have some faith, si? Things will turn out okay in the end."

"I'm sure it will, if the end ever gets here," he said bitterly. His eyes stung and he didn't trust himself to turn round. Instead he headed straight for the door, only giving the briefest of nods and well aware that he'd left Tony staring after him, looking worried sick. He knew Tony deserved better, and as he strode towards the pub he was filled with guilt.

How could he feel any worse? arm. "And by the sound of it, you don't really have that much respect for anyone else's view anyway." She laid the £20 note on the table.

"Look, Rebecca, I—I mean, we were getting on so well—"

"Yes we were. Surprising, really, lame brain that I am. Not a hypocrite by the way, I don't eat venison or veal." She smiled tightly and-ever-so-politely. "Believe me when I say I'm as disappointed at how things have turned out as you are. Who would have thought that one sentence could ruin a whole evening?"

"But does this have to matter? We can agree not to talk about it." A tiny glimmer of hope sparked in his eyes.

In other circumstances, that eagerness would have been fantastically flattering for her ego, she thought. Not now. "That wouldn't change the fact that you do something that's completely against my principles. I can't ignore it." She frowned. "Unlike you. Why didn't you say you were into hunting on your profile? It would have saved both of us time. It specifically asked about things like this under 'ethics and viewpoints'."

「謝謝。」他不知道還能說什麼。「再見。」

「再見。」

她離開後，他坐在那裡很長一段時間，沒有在盯著什麼。一段時間後，他意識到東尼站在他身旁。

「你想要個肉卷嗎？史堤夫。」東尼輕輕地問。「我們有兩個剩下。或者要杯咖啡，如果你想？免費的。但我必須很快就要送你回家，朋友。瑪麗亞在等我。」

史堤夫低頭看了看自己的手錶。剛發生了什麼事？已經差不多九點了。他環顧四周，他意識到其他客人都離開了，坐在靠近門口的一對夫婦，他們正站了起來，並穿起自己的大衣。他站起來，搖搖頭。「不，謝謝你，東尼。我想我需要更強烈的東西。」

他走開，但東尼一隻手放在他的胳膊上。

「照顧好自己，知道嗎？而且不要做傻事。你是個好男孩，史堤夫，但我很擔心你。你得要有信心，嗯？事情到底都會變好的。」

「我敢肯定會，如果終點就在這裡。」他苦澀地說。他的眼神有點刺痛，他不相信自己沒有轉身，相反地直奔大門，只簡單地點了頭，他清楚地意識到，當他離開後，東尼一直盯著看他而且擔心得要命。他知道東尼應得到好點的回應，他大步走向酒吧，充滿著內疚。

他怎麼能感覺更差勁呢？

"I know, and I did!" He looked genuinely perplexed. "That's why I was surprised by your reaction."

Rebecca shook her head. "I'm starting to think that agency couldn't organise a piss-up in a brewery."

He nodded ruefully. "They do seem to like matching polar opposites. My last date hated Italian food, and Chinese. I rarely eat anything else."

"That sounds familiar." She sighed as she pushed her chair in. "It was interesting to meet you, Dean. Sorry I wasn't what you were expecting."

"No, you were fine, I mean I... more than fine," he floundered. "But obviously we're not a good match. I hope you have better luck with your next date."

That wasn't very likely, she thought as she left. Because there wasn't going to be a next date.

不需要此页

Chapter Fifteen

Rebecca leaned on the counter. "Hi."

"Hi." Steve smiled, but there was a weariness about it that meant although it reached his eyes, it didn't make them shine the way they usually did.

Poor Steve. Rebecca saw the shadows under his eyes and that tell-tale stretched look she'd seen on herself in the mirror a few times, when sleep was coming rarely and not giving you any proper rest when it did. She knew how it felt to have grief and worry gnawing away at you.

"Have you got time for lunch?" she asked gently. "I can come back if now's not good."

"Thanks, but I don't think I'm very good company at the moment."

"I wasn't asking if you were good company. I was asking you to have lunch with me." Why did he put these barriers up? She couldn't understand it. She didn't think she'd made a very good job of keeping her distance; whenever he looked sad she felt compelled to touch his arm, or his shoulder. Surely he knew how she felt?

"I'm sure you'd have a much better time with Kevin. I'll probably only take a short break anyway, we're pretty busy today."

"Well, I'm not going to beg, because a lady never does that," she said lightly. "But I am disappointed." A lot more disappointed than you know.

He looked up sharply. "Disappointed? What do you mean?"

"Because I thought we were more than just café supremo and customer lady." She flashed him a small smile. "I thought we were friends. And friends are there for you even when life's not all butterscotch lattes and chocolate sprinkles."

第十五章

麗貝卡靠在櫃檯上。「嗨。」

「嗨。」史堤夫笑著，雖然她看到他的眼睛，但流露著一絲倦意，也沒有了跟平常一樣神采。

可憐史堤夫。麗貝卡看見他眼睛下的陰影，揭穿那個耗盡的表情。她曾經有幾次在鏡子裡看過自己這個樣子，是睡眠不足，而沒有任何適當休息的時候。她知道感覺就像被悲傷和憂慮蛀空了自己一樣。

「你有空吃個午飯嗎？」她輕輕地問。「我可以再回來，如果現在不是很方便的話。」

「謝謝你，但我不認為我現在是一個非常好的夥伴。」

「我沒有要你做好的夥伴。我是問你跟我共進午餐。」他為什麼拒人於千里之外？她無法理解。她沒有想過她做了什麼去保持跟他的距離。而每當看著他傷心，她覺得自己不得不去觸摸一下他的胳膊或肩膀。當然，他會知道她的感覺嗎？

「我敢肯定，你跟凱文一起吃的時間會過得更好。我大概只需要短暫的休息，無論如何我們今天很忙。」

「好吧，我不會去乞求，因為女人從來不會，」她輕輕地說。「但我感到失望。」比你知道的更加失望。

他大幅度地抬起頭來。「失望？你是什麼意思？」

「因為我覺得我們不僅僅是咖啡店掌門和女性客人的關係。」她向他微微地笑了。「我還以為我們是朋友。而朋友就是為了你而在這裡，而生活並非只有奶油糖果拿鐵咖啡和巧克力碎灑。」

他笑了一下，他的臉少了些緊張了。「還有印第安雞卷？」

He smiled, and some of the tension left his face. "And Cajun chicken wraps?"

"Life's definitely not always those. Particularly if you've got clothes you don't want dry-cleaned." She smiled. "You never did talk to Tony about that excess sauce, did you?"

He shook his head. "If you really want to have lunch, then I'll go and ask Tony if I can go now. I might as well, to be honest. I've been cleaning the same bit of the counter for the last ten minutes."

"Mind not on the job?" she asked wryly.

"You could say that."

Steve went to the kitchen door and had a brief muffled conversation.

Rebecca leaned on the counter waiting and pondering. Perhaps he just didn't fancy her. After all, now she knew he'd been unattached all this time, it did raise the question—if he did like her, why hadn't he done something about it before now?

Rebecca could hear Tony rumbling in reply, with the occasional discernible, 'si, si'. A few moments later, Steve came back to the counter and pulled his apron off, closely followed by Tony.

"Rebecca, what would you like today? Something special, eh, that I make just for you? Or perhaps you try my new Caribbean Chicken wrap, and tell me what you think?"

"Thanks for the offer, Tony," she smiled, "But I was wondering if Steve would like me to take him away from all this, and go somewhere else for lunch. Just for a change." She looked at Steve questioningly.

Tony clutched at his chest. "Somewhere else?" he said dramatically. "I cannot believe what I am hearing. Is not good for Tony's heart!" Then he grinned. "She is a wise woman, this one, eh Steve? A very good idea. A change of scenery!"

Steve looked dazed. "Right, that would be great." Then he looked quickly at Tony. "When I say great, I mean different. Obviously the food won't be as good as yours, and the coffee—"

Tony shut him up by flicking him with the cloth he'd left on the side, and pushing him away from the counter. "Go, go, foolish boy! Enough! Take as long as you like."

「生活肯定不是只有那些。尤其是如果你穿了一件你不想拿去乾洗的衣服。」她笑著說。「你從來沒有跟東尼說大多醬汁了，是嗎？」

他搖搖頭。「如果你真的想要吃午飯，我可以去問東尼，我現在可不可以出去。我想一定可以，老實說，在之前的十分鐘，我一直在清潔櫃檯上同一個位置。」

「很用心工作嗎？」她挖苦地問道。

「你可以這麼說。」

史堤夫走到去廚房門，並簡短而低沉地說了幾句話。

麗貝卡俯身在櫃檯上等待和思考。也許他沒有喜歡上她。至少現在她知道他在這個時候沒有被纏住，但這樣就有一個問題，如果他喜歡她，為什麼之前一直都沒有什麼行動呢？

麗貝卡能聽到東尼低沉地回應著，偶爾可聽到「嗯，嗯」。幾分鐘後，史堤夫回來到櫃檯並拉開他的圍裙，緊隨其後的是東尼。

「麗貝卡，你今天想要什麼嗎？一些特別的東西，哎，我為你做一個？或者你試試我的新加勒比雞肉卷，告訴我你想要什麼呢？」

「謝謝你的好意，東尼，」她笑了，「但我在想，史堤夫可能想我帶他遠離這一切，去別的地方吃午飯。只是改變一下。」她一副詢問的表情看著史堤夫。

東尼抓住了胸口。「別的地方？」他戲劇性地說。「我簡直不敢相信我所聽到的。這對東尼的心臟不好的！」說完，他笑了。「她是個聰明的女人，這個，史堤夫，嗯？一個很不錯的主意，改變一下環境！

史堤夫一臉茫然。「是的，這實在是太好了。」然後他趕緊望向東尼。「當我說太好了的時候，我的意思其實是相反的。顯然，食物不會及得上你的，還有咖啡。」

東尼用剛才他放在一邊的抹布抽打他要他閉嘴，並從櫃檯把他推了出去。「走，走，蠢男孩！夠了！你喜歡去多久就多久。」

一陣大笑，麗貝卡和史堤夫急忙跑掉了。

「所以我們要去哪裡？」他問。他還沒有太多的心情，但現在他

Laughing, Rebecca and Steve scuttled out.

"So where are we going?" He asked. He hadn't been in the mood for this at all, but now they were out here on the pavement he was glad she'd persuaded him.

"Where would you like to go?" She smiled into his eyes and he felt the familiar lurch inside him.

"You choose."

"Alfresco, or is that a bit optimistic?"

He squinted upwards to where a weak sun was managing to shine hazily through a thin layer of cloud. "Alfresco. I don't think it's going to rain. I'm not sitting on grass though, everything's still wet."

She punched him gently on the arm. "I invited you out for lunch, not a picnic. What do you take me for?" She smiled. "I know just the place. It's a ten minute walk though."

"That's okay."

They walked in companionable silence for a while, only exchanging the odd remark until they came to the canal. Rebecca turned on to the bridge and Steve raised his eyebrows.

"Where are you taking me, woman?"

"It will be worth it, you'll see. I know it doesn't look very promising at the moment."

He smiled. "I'm glad you said it first."

"You don't have a favourite café, then? Other than Tony's?"

He shrugged. "I've not really explored the cafés around here, to be honest."

"How come?"

"I haven't lived here that long."

"So where you're living now—it's not your father's house?"

He nodded. "No. He wanted to downsize, release some money

們在人行道上，他很高興她有勸他出來。

「你想去哪裡？」她看著他的眼睛微笑著，他感覺得他熟悉的東西進入了他的心。

「你選擇。」

「露天的，會不會有點太樂觀？」

他瞇起眼睛向上看著微弱的太陽透過一層薄薄的雲閃耀著。「露天的吧。我不認為會下雨，但我不會坐在草地上，都是濕濕的。」

她輕輕地打了他手臂一下。「我邀請你出去午餐，而不是野餐。你想帶我去哪？」她笑著。「我知道有個地方，但從這裡要走十分鐘的路程。」

「那好吧。」

他們沉默地走了一陣，只是間中說了些奇怪的言論，直到他們來到了運河。麗貝卡開啟了橋樑，而史堤夫揚起了眉毛。

「這位女士，你要帶我去哪裡？」

「你將會明白這是值得的。我知道在這刻看起來並不是非常有前景。」

他笑了。「我很高興你先跟我說了。」

「你沒有喜愛的咖啡店嗎？除了東尼那家？」

他聳聳肩。「說實話，我沒有在這裡真正探索過周圍的咖啡店。」

「怎麼會呢？」

「我還沒有在這裡住了很久。」

「但你現在住的地方...這不是你父親的房子嗎？」

他點點頭。「沒有。他希望轉一間較小的，那就可以從我們的老房子換一些錢，但其實它並不是很實用的。他病得太重沒辦法處理它。如果我有意識他病得有那麼重，我就不會上大學，但他隱瞞得太好了。」

from our old house, but it wasn't practical. He was too ill to handle it. If I'd have realised how ill he was, I would never have gone to uni, but he hid it from me too well."

"He didn't want to stop you living your life," she said gently.

"No, he didn't." He paused. "Anyway, in the end it was Laura and I who downsized eight months ago, because the old house was high maintenance. And," he said, "Laura wasn't earning any money. I didn't want to, but..." he shrugged. "Needs must. Our new place is tiny."

"At least your Dad knew he was leaving you a home."

"Yes. Although I'd rather have kept my Dad. Sod the house."

"I can understand that. Losing a parent is awful."

He touched her arm. "I'm sorry. It must have been a lot worse for you."

She shook her head. "Don't worry. The fact I've lost my parents too doesn't change the fact you've lost yours, or negate your feelings. It just means we both know how painful it is. That's what I wanted to talk to you about... whoops!" She grabbed his elbow and he stopped. "What?"

She grinned. "That's what I get for talking too much. We need to go down there."

"Down there? But that just leads to the canal."

"Yep. Lead on cowboy," she said, attempting a Wild West accent.

"That was terrible," he said, looking around, puzzled, as they started down a paved slope.

"I know, sorry! I love cowboy films."

"Me too. I watch them for the horses." He kept his face straight. "What about you?"

"Oh absolutely. Horses, every time." She said innocently.

The sun came out as they reached the canal, making the water sparkle.

"Perfect," she breathed. "Now that's good timing."

「他不想防礙你的生活。」她輕輕地說。

「不，他沒有。」他停頓了一下。「無論如何，羅拉和我在八個月前就搬走了，因為老房子要高額維修。」他說，「羅拉並沒有任何收入。我雖然不想，但是...」他聳聳肩。「一定要這樣了。我們的新房子很小。」

「至少你爸爸知道他有留給你一個家。」

「是的。雖然我寧願留下的是我爸爸。該死的房子。」

「我可以理解，失去父母實在是太可怕了。」

他摸著她的手臂。「對不起。你的情況一定是更差。」

她搖搖頭。「別擔心。事實上，我失去我的父母也不會改變你失去了你父母這個事實，亦不能去抵消你的感覺。這只是意味著，我們都知道這是多麼痛苦的事情。這就是我想和你談的...哎呦！」她抓住他的手肘，他停了下來。「什麼？」

她咧嘴一笑。「這就是我說話太多了，我們是要下去那裡。」

「下去那裡？但是，這只是走向運河。」

「沒錯。帶領牛仔繼續前進。」她嘗試用狂野西部的口音說。

「很可怕。」他說，困惑地環顧四周，他們開始了走上了一條鋪成的斜坡。

「我知道，對不起！我愛牛仔電影。」

「我也是。我喜歡看他們的馬。」他保持正經的樣子。「你呢？」

「哦，絕對是。馬，每一次都是。」她天真地說。

當他們到達了運河，太陽出來了，照在水上閃閃發光的。

「完美，」她低聲說。「現在是很好的時機。」

他停了下來。「對，但我們是在運河。你要帶我上船嗎？雖然我知道東尼說只要我想多久都可以，但...」

「噓！我們沿著這裡。」她拉著他沿著很短的纖道走，然後把他停住。「嗒－噠！」

He stopped. "Right, we're at the canal. Are you taking me on a boat? I know Tony said to take as long as I want, but—"

"Shh! We turn along here." She tugged him along the towpath for a short distance then brought him to a stop. "Ta-da!"

"Neat." Steve shook his head and stared in amazement. "I had no idea this was here." At the ground level of a large industrial building, a long, skinny café squeezed itself along the side of the towpath. Several brightly coloured tables stood outside, some protected under large red canopies.

"Ah." She tapped the side of her nose. "London's best-kept not-so-secret secret. The Towpath café." They took a seat at a small, square table, painted postbox red.

"Do you come here often?"

She giggled and Steve buried his head in his hands. "Oh God," he said, his voice muffled. "I can't believe I just said that. That wasn't me trotting out the most cheesy chat-up line known to man, honest. It was a genuine question."

"It's shut in the winter, more's the pity," she answered, still laughing. "But I come fairly often once it opens. Usually on the weekends when I've got more time, but sometimes I come here for a change in the week, if I've got time. Or if I'm working on a site nearby. They do a great breakfast."

"Just you? Doesn't Kevin come too?" What strange compulsion made him ask that, when he didn't want to know? Just the thought of them together in the sunshine, enjoying a long, lazy lunch, provoked a hot surge of jealousy in his chest. The last thing he wanted to do was picture the pair of them here, but his stupid brain seemed to have other ideas.

"No. This is a me thing. A place I like to come by myself."

It was ridiculous that he felt a ridiculous wave of relief wash over him when she said that. In that case, I'm honoured m'lady," he said, touching an imaginary hat to her.

She smiled back at him in a way that stirred up all the feelings he'd been trying to put to rest. "So you should be," she said. "I've never brought anyone else here."

"Really? Nobody?" His throat felt tight.

"Yep."

「太棒了。」史堤夫搖了搖頭,驚奇地盯著。「我不知道在這裡有這個地方。」在地面上有一座大型的工業建築物,長而窄的咖啡店在纖道的一側。在大紅色的簷篷保護下,有幾張顏色鮮豔的桌子在門外。

「啊...」她一邊輕叩著鼻側。「倫敦保持得最好的就是不太秘密的秘密,就像在纖道的咖啡店。」他們坐了下來,在紅色頂篷下的一張小方桌。

「你常來這兒嗎?」

她咯咯地笑,史堤夫把他的頭埋在手中。「噢,天啊。」他悶悶的說。「我簡直不敢相信我剛才說了什麼。那我不是反覆說著一個男人與人搭訕時的套話,說實在的,這是一個真正的問題。」

「它在冬季不營業的,很可惜,」她回答說,但還在笑。「但是,如果有營業的期間,我來得相當頻繁。通常是在週末,因為我有更多的時間。但有時我也會在週日來到這裡吃點不同的,如果我有時間的話,或者如果我在附近的場地工作。他們做的早餐很棒。」

「只有你嗎?凱文不來?」什麼奇怪的衝動令他問了這個他其實不想知道的問題?只要想到他們一起在陽光下,享受著一個長而休閒的午餐,就在他的胸口挑起了一陣刺熱的嫉妒。最後一件事他想去做的就是想像他們兩人在這裡,但他那個愚蠢的大腦似乎有其他的想法。

「沒有。這是我的東西。一個我喜歡自己來地方。」

很荒謬地,當她這樣說的時候,他覺得自己被一波荒謬解救了。在這種情況下,「我很榮幸,我的女士」他說,碰一下她那頂虛構的帽子。

她微笑地望著他,激起了所有的感情,那是他一直試圖放在一旁的。「所以,你應該是,」她說。「我從來沒有帶任何人來過這裡。」

「真的嗎?沒有任何人?」他的喉嚨發緊。

「沒錯。」

她目不轉睛地看著他,而史堤夫認為,他們之間的氣氛比以往任何時候都更加親密。他的大腦一片空白,他設法不看她去看其他

She looked at him intently and Steve felt that the atmosphere between them was more intimate than ever. His brain went blank, and he tried to look at anything but her. "It's a great location, right by the water," he said, voice hoarse.

She leaned back in her chair. "Yes, it is." Her voice seemed a little flat. "In the summer, it gets heaving. People bring picnic blankets and put them on the towpath."

"Sounds great."

"Yes, although there's always a few people who put their rugs too close to the canal edge so that nobody can get past. Nutters! Sometimes it's so hot here in the summer, though, that people sit in that alcove back there." She pointed awkwardly back over her shoulder. "It gets crammed in there when it rains, too, although it's too shallow to keep you properly dry."

"I can see that." he smiled. "Now as you're a regular, what do you recommend?"

"Well as a frequent visitor, more than a regular, I can tell you that the menu changes frequently – they try and keep it seasonal, and buy local – and that nearly everything here is homemade. Oh, and gorgeous. I can particularly recommend the ginger beer, sir, if you're feeling brave."

"Brave?"

"It'll put a fire in your belly. It's fierce." She sounded like a pirate and Steve laughed.

"What is it with you and accents today?"

"No idea. The canal air's obviously gone to my head."

"What about food?"

"There's the menu..." she craned her neck to look past him and Steve realised there was a blackboard on the wall.

"Ooh, I can definitely recommend the salmon terrine and salad. Well, if you like fish, I can." she eyed him doubtfully.

"I love fish." He twisted round in his chair. "Hmm. Decisions, decisions. They've got kedgeree, too. I love kedgeree."

"Theirs is great."

東西。「這是一個很棒的地方，又鄰近水。」他聲音嘶啞地說。

她靠在椅背上。「是的，」她的聲音顯得有些平淡。「夏天，會有一些波濤起伏。人們會帶野餐毯子來，並把它鋪設在纖道上。」

「聽起來不錯。」

「是的，雖然總是有些人會把他們的毯子放得太靠近運河邊緣，而令其他人不能過去。瘋子！夏天的時候，這裡有時會很熱的，所以那些人會坐在涼亭，在那裡。」她彆扭地指指她的身後面。「下雨的時候它都擠得很滿，但其實它不能讓你不淋濕。」

「我明白這點。」他笑了。「作為一個常客，你有什麼提議嗎？」

「是經常光顧的客人，比常客更多一點。我可以告訴你，這裡的菜單經常變化，他們試圖保持季節性，而且食材都是在本地購買和自製。噢，而且太好了。我特別推薦是薑汁啤酒，先生，如果你夠勇猛。」

「勇猛？」

「它會在你肚子裡放一把火，激烈的。」她聽起來就像一個海盜，史堤夫笑了。

「你今天的是什麼口音呢？」

「不知道。顯然是運河的空氣走進了我的頭。」

「那麼吃的呢？」

「有菜牌。」她伸長脖子望看過去他的身後，而史堤夫也發現在牆上有一塊黑板。

「啊，我絕對可以推薦三文魚肉批拌沙拉。很好吃的，如果你喜歡吃魚，我可以。」她疑惑地看著他。

「我愛吃魚。」他在他的椅子上轉過身來。「嗯。決定了，決定了。他們也有印度燴飯。我愛印度燴飯。」

「他們的很好吃。」

「我要那個。」

"I'll have that then."

"Sorted!" She grinned. "You can always have the terrine next time, if it's on." She bounced out of her chair and went to the counter.

Next time? There was going to be a next time? That sounded marvellous, but Steve didn't know if he could stand anymore. It was wonderful to spend time with her like this, but it was torture as well. He wasn't sure he could cope with a close friendship. His heart was too involved already, and it was proving it right now, thudding in his chest as he looked at her. He hadn't seen her in a skirt or dress before, but she was wearing a dress today, white with tiny blue flowers embroidered all over it. The material was blowing against her legs in the breeze and he saw her pull her denim jacket more tightly round her and smooth down her hair.

He took a deep breath, releasing the tension that had built in his stomach as he looked at her. He made himself lean back in the chair and relax, taking the opportunity to have a good look round, preferably not at Rebecca; far too dangerous, because she was just too beautiful.

It really was a unique little place, nestled into the industrial buildings as though it had burrowed in, hoping to go unnoticed. There was a floating pontoon tethered nearby with a few tables on it, too. He had a great view along the canal, and Steve couldn't help smiling at the little fleet of ducklings who came paddling by placidly following their mother, unperturbed by all the attention they got from their ready-made audience.

"Cute, aren't they."

Steve started.

"Sorry. Me and my ninja feet! Kevin's always complaining about them." She put the drinks on the table, leaning close. Steve swallowed and looked away as she sat down.

"Yes, they're very, very cute. I bet they don't go short of food."

"You bet correctly." She smiled, and took a drink.

He peered at her glass, suspicious. "Hold on, yours doesn't look like mine."

"That's because mine's not ginger beer. I went for watermelon juice."

「排序了!」她笑了。「你可以下一次才吃肉批,如果還有的話。」她彈了起身,離開了椅子並走到櫃檯。

下一次?還會有下一次呢?這聽起來真是絕妙,但史堤夫不知道他能不能忍受到。跟她這個樣子在一起是非常好,但亦是一種折磨。他不知道他能否應付這親密的友誼。他的心已經陷入得太多了,而且證明是沒錯的,因為現在他看著她的時候,胸腔裡劇烈地跳動著。他之前沒見過她穿裙子或穿連衣裙,但她今天穿連衣裙,白色伴著小藍花繡在上面。在她的腿上被微風吹動著,他看到她拉了一下牛仔夾克緊緊地包著自己,撥了一下頭髮。

他深吸了一下,看著她之時用肚子的力呼出來。他讓自己往後靠在椅子上,放鬆一下,利用這個機會好好看看四周的環境,最好不要看麗貝卡,太危險了,因為她太美麗。

這的確是一個獨特的小地方,靠著工業建築物,雖然要尋找一下才找到,好像不想被人發現似的。旁邊拴著一隻浮船,有幾張桌子在上面。他沿著運河看過去,史堤夫忍不住笑了,那裡有幾隻小鴨一面平靜地跟隨他們的母親一面玩水,他們泰然自若地得到了所有現場觀眾的注意力。

「他們很可愛,是不是?」

史堤夫望向她。

「很抱歉,對於我和我的忍者腳!凱文總是埋怨它們。」她把飲料放在桌上,靠近了一點。當她坐下來,史堤夫吞嚥了一下並看著遠處。

「是的,他們是非常、非常可愛。我敢打賭,他們不缺食物。」

「你打賭得沒錯。」她笑了,她喝了一口。

他疑惑地凝視著她的玻璃杯。「等一下,你的看起來並不像我的。」

「那是因為我的不是薑汁啤酒,是西瓜汁。」

「西瓜汁?喝不下薑汁啤酒,是嗎?懦夫!」

「當然可以。我已經喝了一杯你做的奶油糖果拿鐵咖啡,而你似乎加了過多的糖漿,如果我能...」

她的厚臉皮令史堤夫氣急敗壞地虛張聲勢,把薑汁啤酒一飲而

"Watermelon juice? Couldn't handle the ginger beer, huh? Wimp!"

"Of course I can. I've had one of your butterscotch lattes when you've way overdone the syrup, and if I can handle that..."

Steve's splutter was as much a result of her cheekiness as it was the huge gulp of ginger beer he'd taken in a burst of bravado.

Rebecca giggled. "It's traditional to drink ginger beer, you know, not inhale it."

Steve coughed. "You'll never have to suffer my butterscotch latte again, I assure you," he said darkly. "You're barred."

She stuck out her tongue, and he reciprocated.

"Behave yourself. The food will be here in a minute."

"Good, I'm starving."

"It's all this fresh air."

"It's all this walking you've made me do!" He pretended to glare.

She put her hands on her hips, unconsciously drawing attention to her figure, which was curvy in all the right places, thought Steve. "Well, that's gratitude for you!" she laughed. "In that case, I bar you from here!"

"Good. We're quits." On an impulse he instantly regretted, he held out his hand for her to shake. The feeling of her strong, warm hand in his did nothing to slow his heart rate. Even worse, she seemed in no rush to take away her hand. Steve was only saved by the arrival of the food.

He busied himself with the kedgeree, which was just as delicious as Rebecca had promised. After a while he thought his face was probably a more normal colour, and he risked a look at her. She looked like she was enjoying her lunch, which seemed to be a tart of some kind with a salad.

"Good?" He nodded at her plate.

"Gorgeous."

"Is it goat's cheese?" She nodded, mouth full, then swallowed. "Uh-huh. With sweet red onion relish and sundried tomatoes. What's not to love?"

盡。

麗貝卡咯咯地笑了起來。「這是傳統喝薑汁啤酒，你知道是用喝的，不是用倒的。」

史堤夫咳了一聲。「你永遠再不會喝到我的奶油糖果拿鐵咖啡了，我向你保證，」他陰沉的說。「你被禁止了。」

她伸出她的舌頭，他亦禮尚往來。

「規矩點。食物會在一分鐘內到。」

「很好，我餓了。」

「這裡全是新鮮的空氣。」

「是你讓我走到這裡來的！」他假裝怒視著。

她雙手扠腰，不知不覺中突出了她的身材，史堤夫認為在所有適當的地方都有線條。「嗯，這是對你的謝意！」她笑了。「在這種情況下，我禁止你來這裡！」

「好。我們就此了結吧。」他立刻就後悔自己的一時衝動，他伸出手還她搖著。他感到她的強壯而溫暖的手令他沒法減慢心跳。更糟的是，她似乎並不打算拿開手，史堤夫的手被拖著直到食物來到。

他忙著吃印度燴飯，它跟麗貝卡說的一樣好吃。過了一會兒，他覺得自己的臉色可能已經變得比較正常，他冒險看看她。她看起來像很享受她的午餐，這似乎是某種水果餡餅拼沙拉。

「好吃嗎？」他向她的碟子點點頭。

「非常好。」

「是山羊奶酪？」

她點點頭，嘴裡塞得滿滿，然後吞嚥。「嗯。有香甜的紅洋蔥調味，又有乾番茄。有什麼理由會不愛？」

「我差點就要妒忌了，但這個印度燴飯也很美味。」

「告訴過你了。」她看著他眨了眨眼睛。

史堤夫凝視了她好一會兒，直到她突然放下她的刀叉，坐了回

"I'm almost envious, but this kedgeree's delicious."

"Told you." Her eyes twinkled at him.

Steve held her gaze for a long moment, until she suddenly put down her knife and fork and sat back.

"Full up already?"

She shook her head. "No. I want to talk to you about something, and I want to do it now in case you come over all virtuous in a minute and tell me we have to leave our lunch and get back."

"I wasn't planning to, but go on." Steve felt uneasy. She looked quite solemn. He put his own knife and fork down and sat back, sipping his ginger beer.

"It's about Laura. The whole situation's been worrying me since you told me about it."

Worrying her? Why? And what was worrying her, specifically? It was too much to hope for that this was where she revealed she was crazy about him, and would leave Kevin for him in a flash if it weren't for how complicated his life was. He wouldn't blame her. Laura was a major complication. Thinking about her now, Steve's heart began to thud again for totally different reasons. He felt sweat break out at his hairline and his mouth was bone dry.

"Go on," he said croakily, raising the ginger beer to his lips. A drink would help.

"I'd like to help her. Help you with her, I mean. When she comes home."

He stared. What did she mean? "What? How?"

"Those two days you can't cover. I checked with Tony when they are." She sounded calm but her cheeks were flushed. "I can have Laura with me on those days, and a few others too if you like."

"But..." Steve held out his hands, not sure how to say all the things clamouring in his head. He was finding it hard to take in. Rebecca's voice sounded strangely tinny.

"Don't worry, I'm CRB checked and everything," she said, obviously misunderstanding his hesitation. "I have been for years. I'm involved with The Young Archaeologist's Club YAC, for a start. That's how I met Tony Robinson."

去。

「已經飽了？」

她搖搖頭。「沒有。我想和你談點事情，我想現在就要說，怕你在下一分鐘突然良心發現說我們不得不離開並回去了。」

「我沒有這個計劃，但請繼續說下去。」史堤夫感到有點不安，因為她看起來很嚴肅。他把自己的刀叉放下，坐了回去，喝著他的薑汁啤酒。

「是關於羅拉的。自從你告訴了我之後，我很擔心整個情況。」

令她擔心？為什麼？她擔心什麼，確切地？有太多的希望以為她透露她已經迷戀上他了，並會為他快速地離開凱文，如果他的生活沒有這麼複雜的話。他不會怪責她。羅拉是一個重大的難題。現在想著她，也令史堤夫的心劇烈地跳動，但原因是完全不同的。他感覺之前在髮線上汗水和嘴唇已經乾透了。

「繼續吧，」他啞著嗓子說，並把薑汁啤酒提到唇邊。喝點酒會有些幫助。

「我想幫助她。我的意思是為你去幫助她，當她回家的時間。」

他瞪大了眼睛。她的意思是什麼呢？「什麼？怎樣？」

「我已經跟東尼談過了，有兩天你不能看管她。」她聽起來很平靜，但臉頰泛紅。「我可以在那幾天裡跟羅拉一起，如果你喜歡，再多幾天也可以。」「可是...」史堤夫伸出他的手，不知道怎麼說好像有些東西在他的腦袋裡叫囂。他發現自己很難聽得清楚，麗貝卡的聲音聽起來奇怪地刺耳。
「不要擔心，我已經做過刑事紀錄檢查和其他的一切，」她說，很顯然是誤解他的猶豫。「我很多年前已經做了。我在一開始參與過年輕考古學家俱樂部的青年中心。我就是在那裡遇到東尼．羅賓遜。」

「誰？」是薑汁啤酒的酒精作怪嗎？所有東西都好像在移動。

「你認識東尼．羅賓遜的，他是在《黑爵士》扮演鮑德里克...」「但羅拉與你無關，」他脫口而出。他的耳朵突然嗡嗡作聲，突然他很肯定他快要哭了，就在這裡，在有很多陌生人浩浩蕩蕩走過的纖道上一家繁忙的咖啡店。他的胸部感到很緊，無法呼吸。麗貝卡用手覆蓋住他的手，非常堅定地。

"Who?" Was this ginger beer alcoholic? Everything seemed to be moving.

"You know, Tony Robinson, he's the guy who played Baldrick—"

"But Laura's nothing to do with you," be blurted. There was a buzzing in his ears. A sudden certainty he was going to cry, here, outside a busy café with lots of strangers trooping past on the towpath. His chest felt tight. He couldn't breathe. Rebecca closed her hand over his, very firmly.

"Steve, listen. It's going to be okay."

He curled his fingers tightly round hers, although he couldn't see them anymore, just swirls of purple.

"Take a minute. Close your eyes, just for a moment. Breathe slowly, in through your nose, out through your mouth." Her voice was very calm and she was rubbing her thumb soothingly, slowly across the back of his hand. "Think about what how cool the air feels. Think about what you can smell. Hot cheese. Apple crumble. Your ginger beer." He felt his other hand lifted towards his face. "Smell that?"

He nodded. "Now take a slow, deep breath in and try opening your eyes."

He opened them and saw the coloured squiggles receding to the corner of his vision and then disappearing altogether. To reveal Rebecca's face only inches from his.

"Feeling better?" He nodded. He could feel his chest ease and his heartbeat slowing.

"Good," she said, bending forward. For a split second he thought she was going to kiss him on the lips, but instead she kissed him lightly on the cheek. He was sure she'd thought about it though. It had been in her eyes – hadn't it?—and she was still holding his hand.

"I know Laura's nothing to do with me," she said quietly, "but we have a lot in common. We've both lost our parents, and I'd love to help her if I can." She smiled. "I'm actually pretty good with young people, you know."

He nodded. "I can imagine that." He blinked, hard.

"And even though she's nothing to do with me, she's a lot to do with you, and I want to help you, too. Will you let me?"

「史堤夫，聽著。會好起來的。」

他蜷縮他的手指緊緊地包著她的，雖然他看不到，他只看到紫色的漩渦。

「花一分鐘時間，閉上你的眼睛，一會先就好。慢慢呼吸，用鼻子吸，再用口呼出。」她的聲音很平靜，用拇指慢慢地撫慰著他的手背。「想想空氣的感覺是如何的好，想想可以聞到什麼，熱奶酪，蘋果酥，還有您的薑汁啤酒。」他覺得她另一隻手正朝他的臉抬起。「聞到嗎？」

他點點頭。

「現在來一個緩慢而深的呼吸，並嘗試打開你的眼睛。」

他睜開雙眼，看到彩色的波浪線退縮到他視野的角落，然後完全消失了。之後就發現麗貝卡的臉離開他的臉只有幾英寸。

「好點了嗎？」他點了點頭。他能感覺到他的胸部放鬆了，而心跳也放緩了。

「好，」她說，然後向前彎腰。有那麼一瞬間，他以為她要吻在他的嘴唇上，但她只是輕輕地吻了他的臉頰。他相信她真的有想過，因為在她的眼裡看到，不是嗎？而她仍然握著他的手。

「我知道羅拉與我無關，」她平靜地說，「但我們有很多共同點。我們都失去了父母，我很想幫助她，如果我可以。」她笑著。 「我其實跟年輕人相處得很好，你知道。」

他點了點頭。「我能想像到。」他生硬地眨了眨眼。

「即使她的事與我無關，但她跟你有很大的關係，而我很想幫你。你會讓我幫你嗎？」

他點點頭。麗貝卡舉起她的手，並用她的拇指擦乾從他眼中逃了出來的眼淚。然後，就好像什麼也沒有發生，她繼續吃她的午餐。

一分鐘後，史堤夫也跟著吃，直到吃完了，他認為他可以再次信任自己的聲音。

「麗貝卡，你確定你樂於讓羅拉留在你的房子嗎？」

「是的。我在家裡也有很多工作要做，所以甚至不會讓我慢下

He nodded. Rebecca put her hand up and wiped away an escaping tear with her thumb. And then, as though nothing had happened, she went back to her lunch.

After a minute, Steve followed suit and by the time he'd finished, he thought he could trust his voice again.

"Rebecca, are you sure you're happy to have Laura at your house?"

"Yes. I've got lots of work to do from home, so it won't even slow me down."

"And nobody else will mind?"

"Like who?"

Steve shrugged. "I'll be in the café until late on those two nights, and if anyone else will be in your house with Laura for any length of time, they would have to have a CRB check too." And here's where she mentions Kevin, he thought.

"Lucky I live by myself, then." She raised an eyebrow. "I can check the calendar, but I don't think I've planned any wild parties."

So Kevin didn't live with her.

"You're really sure about this?"

She nodded.

"I'm afraid you'll have to come to a meeting next Thursday morning, with a social worker and a police officer. Will that be okay?"

"That's fine."

"And probably another one with Laura there, too."

"Not a problem."

He shook his head. "I don't know how to thank you. I can't believe you're doing this."

"Well believe it, buddy. What are friends for?" She smiled and reclaimed her hand. "Anyway, it keeps me out of Marcie's way. She's throwing her weight about on site at the moment, so Kevin can have that joy for a couple of days." She crossed her arms. "As for thanks, well, next time lunch is on you. Talking of which, if

來。」

「沒人會介意嗎？」

「誰？」

史堤夫聳聳肩。「在那兩個晚上，我會在咖啡店直至深夜，如果有任何人在任何時間會在你的家裡跟羅拉在一起，他們就必須做刑事紀錄檢查。」這裡她應該要提到凱文了，他在想。

「那麼幸好我是獨居的。」她揚起一邊眉毛。「我可以檢查一下日程，但我不認為我有計劃過任何瘋狂派對。」

凱文不是和她一起住。

「你確定嗎？」

她點點頭。

「我恐怕你下週四早上要來開會，跟一名社會工作者和一名警官。沒問題嗎？」

「沒問題。」

「很可能還另一個人，就是羅拉。」

「這不是問題。」

他搖搖頭。「我不知道該怎麼感謝你，我不能相信你會這樣做。」

「相信吧，老兄。什麼是朋友？」她微微一笑並收回她的手。「不管怎麼說，這也是讓我避開瑪西的方法。她這些日子都在場地仗勢欺人，所以，凱文也可以有一兩天喜悅了。」她交叉雙臂。「作為感謝，很好，下一次午餐是你的。話說如果你還想吃布丁，就得快點兒了。雖然你的老闆告訴你去多久都可以，但我的會議在四十分鐘後就要開始了。」

want pudding, make it snappy. Your boss might have told you to take as long as you want, but mine's expecting me at a meeting in forty minutes."

不需要此页

Chapter Sixteen

"Sorry. I'm sure the last thing you want to do on your day off is babysit a waste of space," said Laura, with a tight smile. She took off her boots and followed Rebecca into the kitchen.

"You're way too old to need babysitting, and it's not my day off, I'm working from home. Coffee?" Rebecca smiled and turned the kettle on.

"Yes please. It's the strongest thing I'm allowed to have." She gave a harsh little laugh which Rebecca ignored.

"I've got cappuccino sachets." She flicked through the packets. "Cappuccino, mocha, caramel?"

"Caramel sounds good, thanks."

"Good choice. Think I'll join you." Rebecca made the coffees and grabbed a pack of biscuits. "Hope you like Gingernuts, they're all I've got at the moment."

"I love them. Thanks."

"Me too, and they go great with caramel latte. Dip 'em and see."

Laura sniffed the coffee appreciatively. "It smells really good."

"I know. Don't tell your brother, but I think they're nearly as good as the real thing. Plus I can buy a box of sachets for the price of one cup at Tony's," Rebecca grinned. "Sometimes the thrifty ex-student in me rears her ugly head."

"Where did you go to uni?"

"Bristol."

"Was it good?"

"Fantastic. I had a blast. Hard work, though, and a lot of summer

第十六章

「對不起。我敢肯定，你放假的日子裡最不願意做的事情就是代人看顧一個無用的人。」羅拉說，緊張地微笑著。她脫下靴子跟著麗貝卡進了廚房。

「如果你需要保姆的話，你有點太老了，而且這不是我的假期，我要在家工作。要咖啡嗎？」麗貝卡微微一笑，轉身打開電熱水壺的電源。

「好啊。這是我可以喝的東西之中最強的了。」麗貝卡無視了她這個苛刻的玩笑。

「我有袋裝卡布奇諾咖啡。」她打開包裝。「卡布奇諾、摩卡、焦糖？」

「焦糖聽起來不錯，謝謝。」

「不錯的選擇。我想我也要跟你一樣的。」麗貝卡沖泡咖啡，然後抓起一包餅乾。「希望你喜歡薑汁餅，這一刻我就只有這個。」

「我喜歡。謝謝。」

「我也是，跟焦糖拿鐵咖啡配在一起很棒，蘸一下試試看看。」

羅拉感激地聞了聞咖啡。「味道真的很不錯。」

「我知道。不要告訴你哥哥，但我認為它們跟真實的幾乎一樣好。另外，在東尼那裡買一杯的價錢，我可以買到一盒袋裝了，」麗貝卡笑了。「有時那個節儉的前學生又再出現了。」

「你去哪兒讀大學的？」

「布里斯托爾。」

holidays spent volunteering on digs instead of getting holiday jobs and earning. But yeah, I loved it."

Laura smiled, and silence fell for a while.

Rebecca shook the biscuit packet at Laura.

"I shouldn't."

"Why? There's nothing of you! Go on."

"Okay then, thanks. You're right, they do go well with this coffee."

"Did you ever think about going to uni, Laura?"

She shrugged. "I suppose it's what I thought I was working towards when I started sixth form. But I soon screwed that up."

"What did you want to study?"

"I was doing A levels in Art, History, Graphic Design and IT, just because they were the things I enjoyed really."

Rebecca smiled. "That's the best reason for doing subjects— well, that and obviously choosing subjects that'll get you on the uni course you want. I had some friends whose parents dictated their A level choices because they wanted them to do degrees that would make them 'successful'." She grimaced.

"That's one problem I didn't have." Laura gave a small, crooked smile. "Steve got on my case a bit about studying, but he never tried to dictate what I should study."

"He's not all bad, then." She smiled.

"No. He's not bad, full stop. I'm lucky. I know that, deep down, even if I don't show it." She looked down.

Rebecca steered the conversation back to safer waters.

"So what did you see yourself doing at uni?"

"I didn't get that far. I always thought I'd love to have a job where I could combine the subjects I loved, but they don't exactly go together."

"You'd be surprised," said Rebecca thoughtfully.

"I love IT and history, but how would I combine them—unless

「好嗎？」

「太棒了。我得到了很多樂趣。雖然很辛苦，而且暑假花了很多時間去做志願發掘工作，雖然沒有做暑假工而沒有收入。但是，我喜歡。」

羅拉微笑著，沉默了一段時間。

麗貝卡向羅拉搖搖餅乾包裝。

「我不應該再吃了。」

「為什麼？你沒有什麼可以吃！繼續吃吧。」

「那好吧，謝謝。你說得對，這個跟咖啡很配。」

「你有沒有想過要讀大學？羅拉。」

她聳聳肩。「當我完成了六年級就直接去找工作了，那時候我有想過去，但我很快就搞砸了。」

「你有想過要讀什麼嗎？」

「我高中時是讀藝術、歷史、平面設計及資訊科技，因為這些都是我真正喜歡的。」

麗貝卡笑了。「這是選科的最好理由…對了，無疑地選擇科目可以令你在大學選到你想修的科目。我有一些朋友的父母高中時已經幫他們做了選擇，因為希望他們這樣做會令他們「成功」讀到學位課程。」她做了個鬼臉。

「問題就是我沒有。」羅拉給了一個小而邪惡的笑容。「史堤夫跟我會談一點關於學習的事，但他從來沒有試圖強行規定我應該讀什麼。」

「那麼他沒有很差。」她笑了。

「是，他不壞，就這樣。我很幸運，在內心深處我是知道的，只是我沒有表現出來。」她低下頭。

麗貝卡把談話轉回到安全範圍。

「那麼你想過自己在大學讀什麼嗎？」

「我還沒有到這一步。我一直以為我可以找到一份工作，是將自

someone pays me to make a giant database, and that sounds really boring! But I loved art and graphic design too and I was pretty good at it." She shook her head. "I know I'll never get a job that combines all those. Steve says that's my problem, wanting everything to suit me."

"Hmm." Rebecca got to her feet. "I'm just going to go and grab something, but help yourself to more biscuits, I won't be a minute. Make yourself another coffee if you like—if you want a frothy one, the sachets are in the cupboard above the kettle."

"Thanks." Laura smiled. "Not sure I should though. I bet those coffees are mega fattening."

"But compared to an all-milk latte, they're positively healthy!" Rebecca went into the tiny second bedroom that served as her study and picked up her laptop and field report from her desk, then pulled a book off the shelf. When she came back, Laura had disappeared and she could hear the sound of the kettle. She fired up her laptop and flicked through the report until she found the page she wanted. She paper-clipped the page in place.

"Can I get you another coffee, Rebecca?" Laura called shyly.

"Go on then. Mocha, please." She started up CorelDraw. By the time Laura reappeared, Rebecca had moved the long coffee table parallel to the settee and laid out the laptop, report and book.

"Oh!"

Rebecca looked up. "Thanks. Pop the coffees on the mantelpiece a minute." She smiled encouragingly. "I think you might find this interesting."

Laura sat down beside her and frowned at the laptop, which was showing a blank screen framed on all sides by toolbars. "What am I looking at?"

"Nothing, yet." Rebecca picked up the field report. "This is a photograph of a pottery sherd I found last year."

"Right." Laura glanced at her. "That's... great," she said, trying to sound enthusiastic. "Sherd? I thought it was shard."

"Similar word, but sherds are pottery pieces."

"Okay."

"Because of other material we found at the same level in the

己所喜歡的科目結合在一起，但原來是不能夠全部放在一起。」

「你也許會驚訝。」麗貝卡若有所思地說。

「我喜歡資訊科技和歷史，但我要如何將它們合併，除非有人可以給我一個龐大的數據庫，這聽起來真的很無聊！但我又喜歡藝術和平面設計，是我最擅長的。」她搖搖頭。「我知道我永遠也找不到一份工作，將這些結合在一起。史堤夫說，這就是我的問題，希望所有東西都可以滿足自己。」

「嗯。」麗貝卡站起身來。「我只是去拿些東西，你可以繼續吃多一點餅乾，我只是離開一分鐘。如果你喜歡，你可以自己去沖咖啡的。如果你是想要有泡沫的，小袋裝咖啡就在櫥櫃的水壺上面。」

「謝謝。」羅拉笑著。「不知道我是否應該喝。我敢打賭，那些咖啡是非常容易使人發胖的。」

「但是，跟全脂牛奶拿鐵相比，它們肯定是健康的！」麗貝卡走進另一間很細小的臥室，是給她做研究用的。她從她的辦公桌上拿起她的筆記本電腦和現場報告，然後從書架上拿了一本書。當她回來時，羅拉不見了，她可以聽到水壺的聲音。她打開了她的筆記本電腦，翻閱報告，直到她找到了她想要的頁面，用紙夾夾住那頁。

「我能為你沖杯咖啡嗎？麗貝卡。」羅拉害羞地叫道。

「那好吧，我要摩卡，謝謝。」她開啟一個繪圖軟件。羅拉再次出現的時候，麗貝卡已經把長茶几移動到沙發前面，並放好了筆記本電腦、報告和書籍。

「噢！」

麗貝卡抬頭。「謝謝你。請把咖啡放在壁爐上一分鐘。」她笑笑地催促著。「我覺得你會對這個有興趣。」

羅拉在她身邊坐下，望著筆記本電腦皺起了眉頭，上面顯示著一個空白的框架而旁邊是各樣的工具欄。「我在看什麼？」

「沒什麼，暫時。」麗貝卡拿起現場報告。「這照片是我去年發現的一個陶器的陶片。」

trench, we knew it dated to the tenth century. Pottery was limited at the time, and because of the colour and chemical composition of the glaze, we could tell this was a piece of Stamford ware. So pots already discovered, from the same era and area, could give us an idea of how it looked originally." She pointed to the book. "This pitcher was found in Oxford." Laura looked at an image of a bright yellow pot with a strange flaring spout near the neck. "It's in the British Museum."

"Cool. The piece you found looked tiny, though. How would you know what the whole pot looked like?"

"A-ha." Rebecca grinned. Great, Laura was looking interested. She turned to the paper-clipped page in the report. "These are photos of more sherds we found nearby—can you see the way this one's curved?—and we also had some idea of what they were used for, because of their location and evidence of nearby activities." She leant over in front of Laura and pressed a key on the laptop. "So we think it looked like this." A short animation started, showing all the sherds separately at first, large in the foreground, until they zoomed backwards into position, with the rest of the pot appearing around them.

"Wow, that's so cool." Laura leant forward. "I can't believe you reconstructed that huge pot just from those pieces, they were tiny!"

Rebecca sat back, smiling. "Our graphics and design team do this kind of stuff all the time. Pots, buildings, skeletons; even whole villages."

Laura's eyes were wide. "Whole villages? That's amazing."

"Uh-huh. And they do it using their art, history and graphic design talents," she said lightly, "normally with software like this, using their I.T skills." Laura nodded slowly. "So what you're saying is..."

"What I'm saying is, this is a job you could do. That combines all the things you love."

Laura looked wistful. "I wish someone had told me about this at school. I didn't have a clue what I wanted to do. It all seemed a bit pointless, in the end."

"Well you know now," said Rebecca lightly. She nodded at the laptop. "This programme's called CorelDraw. I'm by no means as expert as my graphics colleagues," she laughed, "but would you like a quick tutorial?"

「很好。」羅拉瞥了她一眼。「這是...真的很好,」她試圖聽起來很熱烈地說,「陶片?我以為這是的碎片。」

「類似的詞語啦,但陶片是陶器碎片。」

「好吧。」

「因為我們在同級別中的坑道發現其他物料,我們知道它是來自於十世紀的。陶器在那個時候是有限的,因為從顏色和釉料中的化學成分,我們可以知道這是一塊史丹福的餐具。所以從同一個時代和地區已經發現的壺中,可以給我們想像它最初的樣子。」她指著書。「這個陶壺在牛津被發現的。」羅拉看到一個明亮黃色的壺,有一個奇怪的火炬噴口靠近頸部。「這是在大英博物館。」

「酷。但你看著這一塊細小的,你怎麼知道整個壺看上去會是怎麼樣呢?」

「哈哈。」麗貝卡笑著。太好了,羅拉找到感興趣的地方了。她翻開在報告中紙夾間著的頁面。「這些是更多陶片的照片,我們在附近發現的,你可以看到這一塊彎曲的地方嗎?我們已經有一些想法知道是什麼來著,因為他們的位置和附近活動的證據也可以顯示出來。」

「哇,太酷了。」羅拉靠前上去。「我不能相信你可以重新構建出這麼巨大的鍋,只是從這些細小的碎片!」

麗貝卡坐了回去,臉帶微笑。「我們圖形及設計團隊都是做這樣的東西。壺、建築物、骨骼,甚至整個村莊。」

羅拉眼睛睜得大大的。「整個村莊?太不可思議了。」

「嗯。而且他們是使用他們自己的藝術、歷史和平面設計的天賦,」她輕輕地說,「通常要用這類軟件,再加上他們的資訊科技技能。」羅拉慢慢地點了點頭。「那麼你的意思是...」

「我想說的是,這就是你可以做的工作。結合了所有你喜愛的東西。」

羅拉充滿渴望地看著。「我希望我還在學校時有人告訴我這些。我那時候一直沒有什麼頭緒我想要做什麼。最終那一切似乎都沒有意思。」

麗貝卡輕輕地說:「嗯,你現在知道了,」她向筆記本電腦點點

"Really? Yes please!"

Rebecca gave her a rudimentary tutorial and then let her have a try herself. She was impressed with how quickly Laura picked up the basics. Later, sitting at Rebecca's tiny dining table and tucking into the chicken and mango salad Rebecca had prepared, all she talked about was archaeological reconstruction. She bombarded her with questions until Rebecca threw up her hands, laughing.

"Laura, stop! I feel like you're turning my brain inside out!"

Laura went pink. "Sorry. It's just really interesting. I never knew this stuff could be so, well, cool."

Rebecca smiled. "Glad to have been of service."

"I suppose I'd need a degree to do this for a job."

"Afraid so. Archaeology's a great degree though, even if you change your mind about what you want to do, because it teaches such a wide skill set."

"Would it teach me how to do all the IT stuff too?"

"Courses vary. They'll all touch on it, but it's best to go on separate courses for the different programs as well. Preferably ones that give you a piece of paper at the end."

Laura nodded. "I don't think I'd mind that. Three years seems a long time, but if I could do something I loved at the end of it..."

"Competition can be fierce for some jobs, but the important thing is field experience."

"Cool."

Rebecca hesitated, about to make a suggestion, but thought better of it. Let's see how today goes first, shall we, she thought.

"Well I've got work to get on with—I'm going to need my laptop, I'm afraid! But there are lots of archaeology books in the hall or study. See what takes your fancy. They're not all really highbrow, some at the bottom of the hall bookcase are ones I've written for the public."

"Ones you've written?" Laura stared.

"Yep. It's no big deal, most project leaders have stuff published," she said quickly, embarrassed. She hadn't meant to big herself

頭。「這一個軟件稱為CorelDraw。我比起我的平面設計同事，絕不是這方面的專家，」她笑著說，「但你會想要個快速教程嗎？」

「真的嗎？要啊，有請！」

麗貝卡給了她一個基本的教程，然後讓她自己試一試。她很欽佩羅拉很快就抓到了基礎。後來，她們坐在麗貝卡的小餐桌前，吃著麗貝卡準備好的雞肉和芒果沙拉，她談到考古的重建。羅拉連珠炮地向她發問，直到麗貝卡扔了一下手，大笑。

「羅拉，停止！我覺得你要把我的大腦翻轉了！」

羅拉臉色泛紅了。「對不起。我只是真的覺得很有趣。我從來不知道這個東西可以這樣，好吧，這樣是很酷的。」

麗貝卡笑，「很高興為你服務。」

「我想我需要一個學位來做這個工作。」

「恐怕是要的。不過考古學是一個很好的學位課程，即使你改變了你想要做其他的工作，它仍然教了你很廣泛的技能。」

「教我如何使用所有資訊科技的東西？」

「課程很廣泛。他們都會接觸到這些，但最好是去上一些獨立的課程去學不同的軟件。最好是一個最後可以給你張證書的。」

羅拉點頭。「我認為我不會介意。三年似乎很長一段時間，但如果我最後可以做到一些我喜歡的東西…」

「有一些工作，競爭是很激烈的，但最重要的是實地經驗。」

「酷。」

麗貝卡猶豫了一下，想要提出一個建議，但認為更好的是，先看看今天過得怎樣，我們應該可以，她想。

「嗯，我要繼續回去工作了，我恐怕我需要拿回我的筆記本電腦！但這個大廳也有大量的考古學書籍可以給你研究一下。看看什麼是你喜愛的。他們不是全部都很學術性，在書架底部有一本是我寫給大眾看的。」

「你寫的？」羅拉瞪大了眼睛。

up. "There's palaeontology stuff, too, if you're interested."

"Thanks."

Rebecca was quickly embroiled in her work. It was lucky that she had so much report-writing to do, and work on the new GLAM publications; otherwise she couldn't have taken time away from the Museum. When she went to check on Laura later, she was on the sofa, legs curled beneath her, with what looked like the Jubilee Line Excavation reports open on her lap and a large pile of pamphlets and books beside her.

Rebecca tiptoed away, smiling. She might just have done her good deed for the decade.

Laura spent the next morning checking out websites that Rebecca recommended to her, and looking through more files and books. She even asked Rebecca if she could spare some paper so that she could take notes. Rebecca went one better and given her a shiny new notebook and a pen emblazoned with the GLAM logos.

"They cost a fortune in the gift shop." She winked. Perks of the job."

The morning shot past. Rebecca had been making notes and planning out pages for a joint publication with Crossrail.

"How's your morning been?" Laura asked her politely as Rebecca stood in the kitchen, heating soup.

"Fine thanks, I think I've got it all clear in my head. I'll need my laptop again, though."

"Of course! Sorry, I didn't mean to hog it."

"No, I didn't need it this morning, honest. I'd soon have said if I did!"

She filled two bowls and they carried them to the dining table, where they fell silent for a while, enjoying the soup and crusty rolls.

"Laura, how would you like to come to work with me next week and see this stuff being done for real?"

Laura stopped eating, eyes like saucers. "Would I be allowed?"

「沒錯。這沒什麼大不了，大多數項目領導人都有發表過什麼，」她趕緊說，感到有點尷尬，她並不是想自誇什麼。「古生物學的東西也有，如果你有興趣的話。」

「謝謝。」

麗貝卡很快就被陷入了她的工作。很幸運的是，她有這麼多的報告要寫，還有博物館新出版的刊物工作，否則她可能不可以花時間遠離博物館。後來當她前去查看羅拉，看見她在沙發上，雙腿蜷縮在腳下，看起來像是在她的膝蓋上打開了銀禧線的發掘報告，她旁邊邊有一大堆小冊子和書籍。

麗貝卡躡手躡腳地走回去，微笑著。在十年內，她一定做到她喜愛的事。

第二天羅拉花了一個早上查看麗貝卡向她推薦的網站，並希望有更多的文件和書籍可以閱讀。她甚至問麗貝卡如果她能給她一些紙張，那樣她就可以做筆記。麗貝卡給了她更好的，是一本全新的筆記本和一支印有GLAM標誌的筆。

「他們花了一大筆錢在禮品店。」她眨了眨眼。「是工作的額外津貼。」

早上很快就過去。麗貝卡已做好了筆記和定好了幾頁與東西橫貫鐵路聯合出版的刊物版面。

「你的早上過得怎麼？」羅拉禮貌地問，麗貝卡正站在廚房裡把湯加熱。

「我很好，謝謝。我想我已經在腦海清楚地整理好所有東西。不過我需要將要拿回我的筆記本電腦。」「當然！對不起，我不是想一直霸佔它。」

「不，今天上午我沒有需要，真的。如果我做好了，我再叫你吧！」

她盛了兩碗湯，拿到餐桌進行她們的午餐，在那裡陷入了沉默一陣子，她們正享受湯和硬麵包。

「羅拉，你下週會不會想跟我去上班，看一下真正正在做的東西？」

"Wouldn't have offered if you weren't," Rebecca grinned. "I can pull a few strings. We'd have to fill in some paperwork"

Laura looked uncomfortable.

She's wondering whether it's because of her criminal record, thought Rebecca. She smiled at her. "Don't worry, we get all our work experience and volunteer people to do it, just to say you've read all the health and safety procedures, things like that."

"Oh. Okay."

"If you want you can stay with me at first, though we'll have to find you something to do when I'm in meetings. Then you can spend time with the graphics team—Kev's got a heap of work to talk through with the graphics team, so he could look after you.. He's a sweetie. Would that be okay?"

"Ok? Are you kidding?" Laura's eyes were glistening. "It would be great."

"Good! That's settled, then." Rebecca got up.

"Rebecca, why are you doing this for me?"

"Because you're interested in this stuff, and it will give you an idea of what the job's like."

"But..." Laura looked down, blushing. "I'm hardly reliable, am I," she said, sounding bitter. "How do you know I won't let you down?"

"You won't."

"But why are you going to so much trouble for me? Someone you barely know? Is it for Steve?"

"No. Steve's a great guy, Laura, but you're a person in your own right. Plus..." The lump in her throat seemed to come from nowhere. She swallowed.

"Plus what?" It was almost a whisper.

"Plus I know how it feels to lose your parents when you're young," said Rebecca. Her voice shook a little and she blinked away tears. She tried to make her voice light-hearted as she looked at Laura. "Us orphans needs to stick together."

"Thanks!"

羅拉停止進食，眼睛像碟子一樣大。「我可以得到批准嗎？」

「如果你不想就不會，」麗貝卡咧嘴一笑。「我可以拉一下關係。但我們不得不先填寫一些文件。」

羅拉看起來有點不自在。

麗貝卡認為她在擔心因為她有犯罪記錄。她微笑看著她。「不要擔心，我們所有有工作經驗和志願者都要填寫的，只是一些關於你讀了所有健康和安全的程序，就這樣而已。」

「哦。好吧。」

「如果你想，你開始時可以跟我呆在一起，雖然當我有會議時，我們得找一些事給你做。然後你就可以花時間跟繪圖團隊…凱文有些工作，是要跟繪圖團隊談一下，這樣他就可以照顧你了…他是個甜心。這樣好嗎？」

「好嗎？你在開玩笑吧？」羅拉的眼睛閃閃發光。「這是非常棒的。」

「好！那就這樣決定。」麗貝卡起身。

「麗貝卡，你為什麼要為我這樣做？」

「因為你對這些東西感興趣，而且可以令你對你想做的工作有多點體會。」

「可是…」羅拉低頭看著，紅著臉。「我幾乎沒有什麼誠信了，我…」她說，聽起來很苦澀。「你怎麼知道我不會讓你失望？」
「你不會。」

「但是，為什麼你要這麼麻煩為我做這些？你幾乎不認識我呢？是為了史堤夫？」

「沒有。史堤夫是一個很好的傢伙，羅拉，但你是一個人，亦有自己的權利。加上…」好像有些東西突然哽在喉嚨裡，她吞嚥了一下。

「加上什麼？」幾乎很小聲地。

「加上，我知道那是什麼感覺，當你還年輕的時候就失去了你的父母，」麗貝卡說，她的聲音有點發顫，而當她眨了眨眼睛，眼淚就掉了下來。她試圖讓自己的聲音輕鬆愉快點，她看著羅拉。

Rebecca started a little as Laura gave her a quick spontaneous hug, and catching the look on Laura's face afterwards she wasn't sure which of them had been most surprised by it.

「我們這些孤兒要站在同一陣線上。」

「謝謝你！」

當羅拉給了她一個快速而自然的擁抱，麗貝卡有點嚇一跳，之後她望一下羅拉的臉，她也不肯定誰才是被嚇到的一個。

Chapter Seventeen

"I wanted you to be the first to hear my news," said Ron, shutting his office door. "Biscuit?" He proffered a pack of smeary chocolate digestives.

"No thanks," said Rebecca, settling herself into a chair.

He looked at the biscuits and winced. "I don't blame you. I should have left them in the fridge." He sat down and rested his elbows on the desk, steepling his fingers.

"Firstly, I'm leaving."

"Leaving?" She sat forward. "Why?"

"Not because I'm unhappy here," he smiled. "But I've had an offer I can't refuse."

"A new job?"

"New everything. Joint director of a new international archaeology team, based in Milan, whose focus will be on urban archaeology."

"Wow."

"Wow indeed."

"We'll miss you round here."

"I suppose that's good. It must mean I've done something right."

She hardly heard him. A cold, uneasy feeling settled in her stomach. Had Marcie known about this? This must have been what she'd meant. Was she really going to take over Ron's post?

Ron cleared his throat. "Anyway, with my leaving, the powers that be have decided it's a good time for restructuring.

"Sounds scary." She tried to smile.

第十七章

「我希望你是第一個知道我的事情的人，」羅恩說，他關上他辦公室的門。「要餅乾嗎？」他遞上一包髒髒的巧克力消化餅。

麗貝卡說：「不，謝謝。」她坐到椅子上。

他看著餅乾和畏縮了一下。「我不怪你。我應該把它們放在冰箱裡。」他坐了下來，手肘放在桌子上，喀喀了幾下他的指骨。

「首先，我要離開了。」

「離開？」她坐了上前。「為什麼？」

「不是因為我在這裡不開心，」他笑著說。「但是，我有一個我不能拒絕的提案。」

「一份新的工作嗎？」

「新的一切。一個新的國際考古團的聯合董事，他們的總部設在米蘭，重點將會是對城鎮的考古發掘。」

「哇。」

「的確要哇的。」

「我們在這裡會想念你的。」

「我覺得這樣很好，意思是我一定做過了一些正確的事。」

她很難聽到他說什麼。一個寒冷而不安的感覺入侵她的肚子。瑪西知道這件事嗎？這一定是她上次說的事。她真的要接管羅恩的職位嗎？

羅恩清了清嗓子。「不管怎麼說，因為我的離開，這是一個很好的時機，管理層決定去重組。」

He grinned. "Not at all. For once, I think the powers that be are talking sense. My role will disappear."

She looked at him incredulously. "There's going to be nobody in overall charge? Seriously?"

He shook his head. "No, that's not it. Much as that might appeal to those whom I have to nag when their reports are late."

"Can't think who that would be. Mine are always on time," she said innocently.

"Just."

She waggled her head in a non-committal way.

"There will be two posts—a Director of Fieldwork, who will oversee surveys, digs, liaison with other agencies, site management etcetera, and a Director of Analysis; any follow-up work that gets done here, including graphics and design, and our publications, archives. Exhibitions and fun days will be a joint enterprise."

"Okay." She nodded. "I can see that might work, although they'll have to be people who work well together."

"Ultimately they'll report to the head of GLAM."

"Oh," said Rebecca archly, "That'll be fun for them."

He leaned forward. "Do you think it would be fun for you?"

"No, I think it will be hell for me if my boss is Marcie, frankly, which I suspect you're about to tell me is the case."

"What?" His eyebrows shot upwards.

"Marcie hinted she might have a position of authority over me, very soon. I guess this is it."

"Believe me, that would never happen," he said grimly. "Particularly with some of the things I've been hearing."

She frowned. "Like what?"

"I can't go into details. Let's just say that those in charge of her have noticed some... erratic behaviour. She certainly won't be assuming a more senior position any time soon. Not anywhere."

"I thought she was just that way around me. Is that why the

「聽起來很嚇人。」她試著微笑。

他咧嘴笑了。「不是。這一次,我覺得管理層講得合情合理。我的角色將會消失。」

她懷疑地看著他。「即是這裡沒有全面負責的人?認真的嗎?」

他搖搖頭。「不,不是這樣的。對一些人有一定的吸引力,就是那些是我嘮叨他們遲交報告的人。」

「沒想到那會是誰。我的一向很準時。」她若無其事地說。

「只有你。」

她不置可否地搖晃著頭。

「將會有兩個職位:一個實地調查的董事,將負責調查、挖掘、與其他機構的聯絡,場地管理諸如此類。而另一個就是業務分析董事,負責任何會在這裡完成的後續工作,包括圖像和設計,以及我們出版的刊物和檔案館。展覽和同樂日將是一個合作活動。」

「好吧,」她點了點頭。「我看應該也可以運作到的,雖然他們必須要是可以互相協調的人。」

「他們最後都要向GLAM的負責人直接報告。」

「哦,」麗貝卡狡猾地說,「那一定很有趣。」

他俯身向前。「你認為這可以為你帶來樂趣嗎?」

「不,我認為這將會是我的地獄,如果我的老闆是瑪西,坦白說,我懷疑你是要告訴我這件事。」

「什麼?」他的眉毛迅速上揚。

「瑪西暗示過她有可能得到一個在我之上的職位,很快。我想就是說這個。」

「相信我,這永遠不會發生,」他冷冷地說。「特別是我已經聽到的一些事情。」

她皺起了眉頭。「什麼事情?」

「我不能詳談。我們只能說那些看管她的負責人已經注意到了一

exchange ended early?"

"I can't say." He looked uncomfortable.

"That's a yes."

He let that go. "Anyway, when I asked if it would be fun for you, I meant the Director of Fieldwork post. I thought you might apply."

She stared at him. "You're joking."

He shook his head, smiling.

"You're not joking." She fell back in her chair. "I don't think so."

"Why not? I thought that would appeal more than heading up analysis."

"Oh it does. Of the two, that's the one I'd go for, but there's no way I'm ready for a role like that."

"Hmm. You might be interested to know you're in a minority with that opinion. Everyone upstairs seems to think you're not only ready, you're the ideal candidate."

"They're mad then."

"Come on Rebecca. You've been basically doing the job, on and off, for this past year."

"But you've inspected the sites first—"

"Something you're more than capable of doing."

"Liaised with the other agencies—"

"As have you, very successfully, after the initial meet."

She waved a finger. "Decided trench positions, test pits—"

"After asking your opinion," he amended.

"I'm flattered by your confidence in me, but I'm not sure I share it." Her? In charge of all those other people?

He sighed. "Will you at least promise me you'll give it some thought?"

She nodded. "I will. You have to admit it's a lot to get my head

些...古怪的行為。她肯定不能在短時間內得到一個更高級的職位，沒有任何地方可以做到。」

「我還以為會放置她在我周圍，因為這樣交流才會提前結束？」

「我不能說太多。」他很不自在地說。

「那就代表對的了。」

他不管她。「不管怎麼說，我剛才問你是否覺得有趣，我的意思是實地調查董事的職位。我覺得你一定要去申請。」

她盯著他。「你是在開玩笑。」

他臉帶微笑地搖搖頭。

「你不是在開玩笑。」她坐回到她的椅子裡。「我不這麼認為。」

「為什麼不呢？我認為這個的吸引力比起只做分析的多很多。」

「哦，那的確是。在兩個之中，我會選這一個，但有這不代表我已經準備好做這樣的一個角色。」

「嗯。你一定是屬於少數有這個想法的人。樓上的每個人都似乎認為你不僅準備好，而且是個理想人選。」

「他們瘋了。」

「來吧，麗貝卡。基本上是你已經在做的工作，斷斷續續地，在過去的一年。」

「但是你一開始已經視察好場地...」

「你能夠做的比你的能力更多。」

「跟其他機構聯繫...」

「就是因為有你，在最初的見面都非常成功。」

她揮舞著一根手指。「決定坑道的位置，探坑...」

「在問你的意見之後。」他修正。

「你對我這麼信任，我有點受寵若驚，但我不能肯定我可以做

around."

"Hmm. If you think that's a lot to get your head around, perhaps I shouldn't tell you about my other proposition."

"Don't tell me, NASA wants an archaeologist on the next shuttle flight," joked Rebecca weakly.

"No. If they did, I'd fight you for it."

"Sounds fair."

"The team I'm joining need two more archaeologists, capable and experienced in urban archaeology. I know I shouldn't be discussing this with you—it smacks of poaching, I suppose—"

"Why? Which member of my team are you hoping to entice away?"

"You."

She shook her head slowly. "Wow. Again."

"I know it's a big deal; it would mean moving to Milan. But you're made for the job. I've already told Francois you're the ideal candidate."

"Francois Villeneuve?"

"Sorry, I should have mentioned that. He's the other joint director. He'll probably ring you soon himself."

"I should hope so." She smiled. She'd heard nothing from him since Christmas, and he was the only remaining link to her parents. Other than Marcie and her mother, of course.

"The thing is, not only will we benefit tremendously from having you on the team, but it's a fantastic opportunity for you, and... well there's not much keeping you here, is there? It could be a new start for you." He looked awkward. "Sorry, that didn't sound quite how I intended, I just meant—"

"No, you're quite right," she said quickly. "Most people have family, or a partner. Or both. I have neither. You're only telling the truth, Ron." She smiled at him, covering the stab of hurt she'd felt, and he leaned back in his chair, relieved.

"Milan," she said into the silence that followed. "It does sound appealing. What a great opportunity."

到。」她？負責看管所有其他的人？

他嘆了口氣。「你至少答應我，你會考慮一下？」

她點點頭。「我會的。你不得不承認，這是很大機會讓我不能不去考慮。」

「嗯。如果你覺得這是一個很大的問題你要去想，也許我不應該告訴你關於我的新職位。」

「不要告訴我，美國宇航局希望下一次航天飛行要帶上一個考古學家。」麗貝卡勉強地開玩笑說。

「沒有。如果他們這麼做，我會幫你爭取。」

「聽起來很公平。」

「我加入的團隊需要更多的考古學家，對城鎮考古有能力而且有經驗的。我知道，我不應該與你討論這個，這意味著挖角。」

「為什麼？你想挖走我團隊哪一個成員？」

「你。」

她慢慢地搖了搖頭。「哇。再說一次。」

「我知道這是一個大問題，這將意味著要搬到米蘭。但是你可以得到一份工作，我已經告訴了弗朗索瓦你是理想人選。」

「弗朗索瓦．維倫紐夫？」

「對不起，我應該提到這一點。他是另一位聯合董事。他可能很快就會打電話給你。」

「我也希望如此。」她笑了。自聖誕節之後，她就沒有聽到他的消息，他是僅餘唯一一個跟她父母有關聯的人。當然除瑪西和她的母親。

「這事情是，你不但會從你對團隊中獲益良多，它也是一個極好的機會給你，而且...沒有太多的東西讓你在這裡，是不是？這可能是一個新的開始。」他尷尬地看了看。「對不起，這聽起來不是我打算說的，我剛才的意思是...」

「不，你說得對，」她很快地說。「大多數人都有家庭或伴侶，或者兩者都有。但我都沒有。你只是說實話，羅恩。」她微笑著

Ron nodded eagerly, obviously sensing she might waver. "Of course there will be interviews—a selection process—but being a director, my recommendation will carry a lot of weight." He grinned. "I think you can safely say you have the backing of the other director, too."

She stared at the edge of his desk for a while, lost in thought. "You've given me a lot to think about."

"Yes, and I'm sorry to spring two such very different options on you at the same time. I know it's not ideal, and I'm in two minds myself which one I want you to take! The noble me would love to hand over the fieldwork to you, knowing I'd leave it in such capable hands. But the selfish me—the one that thinks of myself as not only your boss, but your friend—thinks the Milan job is such a great opportunity for you, and that you'd be such as asset there as well as good company, that I can't not want you to go for it."

"Well all I can say is thank you so much for considering me—for both jobs. I'm flattered."

"You're the best person for the job. Both of them, unfortunately." Ron grinned. "If only we could clone you!"

"Now there's a scary thought. I think one of me is quite enough for the world!" She got to her feet. "I think I'll go for lunch early. I feel the need for a strong cup of coffee!"

"Don't go to our café, then."

She shuddered. "I rarely do. I usually go to Tony's, round the corner." She made for the door. "I'll do some thinking and let you know."

"Ah, about that—" Ron rose from his chair and she turned. "I'm afraid you haven't got very long to ponder."

"How long, exactly?"

"They want the new directors to be in place before I leave, so there's plenty of time to hand over the reins, particularly with the new distinct roles. So we're advertising straight away. Application deadline is next Friday, with short-listing by the end of the week after."

"That doesn't give me long."

"I know."

看著他，涵蓋了她感到的傷害，他靠回在椅背上鬆了一口氣。

「米蘭，」她說，隨後陷入了沉默。「很動聽。真是一個非常好的機會。」

羅恩急切地點了點頭，明顯感覺到她可能會動搖。「當然會有面試，一個甄選過程，但作為一個董事，我的意見將會很有份量。」他咧嘴笑了。「我認為，你也可以放心地說，你有其他董事作為後盾。」

她盯著他的辦公桌邊緣一段時間，陷入了沉思。「你已經給我很多要思考的問題了。」

「是的，對不起突然告訴你兩個非常不同的選項。我知道這是不很理想，而我自己有兩個想法是我想你去做！高尚的我希望可以交付實地考察的工作給你，因為我知道要留給的是個得力手下。但自私的我認為自己不僅是你的老闆，也是你的朋友，所以又認為米蘭的工作對你來說是一個很好的機會，你會成為一家好公司的資產，我沒辦法不想你去。」

「嗯，我只能說非常感謝你為我考慮了兩個工作。我受寵若驚了。」

「你是最好的人選，對於兩份工作都是，很遺憾。」羅恩咧嘴笑了。「如果我們能複製你就好！」

「現在有一個可怕的想法。我覺得只有一個我的世界很不足夠！」她站起身來。「我想我會早點吃個午餐。我需要有一杯強而有力的咖啡！」

「那就去我們的咖啡店吧。」

她打了一個寒顫。「我很少這樣做。我通常去到東尼的店，在拐角處。」她打開了門。「我會先考慮一下，並讓你知道我的決定。」

「嗯，關於這個...」羅恩從椅子上站起來，她轉身。「我怕你沒有很長的時間考慮。」

「多久，準確說？」

「他們希望在我離開之前新董事已經到位，能有充足的時間交出大權，特別是與新的個別角色。因此，我們會立即出廣告，報名截止時間是下週五，短名單會在下周後期做好。」

"And the Milan post?"

"If you're interested, I need to know by the end of next week too. Sorry."

"Oh well, I suppose at least my agonising will be short-lived," she said lightly.

He smiled. "There's that."

Her head was spinning as she walked back to her office. Her first instinct was to go and find Kevin; drag him off to lunch and talk everything through with him. Ron hadn't said to keep any of it quiet, and by the sound of it everyone would know by tomorrow. She wanted to talk to him about Laura too. But Kevin wasn't around; he'd gone out to help on a dig. She left him a note and headed out for lunch.

"So you don't mind taking Laura under your wing, the week after next?" Today she'd found Kevin but he was sitting in front of a huge pile of paperwork, which wasn't like him at all.

"No, that's fine." Kevin shuffled things aimlessly.

Rebecca folded her arms, leaning against the bench. "Sure? You're not exactly bowling me over with your enthusiasm."

"Honestly, it's fine. She sounds great." He glanced up at her quickly, giving a very unconvincing smile. "So what about these new director posts then?"

"Kev what's up? Because something is."

He ran his hands through his hair and sighed. "Just the usual."

"Oh dear. Has the course of true love not run smooth?" She sat down beside him.

He laughed humourlessly. "The course of the third date hasn't even run smooth. If I ever manage to get to the true love bit, I'll tell you."

She tucked her arm in his. "Aw, I'm sorry."

"It's okay. I suppose it's better to be dumped sooner rather than later. Less gain but less pain."

「這並不讓我有很多時間的考慮。」

「我知道。」

「米蘭的職位呢？」

「如果你有興趣，我需要下週結束前知道。對不起。」

「噢，我至少知道我的折騰將不會持續很久。」她輕輕地說。

他笑了。「就這樣。」

當回到她的辦公室，她的頭在旋轉。她的第一個反應是去找凱文並拉他去吃午餐，與他談論這一切。羅恩沒有說要保密，聽上去應該到明天每個人就會知道。她想和他談談關於羅拉的事，但凱文不在，他出了去幫忙發掘的工作。她留下了一張紙條，然後出去吃午飯。

「那麼，你不介意帶著羅拉在身邊嗎？再下一個星期。」今天，她找到了凱文，但他坐在一大堆文書工作前面，這是他最不喜歡的。

「不，這很好。」凱文漫無目的地翻著文件。

麗貝卡抱起雙臂，靠在板凳上。「確定嗎？你完全沒有用你的熱情來擊退我。」

「說實話，這很好。她聽起來很不錯。」他很快地抬頭看了看她，給了她一個非常牽強的微笑。「所以新的董事職位怎麼樣呢？」

「凱文怎麼了？因為其他事情。」

他用手插入他的頭髮，嘆了口氣。「就跟往常一樣。」

「哦，親愛的。在真愛的道路上不順利嗎？」她在他身旁坐下。

他一本正經地笑道。「第三次約會的道路上，甚至還沒有順利過。如果我有靠近了一點真愛，我會告訴你。」

她把手臂擠進他的臂內。「噢，對不起。」

「沒關係。我想，最好還是早點扔掉。 收穫越少，但痛苦也越

"Oh no, it must be bad. You've started torturing idioms." As she hoped, that raised a small smile. "You know what you need," she said, dragging him to his feet.

"A makeover? Inside and out? A shrink?"

"Nope. Cake. Come on."

少。」

「哦，不，這一定是很差。你已經開始在曲解成語了。」正如她希望的，他給了一個小小的微笑。「你知道你需要什麼嗎？」她說，拖著他起來。

「改頭換面？內部和外部？一名精神病醫生？」

「不是。是蛋糕。來吧。」

Chapter Eighteen

"Don't tell me. Butterscotch latte with chocolate sprinkles. Would you like a blueberry muffin with that?" Steve grinned, hands frozen in front of the coffee, just waiting for her to say the word.

"No. I'd like a caramel latte with cinnamon please, and a hazelnut latte for Kevin."

Steve put on what Laura called his 'mock-shock' face. "Ooh... she's living dangerously today. Large?" he slid a bowl-sized cup under the jet and jabbed at the buttons.

She nodded. "Well, what can I tell you? I need some excitement in my life."

Steve felt his cheeks flush a little and was glad he had his back to her. He felt that they were on a new footing now, although he wasn't quite sure what it was. But she sounded tense and cross. He watched the froth come up the top of the cup, trying to work out what to say. He cleared his throat as he gave the top of her latte a quick dusting of cinnamon.

"There you go."

"Thanks. It looks gorgeous." She took a long drink and Steve was mesmerized by her oh-so-perfect mouth on the edge of the cup. When she put her head up, though, he had to suppress a chuckle. He handed her a serviette.

"Here, you've got a foam moustache."

"Oh! That must look glamorous," she dabbed at her mouth.

"So he's not very exciting company then?"

"Who, Kevin?" She looked over her shoulder. "You must be joking!" She searched in her purse. "How much is that?"

"Two pound fifty for Kevin's but yours is on the house."

第十八章

「不要告訴我。奶油糖果拿鐵咖啡加巧克力碎灑。你還想要個藍莓鬆餅嗎？」史堤夫笑了，手停在咖啡的前面，只是等著她說一句話。

「不是。我想要杯焦糖拿鐵加肉桂粉，麻煩你，和一杯榛子拿鐵給凱文。」

史堤夫露出一副羅拉稱為「模擬震驚」的樣子。「噢…她今天活在危險中。大的嗎？」他滑了一個如碗大小的杯在噴嘴下，並按了一下按鈕。

她點點頭。「嗯，我可以告訴你什麼嗎？我的生活中需要一點令人興奮的東西。」

史堤夫覺得他的臉頰有一點點泛紅，很高興他是背對著她。他認為，他們現在是一個新關係，雖然他不太清楚它是什麼。但她聽起來緊張和複雜。他看著泡沫已到杯頂，試圖找出該說些什麼。他清了清嗓子，給她拿鐵的頂部快速撒了肉桂粉。

「是你的。」

「謝謝你，外表非常華麗。」她喝了一大口，史堤夫被她迷住了。哦，這麼完美嘴就貼在杯的邊緣。但當她把她的頭抬起，他不得不抑制住偷笑。他遞了餐巾紙給她。

「這裡，你有了泡沫的鬍子。」

「哦！看起來一定很光鮮亮麗。」她擦了擦她的嘴。

「所以，他不是非常令人興奮的夥伴？」

「誰？凱文？」她轉頭看著。「你一定是在開玩笑！」她搜尋她的錢包。「多少錢？」

She looked at him. "You don't have to do that, you know."

"I know. But I want to." He smiled. "Don't get too used to it though. Temporary privilege."

"Great. A new taste experience and I saved some money too." She passed him a £5 note and he scooped change out of the till.

"So what's up with Kevin then?" he asked. "For someone who's not exciting, you spend a lot of time with him." Ouch. Too far. He started to clean imaginary spills off his side of the cake counter.

"Oh no, don't get me wrong. He can be exciting."

Great. Just what he wanted to hear.

"Just not at the moment."

"Oh? Why's that?"

"Actually, hold on a minute." She walked back to Kevin, resting a hand his shoulder as she bent to talk to him. Then she came back.

"I was going to be good and leave the cakes alone today, but he needs a cake and I can't sit there and watch him eat one by himself. It'll kill me." She smiled. "Besides, it would be rude not to keep him company."

Her eyes moved along the counter. "I'll have an apricot Danish and he'll have an almond and pecan slice, please. If that doesn't cure him, nothing will."

"Cure him?" Steve took two plates off the stack and picked up the tongs. "Of what?" He carefully extracted the cakes.

"He's a bit depressed."

"Oh. Sorry to hear that."

"Well thanks, but there's no need for you to be sorry. You're not the guy who strung him along and then dumped him."

Steve's head whipped round and his arm knocked against the cake cabinet, shooting Rebecca's apricot Danish on to the floor.

"God, I'm sorry." He said, tilting the other plate before he lost Kevin's slice too.

「凱文的兩磅五十，但你的免費。」

她看著他。「你不必這樣做，你知道的。」

「我知道，不過，我想。」他笑了。「不過不要太習慣。只是暫時的特權。」

「太好了。一種新的味覺體驗，而我也可以存一些錢。」她遞給他五元硬幣，他在錢櫃拿出找回的零錢。

「那麼凱文有什麼事嗎？」他問。「如果有誰是不令人興奮的，但你又花這麼多時間跟他一起。」哎，太遠了。他開始清潔他身邊的蛋糕櫃上根本不存在的碎屑。

「哦，不，不要誤會我的意思。他可以是很令人興奮的。」

太好了。正是他想聽到的。

「只是不是現在。」

「哦？為什麼？」

「其實，請稍等一分鐘。」她走回去凱文身邊，把手放在他的肩膀上，因為她彎腰跟談了幾句。然後，她回來了。

「我本來打算不吃蛋糕，但他需要蛋糕，而我不能坐在那裡只看著他吃，這會殺了我的。」她笑了。「此外，不陪他吃會是有點無禮。」

她的眼睛沿著櫃檯看過去。「我要一個杏味丹麥酥，他要一件杏仁和山核桃的，麻煩你。如果不治好他的病，什麼都不能做。」

「治好他？」史堤夫從一疊碟子中拿了兩個，並拿起鉗子。「什麼？」他小心翼翼地鉗起了蛋糕。

「他有點鬱悶。」

「哦。很難過聽到這事。」

「嗯，謝謝，但沒有需要令你感到難過。你又不是那個綁起他，然後把他甩了的男子。」

史堤夫的頭部猛烈搖晃了一下，他的胳膊撞到了蛋糕櫃，令麗貝卡的丹麥酥掉到地板上。

"Don't worry. You know I told you about that stint I did as a waitress? I was useless." She took Kevin's cake.

Steve opened the cabinet to get her a fresh pastry, trying to focus on what his hands were doing. Once it was on the plate, he felt brave enough to say what was hovering on his tongue.

"Guy? So he's..."

"Gay. Yes," she said, keeping her voice low.

Steve shook his head, bewildered. "I had no idea. You never mentioned it."

"Well, I wouldn't have done, before. It's Kevin's business, not anybody else's." She took her plate and put it on the tray.

"But you're mentioning it to me now."

She smiled. "I think I know you well enough by now to trust you with that piece of information, don't you?"

"I hope so," he smiled back. She turned to go but he stopped her. "You'll probably think I'm daft, but I'd always presumed you two were a couple."

"Us two? Kevin and me?" Rebecca dissolved into giggles. "Now there's an unlikely combination!'

"You seemed to get on so well, and you spend so much time together, and, I mean, I had no idea that he gay. At all." He shook his head, knowing he was blushing. "You must think I'm a complete idiot."

"No. I don't know anyone who's pegged Kev as gay unless he's told them. Contrary to the stereotype, not all gay men are camp." Her eyes twinkled. "And he doesn't particularly like musicals, either."

Steve spread his hands. "Hey, I don't buy into that attitude either. I just can't believe I've presumed you two are a couple all this time."

"It's ironic really, because I'll let you into a secret. So far away am I from being part of a couple, that I've been using a dating agency in my efforts to become one."

"And how's that going for you?" he asked croakily.

「天啊，對不起。」他說，在掉了凱文的那片蛋糕之前，他穩住了另一隻碟子。

「別擔心。你知道我曾經告訴你，有一段時間我也當過一名女服務員？我是很沒用的。」她拿起了凱文的蛋糕。

史堤夫打開櫃，給她拿了一件新鮮出爐的，試圖把重點集中在他的手。放到碟子上之後，他覺得自己夠勇氣說出徘徊在他的舌頭上的說話。

「男子？所以，他是…」

「同性戀。是的。」她說，把聲音壓得很低。

史堤夫搖了搖頭，一臉茫然。「我完全不知道。你從來沒有提過。」

「好吧，我不會這樣做，之前。這是凱文的事，而不關別人的事。」她接過碟子，並把它放在托盤上。

「但你現在向我提到了。」

她笑了。「我覺得現在我知道你有足夠的好，而相信可以把真相告訴你，不是嗎？」

「希望如此，」他笑著。當她轉身要走，他叫住了她。「你可能會覺得我很愚蠢，但我總是假設你們是一對的。」

「我們兩個？凱文和我嗎？」麗貝卡禁不住咯咯地笑了起來。「這是一個不太可能的組合！」

「你們看起來這麼好，而且花這麼多時間在一起，我的意思是，我完全不知道他是同性戀，在任何方面。」他搖搖頭，知道自己臉紅了。「你一定認為我是個十足的傻瓜。」

「沒有。我不認識有誰看得出凱文是同性戀，除非他告訴了他們。恰恰相反的印象，不是所有的男同性戀者都是娘娘腔的。」她眨了眨眼睛。「而他確實不是特別喜歡音樂劇。」

史堤夫攤開雙手。「嘿，當然我接受不到這種態度。我簡直不能相信我一直假設你倆是一對的。」

「這是真是諷刺，因為我會讓你保守一個秘密。我要成為一對戀人中的一部分還有很遠路，而我一直有使用一個約會機構努力令

"Disastrously. That's why I'm not doing it anymore."

"Sorry to hear that."

"Probably for the best. I think meeting people naturally is the best thing, after all. It always felt false." She smiled at him and his heart did its usual little flipping over thing. She turned to go again, and Steve felt a wave of panic. For some inexplicable reason, he felt that if he missed his chance to say something now, he'd never get it again."

"Rebecca."

"Yes?"

"Look, er... if I'd known you weren't with Kevin before- "

"You'd have asked him out?" said Rebecca innocently.

He gaped. "No, no! I'm not gay—"

He stopped. Rebecca was killing herself laughing.

"Very funny."

"Sorry. Look, could we talk later? Will you be around? These coffees are going to get cold, and I'd better get back to Mr Cheerful."" She jerked her head.

"Sure. I'm here until 6."

"That's a date, then." She gave him a brilliant smile and walked off.

Steve watched her go, grinning like an idiot.

At first, Steve couldn't wait to see Rebecca at the end of the day, but as the hours went by, he got more and more worried. Rebecca had been single all that time, but had given no clear signals that she fancied him. Maybe she just saw him as close friend material.

He leaned through the hatch. Good. Neil was standing close by sealing up salads. "You were right. They're not together!" Steve hissed.

He looked up. "Who?"

自己可以成為其中一體。」

「最後怎麼樣了？」他聲音沙啞地問。

「慘敗。所以為什麼我沒有再這樣做了。」

「很遺憾得知這一點。」

「也許這是最好的。畢竟，我認為自然而然地遇上一個人是最好的事情。那樣感覺總是很假的。」她微笑著看著他，他的心臟跟平常一樣在翻騰。她再次轉身過去，而史堤夫感到一陣恐慌。莫名其妙的原因，他認為，如果他錯過了現在這次機會去跟她說，他永遠不會再有機會了。

「麗貝卡。」

「嗯？」

「你看，呃...如果我之前知道你跟凱文不是在一起...」

「你會去約他嗎？」麗貝卡天真地說。

他目瞪口呆。「不會，不會！我不是同性戀...」

他停了下來。麗貝卡自己在笑慘了。

「非常有趣。」

「對不起。你看，我們可以晚一點再談嗎？你會在這裡到幾點？咖啡快變冷了，我得回去開朗先生的身體。」她動了動她的頭。

「當然可以。我直到六點都在這裡。」

「那麼，這是一個約會啊。」她給了他一個燦爛的笑容，然後走了。

史堤夫目送她離去，笑得像一個傻瓜。

起初，史堤夫急不及待地想快點結束這一天見到麗貝卡，但隨著時間過去，他越來越擔心。麗貝卡一直都是單身的，但總覺得她沒有給他明確的信號表示過喜歡他。也許她只是待他為密友。

他俯身通過小窗口。很好。尼爾站在附近正把沙拉封起來。「你

"Rebecca and Kevin!"

Neil shrugged. "Told you so."

"You said you didn't think they were. I don't why you were so sure." He frowned. "Unless... you know, don't you?"

"Know what?"

"About Kevin?"

He turned away and started to clean the worktop. "What about him?" he asked gruffly.

Steve lowered his voice. "That he's—"

"Gay?" finished Neil. "Yeah. I suspected."

"How? I can't see it at all."

"I saw him leaving a gay bar a couple of times. That was a clue."

Steve glared at Neil's back. "And you didn't think to mention it?"

Neil turned round. It was the first time Steve had ever seen him look cross. "No. I'm not your spy, Steve, and I didn't think Kevin's personal life was any of your business!"

"No, I... sorry. You're right. It's just if I'd known... "

"If you'd known? Dude, you were too tied up with Laura, and of course, you could always have asked Rebecca if she was single," said Neil wryly.

Steve felt like an idiot. He shrugged and went back to the counter. Neil was right, both about Kevin's personal life and his own reticence with Rebecca, but he didn't have to be so bloody touchy. What was up with him lately?

When Rebecca eventually walked in, he felt more nervous than pleased.

"Nearly done?"

"I'll be five minutes. Are you okay waiting?"

"I'll go and tuck myself in the corner."

是正確的。他們不是在一起！」史堤夫發出噓聲。

他抬起頭來。「誰？」

「麗貝卡和凱文！」

尼爾聳聳肩。「告訴過你了。」

「你說你不認為他們在一起。我不知道你為何那麼肯定。」他皺起了眉頭。　「除非…你是知道的，是嗎？」

「知道什麼？」

「關於凱文？」

他轉身離開，並開始清理櫃面。「他怎麼樣？」他粗聲粗氣地問。

史堤夫壓低聲音說：「他是…」

「同性戀嗎？」尼爾說。「是啊。我懷疑是。」

「你怎麼知道？我無法看出來。」

「我見過了幾次，他離開同志酒吧。這就是線索。」

史堤夫怒視在尼爾的背面。「你不覺得要說出來嗎？」

尼爾轉身。這是第一次史堤夫見到他看起來這麼生氣。「沒有。我不是你的間諜，史堤夫，我不覺得凱文的個人生活關你什麼事！」

「不，我…對不起。你說得對。只是，如果我知道的話…」
「如果你知道的話？老兄，你跟羅拉的關係太複雜了，而當然，你可以隨時追求麗貝卡，如果她還是單身。」尼爾挖苦地說。

史堤夫覺得自己像個傻瓜。他聳聳肩，又回到櫃檯。尼爾是對的，凱文的個人生活和他自己不想輕易暴露對麗貝卡感情。但他根本不用那麼該死的小心眼。他之前究竟是怎麼了？

當麗貝卡最終走了進來，他覺得緊張多於開心。

「快完了？」

"Okay. I'll bring you a coffee."

He refilled the chilled cabinet and made sure there were just a few of each kind of pastry and cake. They didn't sell so well in the evening so most of them were best left wrapped.

He carried two butterscotch lattes over to her table and sat down.

She bent over her coffee and inhaled. "Mmm. Butterscotch. Thanks."

"That's okay." He leant back and sipped his coffee. "Ah. That's better."

"Hard day?"

"Very busy, for some reason. This afternoon's been crazy. What about yours?"

She rolled her eyes. "I was on the site with Marcie this afternoon, and she took great delight in arguing with every single thing I said. I think even if I'd just said 'well here we are on a dig site' she'd have said 'no, I think you'll find it's an archaeological excavation. The woman's so petty."

"Sounds stressful."

"I've had better afternoons."

He desperately tried to think of a way to lead the conversation in the direction he wanted. "How was Kevin's afternoon?"

"I hope it was okay. I took pity on him and asked him to do some writing up at the museum. Marcie's not keen on him by association, and I thought he could do without that today."

"What a kind boss." He smiled. "I still can't believe you two aren't together. I can't believe you tried internet dating, either."

"Tried being the operative word. It's not for me, I've decided it's far better to see who crosses your path."

"I crossed your path a while ago," he said quietly, "and of course it turns out you were single all that time, so I guess that I wasn't your type, and you just let me carry on walking." He tried to laugh and make it sound like a jokey comment, but failed utterly.

She rested her elbows on the table and put her chin on her joined hands. "I did decide you weren't my type, as a matter of fact," she

「我還有五分鐘。你等一下可以嗎？」

「沒問題，我會自己先坐到角落去。」

「好吧。我會為你帶一杯咖啡。」

他重新裝滿冷凍櫃，肯定各種糕點和蛋糕只僅僅是幾個。它們大多在晚上都沒有賣的那麼好，所以最好只剩下肉卷。

他帶著兩杯奶油糖果拿鐵咖啡去到桌子前坐了下來。

她俯身聞了一下咖啡。「嗯。奶油糖果。謝謝。」

「沒關係。」他仰身向後，啜著咖啡。「嗯。這樣有比較好。」

「辛苦了一天嗎？」

「非常忙，出於某種原因。今天下午是瘋狂的。你呢？」

她翻了翻眼睛。「我今天與瑪西去了場地工作，她跟我爭論我說的每一件小事，得到了很大的樂趣。我想即使我只是說：『我們在一個挖掘現場。』她也會說：『不，我想你會發現它其實是一個考古發掘。』小心眼的女人。」

「聽起來很緊張。」

「我下午比較好了。」

他拼命地想辦法，將話題帶領到他想要的方向。「凱文下午如何？」

「我希望是好的。我都很同情他，所以叫他留在博物館做一些文書的工作。瑪西不喜歡跟他合作，而我想今天他也不應該去。」

「這個老闆太仁慈了。」他笑著說。「我仍然不能相信你們兩個不是在一起的，我更不能相信你嘗試過網絡約會。」

「嘗試是個關鍵字。但它不適合我，我已經決定最好還是去看看誰會出現在我的路上。」

「前一段時間，我有出現在你的路上，」他平靜地說，「當然事實證明了，原來一路以來你都是單身的，所以我想我不是你的類型，你只是讓我繼續走下去。」他試圖笑，希望聽起來像一個詼諧的感想，但完全失敗了。

said, looking him in the eye. "Because my type is single."

"But I am single!"

"I know that now," she said, giving a rueful smile. "Ever since Tony told me Laura was your sister. Before that, I presumed that Laura was—"

"My girlfriend?" Steve gaped at her. "You're joking!"

"Oh, worse," said Rebecca cheerfully. "When we overheard the police say Laura Reynolds, Kevin and I presumed she was your wife."

Steve put his head in his hands. "This is crazy," he said softly, "If I'd know you were single, I would have asked you out ages ago."

"And if I'd known you were single, I would have beaten you to it," she said lightly.

His head shot up. "Really?"

"Really. I definitely noted you crossing my path." She smiled at him and Steve felt like one of the people on those old Ready Brek adverts who visibly glowed. "But I got involved before with someone whose relationship was in a mess, all but over, apparently, I was the only person he could talk to...." She shook her head, looking embarrassed. "It didn't end well, not for me anyway, and I didn't want to go through that again. Then when I found out Laura was your sister, I figured that if you were single, you'd obviously never shown any interest in me because... well, because you weren't interested in me."

"Never shown any interest in you?" He protested, smiling. "What are you, blind?"

She laughed. "Sorry. You did sometimes. I was getting very mixed signals, and I felt I was being a bit of a strumpet, kissing you on the cheek that first time. Though back then I hadn't heard of Laura."

"Ah. Whereas I didn't think you were a strumpet until you kissed me the second time." He grinned, leaning forward.

"Well you were fair game by that time, because by then I knew Laura was your sister. And you looked like you needed it."

"Ah, I see. It was charity."

她把手肘放在桌子上，讓下巴放在交疊的雙手上。「我有確定了你不是我的類型，事實上，」她看著他的雙眼睛說。「因為我喜歡的類型是單身的。」

「但我是單身的！」

「我現在知道了，」她說，帶著心懷悔意的笑容。「直至東尼告訴我羅拉是你的妹妹，在此之前，我假設認為羅拉是…」

「我女朋友？」史堤夫目瞪口呆的看著她。「你是在開玩笑！」

「哦，更糟糕的是，」麗貝卡興致勃勃地說。「當我們無意中聽到警方說羅拉．雷諾茲時，凱文和我假設她是你的妻子。」

史堤夫把他的頭栽在手中。「這太瘋狂了，」他輕聲說，「如果我知道你是單身的，很久以前我就已經追求你了。」

「如果我知道你是單身的，我會比你搶先行動。」她輕輕地說。他突然抬起頭。「真的嗎？」

「真的。我絕對有注意到你出現在我的道路上。」她微笑著看著他，史堤夫覺得自己像那些老舊的谷物早餐廣告中明顯發亮的人。「但是，我之前捲入了某人一塌糊塗的關係中，但現在結束了，很顯然我是唯一的人，他可以跟…」她搖搖頭，滿臉尷尬的。「沒有好下場，無論如何不是為我，而我不想再經歷一遍。後來，當我發現出羅拉是你的妹妹，我想通了並認為如果你是單身的，你很明顯從來沒有表現出對我有任何的興趣，因為…嗯，因為你對我沒有興趣。」

「從來沒有表現出任何對你有任何的興趣嗎？」他面帶微笑地抗議道。「你是盲的嗎？」

她笑了起來。「對不起。有時你會。但我收到的信號非常混亂。我覺得我自己已經有一點似妓女般，親吻你的臉頰，在那一次。雖然當時我還沒有聽說羅拉。」

「嗯。但是我沒想過你像妓女直到你親吻我第二次。」他咧嘴一笑，身體前傾。

「好吧，那個時候你是個公平的遊戲，因為那個時我知道羅拉是你的妹妹。而你看起來很需要它。」

「啊，我明白了。是慈善事業。」

「當然。」她的眼睛閃閃發亮，她再靠近了一點點。

"Definitely." Her eye twinkled and she leaned a little closer.

"I don't suppose you fancy donating again?"

"Is it for a good cause?"

"The best." He said huskily.

He must have been convincing because she did kiss him. And this time, it wasn't just on the cheek.

"That's a lot more enjoyable when you're not on the verge of a panic attack."

She smiled. "A lot more enjoyable when it's a proper kiss too."

"All the time we've wasted, when we could have been doing that. You have to see the irony."

"Irony? Tragedy, more like." She sighed.

"Better not waste any more, then. What about dinner?"

"Yes please, but not tonight. Girl's night in, sorry. Do you like Mexican?" She looked at him hopefully.

"I love Mexican, there's this great place, Chi—"

"Chilango!"

"You've been there!"

"Yes, and I'd love to go again. Desperado's is good, but Chilango-

"—is the best," Steve finished.

"Yep. Saturday night?"

"Great." Suddenly an unwelcome thought popped into his head. "Oh no," he groaned. Should he tell her the truth? Yes. Start as you mean to go on. "Rebecca, I really hope you can see the funny side of this, but I've got a date on Saturday. An internet date."

Her eyes went wide. "Seriously? You've been internet dating too?"

"Yes. Look, I'll try and cancel."

Rebecca was laughing. "You don't have to, honestly."

「我不認為你想再次捐獻？」

「為一個好的理由？」

「最好的。」他說，聲音已經沙啞了。

他已經很確定，因為她吻了他。而這一次，它不只是在臉頰上。

「這樣更有樂趣，當你不是在恐慌症發作的邊緣上。」

她笑了。「是更有樂趣的，當它是一個適當的吻。」

「我們已經浪費了所有時間，當我們很久以前已經可以這樣做。你一定看出有多諷刺。」

「諷刺？更像是悲劇。」她嘆了口氣。

「那最好不要再浪費了。晚餐怎麼樣？」

「是的，但不是今晚。現在是女孩的晚上，對不起。你喜歡墨西哥餐？」她帶著期望地看著他。

「我愛墨西哥餐，有這個很棒的地方，叫吉...」

「吉浪高！」

「你有去過那裡！」

「是的，我很想再去一次。亡命之徒是很好，但吉浪高...」
「是最好的。」史堤夫把說話完成。

「沒錯。星期六晚上好嗎？」

「太好了。」突然，一個不受歡迎的念頭出現在他的腦海。「哦，不，」他呻吟著。他要告訴她真相嗎？是。開始了就要繼續下去。「麗貝卡，我真的希望你能看到有趣的一面，我週六有一個約會，一個網絡約會。」

她的眼睛睜大了。「真的嗎？你有去過網絡約會嗎？」

「是的。嗯，我可以嘗試取消。」

麗貝卡笑。「你不一定要這樣做，真的。

"I want to. Anyway it's not fair on her, when I've got no intention of seeing her again."

She quirked an eyebrow. "Careful what you're throwing away there. She might be gorgeous."

"Not as gorgeous as you." He reached for her hands.

She smiled. "Much as I'd love to stay here for some more flattery, I'm afraid I've got to go."

"Okay. Will you be in tomorrow?"

"Yes, but only for a quick coffee, tomorrow's mad. You can let me know then if you've cancelled your other woman." She made a face and Steve laughed.

As they said goodbye outside, it occurred to Steve that it was about time he took some initiative, so he took her hand in his and kissed her, just long enough to send a tingle down his spine.

He didn't quite skip home – that would have attracted funny looks – but there was a definite spring in his step, and he sang very loudly as he cooked dinner.

「我想。反正這樣對她是不公平的，我根本不打算再次見她。」

她挑了挑眉毛。「小心注意你放棄了什麼，她可能是很一個美麗的女人。」

「不夠你美麗。」他伸手拉起她手。

她笑了。「雖然我很想呆在這裡聽多一點奉承的說話，但恐怕我要走了。」

「好吧。明天你會來嗎？」

「會的，但只可以喝一杯快速的咖啡，明天真的要瘋了。那麼如果你已經取消你跟其他女人的約會，你可以讓我知道。」她做了個鬼臉，史堤夫笑了。

他們在外面說了聲再見，史堤夫認為是時間應該要採取了一些主動，所以他拉著她的手，吻了她，時間足夠長到令他的脊椎發麻。

他直接回了家，雖然這將引起異樣的眼光，但在他的步伐有一個明確的春天，當他煮晚餐時他唱得很大聲。

Chapter Nineteen

Steve sat at a table in the plush surroundings of the Maharajah's Palace Tandoori Restaurant and wished he was somewhere else. Anywhere else. It wasn't that he didn't like this place; it was cosy and tastefully decorated, with red velvet curtains and subtle wallpaper, and the food had been good when he'd been here before. But he would far rather be waiting for Rebecca, or a friend, than waiting for his Hot Match No.2.

He hadn't been able to cancel the date in the end, because he couldn't contact her. At least, as far as he knew he wasn't contacting her; there hadn't been any response, so unless she was sulking and just not bothering to reply—perhaps she though leaving him sitting there in the restaurant by himself was suitable punishment—then he had to presume that for some reason she hadn't seen his message and still believed the date was on.

If that was true, he could hardly not turn up, could he? That would be unchivalrous in the extreme, and Rebecca had agreed with hi. So they'd delayed their date until tomorrow, and here he was, waiting for Chantelle and wondering how on earth he would explain that he didn't really want to be here, didn't really care if they got on well, and had no intention of seeing her again? As opening lines went, it wasn't a great one. But nor could he think of a subtle way to bring it into the conversation, unless it turned to heartless cads who invited women on dates under false pretences. Then it would fit right in.

The more he thought about it, the more he was inclined to take to his heels and flee. Perhaps standing her up would be nore helpful and more fair, than letting her think this was a proper date, happily anticipated by both parties, that might lead to more dates.

Think positive, Steve, he told himself firmly, filling his glass from the jug of iced water on the table. Perhaps she'll be a really nice person, and understand completely. She might even laugh about it! He might end up with a really good friend.

Idiot, said the cynic in him. Yes, because that's why women sign

第十九章

史堤夫正坐在一個豪華環境中的座位上，這裡是馬哈拉加宮殿中的唐杜裡餐廳。但他希望自己是在別的地方，任何一個地方都好。並不是因為他不喜歡這裡，這裡很舒適，有高雅的佈置，紅色天鵝絨窗簾和柔和的壁紙。他上次來的時候，已經知道這裡的食物是很好吃的。但他寧願自己是在等待的麗貝卡，或者是朋友，而不是他的第二位熱門配對。

他到最後都沒有取消約會，因為他聯繫不上她。至少據他所知，他並沒有聯繫到她。他沒有收到任何回覆，所以她應該是在生悶氣而不想再花心思去回覆。也許她想把他留在餐廳中，當做一個適當的處分。然後他又假定由於某種原因，她沒有看到他的信息，所以以為約會如期進行。

如果這是真的，他很難不赴約，是嗎？這樣是非常沒風度的，而且麗貝卡已經同意了。因此，他們把約會推遲到明天，而他就在這兒等待仙黛爾。他想著究竟如何解釋，他其實並不真的想來到這裡，亦真的不在乎縱使他們相處得很好，也不會再次跟她見面？如果在一開場時就說這些，似乎不太好。但他也無法想到有任何含蓄的方法可以說出來，否則他就要變成一個負心的無賴，用不實理由邀請女士約會。這樣，它就會變得更恰當了。

他越去想，他就越想滑腳溜走。也許其實失約會比赴約更好和更公平，不用讓她以為這是一個適當的約會，雙方愉快地預期可能會有下一個約會。

想得正面一點，史堤夫，他堅定地告訴自己，拿起了桌上的一壺冰水斟滿了玻璃杯。也許她會是個不錯的人，會完全理解是什麼情況。她甚至可能會嘲笑他！最後亦有機會成為很好的朋友。

白痴，內心那個憤世嫉俗的他在說。是的，這就是為什麼一個女人會註冊約會機構嗎？史堤夫，她一定是為了擴大朋友圈呢！很明顯，除非有奇蹟發生，否則你必須要離開這裡。在服務台留

up to dating agencies, Steve—to increase their circle of friends! And that's a pig flying past the restaurant window. You have to get out of this now. Leave a message with the desk, pretend you were called away on an emergency, and then when you get back in touch explain you've met someone now and won't be using the dating site any more. He was just getting to his feet when the door opened and a slender woman in a red dress walked in. She was grasping her matching clutch bag as though it was a lifebelt, scanning the restaurant uncertainly. He had to put her out of her misery. All thoughts of fleeing were put to one side as he rose to his feet and diffidently held up a hand. She looked relieved as she made her way over, but confident too, looking his in the eye and smiling as she came up to the table. Steve had to admit she was attractive. The red dress flattered her figure and her shoulder-length hair shone.

"Hello." Instead of sitting down opposite him, she leaned over kissed him. On the lips.

Since when had that been usual blind date etiquette? Steve hoped he didn't look as flustered as he felt right now.

"Hi. You must be Chantelle," he croaked.

"And you're Steve. Even hotter than your picture."

Floor, swallow me up now. "Er, thanks," he squeaked. Change the topic! ""I ordered some popadoms, I hope you don't mind. I was starving."

"Lovely." She smiled, taking a popadom and putting it in her mouth in an interesting way, while looking at him quite intently.

Her lipstick really was very red indeed. "Shall we look at the wine list?"

"We can, if you're willing to risk it," she raised her eyebrows, her eyes still fixed on his.

"Er.. risk it?" He frowned. "Why? Isn't their wine any good?"

"No, the wine's fine." She leaned forward, showing more cleavage than Steve was comfortable with. "But I'm dangerous after a couple of glasses of wine."

"Re-really?" He tried to smile casually but he'd never been so uncomfortable in his life. "Do you start to sing loudly? Or will I have to drag you down from the tables to stop you dancing?" Well done. Bit of humour. Keep it light.

個言，假裝被臨時叫走了，然後你回來時再跟她聯繫並解釋你遇上了什麼人，而且將不會再使用任何交友網站。他剛站了起身，門就打開了，一個穿紅色裙子的苗條女人走了進來，她拿著跟她很匹配的手拿包，就好像是一個救生圈似的，她不確定地掃視著餐廳。他得去解決她的憂慮。現在所有逃走的想法都放在一邊，他站起身來，膽怯地舉起手。她即時鬆了口氣並開始走過來，但看起來有點過於自信，她看著他的眼睛，面帶微笑，走到桌子前面。史堤夫不得不承認她很有吸引力。紅色的連衣裙襯托得她的身材和齊肩的頭髮更好看。

「你好。」她第一時間並不是在他的對面的位子上坐下，而是俯身吻了他一下，在嘴唇上。

由什麼時候開始這變成了相親的慣性禮儀呢？史堤夫希望他看起來不是那麼神色慌張，因為他現在的確這樣覺得。

「嗨，你一定是仙黛爾。」他聲音嘶啞地說。

「你是史堤夫，你比照片更性感啊。」

不知所措的感覺把他吞噬了。「嗯，謝謝，」他尖聲地說。轉換話題！「我點了一些脆餅，希望你不要介意，因為我有點餓。」

「很可愛。」她笑著，拿起脆餅，用一個有趣的方式放到嘴裡，目不轉睛地看著他。

她的口紅真的有點太紅了。「我們來看看酒單嗎？」

「可以的，如果你願意冒險的話。」她揚起了眉毛，眼睛仍然盯著他。

「呃…冒險嗎？」他皺起了眉頭。「為什麼？是不是他們的酒有什麼問題？」

「不，酒很好。」她俯身向前露出更多的乳溝，令史堤夫有點不自在。「但我喝幾杯之後就會變得很危險。」

「真…真的嗎？」他試圖輕鬆地微笑，在他這一生之中，從來沒有試過這麼不自在的。「你會大聲唱歌？或是要我從桌子上拖你下來，阻止你繼續跳舞？」幹得好，有幽默感。繼續保持輕鬆。

「不是，但如果你喜歡，以後我也可以跟你跳舞的。」她揚起了一邊性感的眉毛。「酒會使我慾火中燒，幾杯之後，我可以讓你帶我去任何地方。」

"No, although I can dance for you later, if you like." She raised one slinky eyebrow. "Wine makes me horny, and after a couple of glasses, I might let you drag me anywhere."

Oh. My. God.

"Look, I think I should tell you that I tried to cancel this date," he said in a rush.

"Oh, yes, I think I remember seeing a message about that." She winked.

"You saw it?" He was flabbergasted. "Why didn't you reply?"

"I thought you were just getting cold feet. And I might be just the woman to warm them up." Steve became aware of her feet, no longer in their spiky heels, twisting caressingly round his ankles.

He moved his feet sharply away. She looked amused.

"I sent that message because I've met someone. I'm not going to be using the dating agency anymore."

"I see. Set a wedding date, have we?"

"No, but—"

"Then why don't you relax and tell me something about yourself?"

"I can't see much point," he said tensely.

"Charming. I made the effort to come here, the least you can do is have dinner with me and make polite conversation. I promise to leave your feet alone."

He flushed. "Right. I suppose we could still have dinner."

She raised her hand and signalled to the waiter. "So what do you like to do in your spare time?"

"Er, I run, go to the gym occasionally—"

"I can tell." She let her eyes travel down his torso admiringly. "Me too." She moved closer to him and lifted her dress up to nearly hip level. "Look how toned my thighs are."

Steve stood up, pulled some notes out of his wallet and let them fall on the table. "Dinner's on me, Chantelle. You have a great evening."

噢。我。的。天。啊。

「好吧，我覺得我應該要告訴你，我本來想取消此約會。他匆匆地說。

「哦，是的，我想我記得有看過一個訊息。」她眨了眨眼。

「你看到了吧？」他深感驚詫。「你為什麼不回覆？」

「我想你只是有點緊張，而我可能就是可以讓你暖起身來的女人。」史堤夫意識到她的腳不再在那尖尖的高跟鞋裡，而是愛撫地扭動並纏住他的腳踝。

他大幅度地動了動他的腳，她看似很逗樂。

「我發這個訊息是因為我已經遇到了一個人。而我不打算再使用的約會機構了。」

「我明白了。但我們現在是要定婚期了嗎？」

「不是，但...」
「那你為什麼不放鬆點，並告訴我你的事情呢？」

「我看不到有這個需要。」他緊張地說。

「有種啊。但我已經來到這裡來，你至少可以陪我一起吃晚飯，並禮貌地交談。我答應不會再碰你的腳。」

他滿臉通紅。「沒錯。我想我們仍然可以吃晚飯的。」

她抬起手示意服務員。「那麼你在業餘時間喜歡做什麼嗎？」

「呃，我會跑步，偶爾去健身房。」

「我可以告訴你，」她眼睛羨慕地沿著他的軀幹看著。「我也是。」她坐近了他，並把裙子拉起到近臀部的位置。「你看我鍛煉得大腿怎麼樣。」

史堤夫站了起來，從他的錢包中拿了錢出來放在桌子上。「晚餐算我的，仙黛爾。祝你有一個美好的晚上。」

「哦，謝謝。」她向他簡單地笑了一下，然後看著年輕的服務員。他才剛走到桌子前面，看起來很困惑。「我敢肯定，我將有一個非常美好的晚上。」

"Ooh, thanks." She smiled briefly in his direction then eyed the young waiter, who'd just arrived at their table and was looking rather confused. "I'm sure I'll have a very good time."

She turned to the waiter without giving Steve a second glance.

As he walked away, he heard her say, "Hi. Are all the waiters here as good looking as you? I'll have to come here more often. Now, can you sit down and explain the menu to me? I never know what to choose."

她轉過身向著服務員，並沒有再多看史堤夫一眼。

當他離開時，聽到她說：「嗨。這裡是不是所有的服務員都有你這麼好看的呢？那麼我不得不經常到這裡來了。現在，你可以坐下來，並為我解釋一下菜單嗎？我不知道該怎麼選擇。」

Chapter Twenty

Rebecca sighed and leant back in her seat. "I couldn't eat another tiny, single, miniscule thing." Half a Chicken Taco topped with roasted tomato salsa and a small pile of salad lay abandoned on her plate. She pushed it away from her. "Oof."

Steve grinned. "And I was going to take you somewhere for an ice-cream. Cool you down a bit."

She fanned herself with a serviette. "I am quite hot."

He smirked. "Yes, you are. Though you could be a bit more modest."

"Hey!" She glared. "I thought I was being very modest, actually. I only said quite hot."

"Hmm, well..." he ran his eyes over her, pondering. "Some days I suppose you score a 'very'. But not when your face is like a beetroot."

Their first proper date had been delayed by a week, in the end, and in that time they'd found plenty of opportunities for coffee or lunch together. That had been a good thing, thought Rebecca, because they were comfortable with each other now, and she'd felt relaxed as she got ready tonight. It was a world away from the tension and dread she'd felt going on her internet dates. She leaned her head against his shoulder and he planted a kiss in her hair.

"So could you manage an ice-cream?"

"Maybe, once we've walked there. Is it far?"

"Is it far, she says. I thought you were fit."

She batted her eyelashes at him. "I'll have you know, I've been told I'm well fit," she said solemnly.

第二十章

麗貝卡嘆了口氣，靠在她座位的椅背上。「我不能再吃任何細小、一塊或者微不足道的東西。」半件雞墨西哥玉米薄餅卷配上烤番茄醬和沙拉仍堆在她的碟子上。她把它推開了。「嗯。」

史堤夫咧嘴笑了。「我還想帶你去一個吃冰淇淋的地方，冷卻一下你。」

她搗著餐巾紙。「我有點熱。」

他傻笑。「是的，你是。雖然你可能有一點太謙虛了。」

「嘿！」她瞪著。「實際上我覺得我真的是很謙虛了。我只是說有點。」

「嗯，嗯...」他看著她，沉思著。「有些日子裡，我覺得你是『非常』，但不是當你的臉像紅菜頭的時候。」
他們的第一個正式約會最終推遲了一個星期，而在期間，他們已經有很多機會一起喝咖啡或午餐。麗貝卡認為這是一件好事，因為他們現在可以相處得很好，她感到輕鬆自在，因為她已經為今晚做好準備了。這一切都不像她在網絡約會前的緊張和恐懼。她湊近他，把頭靠在他的肩膀上，他吻了吻她的頭髮。

「所以，你還可以吃冰淇淋嗎？」

「也許吧，我們可以先走過去看看。很遠嗎？」

「我想你應該夠健美。」

她向他眨了眨眼。「我會讓你知道，我已經告訴過你我很健美。」她鄭重地說。

「究竟我是什麼回事，總是吸引到所有這樣自負的女人？」他嘆了口氣。「這是一個可怕的詛咒。」他拉著她站起來，她咯咯地笑了。

"What is it about me that attracts all these very forward women?" he sighed. "It's a terrible curse." He pulled her to her feet and she giggled.

"I still can't believe you joined Methodical Matches too. What are the chances?"

"Two lonely hearts," he intoned, passing her coat to her, "just looking for love... quite a high chance, I think."

She buttoned up her coat and Steve kissed her very thoroughly.

"Honestly! In public."

He took her hand and led her to the door. "Couldn't help it. You look too gorgeous to resist."

"Really? In my coat? It's not exactly the most revealing thing I've ever worn."

He opened the door and as she stepped out after her, he stopped and pulled her towards him.

"I love you in that coat."

"Only in my coat? I'd better not take it off, then," she said lightly, very aware that he'd used the I word, even if it was in the wrong context.

"You know what I mean," he said, smiling. "You look wonderful in it. It really suits you. And I used to wait for it to appear every day. If there were lots of people milling about outside the café, I'd still know when you turned up because I'd catch a glimpse of this plum coat—"

"It's not plum, it's auberg—"

She was momentarily silenced in the nicest possible way.

"Sometimes, you know," said Steve as he pulled away, "that really is the only way to keep you quiet."

She pulled his head back down again. "I know. Why do you think I talk so much?" she asked huskily.

Steve tried to be quiet as he opened the front door, even though he felt like being loud. Not just because he'd had a few drinks, but

「我仍然不能相信你也有參加井然配對。這有多巧合？」

「兩顆孤獨的心，」他吟誦道，把大衣遞給她，「只是為了尋找愛情…是相當巧合，我覺得。」

她扣上了大衣上的釦子，史堤夫吻了她，非常深入地。

「老實點！這是公眾地方。」

他拉著她的手，領著她到門口。「沒有辦法，你看起來太美麗而難以抗拒。」

「真的嗎？穿著大衣時嗎？這不是我穿過的衣服之中最能表現我的。」

他打開門讓她出去，然後他停下來，把她拉向他。

「我愛你穿這件大衣。」

「只是穿著大衣的我嗎？那我最好不要把它脫下來。」她輕輕地說，很在意他使用了個「愛」字，即使是在錯誤使用的情況下。

「你知道我的意思，」他說，臉帶微笑。「你非常好看，它非常適合你。我每天都在等待它出現。如果有很多人在咖啡店外亂轉，我仍然知道是你打開門，因為我見到這件梅子色的大衣。」

「這不是梅子色，是紫红…」

她再一度被迫沉默了，在最好的方式下。

「有時候，你知道，」史堤夫說，「確實只有這樣，才能讓你安靜下來。」

她再把他的頭拉回來。「我知道。所以你為什麼想我再說多一點？」她沙啞地問。

當史堤夫打開前門時，他試圖想安靜點，儘管他感覺仍是那麼吵。不只是因為他喝了幾杯，是因為麗貝卡。他們在吉浪高過了非常美妙的一晚，仍縈繞著史堤夫的腦海中。

他脫下了鞋子，溜入了廚房。他想睡覺前先喝一杯茶。水壺開始發出了水泡的聲音，他從櫥櫃裡拿了杯子出來，然後幾乎掉了，因為他注意到羅拉靠在門框上。

because of Rebecca. They'd had a fantastic time at Chilango's and Steve was buzzing.

Taking off his shoes he padded to the kitchen. He fancied a cuppa before bed. As the kettle started to bubble noisily he took a cup down from the cupboard and then nearly dropped it as he noticed Laura leaning against the doorframe.

"God almighty! How long have you been there?" He leaned against the counter, recovering.

Laura grinned and he thought how good it was to see some sparkle and life back in her eyes. He'd never realised just how ill she had started to look; these days she practically glowed.

"Sorry bro. I've only been here a couple of seconds. I was reading but I must have fallen asleep on the sofa."

"Just waiting to give me a heart attack, huh?"

"Ah, you guessed my cunning plan. The kettle was in on it too, masking my footsteps."

"Want a cup of tea?"

She shook her head and pushed herself off the doorframe. "I'm getting some water then I'm heading for bed." She pushed herself off the doorframe and went to the cupboard. "So where have you been?" she asked casually. "You're back late."

He couldn't help himself. He could feel a daft grin settling on his face. "I went out for dinner with Rebecca."

"Rebecca?" She turned round. "What, my Rebecca?"

"S'cuse me, she'd not your Rebecca."

"She's certainly not yours," retorted Laura, a little sharply. She got a glass and walked to the tap.

"You're right, she's not. I wouldn't want her to be. She's nobody's Rebecca, she's her own woman. That's why I lo— like her."

She filled her glass and turned to face him, grinning. "Are you drunk, Steve?"

"No, just happy, that's all."

"My my, we have got it bad, haven't we. You do know how brainy

「天啊！你在那裡多久了？」他靠在櫃檯，讓自己平靜下來。

羅拉笑著，他覺得現在終於可以在她的眼裡看到一些火花和生命，這樣是多美好的事。他從來沒有想過她從前是何時開始生病了，但近日她幾乎都在閃閃發光。

「對不起，老兄。我在這裡只有幾秒鐘。我剛才在看書，但我一定是在沙發上睡著了。」

「在等待令我心臟病發作的機會，對吧？」

「啊，你猜到我狡猾的計劃了。那只是水壺滾燙著，遮蓋了我的腳步聲。」

「想要一杯茶嗎？」

她搖搖頭，從門框上站直身子。「我只想喝水，然後我就去睡了。」她往櫥櫃走過了。「所以，你去哪裡了？」她隨口問道。「你回來晚了。」

他不由得自己，他能感覺到一個愚蠢的笑容掛了在自己的臉上。「我與麗貝卡出去吃飯。」

「麗貝卡？」她轉身過去。「什麼？我的麗貝卡？」

「不好意思，她不是你的麗貝卡。」

「她肯定不是你的。」羅拉反駁道，有一點點尖銳地。她拿到了玻璃杯，走向水龍頭。

「你說得沒錯，她不是。我不認為她是任何人的麗貝卡，她是她自己的女人。這就是為什麼我愛…喜歡她。」

她斟滿了她的水杯，轉身面對他，笑嘻嘻地說，「史堤夫，你是不是醉了？」

「沒有，只是很開心，就這樣而已。」

「我的我的，我們都很喜歡她，是不是？你不知道她是多麼的優秀嗎？」

他皺起了眉頭：「那有什麼區別呢？」

「哦，真的沒有，我認為。」她吻了他的臉頰。「我要睡覺了，情人男孩，我會離開你漂浮到你那粉紅色的小雲上面。」

she is, don't you?"

"What difference does that make?" He frowned.

"Oh, none really, I suppose." She kissed him on the cheek. "I'm off to bed, lover boy, I'll leave you to float upstairs on your little pink cloud."

He couldn't think of a dignified riposte, so he growled and made a face.

"Growling? It must be your sophistication that attracts her." Laura's voice floated back to him as she went upstairs, laughing.

He laughed too, but as he drank his tea he thought about Laura's remark and felt uneasy. Okay, Rebecca was very brainy, very capable and very good at her job, and at the moment, he just worked in a café, which admittedly wasn't a stretch intellectually; but that didn't matter.

Did it?

"Five minutes more. I can see the edge of the bone."

"You said that five minutes ago, Bec."

"So I was over optimistic. Sue me." She grinned at Kevin over her shoulder.

"It's getting dark."

She glanced up. "Barely, and we've got lamps, haven't we?"

"Yes, if you really need them. But we don't, and people want to go home," he said pointedly, jerking his head.

She moved sideways to look beyond him and saw a gaggle of surveyors and diggers, mooching about and casting the odd disgruntled look in her direction. "Well they can go home, they don't have to stay!" she protested. She bent forward again, pushing her trowel into the small hole she was working on and shifting the soil with small, careful movements.

"Someone has to, you know that. Health and Safety," Kevin said huffily. "And it's not going to be me." She turned round, meeting his glare, and stuck her tongue out, but he carried on. "The site needs to be locked down, and we're not the keyholders. It's not

他想不出比較有威嚴的還擊，所以他只有咆哮，並做了個鬼臉。

「咆哮嗎？那你一定已經很老練而且吸引到她了。」當羅拉上樓的時候，她聲音飄回到他身邊，然後是一陣大笑。

他也笑了，當他喝著茶時，他想到羅拉的言論而感到有些不安。好吧，麗貝卡是非常聰明，非常能幹，在工作上也非常成功，而此刻的他只是在一間咖啡店工作，這無可否認延續下去不是很理智，但是不要緊的。

不是嗎？

「再過五分鐘，我就可以看到骨的邊緣。」

「你五分鐘前說過了，貝卡。」

「所以，我之前是過於樂觀了。有本事來告我啊。」她咧嘴一笑，凱文站在她的身後。

「快天黑了。」

她抬頭。「似乎是，但我們有燈，是不？」

「是的，如果你真的需要它們。但是，我們不會這樣做，人們都想回家了。」他尖銳地說，搖動著他的頭。

她移動了一下望向他身後，看到擠滿了的測量師和挖掘機，看上去徬徨並心懷不滿地看著她的方向。「那麼，他們可以回家了，他們沒有必要留下來！」她抗議道。她再次俯身向前，推著她的抹泥刀插入小孔內，她正在轉移體積很小的土壤，很小心地移動著。

「有人要留下來，你知道的。健康與安全，」凱文氣鼓鼓地說。「但不會是我。」她轉過身，望著他的眼睛，並吐出她的舌頭，但他仍然繼續說。「這個場地是需要上鎖，而我們不是保管鎖匙的人。這不公平的，要讓每個人閒待著，貝卡。」

她直起腰來。「好了，你說得對。」

「它明天仍然會在那裡的。」

「是啊，是啊。」

當他們回到了帳篷，她驚訝地發現瑪西還在那裡。她應該要跟她

fair to keep everyone hanging around, Bec."

She straightened up. "Okay, fair enough."

"It'll still be there tomorrow."

"Yeah, yeah."

When they got back to the tent, she was surprised to find Marcie still there. She should speak to her; that was the professional, civil thing to do, and anyway they were under scrutiny. She didn't want the surveyors or the site security team gossiping, and they would if there was the slightest hint of discord.

She started to wipe off her trowel and wandered casually over to Marcie. "Good day?"

Marcie glanced up. "Yes thank you," she said coolly. "It's looking very promising." Her eyes were down on her finds again.

Rebecca waited, but Marcie obviously didn't intend to elaborate. "Good." She went to the plastic box with her name on, and carefully put her trowel in the tool belt inside. Her parents had given her the tool belt for her birthday before they died and the compact set of trowels and brushes it held all had her name on the handle. They went to every dig with her.

"Not taking your tools home?" Kevin asked.

"No, I need to buy food on the way home. Besides, we've got the luxury of an onsite security guard, haven't we? They should be safe enough."

Kevin nodded agreement and wandered outside. Rebecca closed the box, grabbed her coat and turned to leave.

"You?"

Rebecca turned, startled.

"Sorry?"

"How was your day?" said Marcie abruptly.

Wow. Was she trying to be friendly? Miracles would never cease.

"Good, thanks. I think I'm coming down on some burials."

"Really?" Marcie couldn't disguise the interest in her voice, but

說些什麼，那是專業、有禮貌的事情，但他們正在看著。她不想那些測量師或場地保安員說什麼閒話，只要他們發現有些微的異樣。

她開始擦她的抹泥刀，隨便地徘徊在瑪西附近。「今天過得好嗎？」

瑪西抬起頭。「好，謝謝你，」她冷冷地說。「這看起來很有價值。」她眼睛再度看著她發掘到的東西。

麗貝卡在等她，但瑪西顯然不打算詳談。「那很好。」她去拿上面有她名字的塑膠盒，小心翼翼地把抹泥刀放回工具帶裡面。她的父母在去世之前送了她工具腰帶作為她的生日禮物，是一套便攜式的抹泥刀和刷子，手柄上都刻有她的名字，她每一次去發掘都帶上它們。

「不帶工具回家嗎？」凱文問。

「不，我回家的路上還要去買食物。此外，我們有奢侈的場地保安員，不是嗎？應該足夠安全的。」

凱文點頭表示同意，並走到外面躊躇。麗貝卡關上盒子，一手抓起外套轉身離開。

「你呢？」

麗貝卡轉身，嚇了一跳。

「不好意思？」

「你今天過得怎樣？」瑪西硬生生地說。

哇。她想表示友好嗎？奇蹟真是隨時都會出現。

「很好，謝謝。我想我未來的日子都要去基地發掘。」

「真的嗎？」瑪西的聲音無法掩飾她的興趣，但當麗貝卡抬起頭來時，她又連忙低下頭了。「很好啊。」她喃喃自語，並開始整理在她的面前一堆凌亂的樣本袋。

when Rebecca looked up, she quickly looked down. "Good," she muttered, and carried on sorting the untidy heap of sample bags in front of her.

"See you tomorrow." Rebecca thought she heard Marcie grunt a reply as she left, but couldn't be sure.

"Thank God!" Kevin exclaimed as she emerged. "I'm starving, woman."

"I didn't make you stay." She punched his arm lightly.

"Oh had to, had to."

"Why?"

"My boss is a complete slave driver." He rolled his eyes. "She would have had me working until dawn if I hadn't stood my ground."

"Really?"

"Yes. You know how it is in these high pressure working environments," he sighed dramatically. "If you leave before the boss, that's it, you're out on your ear in no time."

"How awful for you. She sounds like a nightmare."

"Uh-huh. I have to keep her sweet by wining and dining her, too, and showering her with gifts. It's the only way to hold on to my job." Kevin turned sideways to wiggle through the gap between the security gates. "And on that note—oof, these are a bit close together – forget buying food. KFC, or do you want to share the microwave Indian Buffet For Two that's lurking in my freezer?"

Rebecca slid through after him easily. "Not sure you should have either of those, fatty. Salad for you."

"And I was going to ask what you wanted for you birthday. Shan't bother now."

"Soz." She grinned. "Indian buffet, please, providing you've got wine."

"I haven't."

"We'll stop off and buy some. My treat."

"That's very gracious of you, boss."

「明天見。」當麗貝卡離開的時候，她好像有聽到瑪西咕嚕地回答她，但不太肯定。

「感謝上帝！」當她走出來凱文歡呼道，「我餓了，女人。」

「我沒有讓你留下來。」她輕輕地打了他的手臂一下。

「哦，必須這樣做。」

「為什麼？」

「我老闆是一個完完全全苛刻的上司。」他轉了轉眼睛。「如果我沒有堅持我的立場，她會要我工作直到天亮。」

「真的嗎？」

「是的。你知道在這個環境工作壓力真的很大，」他誇張地嘆了口氣。「如果你在老闆面前離開，就這樣了，你會即時被解僱。」

「令你那麼害怕。她聽起來像是一場噩夢。」

「嗯。我必須用美酒和餐飲去討她開心，也要大量的禮品。只有這樣，我才可以保住我的工作。」凱文側身穿過保安閘門。「說到那個...噢，這裡有點太窄了...我忘記了買食物。肯德基好嗎？或者你想分享在我冰箱裡的速食二人印度餐嗎？」
麗貝卡輕鬆地超越了他。「不肯定，但你應該要吃點別的，不要那麼多脂肪的，你吃沙拉吧。」

「我正要問你生日要什麼，原來是不應該打擾你的。」

「對不起。」她笑了。「印度餐吧，但你要提供酒。」

「我沒有。」

「那我們中途停下來去買。我請客。」

「真的很有風度啊，老闆。」

「我知道。」天開始下雨，她在她的手袋中找傘子。「該死的。」

「忘記拿你的傘子？」

「沒錯。」

"I know." It started to rain and she fished in her bag for her umbrella. "Bugger."

"Forgot your brolly?"

"Yep."

"Shame." He ostentatiously pulled the in-built hood out of his collar and flicked it deftly over his head. "I'll buy you a new brolly for your birthday."

She sped up, resisting the urge to hunch down in her collar against the rain. "No thanks," she called over her shoulder. "I already know what I want."

He jogged a little to catch up with her, and fell into step. "What's that then, m'lady?"

"What I want most of all is another archaeologist to work with who's not uppity," she started to mark off points on her fingers, "or temperamental, or a bit of a slacker, always wanting to knock off early."

"You don't want much, do you?"

She patted his arm. "A nice bottle of Chardonnay will do for now, though."

"Good, because this is no time to be searching for the impossible, especially not on an empty stomach." He stuck his elbow out and she put her arm in his, laughing as they hurried towards the off licence.

「丟臉。」他誇張地把衣領中內藏的風帽拉出來,並巧妙地套在頭上。「你的生日我給你買一把新的傘子吧。」

她加快腳步,抵抗想蜷縮身體在衣領裡躲雨的衝動。「不,謝謝,」她回頭說。「我已經知道我想要什麼了。」

他跑了一點追上她,並調整步伐跟她一致。「那麼是什麼呢,夫人?」

「我最想要的是跟另一個考古學家一起工作,而他不會很難控制的。」她開始她用手指上數著,「或喜怒無常,或一點點懶惰,又總是要提前收工。」

「你不要想太多,好嗎?」

她拍了一下他的胳膊。「那麼我現在要一瓶漂亮的霞多麗幹白葡萄酒。 」

「好,因為這個時間去尋找有點不可能,尤其是空著肚子。」他伸出他的手肘,她把她的手臂伸進去,他們一面笑一面匆匆向賣酒店走過去。

Chapter Twenty One

Steve pushed open the door of Methodical Matches and stopped. It said Methodical Matches on the window, so this must be the right place. But this couldn't be their office. It was tiny, just a lobby area really, with a reception desk on one side—currently devoid of a receptionist—and a staircase disappearing upwards on the other. Perhaps all the cogs turned upstairs, he thought, but then he saw the large sign on the wall pointing upwards to Cooper's Insurance.

Steve had presumed they'd moved out when he'd seen the Methodical Matches signage appear on the front of the building, but it looked like they were still operating upstairs. He frowned. Weird.

"Can I help you?" asked a voice that Steve mentally tagged as 'bouncy'. A head had popped up from under the reception desk, belonging to a woman with a scarily intense suntan.

"I am in the right place for Methodical Matches, right?"

"You certainly are." She flashed him a smile and her teeth glowed fluorescently.

"But Coopers is still based here? Have they let out the first floor to you?"

"No, we only occupy this area. They still have the rest of the building, although it's only their admin department and data centre now. Their public-facing departments have moved to different premises." She smiled tightly. "Being an internet-based company with no physical product, we don't need a lot of floor space."

He frowned. "So where do you keep your computer servers, stuff like that?"

Her eyes narrowed. "We have a separate data centre elsewhere. Can I ask what your interest is?"

第二十一章

史堤夫推開井然配對的大門，然後停了下來。在窗前有寫著是井然配對，所以這一定是正確的地方。但是，這可能不是他們的辦公室。這裡很小，只有一個大堂那麼大，在一旁設有接待處，但沒有接待員。有一道樓梯一直通往樓上。他想也許所有東西都設置在樓上，但後來他又看到一個掛在牆上的大牌子朝上指住是庫珀保險。

當史堤夫看到井然配對的標誌出現在大廈前，他推測庫珀已經搬走了，但看來他們仍然在樓上經營著。他皺起了眉頭，覺得很怪異。

「我可以幫到你嗎？」一個聲音問道，史堤夫心理上標記了這聲音是「充滿活力」。一個頭從接待處彈了出來，是屬於一個曬黑得很駭人的女人。

「我找井然配對，這是正確的地方嗎？」

「肯定是。」她亮出了一個微笑，她的牙齒像熒光色的一樣亮。

「但是，庫珀也是在這裡？他們出租了一樓給你嗎？」

「不，我們只佔用這裡。剩下的地方仍然是他們所擁有。雖然現在都只有他們的管理部門和數據中心，他們對外的部門已經搬遷到其他地方。」她緊緊地笑了笑。「作為一個以互聯網為基本的公司，又沒有什麼實體產品，我們並不需要很多的樓面空間。」

他皺起了眉頭。「所以，你在他們那裡放置你的電腦伺服器和其他東西嗎？」

她瞇起眼睛。「我們在其他地方有一個獨立的數據中心。我可以問下你問這些幹什麼嗎？」

「只是有個朋友告訴我，你們是很小規模的。我現在知道她並不是在開玩笑。」他讓他的目光別有用心地徘徊著，從大堂的一角

"It's just that a friend told me you run a very small operation. I can see she wasn't joking." He let his gaze wander meaningfully from one corner of the lobby to the other.

Her smile was a rictus grin now, her cheeks reddening through the tan. "It's perfectly adequate. You know what they say, quality not quantity."

"Ah yes. Talking of quality and quantity, can you tell me how many people you currently have signed up to your service?"

She blinked and leaned back a little. "How many?"

"Yes, you know. Numbers."

"The system can handle—"

"No, sorry," he broke in, "I wanted to know how many people are signed up right now, with profiles that are live on the site."

"Why do you want to know?"

He shrugged. "Isn't that the first question most people ask? I'd have thought that was your most important statistic."

He gave her what he hoped was a disarming smile, aware the atmosphere had got confrontational. It obviously didn't work.

"I hear what you're saying, Mr...?"

"Reynolds."

"Mr. Reynolds, but I'm afraid our policy is to keep that kind of information confidential except to clients."

"So much for the age of transparency, huh?" This time he went for the apologetic grin. And got not a flicker of a smile or thawing of expression in return. "Luckily, I am a client." He pointed to her laptop. "Reynolds, Steve Reynolds."

It was hard to tell, but he thought she went a little pale. She probably recognised the name, if Rebecca was right, because she did everything.

"Could you confirm your date of birth for me please? And your username?" Her tone had completely changed now to embarrassed and conciliatory. She typed in his replies. "Yes, of course, I can see you are a client, Mr. Reynolds. What can I do for your today?"

到另一角。

她的微笑變了一個露齒裂嘴的笑容，她曬成棕褐色的臉頰發紅了。「這是完全足夠的。你知道是怎麼說嗎？重質不重量啊。」

「是啊。說到質量和數量，你能告訴我，目前有多少人註冊了你們的服務嗎？」

她眨了眨眼，靠在椅背上一點點。「多少人？」

「是的，你知道的。數字。」

「該系統可以處理…」

「不，不好意思，」他打斷了，「我是想知道有多少人註冊了，現在仍在網站上有個人檔案的人數。」

「你為什麼想知道？」

他聳聳肩。「這不是大多數人會問的第一個問題嗎？我還以為這是你們最重要的統計數據。」

他給了她一個他期望是親切的微笑，但他覺察到氣氛變成對立了，微笑顯然沒有奏效。

「我有聽到你在說什麼，…先生？」

「雷諾茲。」

「雷諾茲先生，但恐怕我們的政策是要將這種資料保密的，除非是給客戶。」

「太高透明度的年代了，對吧？」這一次他給了一個帶歉意的笑容。但他得到的並不是一個微笑或一個想緩和氣氛回應。「幸運的是，我也是客戶。」他指著她的筆記本電腦。「雷諾茲，史堤夫．雷諾茲。」

很難說得出來，但他認為她現在的臉色是有點蒼白。她可能記得他的名字，如果麗貝卡是對的話，因為所有的工作都是她做的。

「我能否確認一下你的出生日期？和用戶名嗎？」她的語氣已經變得尷尬和妥協。她根據他的回答鍵入了資料。「是的，我當然可以看到你是我們的客戶，雷諾茲先生。我今天能為你做些什麼嗎？」

He raised an eyebrow. "I'd still like to know how many clients you have."

He had to admire her for meeting his eye as she told him, although her tan was now looking more blood orange than tangerine.

"Locally, 27."

He gaped, then recovered himself. "27. When you say locally... "

"In the London area."

"How is that defined?"

There was no term for the colour she'd gone now. She dropped her eyes. "Er, within the M25," she quavered, and then burst into tears.

"Look, er..." He patted his pockets frantically for tissues and passed one over.

"Th-thanks."

"That's okay. I'm sorry if I upset you."

She shook her head, mopping at her face. "No, you have every right to ask. You're thinking the numbers are pathetic, and you're right. It's a difficult kind of business to get off the ground."

"I can imagine."

"But that's not really what's upset me. I've had a bad day, that's all. You're not responsible for all this wailing." Her smile, wobbly as it was, was the most genuine one he'd seen from her.

Steve felt his resentment melting away.

"Anything I can help with? If it's a leaky tap I'm not a bad amateur plumber, even though I say so myself."

A strange hiccupping laugh escaped between her sobs, which thankfully seemed to be subsiding. "No, there's not a tap down here. I use Cooper's staff kitchen when I want a coffee."

"Right."

"And their loo," she carried on disconsolately. "And Marjorie lets me keep my lunch in the fridge up there." She slumped back in her chair and blew her nose noisily. "I have to put a label on it."

他揚起一邊眉毛,「我還是想知道你們有多少客戶。」

當她告訴他時,他不得不佩服她是有看著他的眼睛,雖然她現在曬黑了皮膚看起來比較像血橙色多於橘紅色。

「在本地,二十七。」

他目瞪口呆,然後回過神來。「二十七。你說本地...」

「在倫敦地區。」

「那是如何定義的?」

現在已經沒有任何可以形容到她臉色的字眼了。她垂下了眼睛。「呃...二十五號公路內的。」她顫抖,然後開始淚流。

「好吧,呃...」他忙亂地拍了拍口袋裡找出面紙,並拿了一張給她。

「謝...謝謝你。」

「沒關係。對不起,如果是我令你心煩意亂了。」

她搖搖頭,擦拭著她的臉。「不,你有權利問的。你可能覺得數字是慘兮兮的,但你是對的。這種業務是很難可以走上軌道的。」

「我能想像。」

「但是,這不是真正令我心煩意亂的事。今天是很糟糕的一天,就是這樣。你不需要為這番哭訴負責的。」她的微笑帶著顫抖,這是他見過她最真實的一面。

史堤夫覺得他的怨恨已經融化了。

「有什麼我可以幫忙嗎?如果是水龍頭漏水,我也是一個不錯的業餘水喉匠,即使只是我自己說的。」

一個奇怪的噴笑從她的嗚咽中逃了出來,令人欣慰的是氣氛似乎已經緩和下來了。「不,這裡沒有水龍頭的。如果我想喝杯咖啡,我也只是用庫珀的員工廚房。」

「是啊。」

「還有他們的廁所,」她悶悶不樂地說。「瑪喬麗讓我存放我的午餐在他們那裡的冰箱。」她頹然地坐回她的椅子上,大聲地哭

There was something so comical about the despairing tone of that final comment that Steve let a small snort escape. Nicola glanced up sharply and then saw the funny side too.

"Sorry," said Steve.

"It's alright. It is ridiculous. This is the only way I could afford office space, if you can call it that. Cooper's don't need a meet-and-greet area any more, now that only back-end stuff goes on here. It's just the employees who need access, and most of them use the staircase at the back. It seemed like a great opportunity, especially when they agreed to let me put signage on the window. But it's pathetic, isn't it. I'm pathetic."

"Not at all. At least you're giving it a go, showing a bit of enterprise. And I'm guessing you're doing that all by yourself..." he asked gently. "Am I right?" He prayed she wouldn't start crying again. Crying women he knew were one thing. Crying strangers were another.

"I wasn't to start with," she said heavily. "That's sort of the problem. I set it up with this guy Andy—he used to work upstairs at Coopers, writing data analysis programmes for them."

Steve's brow furrowed. "Tall? Sandy hair? Skinny?"

"Yes—do you know him?" She leaned forward, eyes bright with hope.

"Not really. I work at Tony's—you know, the café? He used to come in for lunch sometimes."

"Not recently?"

Steve thought for a minute. "He certainly hasn't been in since we did that Mexican day in January. Or at least not when I've been there."

"Oh." She sat back. "You wouldn't know where he's gone then."

"Afraid not. Did he run out on you, then?"

She nodded. "I handled the business and admin side of things, he wrote the client matching program and handled the website. He set it all up, hung around for a week entering the first few clients, and then he left one evening and didn't come back."

"Didn't he leave a message? Or a forwarding address?"

鼻子。「但我必須放個標籤在上面。」

最後的一句中，絕望的語氣中帶著一點滑稽，史堤夫忍不住小哼了一聲。妮科拉大幅度地抬起頭，看到了這有趣的一面。

「對不起。」史堤夫說。

「對啊。是很荒謬。但這是我唯一負擔得起的辦公空間，如果能這樣叫的話。現在庫珀不需要會見和接客區，只是放一些後台的東西在這裡。平常只有職員會經過，但他們大部分都使用在後面的樓梯。看起來就像是一個很好的機會，尤其是當他們同意讓我把標誌貼在窗口。但是很差勁，是不是？我很差勁。」

「不是。至少你有努力地試一把，讓它呈現出一點企業的姿態。我猜所有工作都是由你自己做的。」他輕輕地問。「對不對？」他祈求她不會再哭起來。他知道什麼是哭泣的女人，但哭泣的陌生

人的卻是另一回事。

「我沒有，」她沉重地說。「這就是排序的問題。我跟一個叫安迪的傢伙一起創立這裡。他曾經在樓上的庫珀工作，負責編寫他們的數據分析程式。」

史堤夫的眉頭緊鎖。「高的？沙色頭髮？瘦瘦的？」

「是的，你認識他嗎？」她眼前一亮並帶著期望地把身體傾前。

「不是。我是在東尼的咖啡店工作的，你知道那家咖啡店嗎？他有時會來吃午飯。」

「最近沒有了？」

史堤夫想了一會兒。「他肯定沒有，自從我們在一月份做了墨西哥日之後。或者至少是我在那裡的時候沒有來過。」

「哦。」她坐了回去。「那你應該不會知道他去了哪裡吧。」

「恐怕就是。他拋下你走了嗎？」

她點點頭。「我是負責業務處理和管理方面的東西，而他就寫了一個配對客戶的程序和負責處理網站。他準備好所有東西之後，用了一個星期時間輸入前幾個客戶的資料，然後他有一天晚上離開後再沒回來了。」

She snorted. "Oh yes. I got an email three days later, from a new webmail address, telling me about the 'new life' he'd decided he had to start. I told him the program seemed to be going nuts—I don't know what it's doing but it might as well be one of those randomiser programs for all the success it's having," she said bitterly. Then she slapped her hand over her mouth. "Forget I said that! I shouldn't be telling you any of this. I'll get it fixed, honestly, and if I can't I'll issue refunds."

"Er... don't worry about me. I know this isn't the best time to say it, but I came in to cancel my membership."

She put her head in her hands. "Of course you have. Why wouldn't you? So will everyone else soon, I expect. All 26 of them."

"I thought you said the 27 people were inside the M25? What about your clients elsewhere?"

She laughed hollowly. "Oh yes. Our other clients. We had 30 applications from the whole rest of the country. Right from Northumberland down to Cornwall."

"Ahhh, I see. Tricky."

"Yes."

"So you turned them away?"

"No, I told them we had too many applicants and they would be put on a waiting list. The plan was to put them on area by area once we had enough people there to make it workable." She tilted her head to look at him. "Can you believe that?"

He shrugged, not wanting to condemn her when she was already down. "I can see the logic."

"London was the only place where we had enough applicants to go ahead and make the profiles live, and even that was pushing it. We only had 32."

"So you've lost a few already," said Steve sympathetically.

"Yes, and I can't say I'm surprised, are you?"

Safer to change the subject than answer that one, he decided. "Did Andy ever reply to your message about the program?"

"Yes. He said he'd access the server remotely—he'd already installed the software to do that on his laptop, so that he could

「他沒有留下信息嗎？或轉寄地址嗎？」

她哼了一聲。「哦，是的。我三天後收到了一封電子郵件，從一個新的網上電郵地址發出的，他告訴我他已經決定了開始『新生活』。我告訴他程式似乎有點瘋了，我不知道它是做什麼的，但它應該跟隨機產生程序一樣，這才是成功的地方。」她恨恨地說。然後，她掌摑自己並用手摀住了嘴巴。

「請忘了我說的！我不應該告訴你這些。我會修復它的，說實話，如果我不能，我會退款。」

「呃...不用擔心我。我知道這不是說這些的時候，但是我是來取消我的會藉的。」

她把她的頭埋在手中。「當然，你必須的。為什麼不呢？那麼我相信其他的人都很快都會，全部二十六個人。」

「我在想你剛才是說有二十七個人是在二十五號公路內？其他的客戶是在什麼地方呢？」

她空洞地笑了。「哦，是的。我們的其他客戶，我們有三十份申請是從全國其他地方，從諾森伯蘭郡到康沃爾都有。」

「啊，我明白了，真的非常棘手。」

「是的。」

「那麼，你拒絕了他們的申請嗎？」

「不，我告訴他們，我們有太多的申請人，他們將被放在等候名單上。計劃是把他們逐區分組，一旦我們有足夠的人數，就可以實行了。」她偏著頭看著他。「你相信嗎？」

他聳聳肩，在她已經夠低沈的時候，他不想再譴責她。「我明白是什麼邏輯。」

「倫敦是唯一的地方有足夠的申請人讓我們繼續進行配對並放上更多的個人資料檔。我們甚至認為可以繼續推動它。我們只有三十二個檔案。」

「所以，你已經失去了一些了。」史堤夫同情地說。

「是的，我不能說我很驚訝，你也是嗎？」

work from home when he wanted to—and he promised me he would get it sorted. But it's not. In fact, whatever he did to it seems to have made it worse. It's gone completely haywire, and the questionnaires it generates seem to get longer every week!"

"Have you told him that?"

"Yes, but I've heard nothing from him since. That was two months ago, and I can't track him down. It's like he's disappeared off the face of the earth."

"And you can't alter the program yourself in any way?"

She shook her head. "Not a chance. I wouldn't know where to start! I didn't take an IT qualification at school, I only did the basics—and I wasn't that great at them, to be honest."

Steve knew he should be cross about this, in a disgruntled-customer-who's-been-misled kind of way, but it was all too much like a farce and, looking at Nicola now, all he could feel for her was pity. Andy was a heel, leaving her in the lurch like this. He wished he could do something to help. Suddenly it occurred to him that perhaps he could.

"Nicola, I think I might be able to help. With the matching program, anyway."

Her head came out of her hands and her eyes brightened. "Really? Do you know about computer programs, then?"

"No I don't, but I know someone who does."

"That would be fantastic!" Nicola beamed. Then her face dropped. "But IT experts cost a fortune. I could barely afford to pay them for a morning, and it might take hours."

"Nicola she's not an IT expert, she's my sister. But she does know her way round computers and programs, she has got an A level in IT, and she won't expect to be paid a fortune. Anything but."

"It's got to be worth a try. Do you think she'll do it?"

"I'm sure she will. But," he emphasised grimly, "when you hear what I'm about to say, you might decide you don't want her within a mile of your business."

Her eyes widened. "Tell me more."

他覺得改變話題比回答這個問題更安全。「安迪曾經回覆你有關這程式的信息嗎？」

「是的。他說，他會遠程進入伺服器，他已經安裝了該軟件，他用筆記本電腦就可以做到，這樣他就可以在家工作。而他答應了我他會整理。但並非如此。事實上，無論他做什麼似乎已經令情況變得更糟了。情況已經完全失控，現在生成問卷調查的時間每週比每週長！」

「你有沒有告訴他？」

「有的，但我至今沒有收到他消息。這已經是兩個月前的事，我追查不到他的下落，他就像在地球表面消失了。」

「你自己沒有辦法更改程式嗎？」

她搖搖頭。「絕對不可能。我完全不知道從哪裡開始！我在學校裡沒有拿到資訊科技的資格，我只是做了基本的…和我對這些不在行，說實話。」

史堤夫知道，他應該不要插手此事，一個心懷不滿的客人被她誤導，但它太像一場鬧劇，現在看著妮科拉，他能感覺自己覺得她太值得同情了。安迪腳底開溜了，把她留在這樣的困境。他希望能做些什麼來幫助她。突然間就發生在他身上，也許他真的可以。

「妮科拉，我想我也許能幫忙。配對的程式，不管怎麼說。」

她的頭從她的手中冒了出來，眼睛突然一亮。「真的嗎？那麼你了解電腦程式嗎？」

「不，我不懂，但我知道誰懂。」

「這太棒了！」妮科拉面露喜色，然後她的臉又再下沈了。「但是，聘請資訊科技專家要花費一筆。我可以只能勉強支付他們一個上午，可能只是幾個小時。」

「妮科拉，她不是一個資訊科技專家，她是我的妹妹。但是，不知道她會不會反而害了你的電腦和程式，她在高中有讀過資訊科技，她沒有期望可以收取一大筆錢。絕對不會。」

「這一定值得一試，你認為她能做到嗎？」

「我敢肯定她會的。但是，」他嚴肅地強調說道，「當你聽到我

Much to his surprise – something he felt guilty for afterwards—Nicola didn't turn a hair when Steve filled her in about Laura's track record, and she didn't seem to be just taking a chance to save money, either. She seemed genuinely sympathetic and was happy to have Laura, "in my extensive open plan office," she'd said, laughing self-deprecatingly, for as long as it took take.

Ten minutes and a quick call to Laura later, and the details were sorted. Laura would try to sort out the program, or if not, try to create a simple one that would match Nicola's clients with someone compatible. It might not be the scientific sifting of variables that people had signed up for, thought Steve privately, but who was to say something more basic might not work just as well – and on so few people, it would probably make the same matches anyway.

All it was costing Nicola was the price of keeping Laura in coffees and light lunches. She considered she was getting the best end of the bargain.

"I can't thank you enough, Steve. It's really kind of you." She beamed. "It's a shame you're cancelling your membership, a girl would be lucky to have you."

"Why thank you," he grinned. "I should be off. Nearly time for work."

"Oh, before you go... "

"What?"

"I know it's daft but I'm meant to ask you why you decided to cancel. Customer feedback, and all that." She shrugged. "I'll just put 'incompatible matches', shall I, and leave it at that?"

"You could, but that's not why I wanted to cancel."

"Really?"

"Really. I wanted to cancel because I think I've met the girl of my dreams."

Nicola practically bounced out of her chair. "Fantastic! Can I put it on the website? What's her username? Will she mind?" She clapped her hands together. "Is there a chance there might be the first Methodical Matches wedding in the near future?"

Steve put up his hands. "Hate to disappoint you, but I didn't meet her through the dating agency. I only went on two dates."

將說的話，你可能會決定不讓她在你的業務一英里範圍內。」

她睜大了眼睛。「請告訴我更多。」

完全出乎他的意料之外，之後令他感到有點內疚，當史堤夫提到羅拉的犯罪紀錄時，妮科拉幾乎是面不改色，而她似乎也不只是在爭取一個省錢的機會。她似乎真正的同情，而且很高興可以找到羅拉，「在我廣闊的開放式辦公室內。」她笑著自嘲道，反駁了只是想得到利益之說。

之後的十分鐘裡，他們打了個電話給羅拉，並把細節安排了。羅拉將嘗試解決程式中的問題，如果不能做到，她會嘗試建立一個簡單的程式，來配對可以合得來的客戶。史堤夫私下覺得，對於那些已經註冊的人，根本這不可能有很大的改變。想說的是連最基本的東西已經不可行了，因為就只有這麼幾個人，反正有可能會做出跟之前相同的配對。

妮科拉要付出的就是請羅拉喝咖啡和吃一個清淡的午餐。她認為，她已經得到最好的交易。

「我不能不感謝你，史堤夫。你真的很好。」她笑容滿面地說。「很遺憾你取消了你的會籍，擁有你的那個女孩一定是很幸運。」

「為什麼要感謝，」他咧嘴笑了。「我應該要走了，差不多要去上班了。」

「哦，在你走之前…」
「什麼？」

「我知道很愚蠢，但我想問你，為什麼要決定取消呢？客戶的反饋是一切。」她聳聳肩。「我要將它改為『合不來的配對』，或是不理它了，是嗎？」

「你可以，但是我並不是為了這原因而取消的。」

「真的嗎？」

「真的。我想取消是因為我覺得我已經遇到夢想中的女孩了。」

妮科拉幾乎從椅子上蹦了起來。「太棒了！我可以寫在網站上嗎？她的用戶名是什麼？她會介意嗎？」她拍了拍手。「有機會在不久的將來舉行第一個井然配對的婚禮嗎？」

"Oh." Nicola deflated. "What were they like?"

"Honestly? Awful. Sorry." He smiled. "Although in your defence, I don't think that's got much to do with your matching program. Number one was just after my money and number two, er, was after my body."

"Really? Oh. But there's not a lot I can do about that." Nicola perked up a little. That's something, then. Good luck with the girl of your dreams."

Steve smiled. "Thanks."

He walked out into the street. That was it, then. He couldn't believe he'd said it out loud—and to a stranger! But he honestly felt Rebecca was the girl of his dreams. The One.

He hoped she felt the same about him.

史堤夫舉起他的手。「要讓你失望了，但我不是通過你們認識她的。我只去過兩個約會。」

「哦。」妮科拉洩了氣似的。「她們是怎樣的？」

「說實話嗎？太可怕了。對不起，」他笑了。「雖然你可以辯護，但我不認為你的配對程式可以做得更多。第一個只是在乎我的錢，而第二個，呃，就只是在乎我的身體。」

「真的嗎？噢。那我就沒有什麼可以做了。」妮科拉振作了一點。「那麼就這樣了。祝你與你的夢想中的女孩好運。」

史堤夫笑著。「謝謝。」

他走到街上。就這樣了。他簡直不敢相信他會跟一個陌生人大聲說出來！但他確實覺得麗貝卡是他的夢想中的女孩。唯一一個。

他希望，她有跟他相同的感覺。

Chapter Twenty Two

Rebecca had only just got to her desk when the phone rang.

"Hello, Rebecca Maynard—"

"Bec, it's Kev. Are you coming over to the site this morning?" He sounded strained.

"I wanted to, but I've got these proofs to check—"

"Leave those until later. The site's been vandalised."

"Vandalised?"

"There's, er, a few things been taken and they've destroyed your trench."

Questions were buzzing around Rebecca's head, but she knew asking Kevin all of them over the phone wasn't the best use of her time. "Stay there. I'm coming straight over."

She didn't even stop to tell Ron. She could call him in the cab on the way.

Rebecca stood at the edge of her trench beside Kevin. All her carefully excavated layers were gone, replaced by a heap of sandy soil, with the bones of the skeleton she'd been able to glimpse yesterday sticking out here and there.

She turned, trying to keep her anger tamped down. Losing her rag would accomplish nothing. "And you say none of the other trenches have been touched?"

"No. Nearly everyone who was here digging yesterday is here today, and they all say their areas are exactly as they left them. It's just yours. None of their tools have been taken either." He added hesitantly.

第二十二章

麗貝卡才剛剛到達辦公桌前，手機就響了。

「你好，我是麗貝卡．梅納德…」

「貝卡，我是凱文。你今早會過來場地嗎？」他聽起來很緊張。

「我想，但我拿了一些初稿要檢查…」

「那些先放一邊，場地被破壞了。」

「被破壞了？」

「還有，呃，有幾件東西被拿走了，你的坑道也被摧毀了。」

很多問題在麗貝卡的腦海裏翻騰，但她知道在電話裡問凱文不是最好的方法。「留在那裡，我趕過來。」

她甚至沒有停下來告訴羅恩，她在出租車上才給他打電話。

麗貝卡跟凱文站在她的坑道邊。每一層她精心的挖掘都不見了，取而代之的是一堆沙土，混著骨骼中骨頭，那都是她昨天那些在這裡和那裡看到的。

她轉過身來，試圖壓制住憤怒，勃然大怒也無補於是。「你說沒有其他的坑道被破壞嗎？」

「沒有。幾乎每個昨天在這裡挖掘的人今天都在。他們說，他們的領域都跟他們昨天離開時一樣。就只有你的。而且他們的工具都沒有不見。」他猶豫地補充說道。

她的腦袋有個想法。「你是什麼意思，他們的工具沒事？」她看到他的表情，然後她跑向帳篷裡。她看到有她名字的塑料盒掉在

Her head shot round. "What do you mean, none of their tools?" She saw his expression and then she was running towards the tent. She saw the plastic box with her name on dumped on the floor in front of the others with the lid off. Empty, save for a tatty old pair of gloves.

Kevin came to stand beside her. "I'm so sorry, Becs," he put his hand on her shoulder. "I know how much those tools meant to you. We'll get them back."

"Only my trench. Only my tools," she said through gritted teeth. "Please tell me nobody is dumb enough to think this wasn't Marcie King's doing."

She could hear Kevin swallow. "She hasn't turned up this morning, Becs, but I don't think we should jump to any conclu—"

Rebecca turned and called him a name she'd never called anyone before, and stormed out of the tent. She strode up to the security guard and he took an involuntary step backwards, even before her finger jabbed into his chest.

"And where the fuck were you while this was going on?" she yelled.

"Er, I wasn't on duty Miss, it was Roger—"

Rebecca called him the same name she'd called Kevin.

"Our coffee not good enough for you any more, then?" He leaned on the counter, shoulders squared, and tried to look threatening.

Rebecca grinned. "Dunno, why, has it gone downhill since last time? It's probably the staff. They're pretty useless, so I hear."

He grunted. "So, to what do we owe the honour?"

"Honour?"

"Of madam gracing us with her presence."

"I'm thirsty."

"But you haven't been thirsty for the last two weeks?"

"Oh I have, but as sir knows I've been elsewhere, I'm afraid, working."

地板上，蓋子打開了掉在其他盒子的前面。空的，只剩下一雙簡陋的舊手套。

凱文來到她的旁邊。「我很抱歉，貝卡，」他把手放在她的肩上。「我知道這些工具對你的意義，我們一定會把它們找回來。」

「只有我的坑道，只有我的工具。」她咬著牙說。「請告訴我，沒有人傻到認為這並不是瑪西.京做的。」

她可以聽到凱文的吞嚥聲。「今天上午她還沒有出現過，貝卡，但我不認為我們要妄下任何結論...」
麗貝卡轉身罵了他一句說話，她之前從來沒有這樣罵過任何人，然後她氣沖沖地走出了帳篷，大步走向保安員，他不由自主地倒退了一下，就在她的手指捅到他的胸口之前。

「他媽的你當時究竟在哪裡？」她大叫。

「呃，當時並不是我值班，小姐，是羅傑...」
麗貝卡罵了他一句跟她罵凱文一樣的說話。

「那麼你已經覺得我們的咖啡不夠好了嗎？」他斜靠在櫃檯上，挺直身子，試圖讓自己看上去比較有威脅性。

麗貝卡咧嘴笑了。「不知道為什麼，自從上次之後就已經走了下坡路了？這可能是員工的問題，我聽說，他們毫無用處了。」

他哼了一聲。「所以，這是我們的榮幸嗎？」

「榮幸？」

「夫人蒞臨使我們不勝榮幸。」

「我渴了。」

「但你在過去兩個星期都沒有渴啊？」

「哦，我有的。但爵士要知道我是在其他地方，我恐怕是因為工作。」

「真的。夫人在她工作的地方沒有自來水嗎？」他傲慢地問。

"Really. Madam doesn't have a tap where she works?" he asked haughtily.

"Nope."

"And no coffee machines where you work?"

"Oh, we're drowning in coffee over there," said Rebecca brightly. "But it's not as nice as yours." She batted her eyelashes at him theatrically, very fast. "Ow!" She clapped her hand over her right eye. "Eyelid strain!"

"Serves you right," he said severely. "Well I suppose I could forgive you, even though this is barefaced flattery and cupboard love."

"Cupboard love? Hold on. I wasn't offering that. Coffee really has got expensive here."

"Don't go lowering the tone with your lewd remarks."

"You started it!"

"Ahem." He looked at her sternly. "That's quite enough. What can I do for you?"

Her lips quivered.

He glared. "Don't start! What would you like to drink?"

"A butterscotch latte, please."

"Ah. So long away, yet I see madam still favours the latte avec butterscotch a la Steve." He grinned and reached for the butterscotch syrup.

"Oui."

"Ooh, I like a girl who speaks French," he laughed, his back to her as the cup filled with milky froth.

She grinned. "Moi, aussi."

"Oh? Is there something you're not telling me?"

"Non, monsieur. Rien."

"Phew." He slid her latte over to her. "And would madam like a cake too?"

「沒有。」

「工作的地方沒有咖啡機嗎？」

「噢，我們淹沒在那邊的咖啡裡，」麗貝卡爽朗地說。「但還是沒有你做的好。」她向他誇張地撲閃著睫毛，速度非常快。「噢！」她用手拍了拍在她的右眼。「眼皮拉傷了！」

「你活該，」他嚴肅地說。「好吧，我想我可以原諒你，即使這是厚顏無恥的奉承和另有所圖的親熱。」

「另有所圖的親熱？等等，我沒有啊。這裡的咖啡真的很昂貴的。」

「請你說那些下流的的言論時把音調降低。」

「是你先開始的！」

「咳咳。」他嚴厲地看著她。「夠了。我可以為你做什麼？」

她的嘴唇顫抖著。

他怒視著。「不要再來了！請問你想喝點什麼？」

「奶油糖果拿鐵咖啡。」

「哦，雖然過了這麼長的日子，但我仍然看到夫人是偏愛史堤夫的奶油糖果拿鐵。」他咧嘴笑了，拿起奶油糖果糖漿。

「是的。」

「噢，我喜歡的一個女孩她也會說法語。」他笑了，當她的杯裝滿乳白色的泡沫時他轉了身過去。

她咧嘴一笑說道：「我也是。」

「哦？你是不是有什麼事沒有告訴我呢？」

「不，先生。沒什麼。」

「呼，」他把拿鐵遞給她。「夫人想要吃蛋糕嗎？」

「我覺得這裡應該有很多餡餅。」

「對不起，夫人，我們不是那種機構。」

"I imagine you have plenty of tarts here."

"Sorry madam, we're not that kind of establishment."

"I'll settle for a Danish then." She took a sip of her coffee.

"Ah, you prefer tall, blue-eyed blondes, do you?" He sighed sorrowfully.

"Well I used to," said Rebecca. She stared at him very deliberately over her coffee cup, making his stomach flutter."But I can make exceptions."

"What kind of exceptions?" he asked hoarsely.

She didn't answer for a moment, running her eyes over him.

"Oh, for other shades of hair, towards the darker end of the spectrum. Say, light brown."

"I see."

"And the eyes don't have to be true blue. They could be..." she looked at him meditatively. "Kind of greeny."

He swallowed. "Any other preferences?"

"Definitely. Medium height, about 5'10ish, not too skinny, not too fat."

"I'm beginning to get the picture."

"Looked in a mirror lately?" she asked, raising an eyebrow suggestively.

Get this back on a humorous level, Steve, or else you're going to have a heart attack mate. "Excuse me, madam, but are you coming on to me?" She would laugh now, then he could steer the conversation back to safer waters. "Because if you are, I must warn—"

"Yes."

"— you that you may be charged with harassment..." he trailed off.

"I missed you," she said quietly.

"Good. You seem a lot happier today."

「那我要丹麥。」她喝了一口咖啡。

「啊，你喜歡身材高大、藍眼睛、金髮的，是嗎？」他傷心地嘆了口氣。

「是啊，我一般都是，」麗貝卡說。她很刻意地把目光移離她的咖啡，然後盯著他，他的心怦怦直跳。「但我可以酌情的。」

「怎樣酌情？」他用嘶啞的聲音問。

她沒有即時回答，眼睛在他身上運行。

「噢，例如是其他色調的頭髮，光譜後端比較暗的那種，像是淺棕色。」

「我明白了。」

「眼睛如果沒有真正的藍，也可以是...」她若有所思地看著他。「近似綠色也可以。」
他吞嚥了一下。「還有其他偏好嗎？」

「當然。要中等身高，約五尺十吋，不要太瘦，也不要太胖。」

「我開始想像到了。」

「看著鏡子了嗎？」她問，暗示地揚起眉毛。

找回一點幽默吧，史堤夫，否則你就會心臟病發了。「對不起，夫人，但你是對我有意思嗎？」她現在應該會笑，然後他就可以引導談話回到安全區域了。「因為如果你是，我必須警告...」
「是的。」

「...你可能會被控騷擾...」他拖長說道。
「我很想念你。」她平靜地說。

「好吧。你今天似乎心情好多了。」

「我作出很大的努力了。凱文叫我不要再令使大家苦不堪言和神經緊張了。很抱歉，如果我有這樣的話。」

「沒有。我能理解你的感受。有關場地和一切究竟發生了什麼事？還是我不應該問嗎？」

「如果你讓我帶你出去吃晚飯的話，我就會告訴你，今晚。」

"I'm making a concerted effort. Kevin told me off for making everyone miserable and tense. Sorry if I've done that to you too."

"No. I understood how you felt. What's happening about the site and everything? Or shouldn't I ask?"

"I'll tell you if you let me take you out to dinner tonight."

"That sounds good. Chilango, or would you like to go somewhere different?"

"You choose. It's the company I'm looking forward to."

On an impulse, Steve leaned over and kissed her.

"We'll go to Chilango's again then. Shouldn't be too busy on a Monday. 7.30?"

"Great." She looked down at her coffee. "It's getting cold."

"Shall I get you another one?"

"There's not much left." She smiled. "Can you put my pastry in a bag? I should be getting back, it's mad today. I only came in to see you."

"I'll see you later."

"Bye."

He heard the kitchen door snap back on its hinges as he watched her go.

"About time too, eh? Although if you kiss all the customers, Steve, I get complaints."

"What?" he asked. "I wouldn't, er, Rebecca and I, we're—"

"Going out?" said Tony, wiping down the counter, his back to Steve, "That is why I say, about time. But," he said, raising his voice as he thrust the cloth forcefully into Steve's, "this is work. I'm pleased for you, but save kissing for the break times, not when you're serving, si?"

"Sorry, Tony."

"No problem. I was young man once, too. And skinny man once, also. Is hard to believe now, eh?" He grinned. "Now you wipe down front counter, and refill the coffee machine. The more you

「這聽起來不錯。吉浪高，還是你想去不同的地方？」

「你選擇吧。我只想要一個伴侶。」

一時衝動下，史堤夫俯身吻了她一下。

「那我們去吉浪高吧。週一應該不會太多人，七點半好嗎？」

「太好了。」她低頭看著她的咖啡。「冷掉了。」

「要我給你另一杯嗎？」

「沒剩下多少了。」她笑了。「你能不能把我的糕點放在袋子裡？我應該要回去了，這是瘋狂的一天。我只是來見你的。」

「我會再見到你的。」

「再見。」

當他目送她離去時，聽到廚房門的合頁彈回的聲音。

「是時候了，不是嗎？但如果你要吻所有的客戶，史堤夫，我會收到投訴。」

「什麼？」他問。「我不會，呃，麗貝卡和我，我們是...」

「去約會了嗎？」東尼說，他背著史堤夫在擦拭櫃檯，「這就是為什麼我說，是時間的問題。但是，」他強行把抹布往史堤夫的手裡一塞，提高嗓門地說，「這是工作。我為你高興，但請把接吻留到休息時間，而不是當值時間，好嗎？」

「對不起，東尼。」

「沒關係。我也當過年輕人一次，瘦男人一次。雖然現在是很難相信，對吧？」他笑了。

「現在你去擦拭櫃檯，再填充一下咖啡機。你現在做的越多，白馬王子，我就更快讓你去見灰姑娘了。」他閃爍的眼神似在建議他，儘管是他必須承認那是當之無愧的譴責，但東尼不是真的生他的氣。

他咧嘴笑了。「真有趣，我從來沒有想過你是仙女教母。」

東尼怒視。「有很多人想要你的工作，你知道嗎？那個櫃檯，仍然是骯髒的。」

are getting done now, Prince Charming, the quicker I am letting you go to see Cinderella." The twinkle in his eye suggested that despite the reprimand—well-deserved, he had to admit—Tony wasn't really cross with him.

He grinned. "Funny. I never thought of you as the Fairy Godmother."

Tony glared. "There's plenty of people wanting your job, do you know? And that counter, still it is dirty."

"Yes, boss." Steve raised his hand in mock salute and set to it. But his mind wasn't on dirty counters and coffee machines. It was on kissed Rebecca, and how things would go tonight. He felt contented and stirred up at the same time.

He had plenty of time for happy anticipation, in the end. At 4.30 Tony declared he wasn't fit for anything with his head in the clouds, and sent him home.

"So the police think it's Marcie?" Steve asked, before biting into his burrito.

"They do now. I never had any doubts, myself."

"Barmy woman. Risking her career to get back at you in such a petty way."

"Oh there was nothing petty about it." Rebecca smiled tightly. "She knew how important those tools were to me. How hurt I'd be."

Steve reached for her hand. "I know, honey. I didn't mean that wasn't important. But she must really be off her rocker. She must know her career in archaeology's probably over."

"Yep."

"So do they know where she is now?"

"No. They know she got on a flight to France in the early hours of that morning. She'd been staying in a cheap hotel since she got back from Italy, apparently. She hadn't bothered to find a flat."

"And the security guard wasn't suspicious?"

"No. She filed out at the back of the stragglers, then as she got to

「是的，老闆。」史堤夫抬起手假裝在敬禮，並立正。但是，他的腦袋並不是在想骯髒的櫃檯和咖啡機，而是親麗貝卡那一吻，今晚會發生什麼事呢。他感到很愜意，同一時間又點興奮。

到最後，他有足夠的時間去期待他的幸福。四點半時，東尼宣告他的腦袋已經跑到九霄雲外而不適合做任何事，並叫他回家了。

「因此，警方認為是瑪西做的嗎？」史堤夫在咬下他的捲餅前問道。

「現在他們是，而我從來沒有懷疑過我自己。」

「愚蠢的女人。用她的職業生涯作賭注，就是為了向你用這麼小題大做的方式實行報復。」

「哦，這不是小題大做。」麗貝卡緊緊地笑了笑。「她知道那些工具對我有多重要，可以如何傷害到我。」

史堤夫捉住她的手。「我知道，親愛的。我不是說那些不重要。但她真的有點瘋瘋癲癲。她一定知道她在考古學的職業生涯可能已經結束了。」

「沒錯。」

「所以，他們知道她現在在哪裡嗎？」

「沒有。他們只知道她乘飛機去了法國，就在那天早上的凌晨。她從意大利回來之後，似乎一直住在便宜的旅館。她並沒有找到單位去居住。」

「保安沒有懷疑嗎？」

「沒有。她從留到最後的人群中溜了出來，然後她回去閘門說自己忘了拿東西，而她只是去了幾分鐘時間。保安員看見她回到帳篷裡，然後他站在一邊跟一個測量師談話。從他站立的地方望過去帳篷，有部分會被擋住視線。而且跟閘門有一段距離，所以他沒有聽到什麼並不出奇，而且，他還在談天呢。」

「那麼她離開的時候呢？」

麗貝卡聳聳肩。「她總是拿著一個大袋子出入，她走的時候也是拿著她平常用的袋子。而當她離開的時候，他知道她是名單上的

the gate she said she'd forgotten something and she'd just be a few minutes. He saw her go back towards the tent and then stood there a while talking to one of the surveyors. From where he was standing, the tent would have blocked the view of that section of the site. It's quite a way from the gate, so it's not surprising he didn't hear anything, either, especially as he was talking."

"And when she left?"

Rebecca shrugged. "She always takes a big bag to and from the site. She just walked out with her usual bag. When she left, he knew she was the last person on his list, and he'd already done a perimeter check. So he just locked the gate and went to sit in his little box."

Steve shook his head. "Unbelievable."

"Yet unfortunately true." Rebecca gave him a small smile. "Anyway, on to a happier topic. You've got next Saturday off, haven't you?"

"Sure have. I'm all yours," he grinned.

"Great. Fancy coming to a wedding?"

Tonight had been great, Steve thought. Despite the shadow cast by what he'd now termed the Marcie Goes Mental incident, they'd still had a good time. He didn't think he could be any happier. He stopped the car outside Rebecca's flat and leaned over to kiss her goodnight.

"Would you like to come in for a coffee?"

Wow. That had come out of the left field. "Er..."

"Your enthusiasm's overwhelming," she said, raising her eyebrows.

"No, it's just, er..." he cleared his throat. "Is that coffee with a small c, or coffee with a capital C?" he asked, awkwardly.

"Oh I see," she said sharply. "If it's coffee with a small c, you're not that bothered, thanks, you'll go home and have a drink there? Is that it?"

"No, of course not! You know me better than that!"

最後的一個人，因為他之前已經做了周邊檢查。所以，他只是鎖上了閘門，就坐回他的更亭裡去了。」

史堤夫搖了搖頭。「真是令人難以置信。」

「然而不幸的是，這就是事實。」麗貝卡給了他一個小小的微笑。「無論如何，轉一個快樂的話題。你得下週六休假，可以嗎？」

「當然可以。我是你的了。」他咧嘴笑了。

「太好了。喜歡出席婚禮嗎？」

史堤夫覺得今晚真的很完滿。儘管他有點被瑪西的精神失常事件影響了一點，但他們還是過了很好的一晚。他想不到他怎可以更快樂。他在麗貝卡的大廈外把車停下，俯身吻了她並說了晚安。

「你想進來喝杯咖啡嗎？」

哇。真的是意料之外。「呃…」

「你的熱情真是令人不知所措的。」她揚起眉毛說。

「不，只是，呃…」他清了清嗓子。「那杯咖啡是小寫的c，還是大寫的C？」他笨拙地問。

「哦，我明白了，」她嚴厲地說。「如果是小寫c的咖啡，你就不太想被打擾了，感謝，然後你會回家才喝嗎？是不是這樣？」

「不，當然不是！你知道我不是這樣的！」

她看上去有點心虛。「對不起，這個問題有點太直接了。」

他吻了她。「我也很抱歉，但這個情況我不得不問，我，呃…」
「什麼？」

「需要從手套箱拿些東西。」他尖聲地說。

麗貝卡用手掩著臉一會兒。「哦，上帝。抱歉。你是想表示負責任、關懷和謹慎，而我就在指責你的淺薄。」

她把臉埋在他的胸前，他誇張地嘆了口氣。「我想，我會原諒你。但有一個條件。」

She had the grace to look guilty. "Sorry, but it was a bit of a direct question."

He kissed her. "I'm sorry too, but I had to ask in case, I, er..."

"What?"

"Needed something from the glove box," he said pointedly.

Rebecca out her hands to her face for a moment. "Oh God. Sorry. There was you trying to be all responsible and caring and discreet, and there was me accusing you of being shallow."

She buried her face against his chest and he sighed theatrically. "I suppose I forgive you. On one condition."

She lifted her head. "What's that?"

"Will you please tell me if it's small c or large C, bearing in mind I'm happy with either?"

"I was thinking more medium c."

"Right." He froze, not sure what to do and not wanting her to take offence. In future, Steve, keep some in your pocket, you moron.

"But a good boy Scout should always be prepared," she said mischievously.

"I was never a boy scout, but what the hell," said Steve, yanking the glove box open. "Get in there and put that kettle on, woman. Pronto!"

她抬起頭。「是什麼？」

「請你告訴我，究竟是小c或大C，記著，是那一個我都會很高興的，好嗎？」

「我想是中C。」

「沒錯。」他愣住了，不知道該怎麼做，也不想她生氣。將來，史堤夫，要準備一些在你的口袋裡，你這個笨蛋。

「但童子軍都要時刻做好準備。」她頑皮地說。

「我從來都不是一個童子軍，但是什麼鬼呀，」史堤夫說，猛地拉開了手套箱。「女人，去把電熱水壺打開吧。馬上！」

Chapter Twenty Three

"Hi! You must be Laura."

Laura blinked. That tan was bright. "Yes."

"Would you like a coffee before you start?"

"Yes please."

Fifteen minutes later she was engrossed. The program was a mess, cross-referencing various spreadsheets and web links. She needed to go for Plan B.

"Nicola, do you have the original information from your clients' profiles?"

"Yes." She beamed then frowned, speaking slowly as if remembering something she'd learned by rote. "Plain text file versions of profiles are saved automatically as a back-up."

"And that's still been working?"

Nicola rolled her eyes. "It's about the only thing that has. I print them out too, so there's something on paper if the computer crashes."

"Great. Can I have your print-outs? It's going to be easier to make a new, simpler matching program and abandon this one. I need to start from scratch."

"Whatever you think best. I wouldn't have a clue."

It took Laura the rest of the morning to sift through the mountain of detail the profiles recorded and decide on sensible parameters, and then as promised, Nicola took her out for lunch.

Once she was back, she spent time designing the program and then began to enter data from the print-outs. She expected to find Steve's details, but her eyes widened when she saw Rebecca's

第二十三章

「嗨！你必定是羅拉了。」

羅拉眨了眨眼。那棕褐色曬得真夠明亮。「是的。」

「你想在開始之前先喝杯咖啡嗎？」

「好，麻煩你。」

十五分鐘後，她已經在全神貫注中。該程序真的是一塌糊塗，交叉引用不同的電子表格和網頁鏈接。她需要用到B計劃。

「妮科拉，你有客戶個人資料的原始檔案嗎？」

「是的。」她滿面笑容然後皺起了眉頭，她好像在記住靠死記硬背學到的東西似的，慢慢地說：「個人資料的純文字版本檔有自動保存備份的。」

「還可以用嗎？」

妮科拉翻了翻眼睛。「這是唯一有的東西，我有把它們打印出來了，所以所有都有打印本，以防電腦死機。」

「太好了。我能要你的打印本嗎？這樣就更容易做一個新的、更簡單的配對程式，也可以放棄這一個了。我要從頭開始。」

「只要你認為好就好，我對這些真的一無所知。」

羅拉早上用剩下的時間來篩選堆積如山的詳細個人資料記錄，並定下了合理的參數，然後如之前承諾的一樣，妮科拉帶她出去吃午飯。

她回來就之後開始去設計程式，然後輸入列印本的數據。她希望

找到史堤夫的詳細資料，但當她看到麗貝卡的個人資料時，她眼睛都瞪大了。她知道她有嘗試過網上約會，但沒有想到她一直與

profile. She knew she'd tried internet dating, but had no idea she'd been with the same agency as Steve.

By the time Nicola called a halt for afternoon coffee break—not that there was much for Nicola to be wearing herself out with, as far as she could see—Laura was ready to run the program she had designed and generate new matches.

She began to save the matches for each client in a file, so Nicola could refer to it when she sent out emails. She looked at the next batch. These were from currently inactive profiles but Nicola had asked her to run them through anyway, in case any clients decided to reactivate their profile.

She shifted uneasily. Rebecca and Steve had both come up in each other's top three. She shouldn't be surprised. She'd been dimly aware as she entered the data that they had a lot in common. Laura frowned. She knew they'd only been out once, but thinking about them together made her uncomfortable. They had distinct roles in her life at the moment, and she didn't want that to change. Not when things were going right for a change.

She could change some of their details to make sure they didn't come up as a match. She flushed guiltily, dithering.

In the end she left them exactly as they were. Not because she'd had a sudden attack of integrity, but because she figured it was unnecessary. Their profiles were inactive, and from what they'd both said about their experiences, neither of them intended to try internet dating ever again.

So they'd never know.

"Thanks for meeting me."

"'Meeting me'? That is very formal!" Francois laughed. He had risen to his feet as Rebecca walked over to his table and now he kissed her on both cheeks. "It's my pleasure. I was planning to see you while I was in London, already."

Rebecca settled herself opposite him. Francois never changed, she thought, as he sat down. Still full of old-fashioned courtesy – how many men, these days, would wait for her to sit down before they did?—and still very handsome, even with the grey that was starting to creep through his dark hair. Those cheekbones. That jaw!

史堤夫用同一間機構。

直到妮科拉她叫停下來的時候已經是下午茶時間，不是有很多時候可以看到妮科拉如此精疲力竭，羅拉已經準備去運行她設計的程式，並生成新的配對。

她開始保存每一個客戶的配對去一個文件檔中，這可以給妮科拉在發出電子郵件時作為參考。她在看著下一個批次，這些都是從目前無效的個人資料檔生成的結果，是妮科拉叫她做的，以便有任何客戶決定恢復他們的個人資料檔。

她不自在地轉換著，麗貝卡和史堤夫一直都在對方的前三名位置。她不應該感到驚訝，因為她隱約知道她輸入的數據，他們有很多共同之處。羅拉皺起了眉頭，她知道他們只去過一次約會，但想著他們在一起就使她感到不自在。在她的生活中，他們都在扮演著不同的角色，她不想有任何改變。當事情順利的時候都不想有任何改變。

她可以改變他們的一些資料，去確保他們沒有配對上。她內疚地刷新著，有些猶豫不決。

最後，她還是任由他們配對上，不是因為她突然明白誠信的重要，而是她想通了這是沒有用處的，因為他們的檔案已經是無效的了。而根據他們所說的經驗，他們也不打算再嘗試網上約會。

所以他們根本不會知道。

「謝謝你跟我會面。」

「『跟我會面』嗎？這樣太正式了！」弗朗索瓦笑了起來。當麗貝卡開始向他走過去的時候，他已經站起來了，然後他親吻了她的

雙頰。「這是我的榮幸。當我一到達倫敦的時候，我也打算要去見你了。」

麗貝卡把自己安頓好並坐在他的對面，然後弗朗索瓦再坐了下來，她覺得他從來沒有改變過。他仍然跟從老式的禮節，這個年頭究竟還會有多少男人會等先她坐下來，自己才坐下呢？雖然一點灰色開始悄悄從他深色的頭髮中探了出來，他還是很帥氣。那顴骨！那下顎！

"You look well, Francois."

"You do not just look well, you look gorgeous. And so like your mother," he said with a smile.

She laughed, trying to ignore the nervous churning in her stomach. "French flattery already! Nothing changes."

"Indeed. Now what can I do for you, Rebecca? It sounded important."

He rolled the r in her name beautifully. If he were fifteen years younger, perhaps she wouldn't need an internet dating agency. She sighed inwardly, wondering how many women's knees had been turned to jelly over the years by that accent and those looks. And how many men's, too.

"Oh, I just thought it would be nice to catch up," she said lightly. "You're not in London often. I thought I'd best grab the bull by the horns."

"This is charming, I am sitting here for just five minutes and you call me an animal." His white teeth flashed as he grinned. "Is this English hospitality?"

"Sorry," she smiled.

"I forgive you, cherie. Perhaps coffee before we start to 'catch-up'? Even though I am not sure what I am meant to catch."

She raised her eyebrows. "Your English is excellent, Francois, idioms and all. You don't fool me for a second. It's all for comic effect."

He stood, clutching a hand to his heart. "How can you say such a thing?" He rolled his eyes. "Now, what can I get you?"

"A vanilla latte, please."

He shuddered comically. "An abomination. Vanilla is a flavour for ice creams. But I will order it." Another flash of that brilliant white smile, and he was off towards the counter. Steve was serving behind the counter now. She gave him a wave, hiding her nerves behind a big smile, then wondered how she was going to broach the subject that was on her mind.

"I brought sugar, too."

Rebecca jumped.

「你看來很好，弗朗索瓦。」

「你看來不單止是好，你很華麗，跟你的母親一樣，」他笑著說。

她笑了，試圖不理會她肚子裡的神經攪動。「法國式的奉承！沒有變啊。」

「的確如此。那麼現在我可以為你做什麼？麗貝卡。聽起來是很重要的事。」

他翹舌頭叫她的名字真的很動聽。如果他年輕十五歲，也許她就不會需要網上約會機構了。她暗自嘆了口氣，這麼多年來，不知道有多少女人因為這個口音和長相而雙膝不由得發軟，然而有多少男人可以像他這樣。

「噢，我只是認為可以趕上實在是太好了，」她輕輕地說。「你不是經常在倫敦，我想我最好立馬行動。」

「真是太好了，我坐在這裡只有五分鐘，你就稱我為動物了。」他亮出潔白的牙齒笑著。「這是英式的款待方式嗎？」

「對不起。」她笑了。

「我原諒你，親愛的。也許在我們『趕上』之前，可以先喝杯咖啡？雖然我不知道我要趕什麼上。」

她抬起眉毛。「你的英語是非常出色的，弗朗索瓦，成語和其他的你都懂。你騙不了我的，這只是喜劇效果吧。」

他站起身，用一隻手抓著他的心口。「你怎麼能說出這樣的話？」他轉了轉眼睛。「那麼你想要什麼？」

「香草拿鐵咖啡，麻煩你。」

他滑稽地打了一個寒顫。「真是可怕，香草明明是冰淇淋的口味。但我還是會幫你點的。」另一個閃亮的白色笑容掛在他臉上，然後他朝櫃檯走去。史堤夫現在正在櫃檯後面工作。她向他揮揮手，在大大的笑容背後隱藏著她的緊張，在她的腦海想著如何把話題轉向。

「我拿了砂糖。」

麗貝卡跳了起來。

"I wasn't sure how you took your..." Francois wrinkled his nose, "vanilla latte." He said the words as though he had a nasty taste in his mouth and Rebecca giggled.

He looked over and smiled, stirring his coffee. "That is better. When I walked back to the table, your face—" he shrugged, "I don't know. Angry? Sad? You looked like you were in a black mood, as you English say. If one can still say that?"

"No, I'm fine. Just tired." She leant forward to look in his coffee cup. "Espresso, I presume?"

"Double. What else? It is the only thing they serve in England that gives something close to the, the kick of French coffee. Not like your latte, full of sweetness and froth and strange flavours!"

"I know someone who would agree with you wholeheartedly on that," said Rebecca wryly. "But you'll never meet him, thank God. And I apologise on behalf of England."

"Merci," he laughed. "So, why did you really want to see me?"

"I haven't seen you for ages. Do I need an excuse?" She concentrated on stirring her coffee.

He regarded her steadily. "No, but your tone when you called me—it did not sound like you wanted just a 'catch-up', as you called it." He sipped his coffee. "You knew I was in London at Christmas, Rebecca, yet you did not seek me then."

She smiled. "I was busy at Christmas, and presumed you were too. You weren't over here for long."

His gaze was very direct, and she squirmed under it, realising that she was wringing her hands. With an effort she made herself still, took a deep breath, and met his eyes. She wanted to speak but felt like she was on the edge of a cliff—about to make someone push her over the edge.

"We have known each other for many years, yes? You may say to me whatever you wish. I am your honorary uncle," he said gently. "Your parents would have been happy to know you could talk to me."

"It's about them. When they died. That's what I want to talk about," she blurted.

He nodded slowly. "Yes?"

「我不知道你怎麼喝…」弗朗索瓦皺了皺鼻子,「香草拿鐵。」他說話時做了一個很厭惡這味道的表情,麗貝卡咯咯地笑了。

他看了看,笑了,攪拌著他的咖啡。「那就好了,當我走回來的時間,你的臉,」他聳聳肩,「我不知道怎麼說,生氣嗎?傷心嗎?你看起來像很憂鬱,像你們英語的說法。仍然有人會這樣說嗎?」

「不,我沒事。只是累了。」她仰身看看他的咖啡。「我猜想,是濃縮咖啡嗎?」

「特濃。還有其他選擇嗎?它是唯一一種在英國可以找到,而且比較跟法國的咖啡接近的東西。我不喜歡你的拿鐵,充滿甜味和泡沫,還有奇怪的味道!」

「我認識有一個人會完全同意你的想法,」麗貝卡苦笑著說。「但是你永遠也不會遇到他,感謝上帝。我也代表英國跟你道歉。」

「謝謝,」他笑道。「那麼,為什麼你那麼想見我呢?」

「我很久沒有見你了,還需要什麼藉口嗎?」她專注地攪拌著她的咖啡。

他凝視著她。「沒有,但是你打電話給我時候的語氣,聽起來並不像如你所說的只想要『趕上』我,」他啜著咖啡。「你知道聖誕節我都在倫敦,麗貝卡,但你也沒有找我。」

她笑了。「我在聖誕節正忙著,想你也很忙。而且你也不是待了很長時間。」

他的目光很直接,令她感到有點窘迫不安,她意識到她緊緊地握住了雙手。她努力讓自己深吸了一口氣,然後看著他的眼睛。她想說話,但是覺得自己在懸崖的邊緣,像有人想推她下去似的。

「我們已經認識很多年了,是嗎?你想說什麼就說什麼吧。我名義上也是你的叔叔,」他輕輕地說。「你父母知道你找我傾訴也會很高興的。」

「這是關於他們,他們的死。這就是我想談的。」她脫口而出。

他慢慢地點了點頭。「是嗎?」

「我想知道發生了什麼事。」她忍不住說了出來,她眼睛瞟他一

"I want to know what happened." She couldn't help herself. Her eyes flicked up, wanting to gauge his reaction.

He spread his hands. "You know what happened, Rebecca. There was a car accident and your parents were killed, along with David King. A tragedy, not only for you and friends, family, but also for the archaeological community. You know this."

"I know what I've been told."

"What else is there to tell?"

"I want to know exactly what happened. What caused the accident—"

"Bad roads, an unexpected rainstorm—"

"—and why Marcie King blames my father for her father's death," she finished, her voice quavering.

Francois sat back, putting his hands on the armrests of his chair. "Marcie has never comes to terms with her grief, not in the way that you have, I think." He shrugged. "Whether it is her personality, or how she was supported after her father's death, or the reaction of her mother... who can say?"

"I know that."

"So, she looks for someone to blame. This not new, this anger she has. She has kept it alive all this time. Why is it bothering you now, cherie? Put it out of your mind. It is her problem, not yours."

Rebecca wanted to believe him but she'd noticed how he moved his hands back and forth on the arms of the chair as he spoke, just a little. It flashed a warning signal. Francois was usually so poised and calm.

"It bothers me now because she made it my problem. You must have heard from Ron what happened?"

"I did. I'm sorry about your tools. I know how special they were to you."

"Thanks. But I'm sorry, Francois, I don't believe you."

His eyes narrowed. "Believe me? About what?"

"The accident. What caused it."

眼，想知道他有什麼反應。

他攤開雙手。「你知道發生了什麼事的，麗貝卡。就是一場車禍中，你父母跟大衛．京一起，他們都遇難死亡了。這是一場悲劇，不僅是對你跟你的朋友和家人來說是，對考古界來說也是。

你也知道這一點。」

「我知道，我已經聽說過。」

「那你還有什麼想知道呢？」

「我想知道到底發生了什麼事，是什麼原因造成那場事故。」

「就是很壞的道路情況，以及一場意想不到的暴雨…」

「…和瑪西．京為什麼要指責我父親跟她父親去世有關。」她終於把話說完，聲音顫抖著。

弗朗索瓦坐了回去，他把手放在椅子的扶手上。「瑪西從未學會如何來對待她自己的悲痛，她不是用你用的方式，我覺得。」他聳聳肩。「無論如何這就是她的個性，而她父親去世後，她有什麼想法，或她母親有什麼反應…誰會知道呢？」

「我明白。」

「所以，她就要找個人來責怪。這不是新事，這種憤怒，她一直都有。她一直讓它持續下去。為什麼現在才會令你困擾呢？親愛的。別再把它放在心上了，這是她的問題，不是你的問題。」

麗貝卡很想去相信他，但她注意到當他說話時，他的手在扶手上來回地移動著，就只是這麼一點點，就像閃過了一下的警告信號一樣。弗朗索瓦一般都很泰然自若、平靜的。

「現在困擾我的，是她做了一些事令我很煩惱。你一定有聽羅恩說過發生了什麼事？」

「我有。對於你的工具我很抱歉，我知道它們對你來說是多麼的特別。」

「謝謝你。但是，對不起，弗朗索瓦，我不相信你。」

他的眼睛瞇了起來。「相信我嗎？關於什麼？」

「事故，究竟是什麼原因造成的。」

"You know what the report from the Thai authorities said. They are the facts. Marcie is a bitter woman, but one we must feel a certain sympathy for, oui?"

"Marcie says my father was drunk that night," she said flatly. "That he should never have been driving." The words sounded abnormally loud in her head, as though they were ringing out. She half-expected silence to fall all around them. But the hubbub of the café just carried on as normal.

Francois said nothing. When she looked up, he was drinking his coffee again. "This is excellent."

"Yes. I come here all the time."

"Most surprising, for an English café."

She leaned forward. "Yes, the coffee's great," she said abruptly. "Is it true? Was Dad drunk?"

After a hesitation that felt like years, he nodded. Rebecca collapsed back into her seat, stunned. She couldn't believe it. No wonder Marcie blamed her father. And her, by default. How had Marcie known?

"But this is not the whole story." He put down his coffee and clasped his hands together, elbows on the arms of his chair. "David King was also drunk. So your mother had to drive," he said slowly. "If there's any blame, that's all there is. Your mother was never a confident driver; she rarely drove abroad." He sighed. "But I believe whoever drove, the end result would have been the same. Nobody could have kept that car on the road once the storm hit. Half the road was swept away."

"How do you know?"

"Because I drove out there the next day." Francois looked pale now under his tan. "I waited while the authorities recovered the car, and I identified the bodies," he said softly. "Your mother... well. Let us say from her position, it was obvious she had been in the driving seat."

"And you've never told Marcie? Or her mother?"

"Oh, but I have," he said grimly. "But you know what you English say about the blindness of those who do will not see."

There was a long silence.

「你知道泰國當局報告說什麼的，他們說的都是事實。瑪西是一個懷恨的女人，而我們必須對她有一點同情，是嗎？」

「瑪西說是我父親那天晚上喝醉了，」她直截了當地說。「但這樣他就沒有可能駕駛。」這些話在她的腦袋中異常地響亮，彷彿在鳴響。她半預期周圍會落得沉默一片，但沸沸揚揚的咖啡店仍然在正常運作。

弗朗索瓦沒有說什麼。當她抬起頭來，他再次喝著咖啡。「這裡真是一個好地方。」

「是的。我很多時候都會來這兒。」

「最大的驚喜是，這是一間英國的咖啡店。」

她俯身向前。「是的，咖啡是非常好，」她突然說。「是真的嗎？爸爸喝醉了嗎？」

在他猶豫的時間就像過了幾個年頭的時間一樣，然後他點點頭。麗貝卡倒回她的椅子上，嚇呆了。她不敢相信，難怪瑪西一直指責她父親。而且是在默認情況下，瑪西怎麼會知道的呢？

「但這不是故事的全部。」他放下他的咖啡，緊握著自己的雙手，手肘放在椅子的扶手上。「大衛·京也醉了。所以，你母親不得不駕駛，」他緩緩地說。「如果有任何指責，就只有這樣了。你母親從來不是一個有自信的司機，因為她很少在國外開車。」他嘆了口氣。「但我相信不管誰開車，最終的結果都會是一樣。一旦有風暴打擊，根本沒有人能夠把車停在路上，何況那裡有一半的道路都被一掃而空了。」

「你怎麼會知道的？」

「因為第二天我就開車過去了。」弗朗索瓦雖然曬黑了，但面色仍然顯得蒼白。「我一直等到當局找回了車子，而我就確認了屍體，」他輕聲說。「你的母親......好吧，我們應該說，從她的位置看來，很明顯她之前是在駕駛座上。」

「那你為什麼從來沒告訴瑪西或者她母親呢？」

「哦，我是有的，」他冷冷地說。「但是你要知道正如你們英國人說的話，盲目的人是什麼都不會看見的。」

之後他們沉默了很長時間。

"Was there anything else you wish to ask?"

She shook her head.

"Then, cherie, we shall discuss a happier topic. How can I get you to come and work for me? And if we can arrange it, would a two month trial period in Milan – a sabbatical from your Museum – help you to come to a decision?"

「還有什麼要問嗎？」

她搖搖頭。

「接著，親愛的，我們來討論一下開心的話題。我怎樣才能讓你來為我工作呢？如果我們可以安排你在博物館先休假，來米蘭工作兩個月的試用期，這樣對你做決定會有幫助嗎？」

Chapter Twenty Four

Rebecca took her keys from the ignition and smiled at him. "Ready?"

"What, to play Kevin's stand-in? You've got me here under false pretences."

"Don't complain! Thanks to Mr. Grumpy's absence, you get free food and a night in a hotel. With breakfast, might I add."

"Yeah. Free food I didn't choose," he pouted as he climbed out of the car.

"Kevin chose some Italian thing with chicken. You'll love it." She walked round to his side and Steve looked at her admiringly.

"You look gorgeous."

"Oh, now you notice?" she teased.

"I couldn't see you in your full glory before." He grinned.

"Thanks. It's the same outfit I wore for Anna and Jessica's wedding, but hopefully no one will notice."

"Same crowd, then?" he asked as they started towards the church.

"Not by a long chalk, but there's some overlap."

"I see. Hope I pass muster."

"Oh, you'll do. I'm sure you'll cause quite a stir."

"What, with my rugged charm 'n all."

"No. Well, yes, obviously." She grinned and took his hand. "But mostly because you're not Kevin, and usually it's him I drag to these things."

第二十四章

麗貝卡從發動器上拔出鑰匙，並著看著他微笑。「準備好了嗎？」

「就是要扮演凱文的替身？你用虛假的名義把我帶到這裡來。」

「不要抱怨啦！是因為脾氣暴躁先生缺席了，你才可以得到免費的餐飲和一晚酒店住宿。而且包早餐，是我加的。」

「是啊。免費的餐飲，但不是我自己選擇的。」當他從汽車中爬了出來時，他撇著嘴說。

「凱文選擇了一些雞類的意大利食物。你一定會愛上它。」她繞到他身邊，史堤夫用贊賞的神情看著她。

「你看起來很華麗。」

「哦，現在你終於注意到了嗎？」她取笑他說。

「我之前看不到你穿得如此美麗。」他咧嘴笑了。

「謝謝你。我穿了去安娜和潔西卡的婚禮時同樣的衣服，希望沒有人會注意到。」

「都是同一群相同的人嗎？」他問道，他們開始走入教堂。

「不是相差很多，但也有一些是。」

「我明白了，那希望我可以過關吧。」

「哦，你會做到的。我相信你一定會引起一點轟動。」

「什麼？是因為我強健而且富有魅力。」

「不是。嗯，是的，很明顯。」她笑了，拉著他的手。「但主要是因為你不是凱文，而他通常是被我硬拖來的。」

"Drag? Aren't they normally Kevin's friends as well, though?"

"Often, but unless they're close friends, he avoids weddings."

"Why?"

"Doesn't enjoy them. It's because he always gets cornered and asked when he's going to bring a girlfriend along, and when it's going to be his turn. Especially at family weddings.'"

"Right. Awkward."

"Yes."

"Why doesn't he just tell them? Are his family all hugely anti-gay or something?"

"Not any more than your average family, I don't think."

"So why not make a stand? Tell everyone and get it over with?"

She shrugged. "Because he doesn't see it as anyone else's business. On a personal level, and on principle too."

Steve slipped his arm round her. "Explain."

"Well, do you think it's anyone else's business that you're heterosexual?"

"Er... no."

"And do you think you should be expected to declare your sexual preferences to everyone? To have to come out as straight?"

"No, and I see your point. It's not fair that people make presumptions." He shrugged. "But they do, not always because they're prejudiced, but because they're wired to expect 'the norm'".

"And cause misery for the minority."

"Unfortunately, yes, But a wedding would be a great time to come out, that way everyone finds out at once. Done. Dusted. No more awkward questions."

"No, he'd just get a whole new set!" She laughed. "The more accepting relatives would start asking when he was going to settle down with a nice boy, and he'd hate that!"

「硬拖？他們不都是凱文的朋友嗎？」

「通常是，但是除非他們是親密的朋友，否則他都避免出席婚禮。」

「為什麼？」

「不喜歡。這是因為他總是被追問他什麼時候帶女朋友一起來，什麼時候輪到他結婚了。尤其是在家庭婚禮上。」

「沒錯，是很尷尬。」

「是的。」

「為什麼他不去告訴他們呢？是他的家人非常反對同性戀或其他什麼嗎？」

「比你的家庭更正常，我並不這麼認為。」

「那麼，為什麼不能表明立場？告訴大家，並處理它？」

她聳聳肩。「因為他不覺得這關其他人的事，在個人層面上和原則上也是。」

史堤夫用胳膊摟著她。「解釋一下。」

「嗯，那麼你是不是認為你是異性戀關誰的事嗎？」

「呃...不是。」

「那你是不是認為你應該要向大家申報你的性取向呢？直接地說出來？」

「不是，我明白你的意思了。他們自己作出推測是不公平的。」他聳聳肩。「但他們就是這樣，不是因為他們總是先入為主，而是因為他們都期待『正常』。」

「而造成少數人的苦難。」

「不幸的是，正是這樣，但是婚禮是一個把事情說出來的好時機，所有人都一次過說。說完，拂去灰塵，不需要回答任何尷尬的問題。」

「不，他剛剛找到了一個全新的了！」她笑了起來。「比較開明的親戚開始問什麼時候要跟一個不錯的男孩安頓下來，他討厭這

"Not a fan of commitment then?"

"I wouldn't say that; he's just not found the right person yet."

"Poor bloke. Hope he does, he's a nice guy."

She grinned. "Funny, that. I used to have the impression you weren't too keen."

He blinked at her innocently. "Don't know what you mean."

She raised her eyebrows.

"Okay, perhaps I was a bit jealous."

"Completely without reason."

"I know that now, don't I!"

They reached the back of the queue filing into the church.

"Shh! Behave yourself, we're going in."

"Yes miss." He grinned and swooped for a kiss.

The woman in front was wearing an intricate, bright purple fascinator so huge that as she turned round Steve instinctively ducked, expecting it to either fly off or take his eye out. She glanced at him without recognition, her eyes sliding off him to Rebecca.

"Rebecca! Thought that was your voice! How are you? Where's Kevin? And who is this delightful man?" She moved closer to him, resting a proprietorial hand on his chest.

Rebecca stretched to look at Steve over the top of the woman's head and fascinator. "See?" She mouthed, grinning.

Steve collapsed into the chair beside her and groaned. "I'm bushed."

"No! Really?" She smiled brightly. "What's happened to those dancing feet? Surely they're not worn out?"

He shot her a steely look. "So would yours be if you'd spent the last half hour dancing with *Purple Fascinator Woman*."

樣！」

「不是肯承諾的人嗎？」

「我不懂怎麼說，他只是還沒有找到合適的人。」

「可憐的傢伙。希望他可以找到，他是個好人。」

她咧嘴一笑。「有趣呢，我對你的印象是你對這事情並不是那麼熱心。」

他眨了眨眼睛，傻傻地看著她。「不知道你是什麼意思。」

她抬起眉毛。

「好吧，也許我是有點嫉妒。」

「完全沒有道理的。」

「我現在知道了，可以了吧！」

他們達到教堂排在隊的最後面。

「噓！老實點，我們要進去了。」

「是的，小姐。」他咧嘴一笑，俯衝去吻了她一下。

在前面的女人戴著一個複雜而明亮的紫色頭飾，非常巨大。她一轉身，史堤夫本能地躲開了，因為怕它會飛脫而一直注意著它。她瞥了他一眼，沒有認出來，然後她的眼睛就落到麗貝卡身上。

「麗貝卡！都知道是你的聲音了！你怎麼樣了？凱文在哪裡？這個討人喜歡的男子是誰？」她走近他，據為己有地把手放在他的胸口上。

麗貝卡從那個女人的頭和頭飾上伸出來看著史堤夫。「明白了嗎？」她笑嘻嘻的嘟囔著。

史堤夫崩潰地坐到她旁邊的椅子上，呻吟著說：「我已經筋疲力盡了。」

「不會啦！真的嗎？」她明亮地微笑著。「那些舞足發生了什麼事？筋疲力盡的當然不是她們吧？」

"You mustn't keep calling her that. Her name's Veronica! She's Jason's cousin."

"I don't care if she's Kylie Minogue's cousin. She's got all the grace of an elephant and the charm of a mosquito."

"Better get your net out then, she's headed this way."

"What!" He jolted upright, looking all around. "Where? I can't see her."

Rebecca doubled up with laughter.

"Oh. Very funny." He glared.

"Good meerkat impression. Best I've seen."

"When you're done humiliating me, can we go? That hotel bed is starting to call to me."

"That depends."

"On what?"

"What's all this about Kylie Minogue?"

"She's hot. I'd dance with all of her cousins to get an intro."

"Oh would you now?"

"Wrong thing to say?"

"Not if you're happy to spend all night alone, waiting for Kylie," she said lightly.

He sat bolt upright again. "I didn't know there were other options."

"If you keep talking about Kylie Minogue there won't be, Meerkat Man."

He clamped his lips together and mimed zipping them up. "Shutting up about her right now, ma'am."

"Good. Come on." She pulled him to his feet. "If you're so tired, I'd best get you to the hotel."

He looked down at her. "It's only my feet that are tired. The rest of me is fine. Completely fine."

他用鋼鐵一般的表情看著她。「這麼說，你很樂意花最後半小時跟那個紫色頭飾的女人一起跳舞。」

「你不應該繼續這樣稱呼她。她的名字是韋羅妮卡！她是傑森的表姐。」

「我不在乎除非她是凱莉．米洛的表姐。她已經用一隻蚊子的魅力來得到了一隻大象的恩典了。」

「你最好把你的網撒開，她正在走來這邊。」

「什麼！」他震驚地坐直了，環顧四周。「在哪裡？我看不到她。」

麗貝卡笑得更加大聲了。

「哦。很有趣啊。」他怒視著。

「我見過最狐獴的印象。」

「就當你成功羞辱我了，我們可以走了嗎？這家酒店的床開始打電話給我了。」

「這就要看下。」

「看下什麼？」

「怎麼是凱莉．米洛？」

「她很性感，我可以跟她的所有表姐妹跳舞作為一個前奏。」

「哦，你會嗎？」

「我說錯了什麼了嗎？」

「沒有，如果你想獨自地渡過整個晚上，並快樂地等待凱莉。」她輕輕地說。

他再次坐了起來。「我不知道有其他的選擇。」

「如果你繼續談論凱莉．米洛就不會有了，狐獴人。」

他夾住了他的嘴唇，用動作來示意拉上拉鏈。「現在就開始不再說她了，夫人。」

She kissed him and took his hand. "I'll be the judge of that, thank you."

Steve woke up to find himself lying on his side, curved around Rebecca's back. That was a pretty darn fine place to find himself, he decided. He lifted his head to peer over her shoulder and found her smiling up at him.

"Morning."

"Morning gorgeous. How are you?"

"Marvellous, thanks."

"Good. So," he said solemnly, kissing her shoulder, "Now you've had a taste of my coffee with a capital C, what's your opinion?"

"Hmm, well after experiencing your coffee with a medium c, I had quite high expectations," she said, eyes twinkling, "and I wasn't disappointed. Grande Latte standard, I think."

"Glad madam was satisfied."

Rebecca's smiled. "Oh, she was."

He bent his head and trailed kisses down her side towards her hip, then watched as her knees jerked upwards, her arms flailed and she disintegrated into giggles.

"Oh God, I'm really ticklish! Do that again and I'll kill you!"

"'Do that again and I'll kill you'. Just what every man wants to hear when he's seducing his woman." He tugged her shoulder, rolling her on to her back beside him. "Where are you ticklish?"

"Nearly everywhere, I'm afraid."

He leaned over her, frowning. "Hmm. I'm not convinced." He slid down the bed.

A while later he lifted his head. "You're not giggling."

"No. I'm not ticklish there," she said huskily.

"So you're not going to kill me then?"

She buried her fingers in his hair. "Only if you stop."

「很好。來吧。」她把他拉起來。「如果你累了，我最好還是讓你回酒店。」

他低頭看著她。「這其實只是我的腳累了。剩下的部分都很好，非常好。」

她吻了他一下，拉著他的手。「我會來判斷的，謝謝你。」

史堤夫醒來時，發現自己側身躺著，彎彎地繞住麗貝卡的背部。他覺得自己在一個相當不錯的位置。他抬起頭凝視在她的肩膀，發現她正看著他微笑。

「早上好。」

「早晨，美人。你怎麼樣？」

「非常好，謝謝。」

「好。那麼，」他親吻她的肩膀，一本正經地說，「現在你已經嚐過了大寫c了，你對我咖啡的味道有什麼意見嗎？」

「嗯，經歷過中等c的咖啡之後，我有相當高的期望，」她眨了一下眼睛說，「但我並不失望，有大杯裝拿鐵咖啡的水準，我覺得。」

「很高興夫人滿意。」

麗貝卡笑了笑。「哦，她是。」

他低下頭親吻了她腰側的位置，然後看見她的膝蓋猛烈地向上縮了一下，雙臂在揮動，笑成了一遍。

「上帝啊，我真的很怕癢！再這樣做，我就殺了你！」

「『再這樣做，我就殺了你！』這正是每個男人在勾引他女人的時候最想聽到的呢。」他拽了拽她的肩膀，讓她在他身旁仰躺著。「你哪裡怕癢呢？」

「我恐怕幾乎是無處不在。」

他俯身對住她，皺著眉頭。「嗯。我不相信。」他滑到床的下面。

過了一會兒，他抬起頭。「你沒有在笑啊。」

Laura stretched and looked at the clock. Nearly ten. She should get up, really, but she was comfy, and it felt so good not to have anywhere she had to be, no deadlines. Though she didn't mind going to the Museum, if she was honest. She loved it.

Still, the day was a'wastin, as Steve would say, and she'd planned to cook him a nice dinner today. She wanted to spend some quality time with him; perhaps watch some comedy DVDs or play a board game, prove to him that she could be a nice person to live with instead of a pain in the arse. There was a lot she had to make up for, and she couldn't do that lounging about in bed.

She opened her curtains and sunshine lit up the room. It was a gorgeous day out there. Maybe she should suggest a trip somewhere instead. She showered quickly, pulled on fresh clothes and bounced downs the stairs.

She glanced round the kitchen as she sat at the table with a bowl of cereal and a glass or orange juice. Had Steve been ultra-tidy this morning when he'd had breakfast, or was still in bed—, which wasn't like him at all? And what was that white thing?

There was a note stuck to the worktop beside the kettle—Steve must have expected her to make herself a coffee first thing. She grinned. She would have, normally, but the sunshine had put her in the mood for something cooler... what? The grin slid off her face.

'Don't forget I'm at the wedding with Rebecca today, I'll be back by lunchtime tomorrow. Ready meals and pizza in the freezer, salad in the fridge. Money in the change pot if you need more milk, this carton's the last. See you tomorrow!'

She dropped back into her chair. Great. She was putting time aside to rebuild their relationship, and where was Steve? Off with Rebecca.

Had he even told her he was staying away overnight? He probably had; she couldn't remember. Didn't he realise that what she needed right now was company? Now the bail conditions were lifted, now that he didn't have to spend time with her, was he not going to bother? Laura's nails dug into her palms. Maybe every weekend would be like this now. Her stuck here alone while Steve and Rebecca were off for romantic weekends, weddings, parties...

「不是，這裡不怕癢。」她沙啞地說。

「所以你不會殺了我嗎？」

她把手指伸進他的頭髮中。「如果你停下來我就會。」

羅拉伸展了一下身體，看了看鐘，差不多十點了。說真的，她應該要起床了，但她覺得很舒服，沒有任何地方她一定要去，感覺是多麼的好，沒有任何期限地一直這樣。雖然她不介意去博物館，她誠實地承認她喜歡那裡。

仍是整天在浪費時間，史堤夫應該會這樣說。而她打算今天為他煮一頓不錯的晚餐，她想花一些時間與他相處，也許看一些的喜劇影碟或者玩棋盤遊戲，來向他證明，她可以是一個不錯的同住伙伴，而不是一個討厭鬼。有很多事她要準備，懶洋洋地躺在床上是成不了事的。

她打開了窗簾，陽光照亮了整個房間，這是美好的一天。也許她應該提議去一下別的地方。她很快就洗完澡換上乾淨的衣服，並走下樓梯。

當她坐在桌前吃著麥片和喝著橙汁時，她掃視了一下廚房。今天早上史堤夫是不是已經吃過早餐而且整理過了，或是他仍然在床上…但這並不像他呢？那白色的東西是什麼？
一張紙條粘在水壺旁邊的檯面上，史堤夫一定以為她第一件事一定是沖咖啡。她咧嘴一笑，她一般都會，但陽光令她的心情比較想喝點冷的…什麼？笑容在她的臉上消失了。

「不要忘了我今天與麗貝卡參加婚禮，我會在明天午餐時間回來的。即食食品、冷凍比薩和沙拉都在冰箱。如果你需要買牛奶的話，錢就在零錢罐，因為這已經是最後一盒了。明天見！」

她坐回到她的椅子上。太好了。她留出時間來重建他們的關係，但是史堤夫呢？就休假跟麗貝卡在一起。

他甚至沒有告訴過她要在外面留宿呢？可能他有，她不記得了。難道他沒有意識到，她現在需要的是一個陪伴她的人嗎？現在的保釋條件被解除了，他就不再花時間跟她一起了，他不想被打擾了嗎？羅拉用指甲挖她的掌心，也許以後每個週末都會像現在這樣子，她會獨自被困在這兒，而史堤夫和麗貝卡就去共渡他們浪漫的週末、婚禮、派對……

She was disappointed in Rebecca too. All that stuff about how she understood what she'd gone through. Had everything—helping Steve out by babysitting her, getting her work experience at GLAM—been to show how wonderful she was and impress Steve?

She stabbed her spoon down into her cereal. She couldn't believe how selfish they were being. They had all the time in the world. Was it so much to ask for Steve, at least, to spend time with her until she was back on track?

She chewed her cereal mechanically. How serious were things, anyway? Had they booked a hotel room together? Soon Rebecca would be staying here all the time; or Steve would be staying at her flat. Before she knew it, they'd be moving in together.

She dropped her spoon into her bowl with a clang. Oh God. Say Rebecca was The One? They might get married. Have kids. Would either of them want her hanging around then? No.

She felt sick now, her mind racing as she envisaged a future where she was either pushed out or simply asked to leave. Who would she live with? She wasn't close enough to anyone else to want to share their home. Steve would never have enough time for her if he had a family, and she'd only just begun to appreciate how important he was to her; now she could only see a future where he saw her as a spare part. She pushed her bowl away from her.

It wasn't fair. She folded her arms round herself, frowning. She couldn't cope by herself yet, she still needed Steve. But how could she stop Rebecca stealing him away?

她對麗貝卡感到很失望。她明白她之前經歷的所有事情，照顧她，讓她在博物館工作，都只是為了幫助史堤夫，這樣就可以表現她是多麼美好，而可以打動史堤夫了吧？

她用勺子戳碗子內的穀物，她簡直不敢相信，他們是多麼的自私。他們擁有全世界的時間了。如果叫史堤夫跟她一起直到她回正軌，是很浪費時間嗎？

她機械式地咀嚼她的穀物早餐。反正也不是什麼嚴重的事情吧？如果他們訂了一間酒店房住在一起呢？不久，麗貝卡就會住在這裡，或史堤夫會住在她的公寓。甚至可能在她知道之前，他們就已經搬在一起住了。

她噹的一聲把勺子丟在碗子內。噢，天啊。說麗貝卡是他的唯一？那麼他們可能會結婚，生孩子。那麼他們其中一個都永遠要跟他泡在一起了嗎？不行。

現在她覺得噁心，她的腦海一直在設想未來，在那裡她都會被排擠出來或者被要求離開。那麼她要跟誰住在一起呢？她跟誰都沒有那麼親近到可以分租房子。如果史堤夫有了自己的家庭，就永遠不會有足夠的時間給她了，她剛剛才開始體會到他對她是多麼重要，但現在她只能預見到一種未來，在那裡他會把她當作後備。她把她的碗子推開去。

這樣很不公平。她抱起雙臂摟住了自己，皺著眉頭。她無法自己應付，她仍然需要史堤夫。可是她怎麼能制止麗貝卡偷走他呢？

Chapter Twenty Five

"How are you getting on?"

Laura jumped. "Oh hi. Sorry, I was—"

"—Concentrating?" Rebecca smiled. "It's okay, I just came to see how things were going." She walked over to look at the find Laura had been studying under a magnifying glass.

"Good thanks. It's interesting to see the other side of it all."

"Even the side where you get your hands dirty?" Rebecca grinned.

Laura looked down at her hands and grimaced. "Yeah, that's the one."

This week she'd been working with some uni students, under the guidance of Tasha, learning about cleaning and labelling finds.

Rebecca looked round. "I take it everyone else has gone to lunch?"

Laura smiled ruefully. "I think so. I lost track of time."

"Well if you want to come for lunch with me, I know this great café. Friendly staff."

"Cool! Thanks, I'll just get cleaned up." Laura walked to the sink and Rebecca took her place at the bench, peering through the magnifying glass. Laura had been working on a brooch that Rebecca had tagged when it came in.

"Did you clean this up all by yourself?"

"Yes, start to finish." Laura smiled, going a little pink. She dried her hands and came to stand beside her. "It was so satisfying to see it start to shine. I'd never have guessed it would end up looking like that."

第二十五章

「你進展得怎樣？」

羅拉跳了起來。「噢嗨。對不起，我是...」

「...專注。」麗貝卡笑著。「沒關係，我只是來看看事情做得怎麼樣。」她走過去看羅拉一直在研究放大鏡下面的東西。

「好感謝。看到它的這一面真的很有趣。」

「即使你會弄髒你的手？」麗貝卡笑著說。

羅拉低頭看著她的手，做了個鬼臉。「是啊，這是其中一樣。」

這一周她一直在與一些大學生一起工作，在塔莎的指導下，學習有關清潔和標籤發現品。

麗貝卡看看周圍。「我想找個人去吃午餐呢？」

羅拉苦笑。「我也這樣想，我忘記了時間。」

「好吧，如果你想和我一起去午餐，我知道一間很好的咖啡店，店員也很好的。」

「酷！謝謝，我只要清理一下先行。」羅拉走到洗滌槽，而麗貝卡坐到板凳上，通過放大鏡凝視著。羅拉一直為這個胸針忙著，拿回來時是麗貝卡親自標籤的。

「這個都是由你來清理嗎？」

「是的，從頭到尾。」羅拉笑著，臉上透出一點點粉紅色。她擦乾了手，站到她的旁邊。「看到它開始發亮是多麼有滿足感，我萬萬沒有想到它最後是這個樣子的。」

「你把工作做得非常之好。這之前真的沾滿了泥土。」她把胸針翻轉。羅拉甚至設法把小別針周圍的沙石都清理了，這對一個新

"You've done a brilliant job. This was really caked up." She turned the brooch. Laura had even managed to get the soil out from under the tiny arms of the setting around the stones and that was tricky for a newbie.

As they walked towards the café, Rebecca was glad she'd grabbed her coat on the way out. It was sunny but the breeze was cold. She looked sideways at Laura, only wearing a long-sleeved top, with a thin scarf just visible under her dark wavy hair. "How come you're not cold?"

"Naturally warm-blooded, Steve says."

"Lucky you," Rebecca laughed, pulling her collar up a little. "So how was last week?"

"Great. I thought I'd find all the bones a bit, you know... "

"Gruesome?"

"Yeah," Laura laughed. "But it was so interesting that I just, like, forgot there were bones in the end. Even when Maurice started sawing them up."

"Yes. You do get over being squeamish. Well most people do, anyway!" she laughed.

The café was busy. Laura bagged a table while Rebecca went to the counter.

"And how are my two favourite girls?" Steve asked, smiling.

"We're fine, thank you. But ravenous. We've been working hard."

"Oh yes, I've been hearing about her 'hard work'." He leaned sideway to look past her at Laura, and raised his voice. "If she enjoys dusting so much, perhaps she could so some at home!"

Laura stuck out her tongue at him and grinned.

"Behave yourself and get us lunch or else," said Rebecca firmly.

"Or else what?"

"We'll take our custom elsewhere."

"Right, I'm on it." He scuttled off and returned with two lattes and

手來說是很棘手的。

當她們走向咖啡店，麗貝卡很高興她有拿外套出來。這是陽光普照的一天，但微風吹起仍是有點冷。她側身看著羅拉，她只穿著長袖上衣，在她深色波浪捲髮下只見到一條薄圍巾。「你不冷嗎？」

「天生熱血，史堤夫是這樣說的。」

「你真幸運，」麗貝卡笑了，拉一拉她的衣領。「那麼上週過得如何？」

「太好了。我想所有都是骨頭，有點，你知道…」

「可怕？」

「是啊，」羅拉笑著。「但是很有趣，我只是有點，到最後都忘了是骨頭來的，即使莫里斯要開始鋸起來。」

「是的。之後你就不會再怕了。大多數人都是這樣啦！」她笑了起來。

咖啡店正忙著。羅拉去了找座位，而麗貝卡走到櫃檯。

「我最喜歡的兩個女孩今天好嗎？」史堤夫面帶微笑地問。

「我們很好，謝謝你。但是餓壞了，我們一直在努力工作。」

「哦，是的，我已經聽說過關於她『努力工作』。」他側身俯下從她身後看著羅拉，並提高了聲線說：「如果她這麼喜歡除塵，也許她在家也可以做一下！」

羅拉對他伸出了舌頭，他笑了。

「規矩點，讓我們吃午飯，否則，」麗貝卡堅決地說。

「否則什麼？」

「我們就去其他地方。」

「好吧，我去做。」他急忙地走開了，之後拿兩杯拿鐵咖啡和兩個肉卷回來。「怎麼樣？」

two wraps. "How's that?"

"Marvellous." She flashed him a warm smile and walked back to the table.

Laura took her wrap from the tray. "Thanks, Rebecca, this is great."

"No problem. Not sure about the staff here though."

"Why's that?"

"That bloke serving behind the counter's a bit forward. He said we're his two favourite girls."

"What a cheek!" Laura grinned.

"I know. He thinks he's funny, your brother."

"That's Steve all over," said Laura lightly. "He's all about the fun."

"He is. I love that about him." She grinned. "Did Steve tell you we joined the same dating agency? He was never one of my hot matches, more's the pity, and he should have been because we've got lots in common. I might have had more faith in it if it matched me with Steve."

"Yeah, the program was a mess," said Laura, "but even if it was working, I don't think Steve would have come up on your hot matches."

"Why not?" Rebecca frowned.

"Oh, don't worry – it's just that the program puts more importance on some factors than others, which makes sense."

Rebecca nodded. "And?" Her heart had started to beat uncomfortably fast. Laura's line of conversation was worrying her

"Like you said, Steve's fun, and, well, that's what he was primarily looking for. Fun. He wanted to date someone, of course –he wasn't looking for a series of one night stands – but he's not looking for anything long-term at the moment."

"I see," said Rebecca faintly.

"See? Nothing to worry about. He hasn't got any strange beliefs or anything. It's nothing you didn't know already!" She smiled at her and went back to her food.

「太棒了。」她對他亮出了一個溫暖的微笑，走回桌子去。

羅拉把肉卷從托盤上拿起來。「謝謝你，麗貝卡，真的非常好。」

「沒關係，但是這裡的店員有點問題。」

「為什麼？」

「櫃檯後面的那個傢伙有點無禮。他說我們是他最喜歡的兩個女孩。」

「不要臉！」羅拉笑著。

「我知道。他覺得自己很幽默，你的哥哥。」

「這就是史堤夫了，」羅拉輕聲地說。「他就是喜歡這種樂趣。」

「他是，我就愛他這樣。」她咧嘴一笑。「史堤夫有沒有告訴你，我們加入了相同的約會機構？他從來也不是我的熱門配對，更可惜的是，他本來應該是的，因為我們有很多共同之處。如果它配對了我與史堤夫，我可能對它更有信心。」

「是啊，該程式真的是一塌糊塗，」羅拉說，「但即使是有用，我認為史堤夫也不會在你的熱門配對上面。」

「為什麼不呢？」麗貝卡皺起了眉頭。

「哦，不要擔心。這只是因為程式會認為某些因素比其他的更重要，那是正常的。」

麗貝卡點點頭。「所以呢？」她的心臟已經開始跳得快到有點不舒服，羅拉這一席話令她很擔憂。

「就像你說的，史堤夫的樂趣，而且，好吧，他主要想尋找的就是樂趣。他想和某人約會，當然他不是在找一夜情的對象，但這一刻他也不是在尋找什麼長遠的關係。」

「我明白了。」麗貝卡微弱地說。

「明白了嗎？沒有什麼好擔心的。他沒有任何奇怪的信仰或什麼。而且沒有什麼你是不知道的！」她笑了，然後又繼續吃她的午餐。

Rebecca looked at her wrap. She didn't think she'd ever felt less hungry in her life.

"Good day?" Steve looked up, grinning, from his newspaper as Laura bounced in the door.

"Fantastic!"

"Coffee?"

"Yes please!"

Steve smiled as he made the coffee. He couldn't believe the change in Laura, though he had to admit to some mixed feelings. He was delighted with this new, motivated, cheerful Laura who was so much more open and so much less hostile. But he couldn't help feeling regretful that he hadn't brought about this change himself. He hadn't had a clue how to help her escape her substance abuse, let alone known how to guide her towards becoming this enthusiastic, glowing young woman. Strangers had succeeded where he had failed so miserably. Whenever he looked at her and felt pride and delight, guilt and inadequacy always came hot on their heels.

He shook himself. This was pointless. He was the first to tell other people you could learn from the past but not relive it.

Laura appeared, stretching up to hang her bag on the hook on the kitchen door. "Mmm, latte!"

"Got to give the working girl some treats after a hard day. I bought some more yesterday, since Rebecca's given you a taste for them. Pair of philistines!" He grinned.

"Thanks." She took a sip. "Mmm. Yummy."

"What did you get up to today, then?"

"Loads of stuff. Kevin made me mirror someone this morning, for a start."

"Don't you mean shadow someone?"

She shook her head. "No, dumbo, I know what I mean. I wasn't copying what they were doing, I sat at a computer and was given all the same information they had, to do the same job. Sooo cool!"

麗貝卡看著她的肉卷，她這輩子從未如此覺得這麼不想吃東西。

「今天過得好嗎？」史堤夫從他的報紙中抬起頭來咧嘴笑了，羅拉正在門口進來。

「太棒了！」

「咖啡？」

「好啊！」

當史堤夫沖咖啡的時候，他笑著。他簡直不敢相信羅拉的變化，但他不得不承認他有些感慨。他很高興這個新的、有上進心的、

性格開朗的羅拉變得更加開放了，而且少了一點敵意。但他感到遺憾的是這種變化並不是他自己做成的。他之前沒有辦法去幫助她脫離藥物濫用，更不用說知道怎樣引導她成為這個熱情而發亮的年輕女子。在他如此慘敗的時候，其他人卻成功了。每當他看著她感到驕傲和喜悅的時候，緊隨的卻是內疚和無能。

他搖了搖頭，這是毫無意義的。他是第一個跟其他人說，你可以從過去中學習，但不能重蹈覆轍。

羅拉出現在廚房，把袋子掛在廚房門的鉤子上。「嗯，是拿鐵！」

「是給一個打工妹辛苦了一天後的一些獎勵。自從麗貝卡給你嚐過這個味道之後，昨天我去買了一些。真是一對庸人！」他咧嘴笑了。

「謝謝。」她喝了一口。「嗯。美味。」

「那麼你到今天為止學到了什麼嗎？」

「很多東西。今天上午凱文讓我跟著別人工作，作為一個開始。」

「難道你的意思是跟隨別人來學習嗎？」

她搖搖頭。「不是，笨蛋，我知道我的意思是什麼。我沒有複製他們所做的，我用自己的一台電腦，並有他們有的所有資料，做同樣的工作。太酷了！」

He smiled at her enthusiasm. "What did you have to do?"

"Try to reconstruct a chapel. They've dug the site and know where the main walls were, and there's an old drawing that shows one side, but nothing else in the picture is still there so it's hard to get a sense of proportion. Some of the decorative pieces were salvaged and used on a church three miles away, so we had photographs of those, too, plus an entry in the churchwarden's diary about bell tower renovations."

Steve was impressed. "Sounds intriguing."

"It's amazing! It's like using all these different skills to, to"—she shrugged helplessly—"put together a 3D jigsaw with no definite picture to follow, making sure the inside's right too."

"That's very complicated for a duffer like me."

She punched him on the arm. "You're not a duffer, bro. Haven't you ever watched Time Team?"

"No."

"Nor had I before, but... hold on a sec." She dashed out of the room and appeared seconds later with a slim black case. "Right, sit down. Demo time!"

Steve sat, amused, and sipped his coffee. "Can't wait."

She produced a shiny, very new-looking laptop and Steve raised his eyebrows. "Wow. They let you bring that home?"

She put her head on one side and a hand on one hip. "No, I hid it under my jacket and sneaked out."

He grinned. "Sorry. Just surprised. It looks expensive." kit."

"It is. I'm allowed it because I'm on the intern register now but I still had to sign it out and everything." She opened the laptop.

"So you're all official now."

"Yep." Steve watched her as she frowned at the screen, concentrating. He touched her shoulder. "I'm really proud of you, you know."

She didn't look round. "It's not often you get the chance to say that, is it?" Her laugh was brittle.

他被她的熱忱逗笑了。「那你有什麼要做呢？」

「嘗試重建一座小教堂。他們已經挖掘了那場地，並知道主牆在哪裡，而且還有一個舊的圖紙顯示了其中一側，但上面沒有其他東西，所以很難有比例上的概念。在教堂三英里外也找到了一些裝飾小品，我們也有那些照片，加上教堂執事的日記中提及有關鐘樓整修的事。」

史堤夫非常欽佩地說：「聽起來很有趣。」

「這真是令人驚嘆！就像使用了所有這些不同的技術，」她無奈地聳聳肩，「把3D拼圖放在一起而沒有明確的畫面去參照，還要確保內部的也是正確的。」

「對於像我這樣的一個笨蛋來說，這是非常複雜。」

她打了一下他的手臂。「你不是一個笨蛋，兄弟。難道你沒有看過《考古小隊》[1]嗎？」

「沒有。」

「我之前也沒有，但...等一下。」她衝出房間，幾秒鐘後拿著一個黑色薄薄的東西回來。「坐下來。示範時間！」

史堤夫坐下，被逗樂了，喝著他那咖啡。「等不及了。」

她拿出一部光亮而且非常新的筆記本電腦，史堤夫揚起了眉毛。「哇。他們讓你把這個帶回家嗎？」

她側一側頭，一隻手扠著腰。「沒有，我把它藏在我的外套裡偷偷拿回來的。」

他咧嘴笑了。「對不起。我只要有點驚訝，因為看起來很昂貴。」

「是的，但他們允許我拿起，因為我現在是註冊的實習生，而我拿走它仍是要簽收一些文件。」她打開筆記本電腦。

「所以，你現在是正式員工啦。」

「是啊。」史堤夫看著她，她正皺起眉頭集中在屏幕上。他摸摸她的肩膀：「我真為你而感到驕傲，你知道嗎？」

1　《考古小隊》是英國第4頻道電視台一套關於考古和歷史的系列紀錄片。

"Seriously, I am," he said in a low voice.

She turned round, eyes glistening. "Thanks, bruv," she said huskily. She leant her head against him for a moment and Steve felt the huge knot inside him start to unravel. She's going to be alright, he thought. Crisis over.

Laura pulled away and clicked confidently around the screen.

"These are scans of the renovation bill and the diary entry... "

Steve squinted, trying to read the faded, spidery writing. "Boy, that's not easy to make out."

"No, and the older the writing, the more difficult it is, because the way we form letters and spell words has changed so much over the years."

He nodded. "Can you read what this says?"

"I can now, but I needed help!" she laughed. She read him the documents then brought up photographs of ornate carvings and gargoyles. "These were used when the village got its own church—it's still standing now, see? Our chapel fell into ruin when the family line died out."

"And what's this?" he asked, pointing to a diagram.

"That shows the walls we could definitely place from the archaeology. And this"—she swapped screens – "is a chapel of very similar size, built two years later and designed by the same architect."

"Okay. Have you got the final reconstruction, or isn't it done yet?"

She grinned. "They're not the absolute, final products but I can show you two reconstructions, in fact."

"Two?"

"Yeah. This is mine."

Steve was impressed at how Laura could move the 3D model around and let him view the inside. "Not all the texture work's done, but the structure is all there."

"That's amazing." He looked at her with respect. "You've picked this up really quickly, Laura. You must have a talent for it."

她沒有回頭看他。「這不是你經常有機會說的，是嗎？」她冷笑了一聲說道。

「我是認真的。」他用低沉的嗓音說。

她轉過身，眼睛閃閃發亮，沙啞地說：「謝謝你，兄弟，」她把頭靠在史堤夫的肩上一會兒，他開始感受到他內心那個巨大的結終於解開了。他想，她一切都沒問題了，危機已經結束。

羅拉坐直身子，自信地點擊著屏幕。

「這些掃描是整修的議案和日記記載的東西...」

史堤夫瞇起眼睛，試圖讀那些褪色像蜘蛛般細長的文字。「小子，這是不容易看出來。」

「沒有，而且更困難的是這都是舊式寫作，這麼多年來我們組成字母和拼寫單詞的方式已經改變很多了。」

他點點頭。「那麼你可以看得懂嗎？」

「現在我可以，但有人幫我的！」她笑了。她給他讀文件，然後給他看一些華麗雕刻和滴水獸的照片。「這些是村莊有自己教堂的時候用的，它仍然在那裡，看到嗎？當一個家族滅絕的時候，我們的教堂就變成遺跡了。」

「這是什麼？」他指著一個圖表問道。

「這顯示了我們從古跡中確定了牆壁的地方。而這個...」她轉換到另一個畫面，「這是另一間差不多大小的教堂，是兩年後建成的，由同一個建築師設計。」

「好吧。你已經做到最終的重建了？或是還沒有做好呢？」

她咧嘴一笑。「它們不是絕對的最終成品，但我可以給你看下，其實重建了兩個。」

「兩個？」

「是啊。這個是我的。」

史堤夫很欽佩羅拉可以移動3D模型，而且還可以讓他看到內部。「不是所有的紋理都完成好，但結構都有了。」

「太不可思議了。」他就看著她。「你真的很快學會這東西，羅

She blushed. "Thanks, and look—I can take you on a tour." She grinned as he watched an animation that 'flew' him inside the chapel and turned him round to view the internal structures before flying him out of a side door.

"Wow. Very clever." Steve clapped. "Is that what you meant by two reconstructions – was the tour the second one?"

"No." She opened another file. "This is Ella's reconstruction."

To Laura's credit, the differences weren't immediately clear, and he didn't spot most of them until Laura talked him through it.

She sighed. "Hers is way better than mine, especially the texturing."

"Hey, come on! I bet she's been doing this for years."

"Ten," Laura admitted."

"You can't compare yourself to someone who's got so much more experience, you've only been at it for a couple of weeks! I think yours is incredible."

"Thanks." She shoulder bumped him, looking embarrassed. "She has got a degree in archaeology and one in Graphic and Computer-Aided Design."

"There you go then. You're up against a talented lady."

"Oh yeah. Everyone is, there. They're all really—"

"Cool?" he grinned.

"Yeah!" she laughed, picking up her coffee. "And really friendly too." She took a sip. "Yuck. Cold."

"I'll pop it in the microwave for you." He got to his feet, then on an impulse leant over and kissed the top of her head. "I'm really glad you've found something you love, Lor," he said quietly. "You deserve it."

To his surprise, she stood up and hugged him. "I don't deserve anything. I've been such a cow to you, and you've taken it. I'm so sorry." And just like that, her smile disappeared and she was sobbing into his t-shirt.

"It's not your fault. Things were so tough for you, and I don't think I was that hot as a surrogate parent." He hugged her tight. "I

拉。你一定是很有天賦。」

她臉紅了。「謝謝你，我可以帶你去遊覽一下。」她咧嘴一笑，他看到一個動畫，讓他「飛」進教堂裡，然後轉過來看到所有內部結構，之後從側門飛了出去。

「哇。非常聰明。」史堤夫鼓掌。「那麼你說有兩個重建，第二個的意思就是遊覽嗎？」

「不是。」她打開另一個文件。「這是愛妮雅的重建。」

羅拉值得稱讚的是，差異其實不是那麼大，他甚至沒有發現差異，直到羅拉告訴他。

她嘆了口氣。「她的是比我更好，特別是紋理。」

「嘿，來吧！我敢打賭，她做了很多年了。」

「十年。」羅拉承認。

「你不能跟一個擁有這麼年經驗的人比較，你只做了幾個星期！我認為你已經很了不起了。」

「謝謝。」她用肩膀碰碰他，滿臉尷尬。「她已經有考古學學位，並在圖形和電腦輔助設計也有一個。」

「那麼就這樣了，你遇上一個很有才華的女人。」

「哦，是的。那裡每個人都是，他們都是真的…」

「酷嗎？」他咧嘴笑了。

「對！」她笑了，拿起她的咖啡。「而且非常友好。」她喝了一口。「呸。冷了。」

「我拿去微波爐給你翻熱一下。」他站起身來，然後一時衝動地靠前去吻了一下她的頭頂。「我真的很高興，你已經找到你所愛的東西了，羅拉，」他平靜地說，「這是你應得的。」

他有點意外的是，她站起身來一手抱住了他。「全部都不是我應得的。我給了你這麼多威脅，而你都承受了。我真的很抱歉。」就這樣她的笑容消失了，她埋在他的汗衫上抽泣著。

「這不是你的錯。事情對你來說是如此艱難，我也不認為我是一個熱情的代理家長。」他緊抱住她。「我可能有做錯了事，所以

probably did the wrong thing, fighting to keep you with me. You'd have been better off with someone else."

She tightened her grip, nearly squeezing the breath out of him. "Don't say that. You were fantastic and you were always there for me, even when I cocked up big time."

"That's what brothers are for."

"No, it's not. Brothers aren't there to do your washing, cook your dinner, help you with homework, clean up after you, tell you about contraception... and bailing you out isn't in the job description either." She sniffed. "Can I have a tissue?"

Steve looked at her solemnly. "Sorry, I don't think that's in the description." That made her laugh, just as he'd hoped it would. He passed her some tissues and waited while she blew her nose ferociously and wiped her eyes. "I'm not sure there is a job description for brothers, however old they are," he said quietly. "And when they willingly take on the role of guardian as well, I think it's superseded."

"But I never thought about it!" Laura's lips quivered. "How much you gave up for me and what I put you through. When all your friends were still at uni having a good time, you were working your guts out all day and then spending all evening doing my washing, helping me with my homework..." she shook her head and fresh tears streamed down her face. "You gave up everything to look after me and I've never said thank you..."

"Shh." He hugged her tightly. "I think you just did. All I wanted was for you to be happy, and it seems you're finally there, sis. And that's certainly not down to me."

"Is."

"Is not."

"Is." She poked him in the ribs.

"Is NOT." He poked her back and she slapped him.

He moved away. "Right, I know when I'm beat. I'll make that coffee."

"No, I'll do it. And I'll make you another one too."

"Oh well, if you're offering..." he grinned, lying down on the sofa and putting his arms behind his head. "I could get used to this."

你才會跟我對抗。你已經比很多人好了。」

她牢牢地緊握拳頭，幾乎是擠壓出一口氣來說道。「不要這樣說，你太棒了，你總是為我著想，甚至在我把什麼愉快時光都弄得一塌糊塗的時候。」

「這就是兄弟。」

「不，不是這樣的。兄弟不是負責清理、煮晚餐、幫你做作業，幫你善後、告訴你如何避孕⋯而且幫你保釋也不在職位描述當中，」她抽了抽鼻子。「我可以要張紙巾嗎？」

史堤夫嚴肅地看著她。「對不起，我沒有想到這是在描述中的。」跟他預期的一樣，這令她笑了。他從她身邊走過去拿了紙巾給她，然後等待她狠狠地擤了擤鼻子和擦了擦眼睛。「我不知道有一個叫做兄弟的工作描述，不論是什麼年紀的，」他平靜地說。

「而當他們心甘情願地做一個監護人的角色，我認為這已經足以取代了。」

「但我從來沒有想過這個問題！」羅拉的嘴唇顫抖著。「你為了我放棄了太多了，而我就令你吃苦。當你所有的朋友們仍然在過開心的大學生活，你就要整天拼命工作，然後花整個晚上來幫我清理，幫我做作業⋯」她搖搖頭，一行眼淚又在臉上流了下來。「你照顧我了一切，而我從來沒有說謝謝⋯」

「噓⋯」他抱得她更緊。「我認為你只是做到了，我最想要的就是你快樂，而且看起來你終於做到了，妹妹。這肯定不是我造成的。」

「是。」

「不是。」

「是的。」她戳了他的肋骨一下。

「不是。」他戳她的背部而她拍了拍他。

他移開了。「好吧，我知道我被打敗了。我會去沖喝咖啡。」

「不，我會去沖，也會為你沖一杯。」

「哦，好吧，如果是你提供的服務⋯」他笑了，倒在沙發上並把雙臂放在腦後。「我會去習慣一下。」

"You'll have to. I'm going to start pulling my weight."

"Best start eating cakes then, there's nothing of you." He looked her up and down. "That's worth about one lot of washing up a week."

She put her hands lightly around his neck. "Do you want to drink this coffee or shower in it?"

He laughed. "Back to the kitchen, wench."

"Yes, m'lord."

She reappeared with the coffee and curled herself into an armchair.

"So enough about me. How was the wedding?"

"Good. It didn't rain, the food was spectacular – it must have cost a bomb – and of course I got to spend the weekend with Rebecca." He grinned. "That's a pretty big bonus."

"Yeah, she's great. So friendly, and soooo good at her job. Everyone at the museum thinks she's, like, the goddess of archaeology." She sighed. "It won't be the same without her, but hopefully someone else will take me under their w—"

"What do you mean, without her?"

"Well she's not going to turn down that job, is she, and Kevin said they've offered to let her go out there for a two month trial—"

"What job? Out where?"

"She must have told you..." Laura looked at him, stricken. "Oh God, she hasn't, has she? Steve I'm sorry, I've put my foot in it."

"No, she has told me. There's going to be a restructure and Ron's suggested she applies for promotion. She hasn't got to go anywhere for that, has she?"

"Not that job. Ron offered her that at the same time, apparently. What a choice! But she won't go for the GLAM job, will she, not once she's spent a couple of months in Milan."

"Milan?"

「你必須習慣，我會開始做好我的分內事。」

「最好是我管不了的，你也沒有什麼事可以做。」他上下掃視她。「可以持續負責打掃一個星期。」

她把手輕輕地放在他的脖子上。「你想要喝咖啡還是要淋咖啡浴？」

他笑了。「回廚房去，丫頭。」

「是的，我的主人。」

她拿著咖啡再回來，蜷縮自己在扶手椅中。

「足夠了解完我的事了。婚禮如何？」

「很好。沒下雨，食物又很壯觀，肯定是花了許多錢。當然，我與麗貝卡共渡了一個週末。」他咧嘴笑了。「這是一個相當大的獎金。」

「是啊，她是非常好。如此友好的，工作上也這麼出色。在博物館的每個人都認為她是，像個考古學的女神。」她嘆了口氣。「沒有她肯定會完全不同了，但希望他們仍然會把我當作是他們的…」

「你是什麼意思，沒有她？」

「嗯，她不會拒絕那份工作，凱文說，他們已經提出讓她去那邊試用兩個月…」

「什麼工作？在哪裡？」

「她一定已經告訴你吧…」羅拉看著他，臉色變青了。「噢，天啊，她沒有告訴你嗎？史堤夫對不起，我說錯話了。」

「不，她已經告訴了我。就是將會有一個重組，而羅恩建議她去申請晉升。她不會去任何地方，是嗎？」

「不是這項工作。羅恩同時給了她另一個提議。一個非常好的選擇！所以她不會選擇GLAM的工作，她不會，她肯定不止會花兩個月在米蘭。」

米蘭？」

「對不起。我真的以為她會提到這件事，但你們只是剛在一起不久，是嗎？並

"Sorry. I really thought she'd have mentioned it, but then you've only just got together, haven't you. It's not like it's serious. She probably wasn't intending to tell you until she'd decided."

Not serious? Weren't they? "It would have been nice to know."

"Well she's still young, and she's got a brilliant future ahead of her. Her career comes first at the moment. She was very honest about it on her profile, that's Rebecca all over, isn't it? Said she wasn't looking for a long term relationship at the moment." Laura smiled. "It's brilliant, isn't it? She's going to have a fantastic time in Milan. I'm so pleased for her."

"Yes," said Steve. His heart felt as if it had doubled in size and was trying to escape from his chest. "It's great."

沒有什麼大不了的。她大概打算決定了才告訴你。」

沒有什麼大不了嗎？是嗎？「真的很高興知道這件事。」

「嗯，她還年輕，在她前面的是輝煌的未來。現在她的事業才是第一位。她在個人檔案上很老實說明了一切，這就是麗貝卡，是不是？說她不是尋找什麼長遠的關係。」羅拉笑著。「這是非常好的，是嗎？她在米蘭一定會過得很好，我很為她高興。」

「是的，」史堤夫說。他感覺自己的心臟猶如漲大了一倍，並試圖從他的胸口逃出來，「真的是太好了。」

Chapter Twenty Six

She'd intended to go somewhere different for lunch, because Ron was pushing her for a decision and she wanted time alone; time to stop and think about her future and what was best for her. Seeing Steve would only blur the picture and she couldn't let that happen when he didn't want a serious relationship. She couldn't give up what might be the chance of a lifetime for someone who might get fed up with their 'fun' in a couple of months' time. And now that she had the option of a trial period in Milan, the idea was appealing to her more and more. What did she have to lose?

But she was so deep in thought that she walked to Tony's on autopilot, only realising she'd done so after she'd opened the door and seen Steve look over at her. If only she'd known from the start he only wanted fun. Then she wouldn't have let her heart get so involved.

Well it was too late now, for her heart and her peaceful lunch. Just her luck that today, Tony told Steve he could go for lunch straight away, as it was still early and fairly quiet. Steve needed no second telling and he had his apron off before she'd reached the counter.

But as he came round the counter he didn't look overjoyed to see her.

"Hi."

"Hi. Rebecca, can we go somewhere else for lunch?" He didn't meet her eye, just looked out the window, pulling his jacket on.

"Of course," she replied, bewildered at his abruptness. "Lead on."

He didn't take her hand as he led the way to a sandwich van parked near the canal, and barely spoke.

"I thought we could sit outside."

第二十六章

她打算去別的地方吃午飯，因為羅恩在逼迫她做決定，而她只想獨處一下。讓時間停下來想想她的未來，究竟什麼是最適合她的。去見史堤夫只會令畫面模糊，她不能讓這種情況發生，因為他不想有一段認真的關係。她不能放棄這個千載難逢的機會，因為這個人可能會在兩個月之內厭倦了他們的「樂趣」。而現在，她有一個選擇可以到米蘭作一個試用期，這個想法越來越吸引她。她有什麼損失呢？

但當她陷入了沉思，她不知不覺又走到東尼的咖啡店了，而她意識到的時候，她已經在打開門，而且看到史堤夫在看著她。如果她一開始就知道他只想找點樂趣。她就不會讓自己的心陷入那麼深。

可惜現在已經太晚了，不管是她的心或是寧靜的午餐。還好今天她有一點運氣，東尼跟史堤夫說他可以馬上去吃午飯，因為仍然很早，還沒有很忙。史堤夫二話不說，在她達到櫃檯之前，他已經除下了圍裙。

但是，當他來到櫃檯前，他並沒有喜出望外地看著她。

「嗨。」

「嗨。麗貝卡，我們可以去別的地方吃午飯嗎？」他沒有看著她的眼睛，只是看著窗外，並拿起他的外套上。

「當然，」她回答說，他粗魯的態度令她不知所措。「走吧。」

他沒有拉著她的手，他一路走在前面直到走到運河附近的三明治麵包車前，幾乎沒怎麼說話。

「我想我們可以坐在外面。」

「好。」一個寒冷的恐懼感圍繞著她。她從來沒有見過他這個樣子。有時他會比較寡言，但從來沒有這樣冷漠。

"Fine." A cold feeling of dread was curling around inside her. She'd never seen him like this before. Sometimes he'd been reserved, but never this cold.

He walked to a bench overlooking the water and sat down.

Rebecca sat beside him, automatically leaving a small space between them. Somehow I don't think I'm going to have to worry about breaking my news, she thought dully. I think I'm going to be dumped instead. She closed her eyes for a second, trying to control the tears that stung her eyes just at the thought of it, and took a deep breath.

"Steve, what's wrong?" Better to tackle it head on and get it over with.

"You tell me," he snapped.

The unreasonable retort and his tone made her hackles rise instantly. "If I knew, I wouldn't ask, would I."

"I just wondered when you were going to tell me that you're taking a job in Milan, that's all. Or even that's you'd been offered it."

Oh God. "I meant to tell you—"

"Well, no rush is there? Just because everyone else knows. Lucky me, I found out everything I needed to know from my sister. She thought I knew."

"Steve, Ron told me about the Milan job before we got together. When I still thought you were married."

"And you haven't found time to mention it since? Slipped your mind. Too busy buying a new suitcase and sunglasses?"

"I know I should have told you, but I didn't want to say anything until I'd decided how I felt about it, and I haven't, not yet. I didn't know Laura even knew about it. She must have overheard me and Kevin talking about it."

"Oh because of course, you've sodding well discussed it with Kevin. Why doesn't that surprise me, Rebecca? It must break your heart he's gay, you make such a lovely couple."

"Don't be stupid."

"I'm telling it like it is, that's all. You two are far more of a couple than we'll ever be, because you tell him everything, and your

他走到一張可以俯瞰水的長凳坐了下來。

麗貝卡坐在他的身旁，中間很自然地留下一小道的空間。有時候我不認為我需要擔心去公佈這個消息，她淡淡地想。而我現在覺得我將會被拋棄了。她閉上了眼睛一秒鐘，努力控制住那刺痛了她眼睛的淚水，並深吸了一口氣。

「史堤夫，有什麼問題嗎？」正面地對付它、結束它。

「你來告訴我吧。」他厲聲說。

這個不合理的反駁和他的語氣令她憤怒瞬間上升。「如果我知道的話，我就不會問，不會。」

「我只是想知道，你要什麼時間才告訴我你會接受了一份在米蘭工作，就這樣。甚至可以說你已經接受了。」

噢，天啊。「我有打算要告訴你的。」

「好吧，因為不急嗎？只是因為大家都已經知道了，而我很幸運，要我妹妹告訴我才知道一切，而她還以為我已經知道。」

「史堤夫，羅恩告訴我有關米蘭的工作，是在我們一起之前。而當時我還以為你已經結婚了。」

「之後你沒有時間說了嗎？還是你忘掉了，因為你忙著去買新皮箱和太陽鏡嗎？」

「我知道我應該要告訴你的，但我想先決定了我想怎樣做才說出來，而我沒有決定到，還沒有。我甚至不知道羅拉知道這件事。

她一定是偷聽我和凱文談話。」

「哦，當然了，你已經該死的跟凱文討論完了。為什麼讓我不感到驚呀呢，麗貝卡？他是同性戀真的是太傷你心了吧，你們是這麼可愛的一對。」

「不要傻了。」

「我只是說出事實，就這樣而已。你們兩個比以前更像一對了，因為你告訴了他一切，而這種關係都取代不到你的職業生涯，是嗎？別擔心，我知道我的位置。如果你只是想要一點樂趣，我可以輕鬆地娛樂你，讓你逗樂，直到你溜到米蘭去。」

career doesn't stand in the way of that relationship, does it? Don't worry, I know my place. You just wanted some fun. I'm the light entertainment to keep you amused until you bugger off to Milan."

"That's not how it is, you know that."

"I don't know anything, Rebecca, anymore. That's what hurts. I thought we were going somewhere. When we slept together it meant something to me. It was special. But it obviously wasn't significant for you. I guess I must be old-fashioned. It didn't even earn me sufficient status in your life to be informed, did it?

Her eyes flashed. "Oh I'm sorry, I missed that bit in the contract, I wasn't aware that sleeping with you meant I had to instantly report everything that happened in my life!"

"You don't. But this, Rebecca, this was important."

Silence. Rebecca felt like she was going to throw up any minute. Thank goodness they were near the canal, she thought, feeling strangely unreal and detached. "Perhaps we should talk about this when we've both had time to think."

"If you want. But from where I'm standing, the only one of us who's got thinking to do is you. Because it doesn't matter what I think, does it. You've proved that." He thrust his uneaten lunch into the bin, slamming the lid down savagely when it wouldn't shut, and turned to go.

"Will I see you tomorrow?" She hated her voice for trembling.

"Come round if you want. Laura's out from 7."

He walked away, leaving Rebecca sitting there. She cried so much that after several minutes the owner of the sandwich van came over to see if she was alright, and ended up calling her a cab.

"I'm going to Milan. Just for the trial period, to see how it goes. No definite decisions." She was sitting beside him on his sofa.

"That's it then," said Steve quietly. His chest hurt.

"What?"

He could tell that she knew damn well what he meant. He shrugged. "It's over. Our relationship. If that's what you can call

「根本不是這回事，你知道的。」

「我什麼都不知道了，麗貝卡。這真的傷了我。當我們睡在一起的時候，我在想，我們會一起去什麼地方，這對我來說要很有意義、很特別的。但對你來說就顯然不是什麼大事，我想我一定是太守舊了。甚至我沒有贏到足夠的地位讓你告訴我生活中的大事，不是嗎？」

她眨了眨眼睛。「哦，對不起，我原來沒有看到有合同訂明了，和你上床的意思就是要必須立即向你報告我的生活中發生的一切！」

「你不用。但是，這是，麗貝卡，這是很重要的事。」

一陣沉默。麗貝卡覺得她好像快要吐了。她在想還好他們在運河附近，她感覺異常地虛幻和超脫。「也許我們應該先用點時間去想想再談論這件事。」

「如果你想，但是，在我的立場，需要去思考的人是你。因為我怎麼想都沒有用，是吧。你已經證明了這一點。」他把吃剩的午餐扔進垃圾桶，蓋子沒有蓋上，他就野蠻地砰一聲扔下它，轉身就走了。

「我明天會見到你嗎？」她討厭她的聲音在顫抖。

「如果你想就過來，羅拉七點會出去。」

他離去了，留下麗貝卡坐在那裡。她哭得非常厲害，而幾分鐘後三明治麵包車的店主走過來看看她怎麼樣，然後幫她叫了出租車。

「我會去米蘭，只是試用期，去看看是怎麼回事。還沒有明確的決定。」她走到沙發上坐在他的身邊。

「那麼就這樣吧。」史堤夫平靜地說，他感到胸口痛。

「什麼？」

他可以該死的告訴她是什麼意思。他聳聳肩。「結束了。我們的關係。如果你有稱它為關係。」

她滿臉通紅。「我告訴你，我還沒有任何決定。」

「來吧，你不會只是去一個試用期的，如果你不考慮接受這份工

it."

She flushed. "I told you, I haven't decided anything yet."

"Come on, you wouldn't be going for this trial period if you weren't considering taking the job, would you. And that leaves us nowhere."

"That's not true."

"It's my fault, I suppose, for presuming we were heading in the same direction. Of course you weren't looking for anything serious, because—"

"I didn't say that—"

"—you knew you were considering moving abroad. I wish I'd known that was the deal. I thought things were going well, that we'd carry on." Say all of it, the voice in his head demanded. Get angry. Tell her that you thought she cared for you as much as you do her, and that it breaks your heart that she would even consider moving thousands of miles away.

"I'm committed now, I have to go. All that agonising I was doing went out the window when I got angry." She smiled bleakly. "In the end I said yes just like that. But I don't want us to end like this." Tears were shining in Rebecca's eyes. "I don't want us to end at all."

"What did you think would happen, Rebecca? Did you really think I'd say, 'Great! You're going to live in Milan, we'll have to plan our dates a bit more in advance'? You're the one who's brought this to an end by deciding to move to Italy."

"But I haven't! I'm only going for two months—in 9 weeks time I'll be back in the UK. Are you saying our relationship can't stand 9 weeks without seeing each other? You could come out for a holiday."

"No. I'm saying our relationship can't stand 9 weeks of not knowing if it's the last 9 weeks." He shook his head. "I can't stand to get in any deeper. It's bad enough to know that our relationship – that I – wasn't even a factor when you were considering this, but to wait for 9 weeks, missing you, not sure what's going to happen, and then maybe find out in the end it's all coming to an end anyway... even worse if I come out there on holiday. I can't do that. It's not fair of you to ask me to."

He couldn't look at her. Tears were clogging his throat. He'd

作，是吧。而現在就離開好了。」

「不是這樣的。」

「那麼我想這是我的錯，因為我假定了我們是朝著同一方向。當然，你並不是找任何認真的關係，因為...」

「我沒有說過...」

「你知道你正在考慮移居國外。我希望我知道這是只是一場交易。我希望事情進展順利，而我們會繼續生活下去。」他的腦袋有個聲音要求他把一切說出來。生氣吧，告訴她，你以為她很關心你就像你關心她一樣，而她甚至考慮搬到千里之外，這樣是多麼令你傷心。

「我已經決定了，我現在得要走。當我生氣的時候，我會控制不了做出使大家都很痛苦的事。」她蒼涼地微笑著。「最後，沒錯，我說的就是這樣了。但我不希望我們就這樣結束。」眼淚在麗貝卡的眼裡閃爍著。「我不希望我們結束。」

「你覺得會發生什麼，麗貝卡？難道你真的認為我會說：『太好了！你要住在米蘭啊，那麼我們要提前一點計劃約會了。』？是你讓一切終止的，就是因為你決定去意大利。」

「但我沒有！我只打算去兩個月，就是九個星期，然後我就會回來英國。你是說我們的關係不能繼續下去是因為會有九個星期不能看到對方嗎？那麼你可以來度假。」

「沒有。我是說我們的關係不能繼續下去是因為不知道這九個星期是不是最後的九個星期。」他搖了搖頭。「我不能忍受再陷得更深了。現在已經足夠清楚我們的關係真的是糟糕透了，而我，從來都不是你考慮這件事的其中一個因素，但我卻要在九個星期裡，想念你，確定有沒有什麼事情發生，然後也許發現最後都是要結束...如果我去度假甚至可能會更糟。我不能這樣做，你叫我這樣做也不合理。」

他不能看著她，淚水已經堵塞了他的喉嚨。他之前有過這樣的九個星期，九個星期的希望和害怕，就是當他的父親接受一種新式治療的時候。而在結束時，給他們的又是另外九個星期不確定的假希望，痛苦和折磨。那使他感到完全無助，他是不會主動要自己去再次面對幾個星期害怕和希望。

「我們已經一起幾個星期了，這不算是長期，是嗎？然而，你卻因此而叫我不要花兩個月去嘗試找出我夢想的工作，只是因為它

waited 9 weeks for something before; 9 weeks of hoping and dreading while his Dad underwent a new form of treatment. And at the end, all it had given either of them was an extra 9 weeks of false hope, pain, and torturous uncertainty. It had made him feel completely helpless and he wasn't going to voluntarily put himself through weeks of that awful dreading and hoping again.

"We've been going out a few weeks – not really long-term, is it? Yet on the strength of that you're asking me not to spend two months trying to find out if my dream job lies elsewhere – and you accuse me of not being fair? "

"Long-term? What chance have you given us to become long-term?" He laughed humourlessly.

"So that's it?" she said, after a long silence. "You don't want to see me again?"

"Only as a friend," he said quietly, and ignored the sob that escaped her. "I still care about what happens to you, Rebecca. I can't just turn that off.. I really hope you get what you want." I just wish the thing you wanted most was me, he thought. That I was at least level-pegging with your career, not scrabbling around at the bottom of your list.

"I hope you get everything you want, too." Suddenly she was on her feet, pulling her jacket on. "Although you already have it," she said harshly. "Your cosy little café and Laura, and that's enough for you. How dare I want anything different, anywhere different, that isn't in your picture? I'm a jigsaw piece that doesn't fit into the gap you've got left, so you're right. Best to finish it right now." She fled towards the door. "Bye, Steve."

"Rebecca—" he was on his feet, wrenching open the front door she'd slammed a second before. "Rebecca!" She didn't even turn, throwing herself into her car. She was crying, but he fought the urge to go over and stop her driving away; what else could he say that would make a difference? It was Rebecca who was ruining this relationship. She couldn't expect him to hang around for a couple of months while she swanned round Milan, only for him to find she was abandoning him for good. Her employers might be prepared to do that; he wasn't.

When her car turned the corner, he shut the front door, feeling dazed. It was over. It couldn't be over. He'd spent so long wanting to be with her; had been so happy when they finally got together. How did it go so wrong, so quickly?

Because you should have known better, that's why. Should have

是在其他地方。你這種指責對我公平嗎？」

「長期？你有給過機會我們成為長期的嗎？」他缺乏幽默感地笑了笑。

「所以呢？」經過長時間的沉默之後她說。「你不想再見到我了嗎？」

「只可以作為一個朋友的身分，」他平靜地說，故意不理會她在抽泣。「我依然在乎發生在你身上的事，麗貝卡。我不能只是把它刪掉…我真的希望你得到你想要的。」我只是希望你最想要的是我，他在想。至少可以跟你的事業在同一個級別，而不是在你的列表中最後的一列中苦苦哀求著什麼。

「我也希望你得到你想要的。」她突然間站了起來，拿起她的外套。「雖然其實你已經擁有了，」她嚴厲地說。「你溫馨的小咖啡店和羅拉，你有這些就夠了。我怎麼敢要不在你的畫面裡不同的東西、不同的地方呢？我只是一塊不適合進入你的空隙中的拼圖，所以你說得對。最好還是現在就結束吧。」她走向門口。「再見了，史堤夫。」

「麗貝卡…」他站了起來，打開上一秒鐘她才重重地關上的門。「麗貝卡！」她甚至沒有回頭，直接撲入了車內。她在哭，但他努力克制自己去阻止她離去的衝動。他還能說什麼來扭轉這一切呢？是麗貝卡破壞這段關係的，她不能指望他一定要等她兩個月，而她自己卻在米蘭逍遙自在，所以他還是最好現在就放棄。她的僱主可能會準備要等她回來，但他不會。

當她的車轉過拐角時他把大門關上了，感覺茫然。結束了。不可能就這樣結束的。他想起自己花了這麼長時間就是想跟她在一起，而他們終於在一起的時候，他是多麼的開心。怎麼能這麼快就變得這麼糟糕？

因為你應該更加了解，這就是為什麼。應該早就知道你對她來說是不夠好。跟有事業心的人應該要保持距離的，要知道自己總是第二位。他去了廚房給自己倒一杯茶。

他很可能從痛苦中救了自己。她說到他已經有想要的一切，跟他「溫馨的小咖啡店」。她決不會接受他「只是」在咖啡店工作就可以幸福的，在她的眼中，這工作永遠只能權宜之計。她需要知道他會朝更高的地方去，像她這樣。那麼，這樣結束了是一件好事，總之是在他完全落後於她之前。

也許這不是全是她的錯。她不習慣有情感束縛去影響到她的決

known you weren't good enough for her. Should have stayed clear of someone so career-minded, knowing you'd always come second. He went to the kitchen to make himself a cup of tea.

He'd probably saved himself from a world of hurt. Her remark about him having everything he wanted, with his 'cosy little café', had been telling. She would never accept that he could be happy 'just' working in a café; in her eyes it could only ever be a stopgap. She needed to know he was headed somewhere higher, like her. A good thing, then, that this had ended now, before she left him behind altogether.

Perhaps it wasn't all her fault. She wasn't used to having emotional ties to affect her decisions. Since she'd lost her parents, she'd had nobody important enough to do that. Certainly not Kevin. The poor guy seemed nearly as gutted as he was.

He looked down and realised he was a cup of boiling water, with no sign of a teabag. He threw the teaspoon down and it clanged hard on the worktop. He resisted the urge to throw the cup after it too.

定。由於她失去了父母，她沒有重要的人令她做到這一點。當然凱文不是。這個可憐的傢伙幾乎跟他一樣失望。

他低下頭，意識到他拿著的只是一杯開水，沒有茶包在裡面。他把茶匙叮一聲丟在檯面上，然後再扔下了杯子。

Chapter Twenty Seven

Rebecca put her suitcase down and collapsed on to the bed. She lay on her back looking at the ceiling, waiting to cool down so that she could think straight. Even for Italy, even for April, this was hot. She had a mental image of her head as a red pepper.

Her apartment wouldn't be ready for another week but once she'd decided to go to Milan, she'd wanted to get there as quickly as possible; no time for more doubts or arguments. It also gave her a week's holiday before she started work, time she badly needed to clear her head after everything that had happened. Staying at the hotel would make it feel more like a holiday; if she'd moved straight into the apartment she would have started unpacking and buying food in. She relished the idea of eating out all week. Luxury!

Francois had recommended The Ravello to her. It was roughly halfway between the Castello and the Duomo, two of the city's major attractions, and it was reasonably priced too. The downside was that it didn't have its own restaurant, but that wasn't a problem here; she'd be spoilt for choice.

This was her first visit to Milan, but she wasn't going to rush to see everything at once. She wanted to save some trips for the rest of her time here. If she took the job permanently, of course, her 'time here' could be 'forever'. She shivered. Maybe after two months out here, that wouldn't be such a scary thought. She was grateful to Francois for giving her the chance to try out life here before making such a big decision.

Thinking of Francois made her sit up. If she lounged on the bed much longer, she'd fall asleep and waste the afternoon, and she was meeting him for dinner. She hung up her clothes and grabbed her wash kit. Everything else could wait; Milan couldn't. It was out there waiting to be discovered.

Twenty minutes later she was ready to hit the streets, wearing a much lighter dress and low-heeled sandals. She stepped out of the cool hotel lobby into the blindingly bright sunshine, armed

第二十七章

麗貝卡放下行李箱就倒在床上。她躺著望向天花板，等待自己冷卻下來，這樣她就可以思考。即使是意大利，即使是四月份，這裡仍然很熱。現在她腦海裡有一個心理圖像，就是一隻紅辣椒。

她的公寓要等到下星期才準備好，但她一決定了去米蘭，她就想盡快來這裡，讓自己沒有時間有更多的疑問或爭議。這樣還可以讓她在開始工作之前有一個星期的休假。在所有事情發生之後，她急需要清醒自己的頭腦。而入住酒店會更有度假的感覺，如果她直接入住入公寓，她就要開始拆包和購買食品。但她現在可以津津樂道地在外面享用一星期的餐飲。多豪華！

弗朗索瓦推薦拉斐洛酒店給她。這大約是在城堡和大教堂之間，就是兩個城市主要景點的中間，而且價格也很合理。唯一的缺點就是沒有自己的餐廳。但是，這不是一個問題，她在這裡選擇太多了。

這是她第一次到米蘭，但她不急於立即去遊覽所有地方。她想把一些行程留在她餘下的時間。如果她接受了這份工作，當然，她在這裡的時間就可能是「永遠」。她顫抖著，也許在這裡兩個月後，這就不會有那麼可怕的想法了。她感謝弗朗索瓦讓她有機會嘗試一下這裡的生活，然後才作出這樣重大的決定。

想起了弗朗索瓦，讓她立即坐了起來。如果她繼續懶洋洋地躺在床上更久一點，她就會睡著和浪費了整個下午，而且她還要跟他吃晚餐。她掛起了她的衣服，抓起她的梳洗包。一切都可以等待，但米蘭不可以，它就在這裡等著我去體驗。

二十分鐘後，她準備好出發了，身穿輕便的連衣裙和高跟涼鞋。她走出涼爽的酒店大堂走到刺眼明亮的陽光底下，手持她的指南和一張獨立的地圖。首先，她需要找個地方吃午飯。最好的地方是可以讓她坐下，觀察一下外面的風景，而桌子只要足夠大放她的指南和地圖就好。她想坐在陽光下作出計劃。

with her guidebook and a separate map. First, she needed to find somewhere to eat lunch. Preferably somewhere she could sit and watch the world go by for a while, with a table big enough for her guidebook and map. She wanted to sit in the sunshine and make plans.

She decided to go with the guidebook's suggestions on this first foray. Half an hour later she had walked and window-shopped her way to 'Bagutta', a small restaurant with an attractive terrace. It had felt good to stretch her legs after travelling for hours.

She chose Risotto alla Milanese, a rice and saffron broth. It smelt divine as the waitress put it on the table, and tasted even better. Afterwards she sipped a rich, dark coffee and sat enjoying the sunshine on her face. It was great to be away from the stresses that life had piled on her lately.

Not that was heartbreak was one of them, though. How could it be? She hadn't known Steve that long; it would be crazy to be devastated about breaking up with him. If she'd have thought of him as her other half, she would have told him about the Milan job, wouldn't she, so there was the proof. Why else would she have pushed it out of her mind every time she went to mention it to him?

She should have told him though. That's why she'd cried; they were tears of guilt, she told herself. Yes, that was it. It was lucky he'd only wanted some fun, a 'casual relationship', though she'd been surprised to discover that. She'd thought he was the type of man who would see where a relationship took him, not dismiss long-term relationships out-of-hand. Maybe raising Laura, a long-term commitment in itself, had made him shy away from long-term commitment in romantic relationships; that was lucky because it meant she knew his anger was just because his male pride was dented, nothing else. He'd soon get over it.

They'd had a perfectly civil lunch before she left; she'd given him her Easter cactus to look after and he had given her a trowel with her name on it. That's why she'd cried again, of course, not because her heart was breaking. Then he'd given her a kiss on the cheek and left. No hard feelings.

So why was she so miserable? And if fun was all Steve wanted, why had he been so devastated?

She gave herself a mental shake. This wasn't getting her anywhere. She ate a tiny zabaglione for dessert while reading her guidebook, and by the time she'd finished the last light, delicious bite, she had chosen her excursion for the afternoon. The Museo

在首次進軍此地，她決定去指南建議的地方。半小時後，她邊走邊逛商店到了她的「芭古達」，有一個迷人露台的一家小餐廳。在遊覽了幾個小時後，她伸展了一下雙腿，感覺很好。

她選擇了米蘭燉飯，就是大米加上蕃紅花粉湯。當女服務員把它放在桌子上時她就已經聞到一股神聖的氣味了，而吃起來味道甚至是更好。之後她啜飲著濃郁的黑咖啡，享受著陽光照在她的臉上。真的很開心，她已經把最近的生活壓力拋得老遠了。

然而他們其中一個並不是那麼心碎。怎麼可能呢？她不是認識史堤夫很久，但與他分手真的是瘋狂的折磨。如果她認為他是她的另一半，她應該會告訴他關於米蘭的工作，但她沒有，所以證明了一切。否則為什麼她每次想跟他說的時候都把它推到腦後呢？

她應該要告訴他的。所以為什麼她會哭，因為那是愧疚的淚水，她是這樣告訴自己。是的，它是。很幸運地他只希望找點樂趣，一段「非正式的關係」，雖然她發現這點覺得很驚訝。因為她以為他會是那種可帶她走到某一個階段的人，而且不排除可以建立長遠關係的男人。也許是因為羅拉，她本身就是一個長期承諾，所以令他迴避在戀愛關係中的長期承諾。這是幸運的，因為這代表了她知道他的憤怒僅僅是因為他男性的自尊心受到打擊，而沒有別的原因。他可以很快就挺過去的。

在她離開之前，他們有一起吃了一個文明的午餐，她讓他幫她看顧她的復活節仙人球，而他就送了一把有她名字的抹泥刀給她。這就是為什麼她又哭了起來，當然，不是因為她的心碎。然後，他吻了一下她的臉頰並離開了。感覺已經不再那麼難受。

那麼，為什麼她要如此淒慘呢？如果史堤夫只想找點樂趣，為什麼他看上去如此傷心呢？

她抖了抖精神，但這對她沒有任何用處。她一面在吃一件細小的薩巴里安尼作為甜點，一面讀著她的指南，當她完成了最後美味的一小口的時候，她已經選擇了下午遊覽的地方。米蘭博物館就在拐角處，她發現步行到那裡不用五分鐘。

鼓足勁的她準備出發去進行第一個冒險，但差點忘了拿她的太陽鏡就走了。她轉身撿起來，在餐廳窗口有一些動靜吸引住她的視線。她肯定窗簾之前是拉起來的，亦同樣肯定它剛被猛烈地拉動過。她皺起了眉頭。有人對自己的隱私是相當小心眼，真的是！那他們就不應該在外面吃飯。她戴上太陽鏡上並往博物館出發。

di Milano was just around the corner, she'd discovered; less than five minutes walk.

Fired up at the prospect of her first adventure, she nearly walked away without her sunglasses. She turned back to pick them up and a sudden movement in the restaurant window caught her eye. She was sure the curtain was pulled back earlier, and equally sure it had just been twitched across. She frowned. Someone was rather touchy about their privacy, weren't they! They shouldn't eat out, then. She put her sunglasses on and set off for the museum.

"It's just that I've never been offered this kind of opportunity before."

Steve closed his eyes. He hadn't expected her to ring. He was trying to get over her. "I understand that," he said quietly, keeping all emotion out of his voice.

"It might never happen again."

"I know. That's why I would never ask you to give it up. I wanted the chance to discuss it. Or at least have time to get used to the idea."

There was a long pause.

"Steve, I—I know I've no right to ask this of you, but please could you reconsider coming out here? I've got five days off at the end of the month, and I really need to talk to you. There are a lot of things I haven't said. Questions I need to ask too."

He didn't know what to say.

"I'd love to spend more time with you, Steve. Just the two of us, away from everything else." Her voice wobbled a little. "I miss you."

Away from everything? Not away from Milan, he thought, and Milan was the problem. The elephant in the room. And she was missing him? Huh! Perhaps she should have thought of that before.

And yet.... "I might be able to. I'll ask Tony, although he's not been feeling that well this week."

"What's wrong with him?"

「只是我從來沒有得到過這種機會。」

史堤夫閉上了眼睛，他沒想到她會打電話來。他正在試圖把她忘掉。「我明白。」他平靜地說，保持不把所有的情感從聲音透露出來。

「而且這可能不會再發生。」

「我知道。這就是為什麼我從來沒有叫你放棄它。我只是希望有機會跟你去討論，或至少有時間去習慣這個念頭。」

一個長時間的停頓。

「史堤夫，我…我知道我沒有權利去問你，但你可不可以重新考慮過來這裡嗎？我在月底前有五天假期，我真的需要跟你談談。有很多事情我還沒有說，還有問題我要問。」

他不知道該說些什麼。

「我很樂意花更多的時間跟你一起，史堤夫。只是我們兩個人，遠離一切。」她的聲音有點晃了。「我很想念你。」

遠離一切？不是離開米蘭，他在想，米蘭就是個問題。真是房間裡的大象。那麼明顯，可你還是在忽略，那就一定有原因了。她真的想念他嗎？嘿！也許她之前應該要想到這點。

然而…「我也許可以。我會問東尼，但是他這個星期好像不太舒服。」
「他沒有什麼事吧？」

「我不知道。我會再看看怎樣。」他猶豫了一下。「但是，如果我能有幾天假期，我就會來。」

「謝謝你。」

「謝謝你邀請我，」他說，然後畏縮了一下。這不自然的禮貌是荒謬的。幾個星期前，他們才跟對方一起睡過。他不能再耍酷的了。「我也想你。」

「很好。」她帶哭腔地說。「我的意思，不是很好，但…」
「我知道你的意思。」

「那我得走了。再談吧。再見。」

"I don't know. I'll see how things go." He hesitated. "But if I can get a few days off, I'll come out."

"Thank you."

"Thanks for inviting me," he said, then cringed. This stilted politeness was ridiculous. A few weeks ago they were waking up next to each other. He couldn't play it cool. "I miss you too."

"Good." She sounded tearful. "I mean, not good, but—"

"I know what you mean."

"I've got to go. Talk to you soon. Bye."

"Bye."

「再見。」

Chapter Twenty Eight

Rebecca loved Milan. It was vibrant; a fantastic hub from which to explore this part of Italy, which was why when Steve came he would get a surprise. She'd booked a long weekend on Lake Garda, staying in a wonderful hotel in Sirmione.

She was loving her job, too. Loving the lack of red tape, and loving working for Ron and Francois. They'd gathered a great team around them: friendly, enthusiastic, and genuinely the cream of the crop. She felt overwhelmed, sometimes, by the thought that Ron and Francois considered her a worthy part of such an exalted group.

But she hated being away from Steve with every fibre of her being and missed him more than she thought possible. It was like bereavement; that was her only comparison. A constant dull misery that lurked under every laugh, every good meal, every sunny morning... she still appreciated all the good things, but they never erased that ache. It was always there, underneath.

She couldn't wait to see him. She was going to tell him how she felt, lay all her cards on the table and admit that he was more than just fun, to her, and ask him if he felt the same. She hoped he did. She hoped that's why he'd been so hurt and angry at her before.

If he said no... well, she would still be hurting. But she would stay here, because Steve was the only thing to go back for. She missed Kevin, but he'd already been out for a visit and she was guessing he'd be a regular visitor if she stayed here. If Steve said yes, then in five weeks she would go back to England for good. Steve had ties to England, and her heart had ties to Steve— several billion more than she'd suspected.

Now she was only waiting for Steve to phone and tell her was flight he was on, so she could pick him up at Bergamo airport.

"Tony? Are you okay?" Steve stopped in the kitchen doorway,

第二十八章

麗貝卡喜愛米蘭，這裡充滿生氣，一個夢幻般的中樞，從這裡開始探索意大利的這部分，這就是為什麼她認為當史堤夫到來，他一定會有驚喜。她訂了一個長週末在加爾達湖，住在西爾米奧奈的一間美妙的酒店。

她熱愛她的工作，喜愛這裡不用繁文縟節，喜愛跟羅恩和弗朗索瓦一起工作，他們聚集了一班很了不起的團隊，友好、熱情、真正的精英。有時她覺得有點不堪重負，因為羅恩和弗朗索瓦都認為她在如此崇高的一群人中是有價值的一員。

但她深深地痛恨自己要遠離史堤夫，她非常想念他，感覺就像喪親之痛，這是她唯一想到的比喻。這種沉悶的痛苦持續暗藏著在每一個笑容、每一頓飯、每一個陽光明媚的早晨之中…但她仍然感恩所有在這裡發生的好事，雖然它們永遠不能把痛楚磨滅，因為痛楚總是在那裡，就在深處。

她迫不及待想見他，她要告訴他她的感覺，毫無保留地說出一切及承認她不僅僅是為了樂趣，並問他是否有相同的感覺。她希望他是，她希望這就是他之前會如此受傷害和憤怒的原因。

如果他說沒有…嗯，她仍然會被傷害。但她會留在這兒，因為史堤夫是她唯一回去的理由。她也想念凱文，但他已經來過探望她了，而且她認為如果她要住在這裡的話，他應該會是一個常客。如果史堤夫說是的話，那麼在五個星期之後，她就會回到英格蘭。史堤夫在英格蘭有跟他有聯繫的人，而她的心聯繫著史堤夫，比她所想的多數十億以上。

現在她只等待史堤夫的電話，告訴她航班，那麼她就可以去貝加莫機場去接他。

「東尼？你沒事吧？」史堤夫在廚房門前停了下來，手裡拿著一盒糖漿瓶。

holding a box of syrup bottles.

Tony was sitting on the chair in the corner of the kitchen; Steve hadn't even realised he was there until he turned to push open the kitchen door with his hip. Tony never sat down. He looked grey.

"I'm fine. Fine," said Tony weakly, trying to smile as he mopped his face with his huge red hanky.

Steve frowned. What had been wrong with that picture? "Stay there," he said, pointlessly. Tony didn't look like he was going anywhere. He barrelled through the door and dumped the box beside Neil.

"Great, time for my break—"

"Sorry mate, you're holding the fort, Tony's ill."

He didn't give Neil time to answer. He'd realised what had looked wrong. Tony had been holding his hanky in his right hand, and he was left-handed. He bent down beside him, chilled by the sight of Tony's clammy face.

"Have you got chest pains?"

Tony nodded.

"I'm ringing 999."

"No, do not bother them with this small thing," he said hoarsely, shifting his bulk on the chair. "Is probably indigestion. Perhaps I forget to take tablet."

Steve was already tapping 999 into his mobile.

"Indigestion? So why aren't you using you left hand?"

Tony's eyes slid away. "Just a little pain, probably pulled muscle, is all."

Steve ignored him, asking for an ambulance. He found Tony's GTN spray in his coat pocket and popped an aspirin from the packet in the first aid cabinet, glad of the reassuring voice on the other end of the phone. Tony was weakly insisting that he was always sweaty; "I am a big boy, too big, you know!"

Five minutes later, the paramedics swept in the back door, dealing with Tony kindly and efficiently. Steve only had a couple

東尼坐在廚房角落的椅子上，史堤夫甚至沒有意識到他那裡，直到他轉身用臀部推開廚房門。東尼從來沒有這樣坐下，而他臉色看起來很差。

「我沒事，很好。」東尼微弱地說，試圖微笑並拿出巨大的紅色手帕擦著臉。

史堤夫皺起了眉頭。這個畫面有什麼不妥呢？「呆在那裡。」他說了毫無意義的話，東尼看起來並不像可以去哪裡。他走出門，開始翻著在尼爾旁邊的箱子。

「太好了，我的休息時間…」

「對不起伙計，你要先待著，東尼病了。」

他沒有給尼爾回答的時間，他已經意識到那看上去是有什麼不妥了。東尼用右手拿著他的手帕，但他是左撇子。他在他身旁彎下腰，看到東尼濕冷的臉給嚇了一跳。

「你胸口有痛嗎？」

東尼點點頭。

「我去打電話。」

「不，不要打擾他們，只是小事，」他用嘶啞的聲音說，他倒在椅子上。「可能只是消化不良，也許我忘了吃藥。」

史堤夫已經用手機在打緊急熱線。

「消化不良？那麼，為什麼你不用你的左手呢？」

東尼把眼睛溜開。「只是有點痛，可能是肌肉拉傷，就這樣而已。」

史堤夫不理他，要求救護車前來。他在東尼的上衣口袋裡發現硝酸甘油噴霧劑，並從急救櫃中找出一片阿司匹林，很高興聽到在電話的另一端令人安心的聲音。東尼很虛弱地堅持自己經常也滿身是汗，「我是一個大男孩，太大了，你知道的！」

五分鐘後，醫護人員捲席而至到了後門，親切和有效率地處理了東尼。在他們要送東尼去醫院之前，史堤夫只有一兩分鐘，盡可能地讓他們知道更多細節。他們離開後，史堤夫斜靠在櫃檯上發呆，好讓自己振作起來。醫護人員說，事實上東尼仍然清醒，而

of minutes to give them as many details as he could before they whisked Tony off to hospital. Steve leaned on the counter in a daze after they left, pulling himself together. The paramedics had said that the fact Tony was still conscious and talking was a good sign.

He began to tidy up things that had been moved out of the way to allow the paramedics room to work. The he stopped. What was he doing? He was meant to be ringing Maria, Tony's wife. He dialled her mobile.

Maria alternately cried and berated Tony, in his absence, for not taking his tablets and losing weight. "Always he is eating, enough for thirty men, Steve! I tell him no but he does not listen."

Steve tried to be reassuring, but in the end he had to cut her short. "Maria, don't you think you should be getting to the hospital now? Tony will want you there." He wasn't entirely sure this was true, from what he knew of them both, but it seemed the right thing to say.

"Yes. I must go. You are all right at the shop, Steve? If you have to shut, I understand."

"We'll try and stay open for the usual hours. Ring me when you have news. Take care."

"Of course. Ciao."

A look of relief swept over Neil's face as Steve came through the door. "There you are. What's going on? Someone said they saw an ambulance pull round the back."

"Suspected heart attack, I'm afraid," said Steve quietly.

Neil gave a low whistle. "God, I didn't think it was that serious. I'd have come through, but I was swamped out here. Is Tony going to be alright?"

Steve shrugged. "I hope so. He was still arguing, and the ambulance got here quickly. Fingers crossed."

"Poor guy."

"Yeah. I know it's short notice, mate, but could you stay until 7? Or even 6?"

"I can stay until 8 if you want."

且懂得說話的是一個好兆頭。

他開始收拾剛才為了讓醫護人員工作而移動了的東西。他停了下。他在做什麼？他應該要打電話給東尼的妻子瑪麗亞，他撥通了她的手機。

瑪麗亞趁東尼不在，不停在輪流地哭著然後斥責他，說他不吃藥又不肯減肥。「他總是一直在吃，足夠三十人的份量，史堤夫！我告訴他不要，但他不聽。」

史堤夫試圖讓她放心，但最終他不得不截停她的說話。「瑪麗亞，你不認為你現在應該去醫院嗎？東尼會想你在。」以他認識的他們，他不完全確定這是真實，但現在似乎最正確的就是說這個。

「是的。我要去。你在店裡沒事吧，史堤夫？如果你需要關店，我會明白的。」

「我們會盡量維持正常的開放時間。如果你有消息就打電話給我。保重。」

「當然。再見。」

當史堤夫通過門看看出面的時候，看見尼爾鬆一口氣地望著他。

「你在這裡。怎麼回事呢？有人說他們看到一輛救護車駛了去後面。」

「疑似是心臟病發作，我恐怕是。」史堤夫平靜地說。

尼爾吹了一個低低的口哨。「天啊，我還以為沒有那麼嚴重。我應該要進來看看怎麼回事的，但我在外面忙得不可開交。東尼還好嗎？」

史堤夫聳聳肩。「我希望沒事。救護車很快就來到這裡，那時候他還在爭論著呢。一起祈禱吧！」

「可憐的傢伙。」

「是啊。我知道有點突然，伙計，但你能一直留到七點嗎？或者六點？」

「我可以一直待到八點，如果你想。」

"Cheers. I'm happy to lock up, but I'd like to cash up before you go, so everything's above board."

"Dude, you know Tony would be totally cool with you cashing up by yourself."

"You're probably right, but I'd feel happier if you at least checked my totals."

Neil slapped his shoulder. "Whatever you want. No problem, boss," he grinned.

Boss? That made him feel uncomfortable, but also, strangely—proud, if that was the right word.

What would happen tomorrow? Would Tony want him to be in charge, or would he pick someone else? Or not well enough to even think about it?

He would take charge tomorrow, unless he heard anything to the contrary. Rinaldo had been there longer than him but it was his day off. But then he'd ring Maria and ask her what to do. He loved working at the café, but he didn't feel happy giving the orders without Tony's blessing; laying down the law and dealing with suppliers was Tony's job.

He wasn't sure he could fill Tony's handmade, Italian, and not inconsiderable, shoes.

The phone rang and Rebecca's heart gave a happy jolt. She didn't get many calls to the landline, and she'd already spoken to Francois thus evening. It must be Steve.

Rebecca curled her legs up under her on the sofa. "Hello, you. Everything sorted? Flights booked?" She couldn't stop smiling; it was so good to hear his voice.

"No, they're not, I'm afraid."

There was a pause. A small cold needle of dread dug into her stomach.

"I'm sorry, but I can't get away."

"Can't? Or won't?" She said harshly.

Steve made no reply.

「太好了。我可以負責鎖門，但我想在你離開之前先結算，那麼一切都光明正大的。」

「老兄，你知道東尼會很開心，你可以自己結算了。」

「你可能是對的，但如果你可以檢查一下我的總結，我會覺得更開心。」

尼爾拍了拍他的肩膀。「無論你想要什麼都沒問題，老闆。」他笑了。

老闆？這讓他感到不舒服，而且，奇怪，是自豪，這應該是正確的詞語吧。

明天會怎樣呢？東尼會希望他當負責人嗎？或是他會選別人呢？或者他沒有康復到可以好好地想這件事？

他明天還是會繼續當負責人，除非他聽到任何反對的聲音。里納爾多在這裡工作比他長時間，但今天是他的休息日。但他隨後可能會打電話給瑪麗亞，並要求她做什麼。他喜歡在咖啡店工作，但他沒有得到東尼的准許是不會感到高興的，制定規則和跟供應商打交道都是東尼的工作。

而且他不肯定自己可以做到東尼的手工製作，意大利式的，這是不可小視的部分。

電話響起，麗貝卡的心頭有一陣幸福的晃動。不會有很多人打她的固定電話，而她晚上跟弗朗索瓦已經談過了，這必定是史堤夫。

麗貝卡把腿捲曲在沙發上。「嗨，你好。一切安排好了？預訂了機票了嗎？」她無法停止地微笑，聽到他的聲音是那麼好。

「不，不是這樣，我恐怕。」

停頓了一陣子。一支冰冷而恐懼的小針刺進了她的胃。

「我很抱歉，但我無法脫身。」

「不能嗎？還是不想？」她嚴厲地說。

史堤夫沒有回答。

"Are you telling me Tony won't give you the time off? Or is it Laura?" Rebecca tried to calm down. "Is she okay?"

"Laura's fine. And it's can't, not won't. Thanks for letting me explain."

Rebecca winced at his tone, but knew she deserved it. "Sorry, that wasn't fair. It's just that I've been looking forward to seeing you. And afraid you might change your mind," she added softly.

"I haven't changed my mind. In fact, the more I thought about it..." He took a deep breath. "God, this isn't a good time to discuss this. But I'm not ready to give up on us just yet. Even though I'm probably a fool, heading for a broken heart."

"That makes me feel so guilty." Tears were pricking in her eyes.

"I understand it's not easy for you either, but I'm left waiting to know where my life is going."

"But why? This is what you wanted, isn't it? A casual relationship."

"You said that before. But when did I ever say that?"

"You didn't."

"So I gave you that impression how, exactly?"

"You... well didn't, I suppose, but Laura – never mind."

Steve's voice was sharp. "What did Laura say?"

"Look, I don't want to get her into trouble for giving away your secrets—"

His voice sliced across hers. "What did she say, Rebecca?"

"She said you'd put on your profile that you weren't looking for a long-term relationship."

There was a long silence that Rebecca was too nervous to break.

"Did she now? The lying bitch," Steve spat.

"Steve, don't be angry at her! She probably—"

"Angry? Oh, I'm way beyond angry. How dare she interfere in my life!"

「你是不是要告訴我，東尼不給你休假？抑或是羅拉？」麗貝卡試著冷靜下來。「她還好嗎？」

「羅拉很好。是不可以，不是不想。非常感謝你讓我解釋。」

麗貝卡對他的語氣有點畏縮，但她知道自己是活該的。「對不起，這是不公平的。只是，我一直在期待你過來找我，而且又怕你可能會改變主意。」她輕聲地補充。

「我並沒有改變主意。事實上，我想了更多…」他深吸了一口氣。「天啊，這不是討論這些的時侯，但我還沒有準備要放棄我們的關係。儘管我可能是一個傻瓜，準備要讓自己心碎了。」

「這讓我感到很內疚。」眼淚刺痛了她的眼睛。

「我明白對你來說是不容易的，但我要留下來等待直到我知道人生應該是怎麼回事。」

「但是為什麼呢？這不是你想要的嗎？一段非正式關係。」

「你以前也有提及過。但我什麼時候說過呢？」

「你沒有。」

「所以我給了你這樣的印象，是嗎？」

「你…好吧，不是，我想，但羅拉…沒關係了。」

史堤夫的聲音變得很尖銳。「羅拉說了什麼？」

「你看，我就是不希望因為她說了你的秘密而讓她陷入困境…」

他的聲音劃破了她的說話。「她說了什麼，麗貝卡？」

「她說你在個人資料上是這樣寫的，你不是在尋找一段長期的關係。」

一段長時間的沉默，但麗貝卡因為太緊張而不敢去打破它。

「她做到了？說謊的婊子。」史堤夫吐了下口水。

「史堤夫，不要生她的氣！她大概…」

「生氣？噢，我已經超越了生氣。她怎麼敢干涉我的生活！」

Rebecca hesitated. "So it's not true then?"

"No. I told the truth, which was that I was interested in meeting new people and was happy to see where it went; I wasn't looking for a long-term partner specifically but wasn't opposed to the idea either."

"That's pretty much what I put," she said quietly.

"Really? Because, big surprise, that's not what she told me."

She'd never heard him so bitter, but she was starting to feel the same. "Laura talked to you about my profile too?"

"Oh yes. Said you wanted a relationship, but nothing that would get in the way of your career, because that would always come first. That was when she dropped the Milan job into the conversation."

"She was never meant to know about that. I wanted to discuss it with you properly, although I know I left it far too late." Rebecca's head was spinning, trying to put it altogether. "I know she's done an awful thing, Steve, but she might have a good reason."

"Like what?"

"Maybe she's scared of sharing you, or even worse, losing you. You've always been there for her, and she's always had you to herself. Perhaps she sees me as a threat to that, especially now you two are so close. She's probably not sure where her place would be if we were together. You know," she floundered, "properly together."

"Perhaps." Steve didn't sound convinced. "She could have talked to me about it though."

"How would she start that conversation? Maybe she was afraid you would get angry."

Steve chuckled suddenly. "Do you always have to be so bloody reasonable about everything?"

"Sorry. It's the scientist in me. I look for all possible explanations." She paused. "Steve, I didn't consider the Milan job until Laura told me that. I would never have gone."

"Really?"

"Yes, unless you wanted to try living out here too."

麗貝卡猶豫了一下。「所以，那不是真的呢？」

「不是。我說了實話，就是我有興趣去結識新朋友，並想看看會進展到什麼程度，我不是特別地在尋找一個長期的伴侶，但並沒有抗拒。」

「這幾乎跟我的一樣。」她平靜地說。

「真的嗎？因為，真是一個大驚喜，她不是這樣告訴我的。」

她從來沒有見過他這樣懷恨在心，但她開始有同樣的感覺。「羅拉有跟你談到過我的個人資料嗎？」

「哦，是的。說你想要一段關係，但不可以涉足你的職業生涯，因為它將永遠是第一位。她是在談到你要去米蘭工作的時候說的。」

「她從來就不知道這件事。我是想與你好好討論的，雖然我知道我遲了。」麗貝卡感到有點頭暈，她試圖把所有事情整理一一遍。「我知道她做了一件可怕的事，史堤夫，但她可能是有很好的理由。」

「什麼理由？」

「也許她害怕跟別人分享你，或者更糟的是，失去你。你一直都在她身邊，她總是有你陪伴著。也許她認為我是一個威脅，特別是現在你們兩人如此親近。她也許不知道自己的位置，如果我們在一起。你知道，」她掙扎了一下，「真正的在一起。」

「也許。」史堤夫聽起來還是不服氣。「儘管如此，她應該來找我談。」

「她要如何去談呢？也許她是怕你會生氣。」史堤夫突然笑了起來。「你總是要那麼該死的將一切合理化嗎？」

「對不起。因為我是個科學家。我會尋找所有有可能的解釋。」她停頓了一下。「史堤夫，在羅拉告訴我之前，我從沒有考慮米蘭的工作，不然我絕不會走的。」

「真的嗎？」

「是的，除非你也想試試在這裡過生活。」

「天啊，麗貝卡，我...真是亂七八糟的。這令我心碎了，我以為

"God, Rebecca, I... what a mess. It broke my heart to think I didn't even cross your mind."

"At least we've found out. When we see each other—"

"Rebecca, Tony's had a heart attack."

"Oh my God! Is he okay?"

"It could have been worse, he was lucky. He hasn't been taking his tablets or looking after himself too well. They're doing tests at the moment, but I get the impression it will be a while before he's back."

"That's awful. Poor Maria, too! Give them my love."

"I will."

"So who's running things?"

"Me, at the moment. His brother, Bernardo, is coming over to help out for a couple of weeks, but I don't think he'll hang around indefinitely. He's got his own business to run."

Rebecca was upset about Tony, but the heaviness in her heart came mainly from disappointment at the thought of not seeing Steve, and disappointment in Laura, too. She'd tried so hard to make her feel part of things at the museum, and to give her a sense of pride in herself and a sense of purpose. Despite the excuses she'd made for her, this felt like betrayal; like having everything she'd done for Laura thrown back in her face. Surely she wasn't that horrible. Was the prospect of her as Steve's long-term girlfriend so terrible?

"Rebecca?"

"Sorry. Just trying to take it all in."

"I know the feeling."

"So you won't be able to come out here at all? Because I might be able to save a couple of days' leave and have a long weekend later."

"I don't know. Neil's off back-packing soon—he was meant to go at the end of last week, he's already giving us an extra fortnight. He's a good lad."

Rebecca laughed weakly. "Good lad? Listen to you, Granddad."

你心目中甚至沒有我。」

「至少我們已經知道了。我們是怎樣看待對方的…」

「麗貝卡，東尼心臟病發作了。」

「噢，天啊！他還好嗎？」

「有可能會更糟糕的，但他已經很幸運了。他只是並沒有好好吃藥和照顧自己。現在他們正在做一些測試，但我覺得他要好一段時間之後才可以回來。」

「太可怕了。還有可憐的瑪麗亞！幫我向他們問好。」

「我會的。」

「那麼，誰在運作店裡的事？」

「暫時是我。他的弟弟貝爾納會過來幫忙幾個星期，但我認為他不會無限期地逗留，因為他也有自己的業務要經營。」

麗貝卡對東尼的事感到難過，但她心裡的沉重感主要來自不能見到史堤夫的失望，還有對羅拉的失望。她那麼努力讓她知道博物館的事情，讓她對自己有自豪感和存在感。儘管她為她找了藉口，但感覺就像被背叛了，就像她為羅拉所做的一切，她都毫不

領情。當然，她並不是那麼可怕。她是史堤夫的長期女友這個前景有如此駭人嗎？

「麗貝卡？」

「對不起。我只是在試圖吸收這些事。」

「我知道這種感覺。」

「那麼，你將無法來這裡了？因為我可能可以節省兩天的假期，之後才放一個長週末。」

「我不知道。尼爾很快就要開始他的背包之旅，他本來是在上週;末就要走了，但他已經答應為我們留下來多兩週。他真是個好孩子。」

麗貝卡微弱地笑道。「好孩子？聽你的，爺爺。」

「我知道，」史堤夫沮喪地說。「有一種指揮的壓力，它讓我都

"I know," said Steve ruefully. "It's the pressure of command. It's made me come over all mature."

Hearing him make jokes again made her miss him more than ever. "I can't believe I won't see you for five six weeks."

"It feels like a lifetime." He sighed. "I'll phone when I can, but—"

"You're really busy."

"Yeah, I am. Trying to do Tony's job as well as mine might send me nuts, eventually."

"You're not making the wraps?" She needed to bring some light-heartedness back into this conversation; otherwise she was going to grizzle.

"Sometimes. Neil and I take it in turns."

"Surely they're not as good as Tony's, though?"

"Hey, I've had no complaints!"

"That's because everyone's making allowances."

"Probably. Rebecca, I'd better go. Sorry but I've got orders to look through before bed, and I'm in at 6 to start the breakfasts."

"Ouch. I'll let you go, then. Phone me when you can?"

"Of course. Take care."

"You too. I miss you," she blurted.

"I miss you too. So much," His voice was rough. "Bye."

"Bye."

The tears were streaming down her face before she clicked the handset back into place.

成熟起來了。」

聽到他再次開玩笑，讓她比之前更加想念他。「我真的不敢相信我沒見你已經有五六個星期。」

他嘆了口氣說：「感覺就像過一輩子。如果我可以，我會打電話給你，但是…」

「你真的很忙。」

「是啊，我試著做東尼的工作，希望我最終不會是自找苦吃。」

「你不會要做肉卷吧？」她需要用一些輕鬆的心情回到這次的談話，否則她會開始不停地抱怨。

「有時候會。我和尼爾會輪流做。」

「雖然一定沒有東尼做的好？」

「嘿，我已經沒有任何怨言了！」

「那是因為大家都體諒。」

「應該是吧。麗貝卡，我要掛線了，對不起，但我睡前還有一些訂單需要翻閱一下，而我在六點就要開始早餐時段。」

「哎喲，那麼我讓你去工作了。可以的話會打電話給我嗎？」

「當然。保重。」

「你也是。我好想你。」她脫口而出。

「我也想你，非常，」他聲音沙啞地說。「再見。」

「再見。」

眼淚流在她的臉上，她按了一下話機並把它放回原位。

Chapter Twenty Nine

Rebecca was buzzing. The concert had been fantastic, although she hadn't expected it to be so long. There had been so many encores at the end, and when it was clear that all the singers had left the stage and could not be tempted back yet again, the audience was slow to move. Many of them shuffled in long queues towards the two bars, which were aggravatingly between the auditorium and the exits, their queues stretching back and partially blocking auditorium's exit doors.

By the time she escaped out into the cooler, wonderfully welcome night air, she was over an hour later than she'd expected to be. Under the bright lights, the streets glistened after the showers that had drenched them on her way there in the taxi. She wished Steve was here; she'd brought him a ticket. She'd had to cancel the Lake Garda break.

The sky was clear now and stars were beginning to appear. It was a lovely night. She would walk home, she decided suddenly. There were plenty of people around, and although it was late, it wasn't the dead of night. It wouldn't take her more than twenty minutes, surely, and she'd avoid the narrow, curving alleyways. It would be good for her, she thought, burn off some of the calories she'd consumed this evening—some, not all. She'd had three glasses of wine and a generous helping of gelato.

She set off, sticking to the well-lit main roads; easy to do in this part of the city. As she got further from the opera house, though, the crowds dwindled rapidly, and fifteen minutes later there was only one other person in view, taking the left turning ahead. She got to the corner and checked out the turning. She knew it would take her in the right direction, but it was narrow and more sparsely lit. She took out the small, foldaway street map that lived in her handbag and stood under the streetlight.

Good. She wasn't too far away from home now. But the quickest route was through narrower back roads, likely to contain only rows of houses. Rows of houses that were likely, at this hour, to be as quiet and dark as the small streets themselves. Or she

第二十九章

麗貝卡仍在餘音繞樑。演唱會太棒了，雖然她沒有預料到時間會這麼長。到最後有這麼多次的安歌，當很清楚所有的歌手都離開了舞台，不會再次返回台上，全場人才開始移動緩慢。他們當中有許多人拖著腳大排長龍走向兩個柵欄，就在禮堂和出口之間，這令他們的長隊開始綿延，而且部分更擋住了出口。

直到她逃出來迎接到涼快而奇妙的晚間空氣的時候，已經比她預計晚了一個多小時。經過雨水淋浴後，濕漉漉的街道在明亮的燈光下閃閃發光。她有給史堤夫買了一張票，她希望他在這裡。但她現在不得不取消加爾達湖的假期。

天高雲淡，現在星星開始出現了。這是一個可愛的夜晚。她突然決定要走路回家。雖然已經很晚了，但周圍的人仍然有很多，這還不是夜深人靜的時間。而且不用二十多分鐘就回到去，當然她會避免走進狹窄彎曲的小巷。她在想這也只是為自己好的，這樣就可以燃燒掉今晚她消化掉的一點熱量，但不是全部。她喝了三杯酒和吃了很大的一客冰淇淋。

她啟程並保持在光線充足的主要道路上，在這樣的一個城市裡，這是很容易做到。當她進一步從歌劇院走遠，熙熙攘攘的人群迅速減少了，十五分鐘後，視線內就只剩另外一個人，他準備在前方左轉。她到達的轉角處，確認一下應該往哪邊走。她知道那是她的正確方向，但路很狹窄，而且人煙稀少。她在手袋裡拿出折疊得細小的街道地圖，站在路燈下。

很好。她現在離家不遠了。但最快的路線就是要通過狹窄的小

路，那裡好像只有一排房子。有可能是一排排的房子，在這個時間，小街道本身就已經夠安靜和黑暗了。或者，她可以繼續走半英里到盡頭回到大路去，從那裡她可能需要用更長的時間，走更迂迴的路線回家。

她仔細考慮著，比較安全的路是更長的，在穿著這種高跟鞋的情

could carry on; in half a mile this road ended at a major one, and from there she could take a longer, more circuitous route home.

She debated. The longer route was the safer one, but would take at least another twenty minutes in these heels. The back roads would have her home in under ten minutes. The effects of the wine had worn off along with her sense of joie de vivre. Now she was weary, painfully aware of the burning sensation in the balls of her feet and the beginning of a blister on her right heel. She dithered a moment, then set off down the turning, trying to set a cracking pace. Her handbag was gripped tightly in her right hand, partly to keep it safe, and partly to keep her safe. She would stay alert, and if anyone tried anything it would be a handbag blow to the head, preferably with the pointy metal crossover clasp pointing towards the attacker's eyes.

Five minutes later she was thanking her lucky stars she'd taken this route. Every step was torture now. The few people she'd passed had either ignored her or smiled.. Ahead of her in the distance, she could see the turning that would take her nearly all the way to her front door. She would soon be home, thank God, because she'd been reduced to a hobble and it had taken twice as long as she'd predicted. She didn't dare take her shoes off because in the dim light she might step on anything.

She heard a noise and stopped. Not the most sensible thing to do, she scolded herself. It sounded as if someone had kicked a can. She looked back behind her but could see nobody. Perhaps the noise had been further away than it seemed. She carried on, going a little faster. Even though this road was only two turnings away from her front door, she'd had no reason to take this route before and didn't know the street at all. She hadn't passed anyone for several minutes and the stillness and quiet was starting to freak her out.

In front of her the road curved and became narrower. There was barely room for a car here and the road surface gave way to cobbles. Another noise made Rebecca glance over her shoulder, but again there was nobody there. Maybe it was just a cat prowling the street. But it made her edgy. She tried to urge her feet to go faster, but she'd reached the cobbles now, still slippery from the rain..

Another noise. Louder. Dark space on the left. A flicker of movement within it. Turning her head. A face. A split second of recognition.

Imploding pain in her head. A scream that resounded inside it, unable to escape. Crushing force driving her to her knees. Joints

況下，至少需要再走多二十分鐘。小路就可以讓她十分鐘就回到家中。酒的影響逐漸消失，伴隨著她是貪一時之快的感覺。現在她已經很疲倦，痛苦地意識到在她腳跟上的燒灼感，而她的右腳後跟上開始長出水泡了。

她猶豫了一下，然後轉了個彎，試圖展開一個極快的步伐。她的右手緊握著手袋，一方面是保證它的安全，一方面也讓自己安心。她提高警覺，如果有人嘗試做些什麼事，她會用手袋擊他的頭部，最好是用尖尖的金屬扣攻襲襲擊者的眼睛。

五分鐘之後，她感謝她的幸運之星令她選擇了這條路。現在每一步都是折磨。她一路上有遇到幾個人，他們不是不理會她就是對她微笑...在她前面不遠，她能看到一個轉角處，那裡差不多就要到她家了。她很快就會回到家，感謝上帝，因為她沒那麼步履蹣跚了，之前的路已經用了她預測的兩倍時間。她不敢把她的鞋脫下來，因為在昏暗的燈光下，她可能會踩到什麼。

她聽到一些聲音令她停了下來。這不是一個明智的決定，她在罵自己。聽起來好像有人踢到了一個罐。她回頭看下身後，但看不到什麼人。也許噪音比感覺的還要遠。即使路上只剩下兩彎就到她家，她還要走快一點。在她不知道這街道的情況下，她之前真的沒有理由決定走這條路。在過去的幾分鐘，她沒有遇見任何人，寂靜與寧靜令她感到非常不安。

在她前面的路又彎又窄。只可以勉強讓汽車通過，而路面舖上了鵝卵石。另一下聲音使麗貝卡再回頭看了一眼，但也沒有人在。也許只是一隻貓在街上竄來竄去。但她開始心急如火了，她試圖催促自己的腳走快一點，但她現在走在鵝卵石上，還因為雨水令它變得濕滑了...

另一下聲音，響亮的。在左側的黑暗處有東西一閃已過。她轉頭一看，有一張瞬間就認得出來人臉。

她的頭感到一陣內爆的痛楚。一聲尖叫在裡面響徹了，但逃脫不了。一陣破碎感傳到她的膝蓋，是她跌倒令關節用力撞在鵝卵石上做成的。她腦海閃過一個想法，她真的無法忍受這種痛，太痛了...

漆黑一片。

麗貝卡意識到有聲音和痛楚。她大腦的一部分不斷催促她聽那些聲音，但似乎在這一刻佔著上風的另一部分告訴她留在休息和朦朧狀態，但最終那些聲音似乎變得更加清晰了。

jarring on the cobbles as she fell. The flashing thought that she couldn't endure this pain, it was too much-

Blackness.

Rebecca was aware of voices, and pain. Part of her brain nagged her to listen to the voices, but another part—and it seemed to have the upper hand at the moment—told her to stay in the easy, hazy state she was in. But eventually the voices seemed to become more distinguishable all by themselves.

She still couldn't move or open her eyes, but now she could hear every word clearly.

"That bitch should be locked up," a voice hissed.

"Steve, I—" Rebecca lost track of what was being said for a moment, trying instead to identify that voice. She struggled to retrieve memory. Ron? Was it Ron? But he had said Steve. They hadn't even met, had they? Why were they talking?

"She could have killed her, Ron. And I'm not convinced that wasn't what she intended!"

"I know you're angry and I understand, but this isn't helping Rebecca."

"I can't help her, I'm not a doctor!"

A doctor? What was wrong with her? She tried to reach out a hand but her fingers just twitched feebly.

"It's frustrating for all of us. If- Steve, I think she's coming round."

She knew he was coming closer. She could feel the warmth radiating from his body, smell his aftershave.

"Bec?"

His voice was gentle but urgent at the same time. With an immense effort she opened her eyes and then groaned at the lightning strike of pain.

"What is it, honey? Pain in your head?"

She only just stopped herself from nodding in response. Pure reflex, but she sensed it would have been agony, as would moving

她仍然動彈不得，也不能打開眼睛，但現在她能清楚地聽到每一個字。

「那婊子應該要被關起來。」一個聲音嘶聲地叫道。

「史堤夫，我…」麗貝卡沒法聽到之後的一段說話，她試圖認出那個聲音。她掙扎地尋找記憶。羅恩？羅恩？但他說史堤夫。他們甚至沒有見過面，有嗎？為什麼他們會談話呢？

「她差點就殺死了她，羅恩。而且我相信那是她真的有這個打算！」

「我知道你很生氣，我明白，但是這對麗貝卡沒有幫助。」

「我當然對她沒有幫助，我又不是醫生！」

醫生？她有什麼不妥嗎？她試圖伸出一隻手，但她的手指只是有氣無力地抽搐了一下。

「這讓我們所有人都折騰了。如果…史堤夫，我想她甦醒了。」

她知道他靠近了，她能感覺到從他的身體發放的溫暖，聞到他鬚後水的味道。

「貝卡？」

他的聲音很溫柔，但同時也很迫切。她用了極大的努力，睜開了眼睛，然後閃過一陣疼痛而呻吟起來。

「什麼事？親愛的？你的頭很痛嗎？」

她停止了點頭去回應，那只是純粹的反射動作，但她感覺到這會讓她一直痛下去，她懷疑是因為她想移動下巴去說話…她舉起了大拇指代替了。無論如何她的嘴現在似乎不能動，她的腦海中組成了一些說話，但不知道怎樣說出來。

「我去找護士，看他們是否可以給你些什麼。」他低頭溫柔地看著她。「我不會吻你，因為會傷害到你。但見到你醒了真的太好了麗貝卡。」在他說完整句話之前，他的聲音破了，他的眼睛閃著淚光。

她似乎不能微笑，但在她的眼角被眼淚刺痛了。他拉著她的手，輕輕地撫弄著。

「別擔心，一切會好起來的。你很快就會感覺好多了。」

her jaw to talk she suspected.. She raised a thumb instead. Her mouth didn't seem to be working at the moment anyway, the words forming inside her head but not knowing how to come out.

"I'll go and get the nurse, see if they can give you anything." He looked down at her tenderly. "I'm not going to kiss you because it might hurt. But it's so good to see you awake, Rebecca." His voice broke before he finished, his eyes glistening.

She couldn't do smiling either, it seemed, but a tear prickled in the corner of her eye. He took her hand and stroked it gently.

"Don't worry. Everything's going to be fine. You'll soon feel better."

She tried to squeeze his hand, but something wasn't right. He was speaking but his voice sounded tinny and far away. She couldn't understand the words...

"She's gone again."

When she woke again, it seemed easier to open her eyes, although her head was still pounding. Moving her head and talking still weren't happening.

"Hey, you're awake." Steve was smiling down at her, although she could see the worry lurking in his eyes. He took her hand and she squeezed it. "Ouch. That killer grip is coming back," he teased. He supported her shoulders and got her a small carton of drink with a straw. She managed one or two swallows but it was physically painful and she felt like she might choke at any moment.

By the time he lowered her gently back on to the pillows, she felt exhausted and frustrated.

"Now, you don't have to do this if you don't want to," he said quietly. "But since your hand squeezing is so good, it would be great if you could answer a few questions to help the police." He took her hand. "I thought we could do one squeeze for yes and two for no, keep it simple. What do you think?"

Squeeze.

He smiled. "Brill." He sat down on the edge of her bed. "Do you know I love you?"

Squeeze.

她試圖去捏他的手，但有點不妥。他在說話，但他的聲音聽起來又細微又遙遠。她開始無法理解那些說話…

「她又昏過去了。」

當她再次醒來的時候，似乎更容易打開眼睛了，但她的頭還在怦怦地跳，仍然沒辦法移動她的頭和說話。

「喂，你醒了。」史堤夫笑盈盈地看著她，雖然她可以看得出在他的眼睛裡的擔憂。他拉著她的手，而她捏了他一下。「哎喲。殺人的握力回來了。」他取笑她說。他扶了一下她的肩膀，給她一盒有吸管的飲品。她吸了一兩口，但身體還是疼痛著，她覺得她可能隨時都會嗆到。

他輕輕地把她放下到枕頭的時候，她感到疲憊和沮喪。

「那麼現在，如果你不想，你不用一定要做的，」他平靜地說。「但因為你用手捏得如此有力，這樣很好如果你能協助警方回答幾個問題，」他拉著她的手。「我想我們可以用捏一下作為『是』，而兩下作為『不是』，那樣會簡單點。你覺得如何？」

捏一下。

他笑了。「非常好，」他在她的床邊坐了下來。「你知道我愛你嗎？」

捏一下。

「很好。」他吻了一下她的手。「我不敢吻在你的頭上，怕你一碰就疼。我會打電話給警察。」

一個外表端好的意大利警察走進來並坐在床另一邊的椅子上，向她微笑了一下。

「你還記得什麼發生了什麼事嗎？」

輕力的捏了一下。她希望他能注意到其中的差別。

「嗯。你記得一點點，但並非全部，是這樣嗎？」

捏一下。

「幹得好，」他的聲音變得更加嚴肅。「你知道是誰攻擊你嗎？」

"Good." He kissed her hand. "I daren't kiss your head, it's a bit tender. I'll call the police officer in."

A good-looking Italian policeman cane in and sat on a chair on the other side of the bed, giving her a smile.

"Do you remember anything about what happened to you?"

A lighter squeeze. She hoped he would notice the difference.

"Ah. You remember a bit, but not everything, is that right?"

Squeeze.

"Well done." His voice became more serious. "Do you know who attacked you?"

Squeeze.

"Was it Marcie King?"

Squeeze.

"Did she say anything?"

Squeeze squeeze.

"Had you seen her before, in Milan?"

Light squeeze.

"You're not sure?"

Squeeze.

"Did you think that someone was following you or watching you?"

Squeeze.

She was only squeezing his hand, but it felt like such hard work. She was exhausted now. There was a mutter of voices and she realised there must be other people in the room.

"That's enough for now. You have a rest."

What another one, thought Rebecca wearily. I've only just woken u....

捏一下。

「是瑪西．京嗎？」

捏一下。

「她有沒有說什麼？」

捏兩下。

「你之前有在米蘭見過她嗎？」

輕力的捏。

「你不確定嗎？」

捏一下。

「你有沒有覺得有人跟踪你或監視你嗎？」

捏一下。

她只是捏下手，但已經覺得是很艱苦的工作。她現在覺得精疲力竭了。有人在小聲嘀咕什麼，她才意識到一定還是有其他人在房間裡。

「現在夠了。你休息吧。」

怎麼又是這樣，麗貝卡疲憊地想。我才剛剛醒來...

Chapter Thirty

Once Rebecca was out of danger, Steve had gone back to England. He was needed at the café and before he left, he'd already arranged with Bernardo to do another stint at Tony's so that he could come back to Milan in three weeks' time and spend more time with Rebecca. While he was gone Kevin came out for a week, and Ron, Francois or both were in every day. Other members of the Milan team popped in periodically bringing treats and books.

Steve's timing was perfect. Two days after he arrived back in Milan, Rebecca was allowed home. Steve picked her up in the morning and when she got back to the flat, she slept for ten hours. It wasn't until the evening that Steve got his chance to talk to her.

"Tony's asked me to take over management of the cafe permanently," he said quietly, his arms wrapped gently round her.

"I see." Rebecca tried to swallow the hard lump in her throat. "What have you told him?"

"Nothing, yet, other than I would think about it." He looked down. "The thing is, Rebecca, I really enjoy running the cafe. And I'm good at it. I'm not saying I'll want to do it forever, but to me a job is about earning enough to live on and doing what makes me happy. He's offered me a very generous deal, and at the moment I'm in no rush to go back to uni."

He reached out, taking her hands in his and looking at her intently. "But on the other hand, where I most want to be is wherever you are. That's the most important thing to me, Rebecca Maynard. You."

Her eyes were brimming with tears but she couldn't find any words.

"And I'm thinking that if that's going to be Milan—most of the time—then that's where I want to be, regardless of what I do."

第三十章

當麗貝卡脫離了生命危險，史堤夫就要回到英格蘭了。咖啡店需要他，而在他離開之前，他已經跟貝爾納公平分配了東尼的份內工作，這樣他就可以回到米蘭三個星期，花更多的時間陪麗貝卡。當他走了之後，凱文來了一個星期，每一天還有羅恩、弗朗索瓦來看她，有時或會兩個一起來。而米蘭團隊的其他成員也會時常帶些零食和書籍來給她。

史堤夫的時間配合得很完美。他回到了米蘭兩天後，麗貝卡就可以回家了。史堤夫在早晨接了她回公寓，之後她睡了十個小時。直到晚上，史堤夫終於有機會跟她談一下。

「東尼叫我接管咖啡店的管理工作。」他平靜地說，他用手臂輕輕地摟著她。

「我明白了。」麗貝卡試圖用力咽了喉嚨裡的東西。「那你回覆了他沒有？」

「沒有，還沒，但我會想想。」他低下頭。「這事情是，麗貝卡，我真的很喜歡營運咖啡店，而且我很擅長。我不是說我會永遠做這工作，但在我來說，一份工作就是有足夠的收入維持生活和做些什麼可以讓我感到快樂。他給我一個非常慷慨的酬勞，而且現在我並不急於回去大學。」

他伸手去握住她的雙手，目不轉睛地看著她。「但另一方面，我最想去的地方就是有你在的地方。這對我來說是最重要的，麗貝卡．梅納德。是你。」

她的眼睛充滿了淚水，但她不知道該說些什麼。

「我想著，如果要去的地方是米蘭，在大部分時間裡，那麼，我就去吧，不管我做什麼都好。」他笑著，把她的臉埋在他的手中，並用大拇指抹走她的眼淚。「也許東尼可以跟他在這裡的一個親戚說點好話，無論如何給我一個意大利語速成班。」

He smiled, cupping her face in his hands and wiping away her tears with his thumbs. "Perhaps Tony could put in a good word with one of his relatives out here. I'll have to do a crash course in Italian, though."

She held him tighter. "I've been an idiot," she said, her voice muffled against his shoulder. "I don't need this job, or Milan, to make me happy. I only need you, and I want you to be happy." She pulled back a little. "I know deep down you want to stay in London, and I love working at the Museum. I think I'd like the Director's job."

"Haven't they given it to someone else?"

"Only on a temporary contract. Tasha's taken it, but she'll go on maternity leave in a few months. When it comes up again I'll apply." She shrugged. "Or perhaps not. I loved my old job, and that's still open, so I haven't lost anything. Although you're the only thing I couldn't bear to lose, I realise that now." She kissed him. "And you'll be a fantastic manager. And I'll be fantastically proud of you."

His arms tightened round her so hard that she gasped, and he pulled back, concerned. "Sorry, honey—did I hurt you?"

"I'm okay." She smiled at him. "Of course, I'm only coming back on one condition."

"What's that?" He looked so worried that she felt guilty for teasing him.

"I'll expect all my lattes to be free, of course."

He didn't reply for a while. He was far too busy kissing her. When they finally broke apart, he grinned. "Done. Hell, you can have everything free."

"In that case, I'd better start packing."

"No. The hospital said you need plenty of rest, and there's no rush. You're not going anywhere for at least another week."

She gave in, but by the end of the week she was feeling a lot better and decided she had her own interpretation of bed rest, although it was different from Steve's and he took a little persuading. Rebecca told him you could have too much rest, and after all, the physiotherapist had said she needed regular exercise.

她把他抱緊。「我一直都是個白痴，」她在他肩膀上說著，聲音聽起來有點模糊不清。「我並不需要這份工作或者米蘭來令讓我快樂。我只需要你，我也希望你能快樂。」她靠開了一點點。「我知道，在你內心深處是想留在倫敦，而我喜歡在博物館工作。我想我會喜歡董事的工作。」

「他們沒有把工作給了別人嗎？」

「只有臨時合同。塔莎在做，但她將會休產假幾個月。當招人消息再出現時，我會再次申請。」她聳聳肩。「也許不會。我熱愛我之前的工作，而它仍然都在，所以我並沒有失去什麼。你是我唯一不能忍受失去的東西，我現在才知道。」她吻了他一下。「你會是一個極之出色的經理，而我會很為你感到極之驕傲。」

他收緊手臂緊緊地抱著她，她喘了口氣，他拉了回來凝視著。「對不起，親愛的，我弄痛你了？」

「我沒事，」她微笑著看著他。「當然，我有一個條件。」

「那是什麼？」他看來很擔心，她有點因為戲弄他而感到內疚。

「我希望我所有的拿鐵咖啡理所當然地都是免費的。」

他有一段時間沒有回答她。是因為他忙著吻她。當他們終於分開，他笑了。「好吧，該死的，你可以所有都是免費。」

「那麼這樣，我最好要開始收拾東西了。」

「不用。院方說你需要多休息，用不著這麼匆忙。你至少不會在一個星期內去任何地方。」

她屈服了，但在一個星期結束前，她感覺已經好多了，雖然跟史堤夫的想法有點不同，他是帶著一點點勸說的方法，但她決定自己去解釋臥床休息的意思，而且以後還有很多時間休息，之後物理治療師也說她需要經常鍛煉。

謝天謝地到了星期五。麗貝卡坐在她的辦公桌前等著午飯時間。她完成了整整一個星期的工作，她已經筋疲力盡了。兩個月的旅程過去，並將她帶回這裡，艱苦的都過去了，他給她帶來快樂，同樣也帶來了心碎。

麗貝卡頭部的傷花了很長時間才能完全恢復。她很多工作都需要

Thank goodness it was Friday. Rebecca sat at her desk waiting for lunch time. She had done her first full week at work and she was exhausted. The journey that, over the last two months, had brought her back here, had been strenuous; happy and heartbreaking in equal measure.

It had taken Rebecca a long time to fully recover from her head injuries. Her fine motor skills had needed a lot of work, and the first time she saw her swollen, shaved head in a mirror, she cried. The other trauma was Marcie's arrest and trial. Rebecca couldn't help feeling sorry for her, even after what she'd done. Marcie's problems went way beyond holding an illogical grudge; she was ill. Even so, when she heard Marcie was safely locked away she cried with relief.

But in the midst of that, there were good things. Rebecca had returned to work in gradual stages, and last week she'd applied for the Director's job. She was up against some strong competition, but she was strangely unconcerned about whether she got it.

There was a knock on her door and Tasha waddled in. That was the only word for it, she thought, as she grinned at her temporary boss.

"Hot?" Tasha glared. "Hot. Fat. I've got indigestion and an awful suspicion I've got piles coming on as well, and my only prize for all this pain is a future full of crappy nappies, so don't mess with me Maynard."

"Sorry."

"Huh. Anyway, I'm here to tell you to pack up your things and go." Tasha turned to leave.

"What?" She sat bolt upright.

"Go. Depart. Leave. Go for lunch first or go straight home, it's up to you, but I don't want to see you until Monday morning. You look shattered."

"If anyone goes home, it should be you," Rebecca protested.

"Oh believe me, I am. Now get your stuff because I'm sending in the troops."

The troops turned out to be Kevin, who appeared a minute later. "I've been sent to escort you off the premises."

"Okay, okay. I surrender."

精細動作技能，她第一次在鏡子看到自己腫脹的光頭時，她哭了。還有另一個創傷是瑪西被逮捕和審判。麗貝卡不由得對她感到抱歉，縱使她做了這麼多事。瑪西的問題是在心裡執著一個不合邏輯的仇恨之外，她生病了。即便如此，當她聽到瑪西被安全地鎖起來，她欣慰地哭了。

在這段時間其他一切都很好。麗貝卡已經逐步恢復工作，而上週她申請了董事的職位。她面對的是一些有實力的競爭對手，但她奇怪地並不擔心她是否能得到它。

有人敲她的門，塔莎蹣跚地走進來，她想那只有一個原因，她對這位臨時上司笑了笑。

「熱嗎？」

塔莎怒目而視。「熱。胖。我還有點消化不良，以及我有一個可怕的預感，我很快還會長痔瘡了，而這一切的痛苦給我唯一的獎品就是充滿著糟糕尿布的未來，所以梅納德你千萬不要惹我。」

「對不起。」

「嘿。無論如何，我是來叫你去收拾你的東西離去。」塔莎轉身離開。

「什麼？」她坐得筆直。

「去。出發。離開。先去吃午飯，或直接回家，你自己決定，但我不想看到你，至少直到週一早上。你看上去真的是亂七八糟。」

「如果有任何人要回家，那應該是你。」麗貝卡抗議道。

「噢，相信我，我是。但現在，你要收拾好東西，因為我已經派了部隊來。」

那部隊竟然是凱文，他在一分鐘後出現。「我已經派人押送你出去。」

「好吧，好吧。我投降。」

Chapter Thirty One

The sun shone as Rebecca and Kevin walked to Tony's for lunch.

"Heard from Neil this week?" Rebecca asked, tucking her arm in Kevin's.

"Yep. He's back in two weeks." Kevin beamed and Rebecca squeezed his arm.

"That's great." She felt a little choked to see him so happy.

Neil had stayed in Milan with Steve and Rebecca for a couple of days after she came home from hospital, before he disappeared off exploring again. Much to Steve's surprise, Neil was intending to cut his exploring short and go back to London after a few months. Rebecca, however, wasn't surprised. She knew he and Kevin had gone out a few times, even before she left for Milan, and also knew that since Neil had left they'd been keeping in touch.

But she did enjoy the look of amazement on Steve's face when she told him. He'd spent a lot of time repeating, "Neil? Neil? And Kevin?" Although when he'd thought about it for a while, he admitted that perhaps he should have put the clues together.

"What about your love life, hmm? All set to move into the love nest this weekend?" Kevin teased.

"Yep. All packed up and ready to go," she smiled. After a tense period with Laura, Steve had finally found it in his heart to forgive her. Laura was applying for uni soon and a fortnight ago she'd moved out, and was now sharing a flat with Sarah, one of the students she'd met at the Museum. Steve had waited a week then asked Rebecca to move in with him. She'd been saying yes before he'd finished the sentence

"Well if you need any help, you know where I am..." Kevin grinned as they both said, "in Australia!"

第三十一章

太陽照耀著，麗貝卡和凱文走到東尼的咖啡店吃午餐。

「這個星期有尼爾的消息嗎？」麗貝卡問，她把手臂伸進凱文的臂內。

「有啊。他兩個星期後就回來。」凱文笑容滿面地說，麗貝卡捏了他的胳膊一下。

「這太好了。」她見他如此開心覺得有點哽咽。

在麗貝卡從醫院回到家之後，尼爾跟史堤夫和她留了在米蘭一兩天，是在他再次出發去探索之旅之前。令史堤夫驚訝的是，尼爾打算縮短他的旅程，幾個月後再回倫敦。但麗貝卡並不驚訝，因為她知道他和凱文去過了幾次約會，是在她離開米蘭前，也知道自尼爾離開後，他們有一直保持著聯繫。

但她很享受看到史堤夫驚奇的樣子，就在她告訴他的時候。他有一段時間重複說著：「尼爾？尼爾？跟凱文？」雖然當他想了一段時間，他承認他應該已經有發現到端倪了。

「那你的愛情生活怎樣了，嗯？這週末都把所有東西搬進愛巢了？」凱文戲弄地說。

「沒錯。全部行裝都收拾好了，準備出發。」她笑了。跟羅拉經過一段緊張的時期之後，史堤夫終於從心底原諒了她。羅拉很快就會申請入讀大學，而兩星期前她已經搬出，現在跟莎拉同住，她是她在博物館認識的其中一個學生。史堤夫等了一個星期之後，問麗貝卡要不要搬過去跟他住。在他說完這句話之前，她就已經答應了。

「好吧，如果你需要任何幫助，你知道我在那裡...」當他們同一時間說：「在澳大利亞！」凱文笑了。

她打了他一下。「懶惰的傢伙！真夠朋友啊。」

She punched him. "Lazy sod! Some friend you are."

Tony's looked rather smarter from the outside these days. With Tony's blessing, Steve had ordered some new signage and given the whole cafe a makeover. It was flourishing under his management and Rebecca was incredibly proud of him.

As Kevin pushed open the door, Steve looked up and saw them both walking in. A big smile lit up his face. Kevin turned to Rebecca and smiled. "Happy days, eh?"

She squeezed his arm. "Yep. Happy days," she said quietly.

Rebecca looked at the next box. Her back ached from hours of unpacking and this one could wait. It must be time for dinner.

Steve popped his head round the door. "Are you getting hungry?"

"You read my mind," she smiled, walking over and winding her arms round his neck.

"I thought, as a reward for all our hard work, fish and chips. Unless you'd prefer Mexican," he grinned.

"Fish and chips sounds gorgeous."

"Good, because the chippy round the corner is great. I'll pop round."

"Okay."

"What do you fancy?"

"Other than you?" she grinned.

"Yes, other than me, you insatiable woman! Scampi? Battered sausage?"

She raised her eyebrows suggestively and he smacked her bottom.

"Behave! We've got work to do!"

"Spoilsport. Cod and chips, please."

He disentangled himself. "Your wish is my command." He bent to kiss her, then frowned, looking over her shoulder. He put his

這些日子東尼外表看起來相當醒目。得到東尼的准許，史堤夫已下訂購了一些新的招牌，並給整個咖啡店重新裝潢。咖啡店在他的管理下蓬勃地發展起來，麗貝卡難以置信地為他感到驕傲。

凱文推開門，史堤夫抬起頭來，看見他們一起走進來，一個大大的笑容掛在他的臉上。凱文轉向麗貝卡微笑著。「開心的日子，嗯？」

她捏了捏他的胳膊。「沒錯。開心的日子。」她平靜地說。

麗貝卡看看下一個箱子。經過幾個小時的整頓，她感到有點背痛了，這一個箱子可以慢慢再整理，現在必須要先去吃晚飯。

史堤夫在門前伸了頭出來。「你餓了嗎？」

「你讀到我在想什麼啊。」她笑了笑，走過去摟著他的脖子。

「我想，魚和薯條作為我們所有辛勤工作的獎勵。除非你更喜歡墨西哥餐。」他咧嘴笑了。

「魚和薯條聽起來很好。」

「好吧，因為拐角處的薯條店很好。我會很快可以買回來。」

「好吧。」

「你有看中什麼嗎？」

「除了你嗎？」她笑了。

「是的，除了我之外，你這個貪得無厭的女人！炸大蝦？香腸？」

她挑逗地揚起眉毛，他看穿了她在想什麼。

「老實點！我們還有工作要做！」

「真掃興。鱈魚和薯條，謝謝。」

他讓自己脫身了。「你的願望就是對我的命令。」他俯下身去吻了她一下，然後皺起了眉頭，看著她的身後，兩手扠腰。

「那是不是我之前見過那個未開封的箱子？」

hands on his hips.

"Is that an unopened box I see before me?"

"Might be," she muttered.

"Then get to it, wench, while I gather food and drag it back to the cave! It had better be empty by the time I get back, else there'll be trouble!"

She booted him out the room, and heard him let himself out of the front door a few seconds later. She hadn't asked him if he wanted any money, she realised. She didn't suppose it really mattered, though. She didn't intend to count every penny and argue about who spent what and she didn't think Steve did, either.

With a sigh, Rebecca dropped to her knees and stared at the offending box. The scrawl of black marker told her this box was her CDs. She moved it over to the shelves that housed Steve's CD collection. He'd bought another set of shelves but suggested with a grin that she should slot her albums in beside his, since they both liked their CDs arranged alphabetically.

She ripped off the tape and grabbed the first handful of discs, which turned out handily to be A to C. Top shelf then. She let her eyes run along the other shelves that held Steve's collection. Ah, he had the Art of Noise too. Quirky. She was willing to bet that most people who'd bought that album had binned it long ago. Sometimes she'd wondered why she hadn't done the same thing. Bryan Adams. She had most of his, Steve only had a couple. Blur, Black-Eyed Peas... she frowned. Wow. Steve had lots of the same albums she had, A to C. It was probably just a coincidence. When she got the rest out she'd probably discover all his guilty secrets—he probably had a stash of Dolly Parton albums somewhere.

After she'd slotted D to F in, she stood back and started to look, really look, at Steve's CDs. She couldn't quite believe it. Apart from some notable exceptions (yes, he really did have all Mariah Carey's albums. and she didn't think the worse of him for not owning any Laurie Anderson), their CD collections were scarily similar.

By the time a gorgeous aroma announced that Steve had returned with dinner the shelves were nearly full.

"Steve! I've discovered something really strange."

He put his head round the door and grinned. "I told my neighbour

「可能。」她喃喃自語。

「當我去買食物的時候,你就把它拆掉,丫頭!到我回來的時候,它最好是空的,不然有人會有麻煩了!」

她把他趕出房間,並在幾秒鐘後聽到他從前門出去了。她發現她沒有問過他要不要給他錢。雖然她不覺得這真的很重要。她從來沒有打算要跟他計算每一分錢,或爭論誰付錢買了什麼,她想史堤夫也不會,無論如何。

麗貝卡嘆了口氣,蹲下去盯著那個有問題的箱子。潦草的黑色標記告訴她,這箱子是她的專輯。她把它搬到史堤夫的專輯收藏架前。他買了另外一組儲物架,但帶著微笑地建議她應該把她的專輯插放在他的專輯中,因為他們都喜歡把專輯按字母順序排列。

她扯下膠帶,拿起一小撮的唱片,那是由A到C的唱片,那麼就是在儲物架頂層。她的眼睛沿著史堤夫的專輯收藏架上看過去。啊,他也有嘈音藝術(Art of Noise)的專輯。古怪。她敢打賭,大多數願意買這張專輯的人一定會扔掉它很久了。有時她也不知道為什麼她沒有這樣做。布萊恩.亞當斯。她有他大部分的專輯,而史堤夫只有兩張。布勒(Blur),黑眼豆豆(Black-Eyed Peas)...她皺起了眉頭。哇。史堤夫有很多跟她相同的專輯,只是由A到C已經有很多,這可能只是巧合。當她在看其餘的部分時,她可能會發現他所有罪惡的秘密,他可能有一大批藏匿某處的多莉.帕頓專輯。

之後她開始放入F到D的專輯,她站後了一點看上去,在看史堤夫的專輯。她真的不敢相信,除了一些明顯的例外(他確實有瑪麗亞.凱莉的所有專輯。而她沒有想得更差,他應該不會有任何勞麗·安德森的專輯),他們的專題收藏相似得可怕。

當聞到食物濃厚的香味之時,表示史堤夫拿回來的晚餐相當豐富。

「史堤夫!我發現了很奇怪的東西。」

他把頭探進門口笑了。「我已經說過我的鄰居有一些奇怪的習慣。」

「史堤夫,不要胡鬧了!老實說,真是不可思議。」

「至少我可以先把食物放下吧?」

has some odd habits."

"Steve, stop mucking about! Honestly, this is weird."

"Can I at least put the food down?"

He deposited the bag safely in the kitchen and followed her into the lounge. "Really? You found something weird in here?"

"Yes." She stood by the shelves, and waved her hand at them dramatically. "Look."

"At what? They're my shelves, sorry, our shelves, and now there's more of them."

"No, look at what's on them."

He frowned. "Er... CDs?" Then suddenly his face cleared. "Oh I get it. Very funny. You've found my Mariah Carey albums, haven't you?"

"Yes, but that's not it. Our CD collections are practically identical."

"That's not so weird. We're around the same age, have a similar socio-economic background, we've both lived in London for some time... I bet the majority of people our age have got a couple of Oasis albums, some Robbie, a bit of Coldplay, Blur, Kasabian, Christina Aguilera—"

"I agree, and if that's as far as it went, I wouldn't think it was odd, but—"

Her mobile rang. "Look at them properly! You'll see what I mean!" she hissed, as she picked up the call, too distracted to check the caller id.

"Hello?"

"Hi, is that Rebecca?" The voice was familiar.

"Yes."

"It's Nicola, from Methodical Matches."

She suppressed a grin at Nicola's 'from'; she obviously couldn't get out of the habit of pretending she was just a cog in a larger corporate machine.

他把袋子安全地放在廚房，然後跟她走進休息室。「真的嗎？你發現了奇怪的事嗎？」

「是。」她站在儲物架前，誇張地揮舞著雙手。「你看。」

「什麼？就是我的儲物架，對不起，是我們的儲物架，而現在有更多東西了。」

「不是，你看看上面是什麼。」

他皺起了眉頭。「呃...唱片？」然後，他突然明白了一切。「噢，我明白了。很有趣。你已經找到了我的瑪麗亞．凱莉專輯了嗎？」

「是的，但我不是說這個。我們的唱片收藏幾乎是相同的。」

「這不用那麼好驚奇的。我們生在相約的年代，有類似的社會經濟背景，而且我們都已經在倫敦生活了一段時間...我敢打賭，大多數人在我們時代的人都有好幾張綠洲合唱團（Oasis）的專輯，一些羅比，幾張酷玩樂團（Coldplay）、布勒、卡薩比安樂隊（Kasabian）、克里斯蒂娜．阿奎萊拉...」

「我同意，而這遠遠超過了這種，我不會認為很奇怪，但...」
她的手機響了。「好好去看看它們！你會明白我的意思！」她低聲呵斥道，她拿起手機，太分心而沒有看到來電號碼。

「喂？」

「嗨，是麗貝卡嗎？」一把很熟悉的聲音。

「是的。」

「我是妮科拉，從井然配對打來的。」

她壓制自己想笑妮科拉的「從」，很明顯她無法擺脫習慣去假裝她是一個大企業中的一個齒輪。

「嗨，妮科拉。你工作到很晚。」

「我知道，我整晚一直在這裡做新的熱門配對。」

「新的？」

「是的。」我的工作夥伴終於回來了，而且修復了那個瘋狂的電腦程式，但整理新的結果已經用上幾個小時了。」

"Hi Nicola. You're working late."

"I know, I've been here all evening generating our new Hot Matches."

"New?"

"Yes. My business partner's finally come back and fixed the crazy computer program, but collating the new results has taken hours."

"Oh dear." She tried to sound sympathetic, but she couldn't see that it was anything to do with her any more, and the smell of the fish and chips wafting in from the kitchen was driving her mad. "Of course, my profile's inactive."

"Oh yes, that's fine. We quite understand. It's just that since we finally got the program to work properly, we're running all our client's details through again."

"Er... good."

"It works really well! The problem was, the program was too intelligent."

"Oh?"

"Yes. It was set up to receive new input from sociological studies on relationships. That's why it started asking more and more questions and there were more variables than it had been made to cope with apparently. I don't really understand it all myself."

"No, me neither," Rebecca muttered.

"It was weighting certain sections more than the others, over-writing earlier calculations. At one stage it was matching people purely on what books they read. Can you believe it!"

"Funnily enough, I can."

"Anyway, the reason I'm ringing you is because, it's not only generated everyone's top 2 hot matches, it's generated an ideal match for everyone. Because of the inconvenience, we're telling everyone about these, and letting them have the next three months' membership for free."

"That's very kind, but I'm not interested. I have a partner now—"

"Oh, good for you!" Nicola chirruped.

「哦，親愛的。」她試圖用同情的語氣說，但她看不出跟她有什麼關係，魚和薯條的氣味從廚房飄出來使她有點瘋了。「我的檔案已經是無效的了吧。」

「哦，是的，那很好。我們明白。這只是因為我們終於令程序正常運作了，我們正在再次運行所有客戶的詳細資料。」

「呃…很好。」
「它真的運作得很好！問題是，它太聰明了。」

「哦？」

「是的。它被設定去接收新的資料，有關社會學上的關係。這就是為什麼它一開始問那麼多的問題，因為那樣比起表面上的配對有更多的變數。但其實我自己也真的不太明白這一切。」

「是的，我也不明白。」麗貝卡喃喃地說。

「這個部分的比重會比其他的更多，它會覆蓋早期的計算。在上一個階段，它會配對一些純粹是他們讀什麼書的人。你能相信嗎！」

「真的很有趣，但我可以相信。」

「不管怎麼說，我打電話你的原因是因為現在不僅可以每個人配對出頭兩位的熱門配對，而且每個人還會有理想伴侶。由於之前帶來的不便，我們想告訴大家這件事，讓他們享有未來三個月的免費會籍。」

「這是很親切的，但我不感興趣。我現在已經有伴侶了…」

「噢，對你有益的啊！」妮科拉尖聲叫道。

「…正如我所說，我的檔案是無效的。而事實上，我打算永久取消會籍，如果我有時間。」

「好吧，如果你確定…」
「是的。」

「那麼我明天就幫你取消。在此期間，我敢肯定你還在好奇地想誰是你的理想伴侶是…」
「不是這樣。」

"—and as I say, my profile's inactive. In fact, I was going to cancel my membership entirely as soon as I had the time."

"Well if you're sure..."

"Yes."

"I'll do that tomorrow for you. In the meantime, I'm sure you're still curious to know who your Ideal Match was—"

"Not really."

"Not even the teeniest bit?"

"Look sorry, Nicola, but my dinner's getting cold."

"Oh." There was a lot of hurt in that one small syllable. Then her voice brightened. "Tell you what, I'll just pop them in the email with the confirmation of your membership cancellation, shall I?"

"Great idea. Thanks," said Rebecca hurriedly. "Bye, Nicola."

"Bye."

Steve was looking at her quizzically from the door. "What was all that about?"

"Nicola."

"I thought I could hear her dulcet tones. Are you still trying to pull other fellas? Hmm?" He grabbed her.

"No. I'll explain later! Now let me at the food, I'm ravenous!" She ducked under his arm and ran to the kitchen with Steve chasing after her.

Later, they sat licking sticky fingers—they'd not bothered with knives and forks, they'd just dived in—and enjoying a glass of white wine.

"You're right about the CDs," Steve said, "it is weird." He found a hidden chip in the corner of the bag and swooped.

"What? Oh yes. I'd almost forgotten about that. It's not just the obvious ones, is it? Told you."

"At least we won't argue about what music to play."

「一點點也沒有？」

「不好意思，妮科拉，但我的晚餐要涼掉了。」

「哦。」這個小音節上顯示出很大的傷害，然後她的聲音又變亮了。「我告訴你，我會在確認取消會籍的電子郵件中列出他們，可以嗎？」

「好主意。謝謝你。」麗貝卡匆匆地說。「再見，妮科拉。」

「再見。」

史堤夫疑惑地從門前看著她。「是誰？」

「妮科拉。」

「我想我能聽到她悅耳的聲音。你還在嘗試去認識其他的傢伙嗎？嗯？」他拉住了她。

「沒有。稍後我再解釋！現在先讓我吃東西，我餓壞了！」她躲開了他的手，史堤夫追住她一起向廚房跑過去。

之後他們坐在舔手指，他們並不是介意用刀叉，但他們剛才一開始就猛吃，而現在正享受白葡萄酒。

「有關唱片的事，你說得對，」史堤夫說，「是很怪異。」他發現了袋子的角落裡藏著一張唱片，他飛撲去看。

「什麼？哦，是的。我幾乎忘了這個。這不是太顯眼的一張，是嗎？我已經告訴過你了。」

「至少我們不會爭論放什麼音樂。」

「我可能會，如果你堅持要放瑪麗亞·凱莉。」

「嗯，勞麗·安德森到底是誰？他的聲音是怎樣的？」

「她。」

「什麼？」

「勞麗·安德森是一個她。」

"I might, if you insist on playing Mariah Carey."

"Well who the hell is Laurie Anderson? What does he sounds like?"

"She."

"What?"

"Laurie Anderson's a she."

"Don't care. As I was about to say, in that case he—sorry, she—is banned on principle."

"Even though you might like it?"

He nodded solemnly. "Even though."

She sighed. "Fair enough. I'll just have to make sure I boot you out of the house at regular intervals, then."

"Or use headphones. Then I could stay here..." he grinned and bent down, licking one of her greasy fingers, "and still enjoy your company. There's lot of things that you don't need your ears for," he said mischievously.

She kissed him but pulled away. "Fun as that sounds, at the moment I do have a report to finish. Sorry."

He stood up. "Very virtuous. I should be virtuous too because I've got a spread sheet of orders waiting for me on the computer upstairs."

"Okay." She smiled up at him. "What say we meet back down here to finish the wine at, ooh, let's see... 10.30?"

He kissed her lingeringly. "It's a date."

He disappeared upstairs and Rebecca set up her laptop on the dining room table. She needed to check her email first—she was waiting for some last minute results before she finalised her report, and was praying Kevin had remembered to forward them to her.

He had, just minutes before he left work, by the look of it. Good. She scanned down. Wow, Nicola had been better than her word. She really was working late. The cancellation email was already sitting there in Rebecca's inbox, sent fifteen minutes earlier. Rebecca's fingered hovered over the delete button—after all,

「不要在意。正如我所說，在這種情況下他...很抱歉...是她，原則上是被禁止的。」

「儘管你可能會喜歡嗎？」

他鄭重地點了點頭。「儘管是。」

她嘆了口氣。「真不公平。那麼我就必須確保要每隔一段時間把你踢出房子。」

「或者用耳機。然後，我就可以呆在這裡...」他咧嘴笑了，彎下腰舔她那油膩的手指，「仍然享受作為你的伙伴。有很多事情，你不需要用到你的耳朵來做的。」他桃皮地說。

她吻了他一下，但靠開了一點。「聽起來很有趣，但此刻我還有一個報告要去完成。對不起。」

他站了起來。「很賢惠。我應該也要去賢惠一下，因為樓上的電腦中還有電子訂單等著我。」

「好吧，」她微笑著看著他。「那麼我們一會兒再回到這裡把酒喝完，噢，看看...十點半？」

他戀戀不捨地吻了她。「這是一個約會啊。」

他上了樓上，而麗貝卡在餐桌上打開了她的筆記本電腦。她先要檢查電子郵件，她在等一些緊急的結果去完成她的報告，她祈禱凱文記得將其轉發給她，所以她需要檢查她的電子郵件。

他有，看來就在他下班前幾分鐘。好。她把它掃描下來。哇，妮科拉做的比她說的更好，她真的工作到很晚。取消會籍的電子郵件已經在麗貝卡的收件箱中，是在十五分鐘前發送的。麗貝卡的手指徘徊在刪除按鈕上。畢竟，她已經知道最重要的一點，她的會籍已被取消了，但現在在她面前的電子郵件中有她的理想伴侶，而且只要一點擊就可以看到，好奇的火花在她的心中燃燒著。

稍稍地看一下又沒有害的，是嗎？只是出於好奇。

電子郵件正文跟預期一樣。兩個星期的通知期，直接扣款已取消，報名費不予退還，等等等等。理想伴侶是在附件中，她驚訝地發現她的心開始跳得更快，因為她正點擊打開它。

第一頁包含了一般的熱門配對。「再見．理查德，37和巴里，32。」她嘀咕道。

she knew the important bit already, her membership had been cancelled—but now the email was actually in front of her and her Ideal Match was only a click away, a spark of curiosity was burning in her.

There wasn't any harm in taking a quick look at it, was there? Just out of interest.

The body of the email was much as expected. Two weeks' notice, direct debit cancelled, no refund of registration fee, blah blah. The Ideal Match was in the attachment, and she was surprised to find her heart starting to beat faster as she clicked to open it.

The first page contained the usual hot matches too. "Goodbye Richard, 37, and Barry, 32," she muttered.

At the bottom of the page, in large bold letters, was the message: 'SCROLL DOWN TO SEE YOUR IDEAL MATCH!'

She took a deep breath. Don't be daft. Rebecca. You've proved already that computers are no good at picking potential partners. This is completely insignificant because you've found your perfect partner already.

'CAUTION!' it said across the top, then further down: 'THIS PERSON COULD BE THE LOVE OF YOUR LIFE!'

Rebecca grinned, relaxing. Ludicrous! "Come on then," she said with a smirk. "Show me my Prince Charming." She scrolled down.

'YOUR IDEAL MATCH IS:

*** STEVE REYNOLDS! ***

She stared, transfixed, for ages, before she realised a tear was running down her cheek. She wiped it away and jumped to her feet.

She would run upstairs and tell Steve, for the hundredth and definitely not the last time, that he really was her ideal man.

在頁面較底部分，比較大的粗體字母寫著：「向下滾動就能看到您的理想伴侶！」

她深吸了一口氣。別傻了，麗貝卡，你已經證明了電腦根本不會幫你挑選潛在的伴侶。這完全是毫無意義的，因為你已經找到了你的完美伴侶了。

「小心！」頂部寫著，再之後是：「這個人可能是你一生的摯愛！」

麗貝卡咧嘴一笑，放鬆，真是荒謬！「那就去吧，」她傻笑地說。「告訴我白馬王子是誰。」她向下滾動。

你的理想伴侶是：

＊＊＊　史堤芬·雷諾茲！　＊＊＊

她愣住了，呆了半天，她意識到眼淚順著她的臉頰流了下來。她擦一擦然後彈了起來。

她跑上樓告訴史堤夫，百分之絕對跟上一次不同，他真的是她理想中的男人。

Available in English and simplified Chinese
Available in paperback (pocket book size)
Available as an audio book

Please go to our website:
www.penrose-publishing.co.uk

See also books from our other authors:
Devon Volkel
Joshua Mercott
Les Gates
Aaron Smith
Joanne Smith
Grace Harding

www.ingramcontent.com/pod-product-compliance
Lightning Source LLC
Chambersburg PA
CBHW051935020726
47501CB00001B/131